LILAH STURGES · PO

LUMBERJANES™

TRUE COLORS

Published by
BOOM! BOX™

BOOM! BOX™

LUMBERJANES: TRUE COLORS, October 2020. Published by BOOM! Box, a division of Boom Entertainment, Inc. Lumberjanes is ™ & © 2020 Shannon Watters, Grace Ellis, Noelle Stevenson & Brooklyn Allen. All rights reserved. BOOM! Box™ and the BOOM! Box logo are trademarks of Boom Entertainment, Inc., registered in various countries and categories. All characters, events, and institutions depicted herein are fictional. Any similarity between any of the names, characters, persons, events, and/or institutions in this publication to actual names, characters, and persons, whether living or dead, events, and/or institutions is unintended and purely coincidental. BOOM! Box does not read or accept unsolicited submissions of ideas, stories, or artwork.

BOOM! Studios, 5670 Wilshire Boulevard, Suite 400, Los Angeles, CA 90036-5679. Printed in USA. First Printing.

ISBN: 978-1-68415-617-7, eISBN: 978-1-64668-029-0

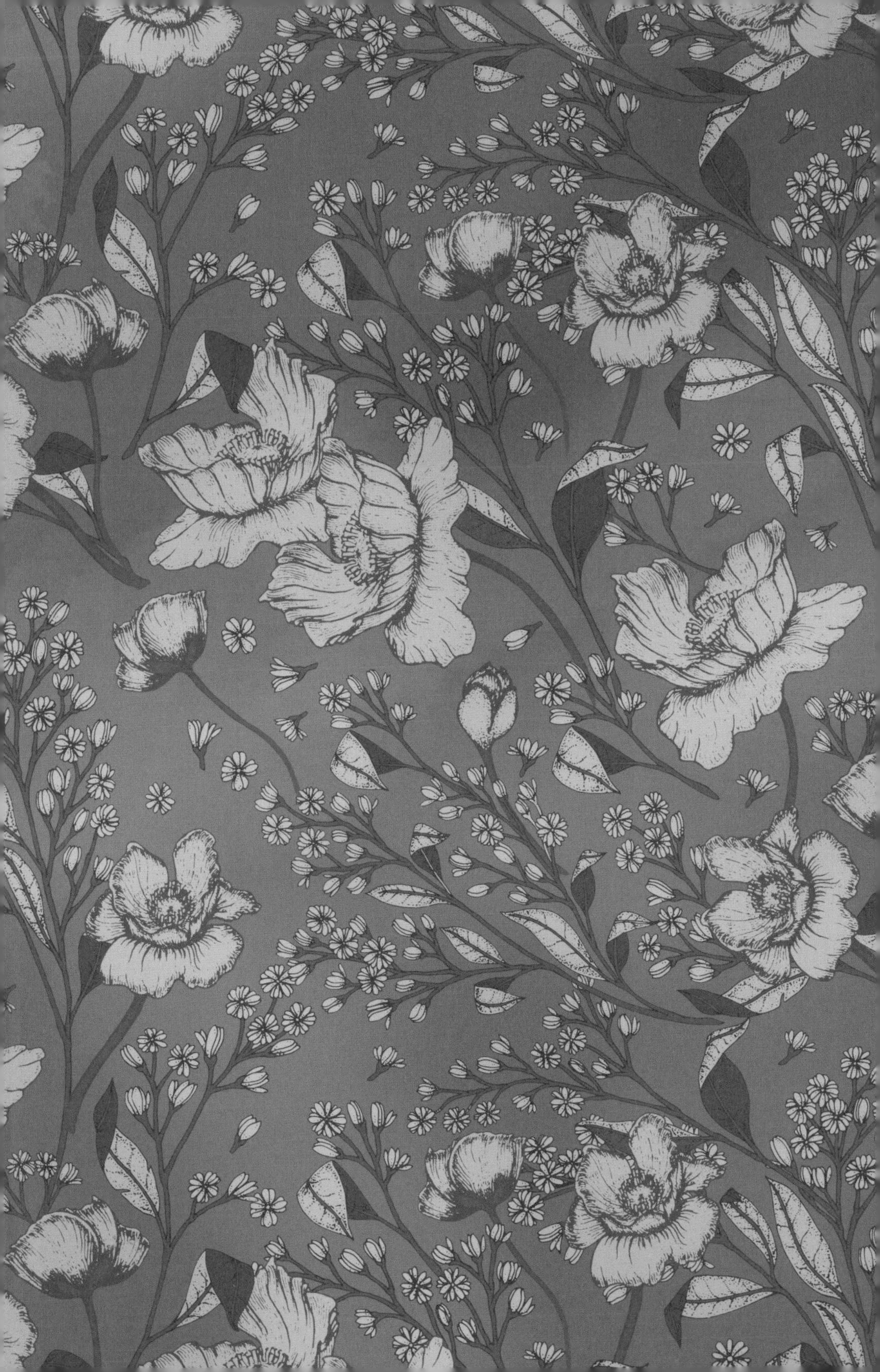

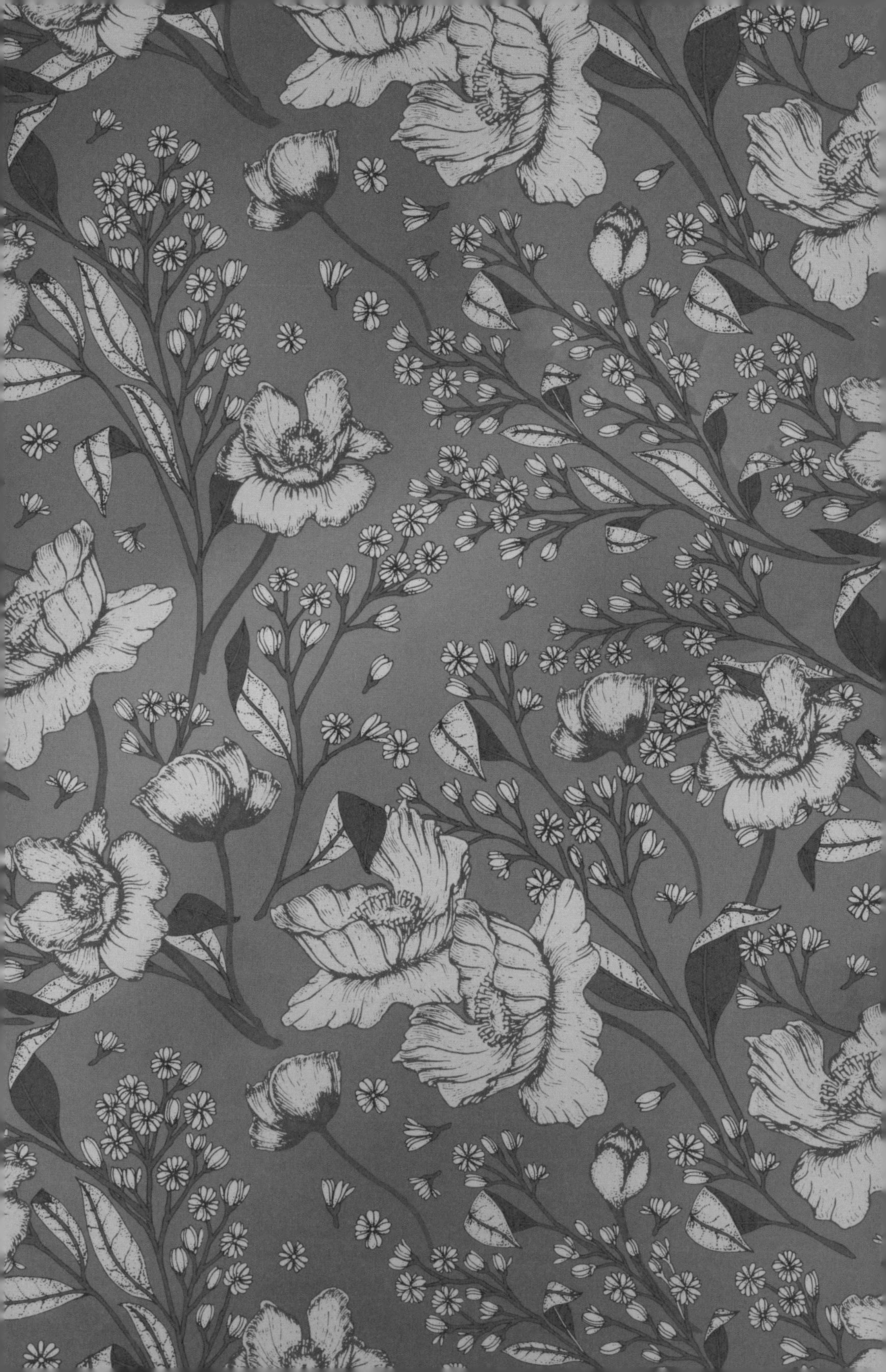

LUMBERJANES™
TRUE COLORS

Written by
LILAH STURGES

Illustrated by
POLTERINK

Lettered by
JIM CAMPBELL

Cover by
ALEXA SHARPE

Designer
MARIE KRUPINA

Editor
SOPHIE PHILIPS-ROBERTS

Executive Editor
JEANINE SCHAEFER

*Special thanks to **Kelsey Pate** for giving the
Lumberjanes their name.*

Created by
**SHANNON WATTERS, GRACE ELLIS,
NOELLE STEVENSON & BROOKLYN ALLEN**

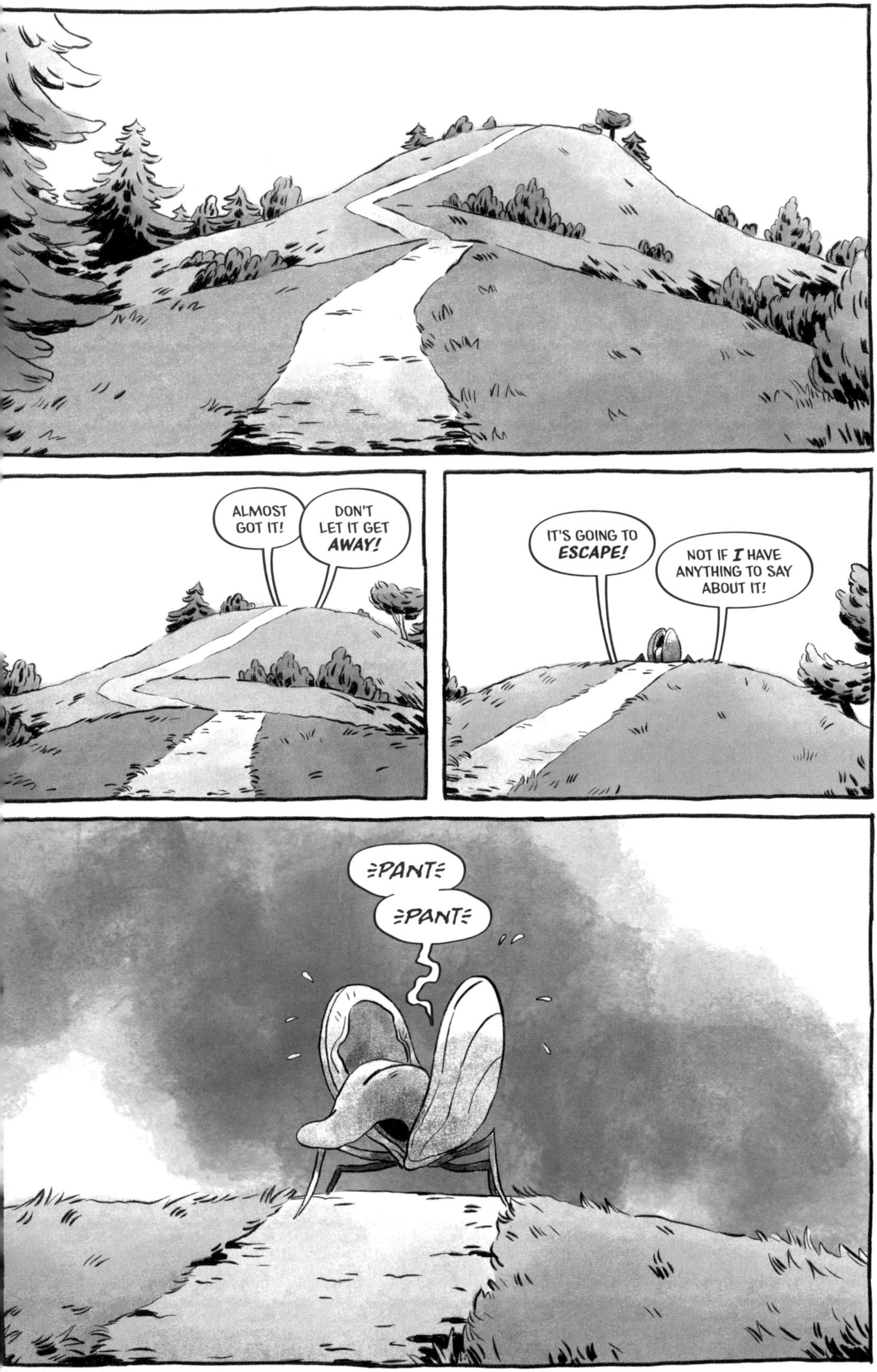
ALMOST GOT IT!
DON'T LET IT GET AWAY!
IT'S GOING TO ESCAPE!
NOT IF I HAVE ANYTHING TO SAY ABOUT IT!
PANT
PANT

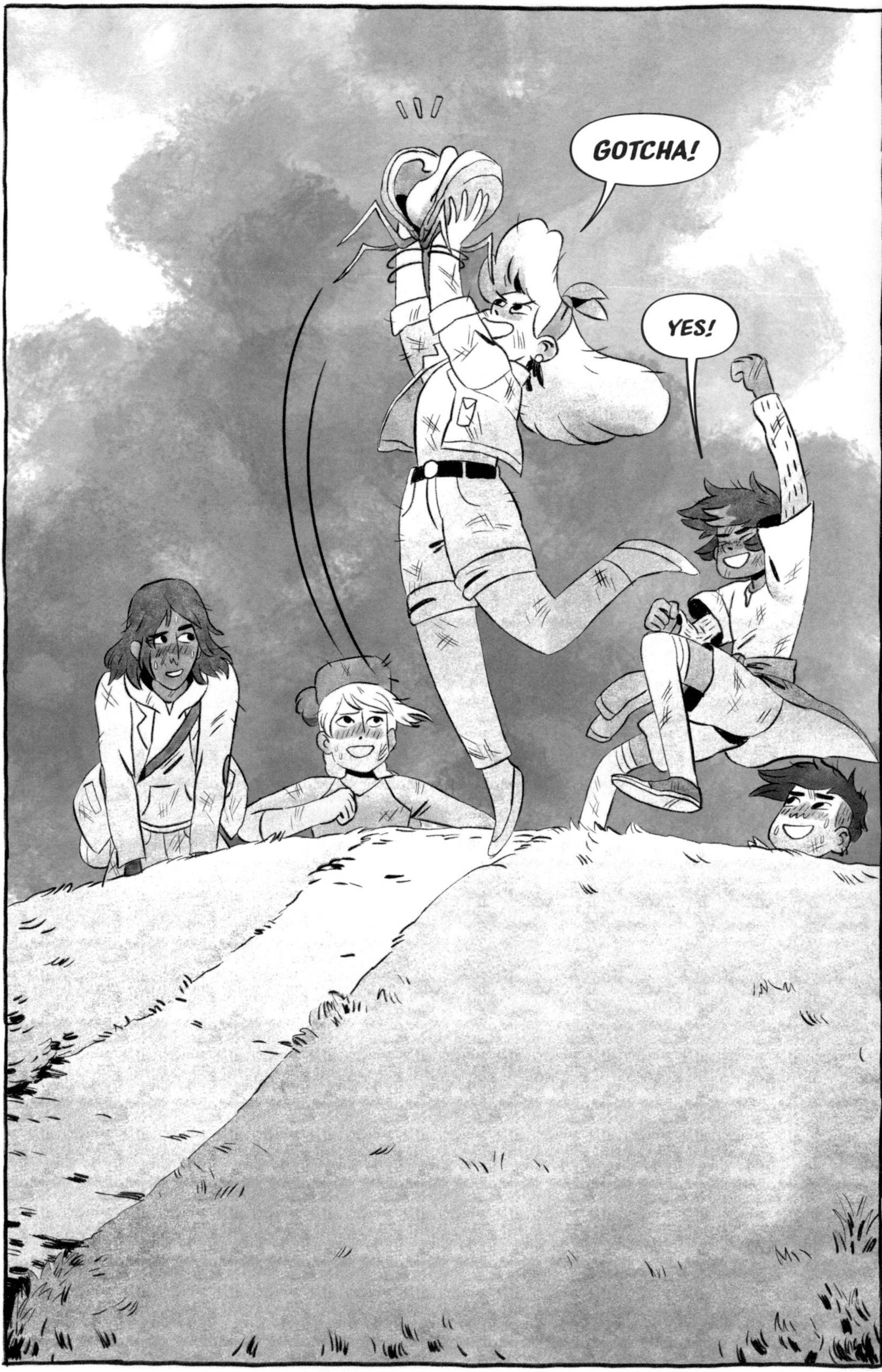
GOTCHA!
YES!

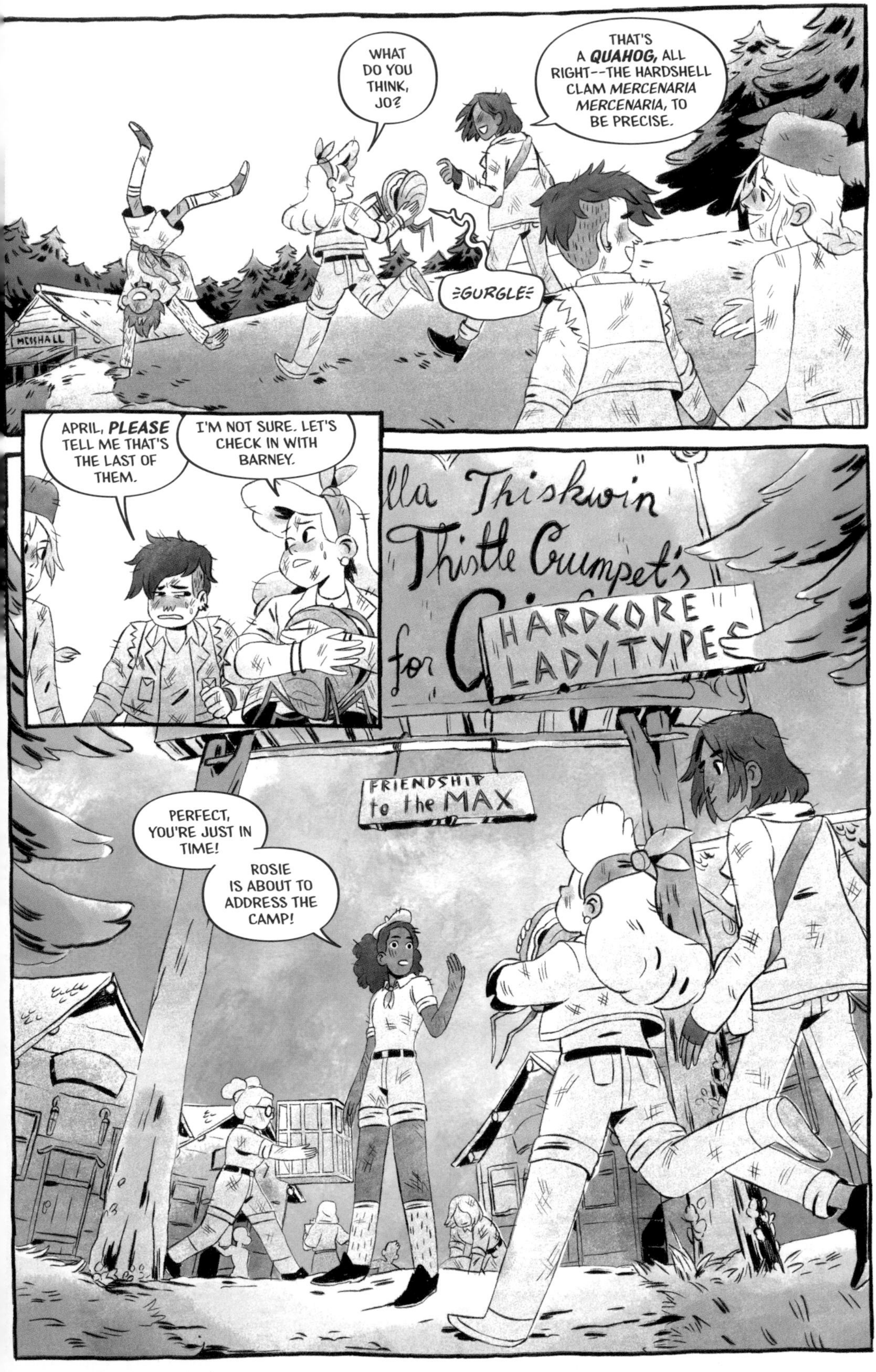
WHAT DO YOU THINK, JO?
THAT'S A QUAHOG, ALL RIGHT--THE HARDSHELL CLAM MERCENARIA MERCENARIA, TO BE PRECISE.
GURGLE
MESSHALL
APRIL, PLEASE TELL ME THAT'S THE LAST OF THEM.
I'M NOT SURE. LET'S CHECK IN WITH BARNEY.
Thistle Crumpet's
for
HARDCORE LADY TYPES
FRIENDSHIP to the MAX
PERFECT, YOU'RE JUST IN TIME!
ROSIE IS ABOUT TO ADDRESS THE CAMP!

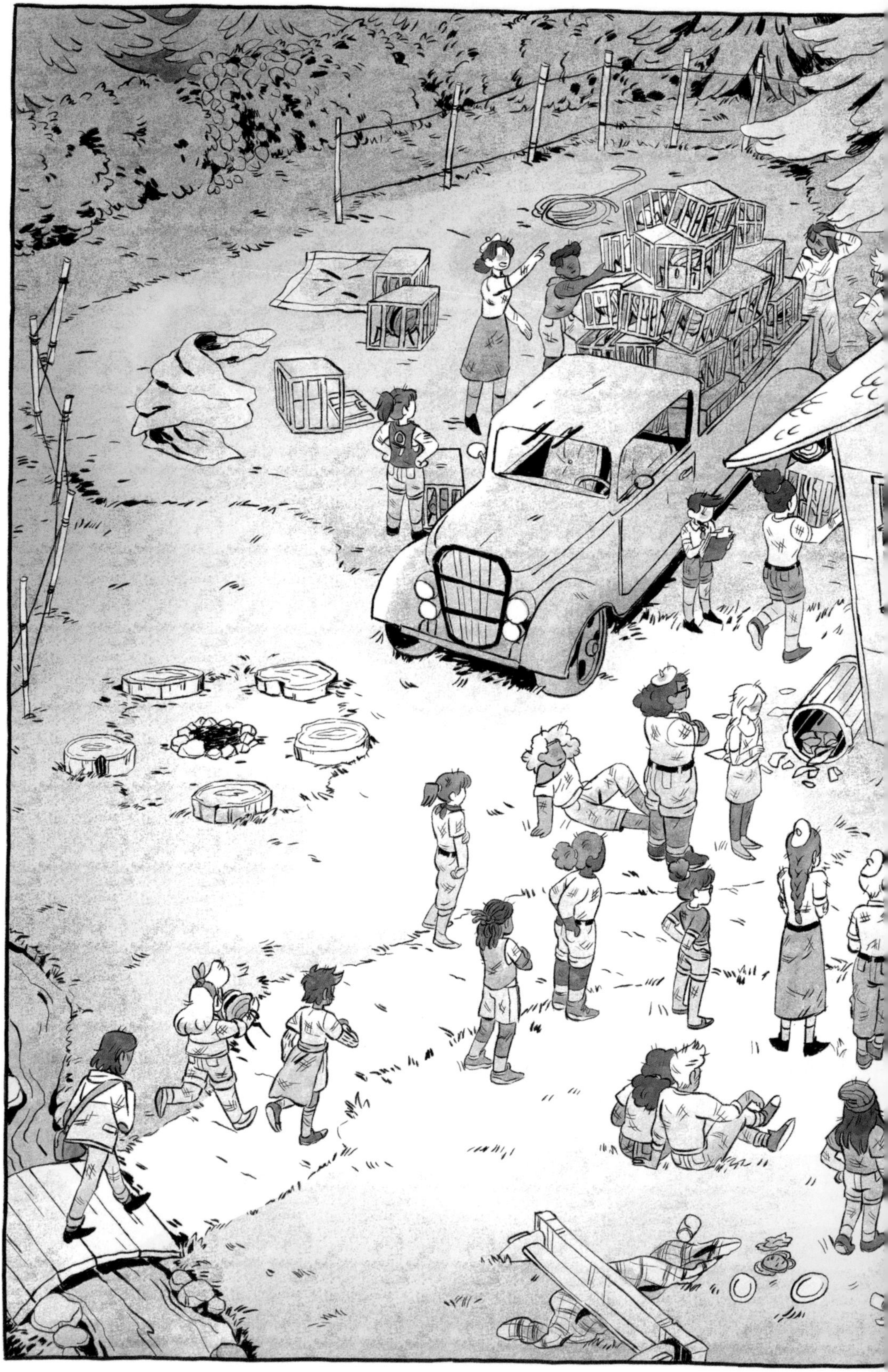

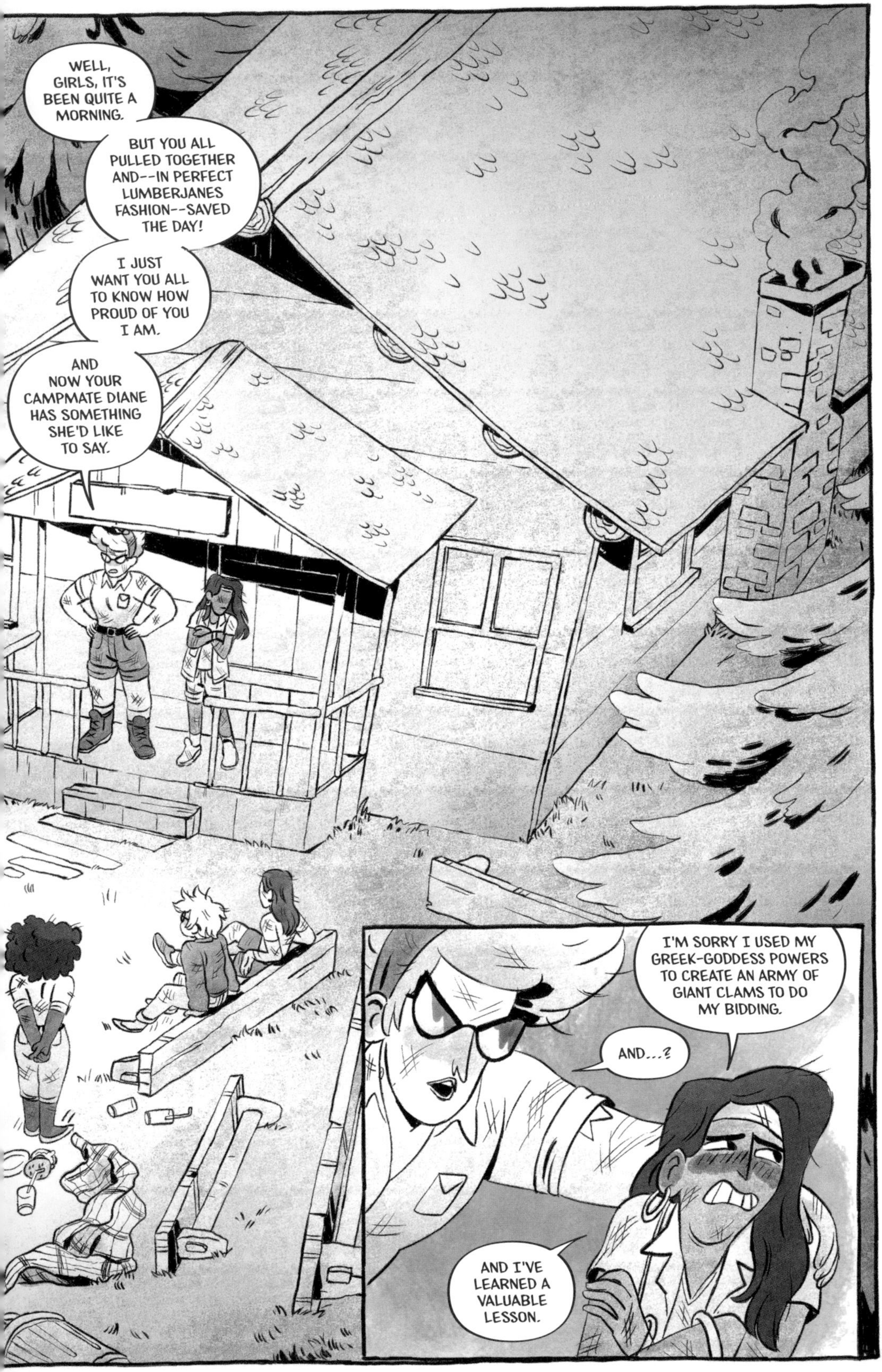
WELL, GIRLS, IT'S BEEN QUITE A MORNING.
BUT YOU ALL PULLED TOGETHER AND--IN PERFECT LUMBERJANES FASHION--SAVED THE DAY!
I JUST WANT YOU ALL TO KNOW HOW PROUD OF YOU I AM.
AND NOW YOUR CAMPMATE DIANE HAS SOMETHING SHE'D LIKE TO SAY.
I'M SORRY I USED MY GREEK-GODDESS POWERS TO CREATE AN ARMY OF GIANT CLAMS TO DO MY BIDDING.
AND...?
AND I'VE LEARNED A VALUABLE LESSON.

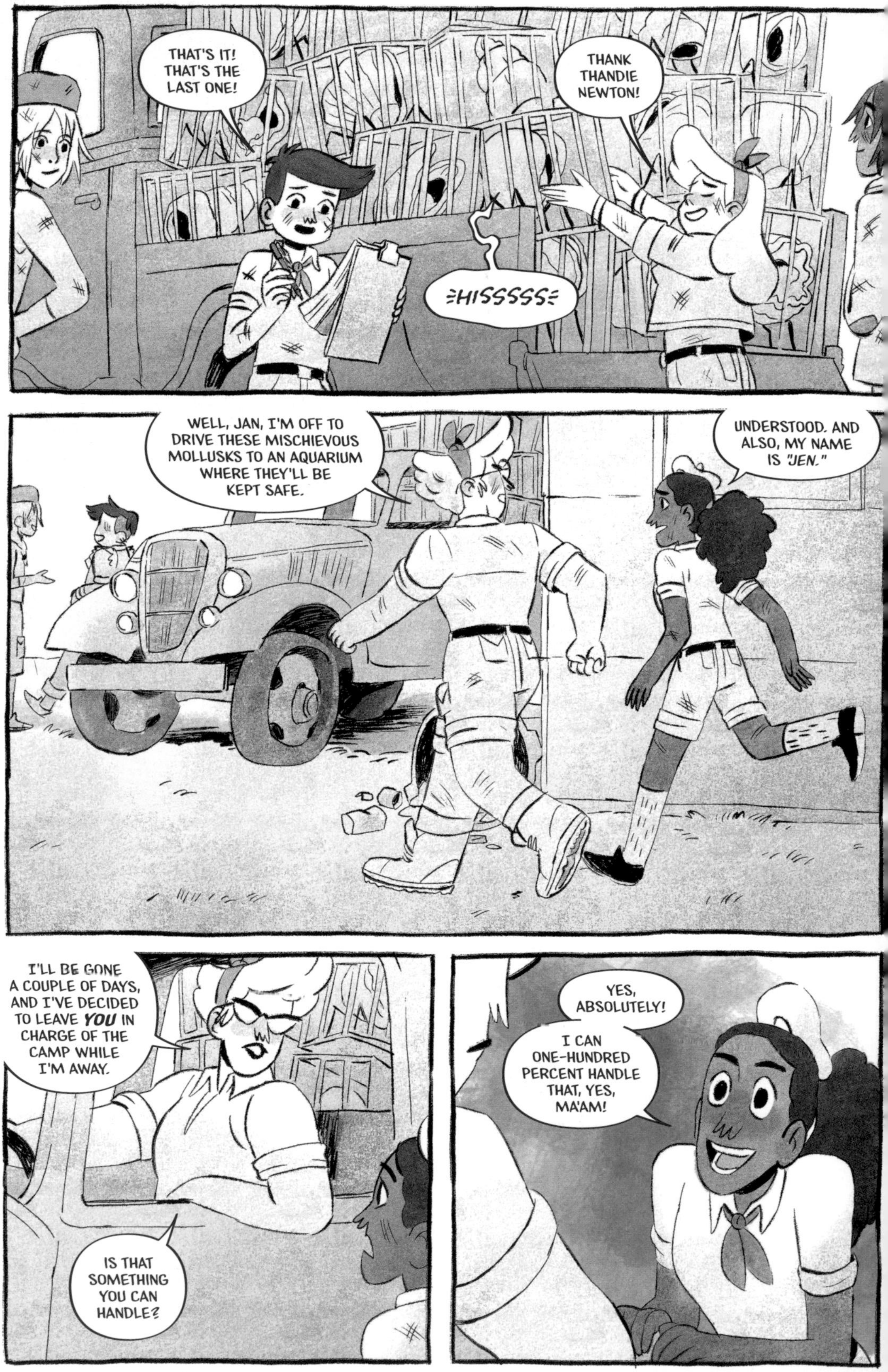
THAT'S IT! THAT'S THE LAST ONE!
THANK THANDIE NEWTON!
HISSSSS
WELL, JAN, I'M OFF TO DRIVE THESE MISCHIEVOUS MOLLUSKS TO AN AQUARIUM WHERE THEY'LL BE KEPT SAFE.
UNDERSTOOD. AND ALSO, MY NAME IS "JEN."
I'LL BE GONE A COUPLE OF DAYS, AND I'VE DECIDED TO LEAVE YOU IN CHARGE OF THE CAMP WHILE I'M AWAY.
IS THAT SOMETHING YOU CAN HANDLE?
YES, ABSOLUTELY!
I CAN ONE-HUNDRED PERCENT HANDLE THAT, YES, MA'AM!

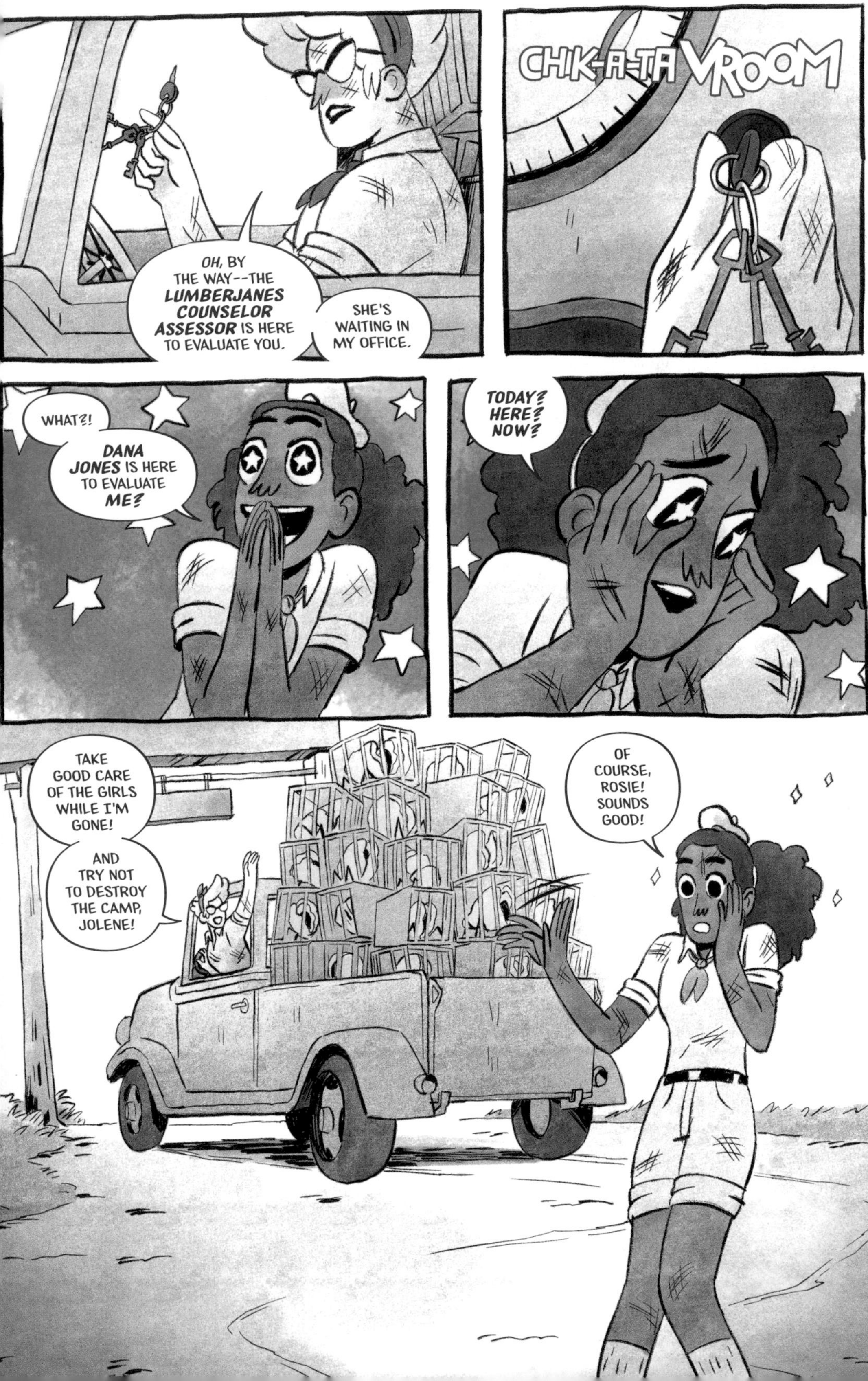

OH, BY THE WAY--THE LUMBERJANES COUNSELOR ASSESSOR IS HERE TO EVALUATE YOU.
SHE'S WAITING IN MY OFFICE.
CHIK-A-TA VROOM
WHAT?!
DANA JONES IS HERE TO EVALUATE ME?
TODAY? HERE? NOW?
TAKE GOOD CARE OF THE GIRLS WHILE I'M GONE!
AND TRY NOT TO DESTROY THE CAMP, JOLENE!
OF COURSE, ROSIE! SOUNDS GOOD!

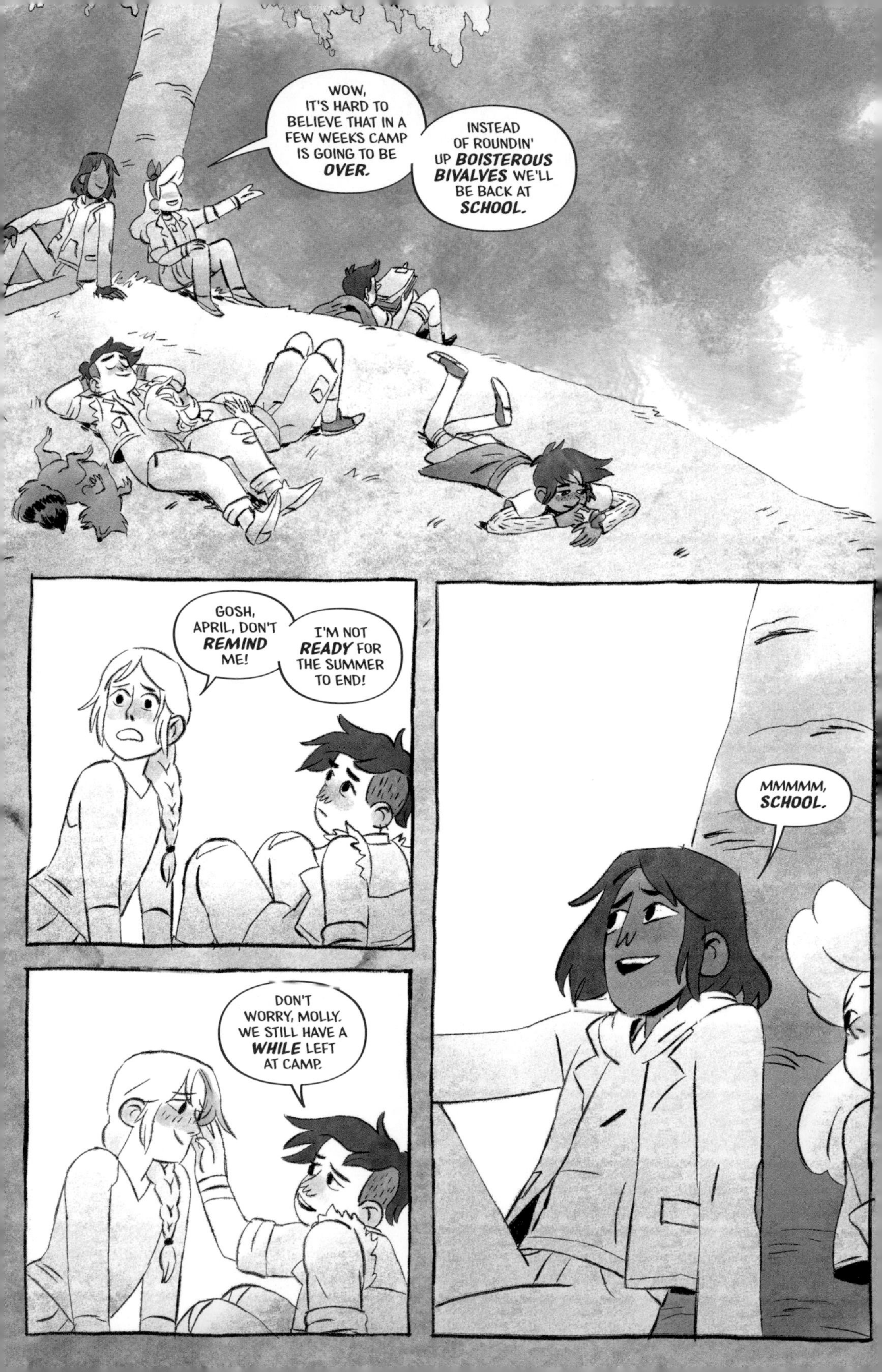
WOW, IT'S HARD TO BELIEVE THAT IN A FEW WEEKS CAMP IS GOING TO BE OVER.
INSTEAD OF ROUNDIN' UP BOISTEROUS BIVALVES WE'LL BE BACK AT SCHOOL.
GOSH, APRIL, DON'T REMIND ME!
I'M NOT READY FOR THE SUMMER TO END!
MMMMM, SCHOOL.
DON'T WORRY, MOLLY. WE STILL HAVE A WHILE LEFT AT CAMP.

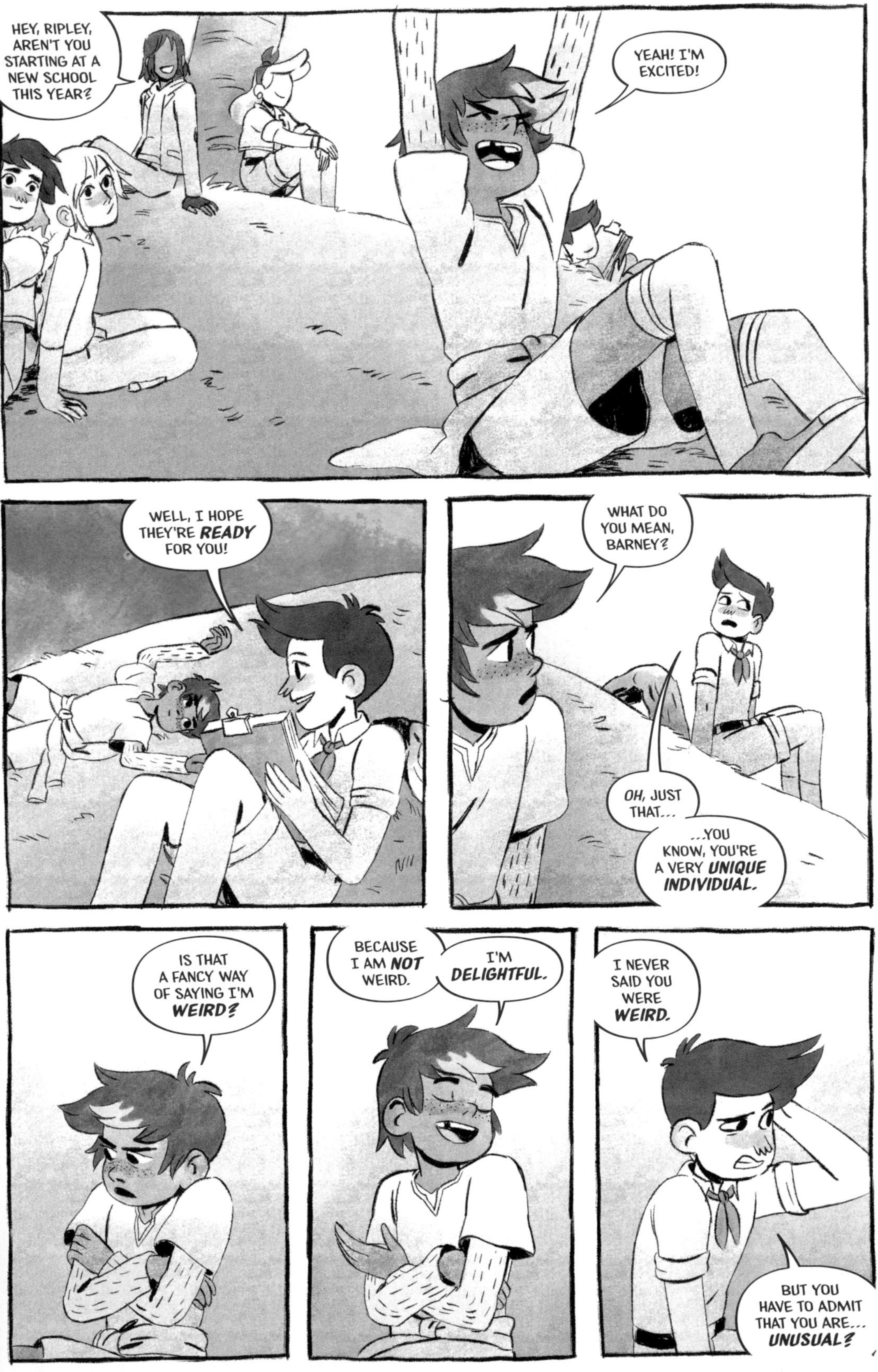
HEY, RIPLEY, AREN'T YOU STARTING AT A NEW SCHOOL THIS YEAR?
YEAH! I'M EXCITED!
WELL, I HOPE THEY'RE ***READY*** FOR YOU!
WHAT DO YOU MEAN, BARNEY?
OH, JUST THAT...
...YOU KNOW, YOU'RE A VERY ***UNIQUE INDIVIDUAL.***
IS THAT A FANCY WAY OF SAYING I'M ***WEIRD?***
BECAUSE I AM ***NOT*** WEIRD.
I'M ***DELIGHTFUL.***
I NEVER SAID YOU WERE ***WEIRD.***
BUT YOU HAVE TO ADMIT THAT YOU ARE... ***UNUSUAL?***

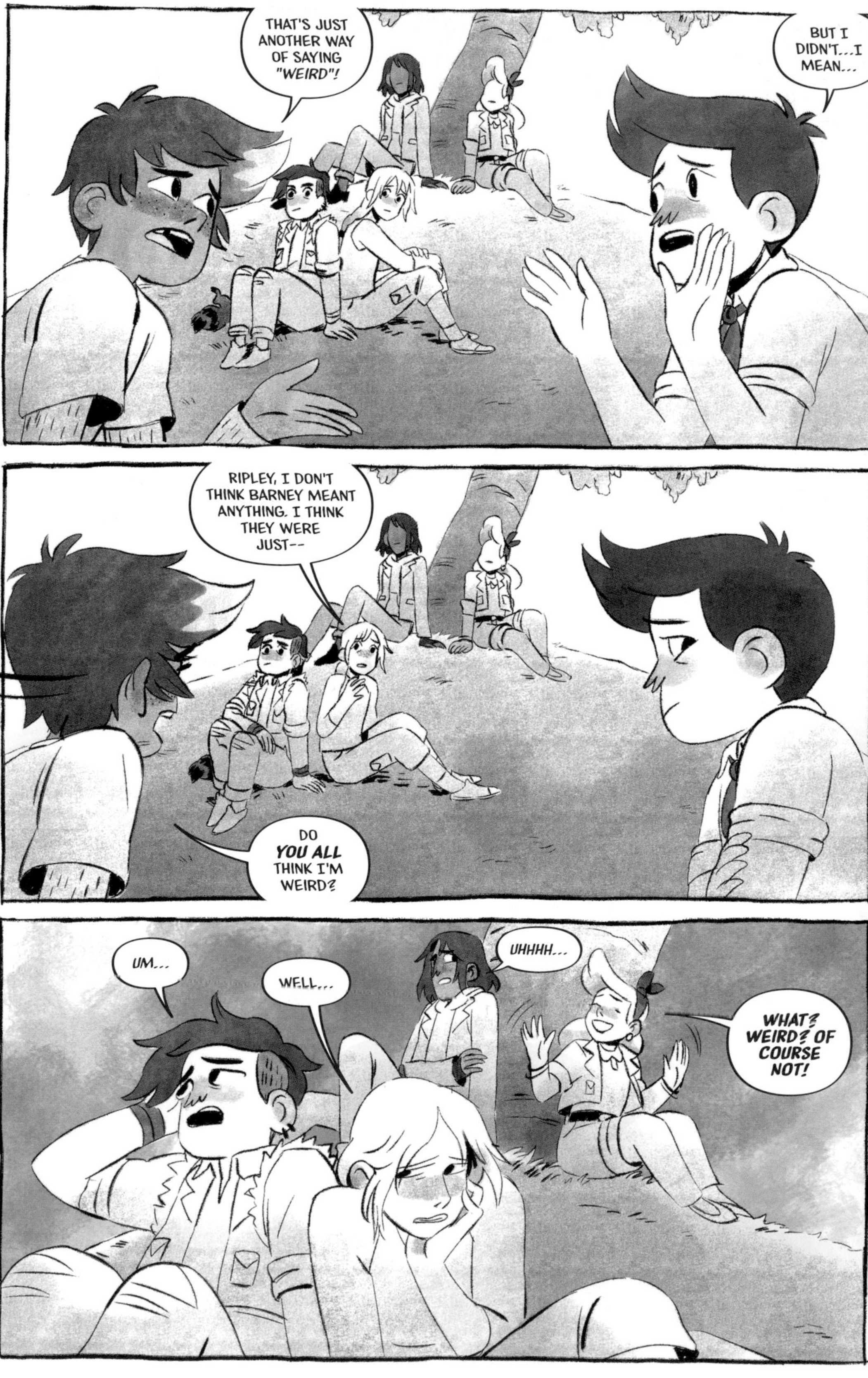
THAT'S JUST ANOTHER WAY OF SAYING "WEIRD"!
BUT I DIDN'T...I MEAN...
RIPLEY, I DON'T THINK BARNEY MEANT ANYTHING. I THINK THEY WERE JUST--
DO YOU ALL THINK I'M WEIRD?
UM...
WELL...
UHHHH...
WHAT? WEIRD? OF COURSE NOT!

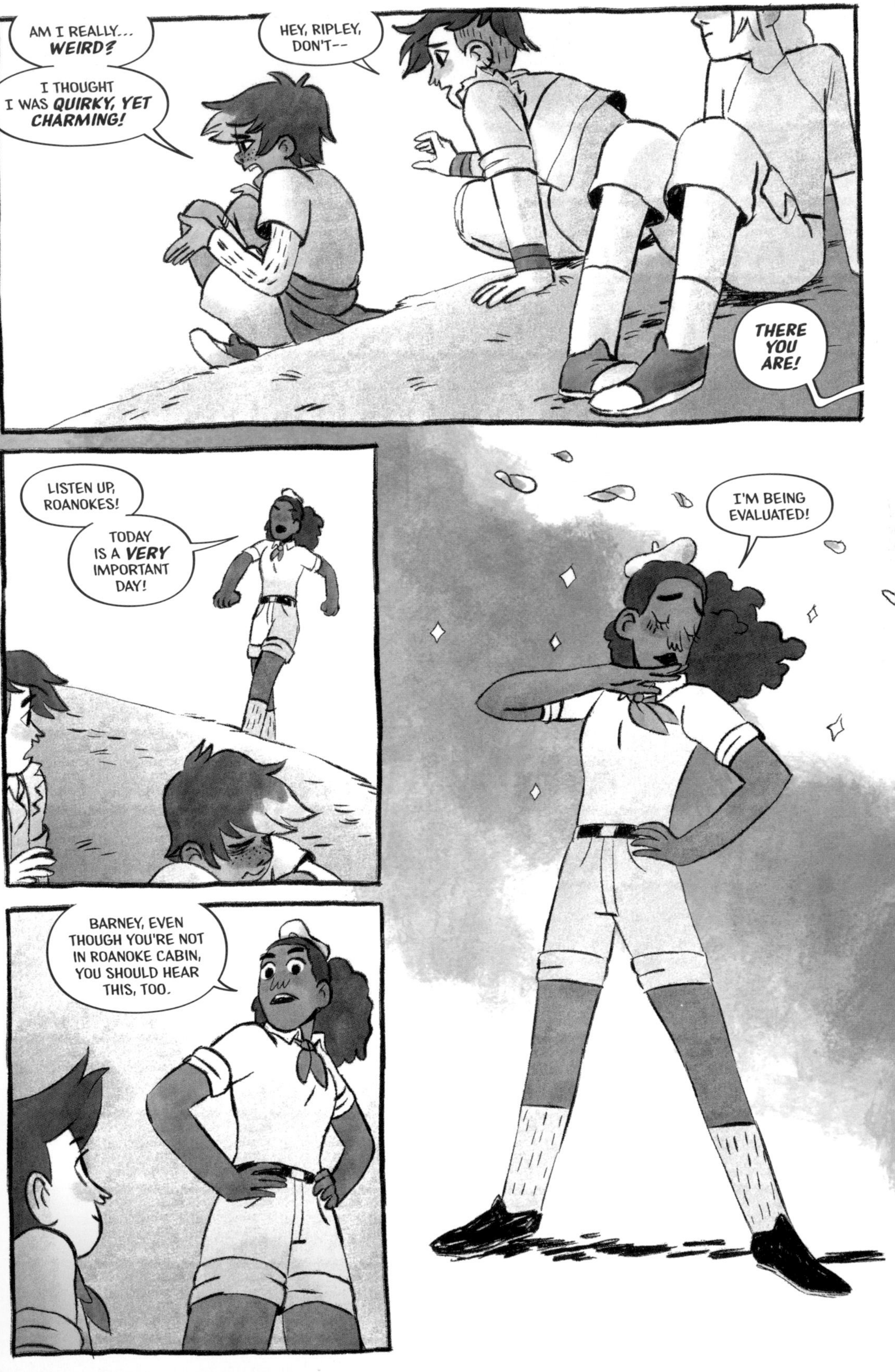

AM I REALLY... WEIRD?
I THOUGHT I WAS QUIRKY, YET CHARMING!
HEY, RIPLEY, DON'T--
THERE YOU ARE!
LISTEN UP, ROANOKES!
TODAY IS A VERY IMPORTANT DAY!
I'M BEING EVALUATED!
BARNEY, EVEN THOUGH YOU'RE NOT IN ROANOKE CABIN, YOU SHOULD HEAR THIS, TOO.

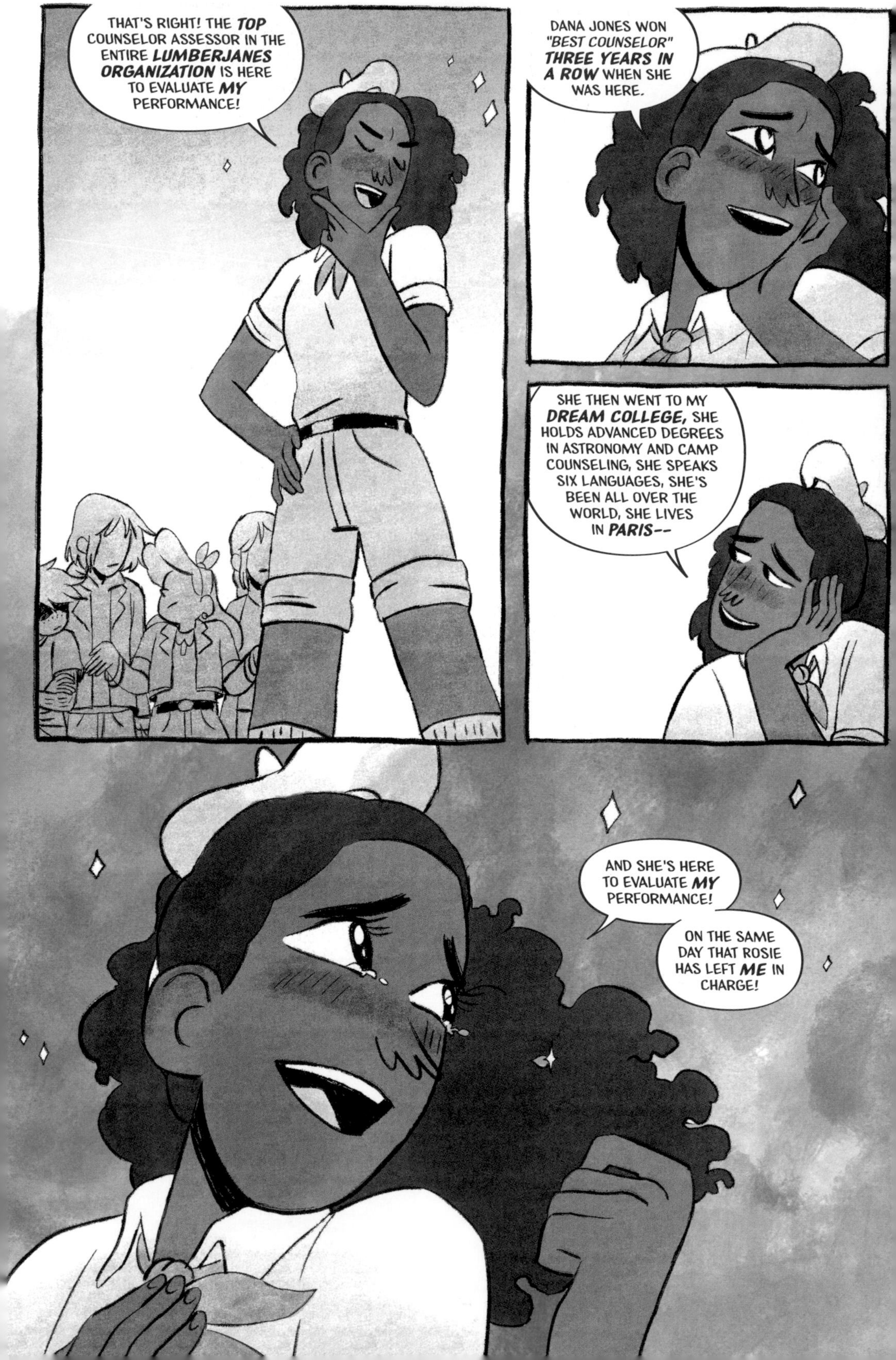
THAT'S RIGHT! THE TOP COUNSELOR ASSESSOR IN THE ENTIRE LUMBERJANES ORGANIZATION IS HERE TO EVALUATE MY PERFORMANCE!
DANA JONES WON "BEST COUNSELOR" THREE YEARS IN A ROW WHEN SHE WAS HERE.
SHE THEN WENT TO MY DREAM COLLEGE, SHE HOLDS ADVANCED DEGREES IN ASTRONOMY AND CAMP COUNSELING, SHE SPEAKS SIX LANGUAGES, SHE'S BEEN ALL OVER THE WORLD, SHE LIVES IN PARIS--
AND SHE'S HERE TO EVALUATE MY PERFORMANCE!
ON THE SAME DAY THAT ROSIE HAS LEFT ME IN CHARGE!

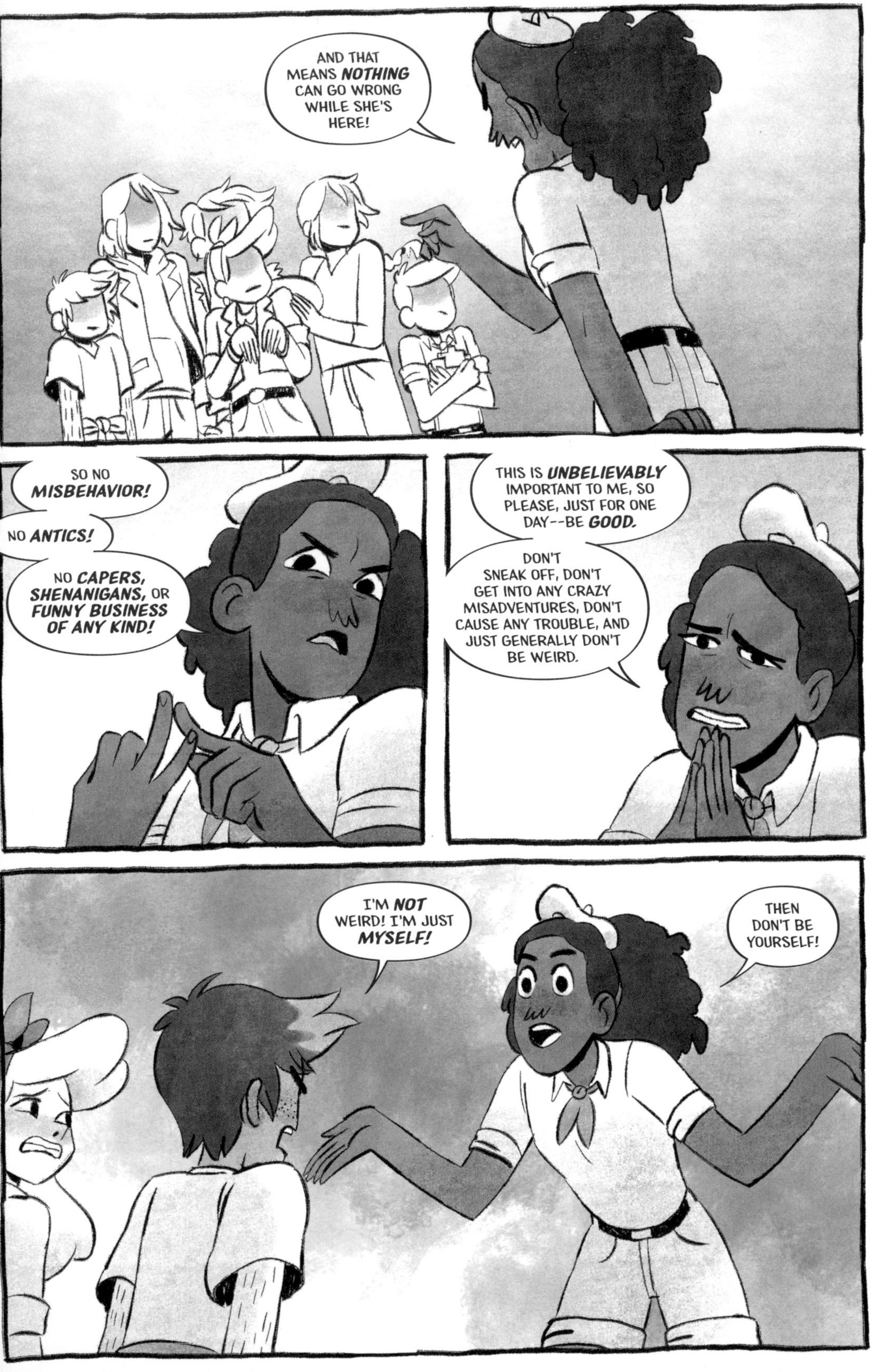
AND THAT MEANS NOTHING CAN GO WRONG WHILE SHE'S HERE!
SO NO MISBEHAVIOR!
NO ANTICS!
NO CAPERS, SHENANIGANS, OR FUNNY BUSINESS OF ANY KIND!
THIS IS UNBELIEVABLY IMPORTANT TO ME, SO PLEASE, JUST FOR ONE DAY--BE GOOD.
DON'T SNEAK OFF, DON'T GET INTO ANY CRAZY MISADVENTURES, DON'T CAUSE ANY TROUBLE, AND JUST GENERALLY DON'T BE WEIRD.
I'M NOT WEIRD! I'M JUST MYSELF!
THEN DON'T BE YOURSELF!

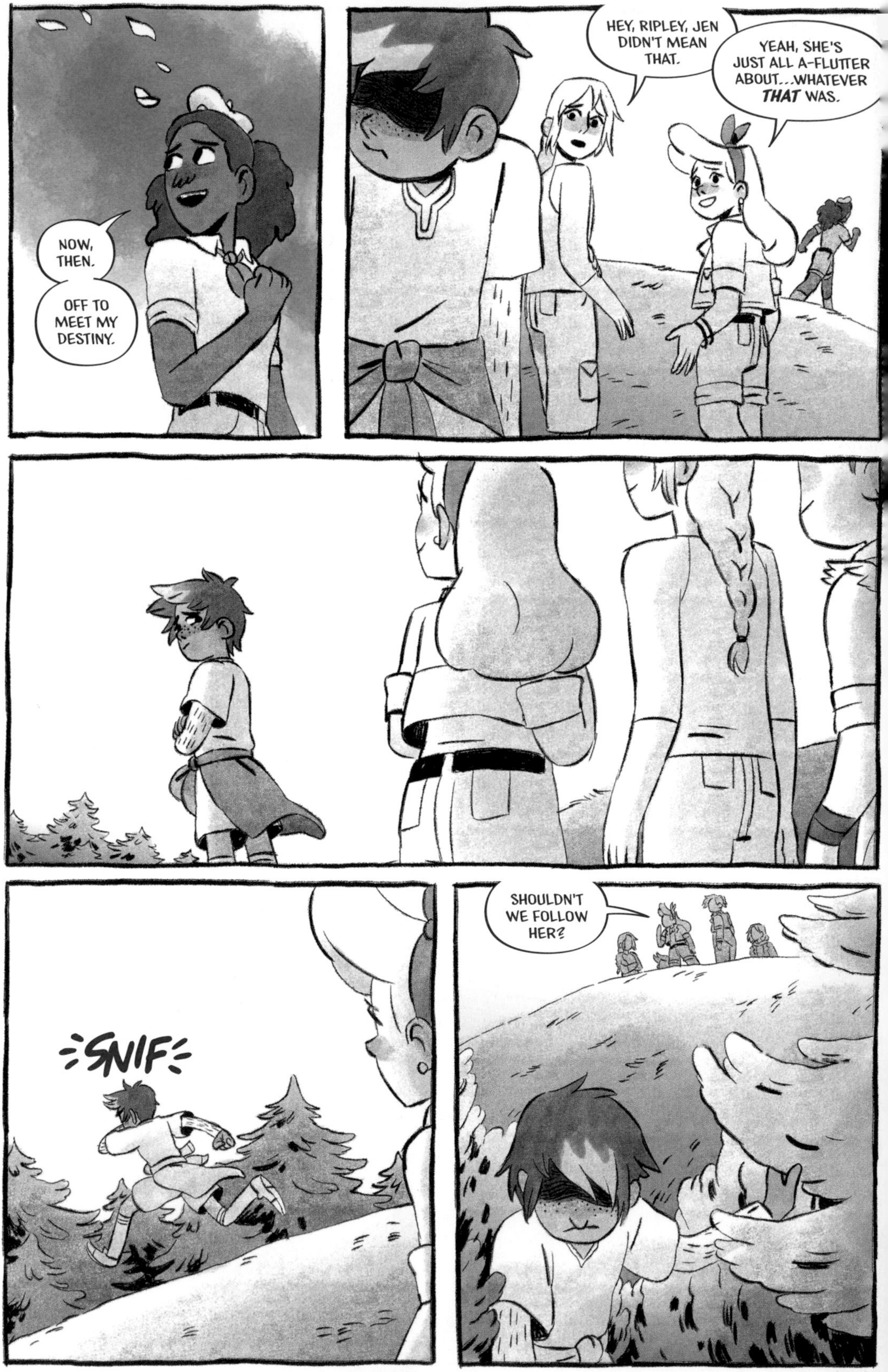
NOW, THEN.
OFF TO MEET MY DESTINY.
HEY, RIPLEY, JEN DIDN'T MEAN THAT.
YEAH, SHE'S JUST ALL A-FLUTTER ABOUT...WHATEVER *THAT* WAS.
SNIF
SHOULDN'T WE FOLLOW HER?

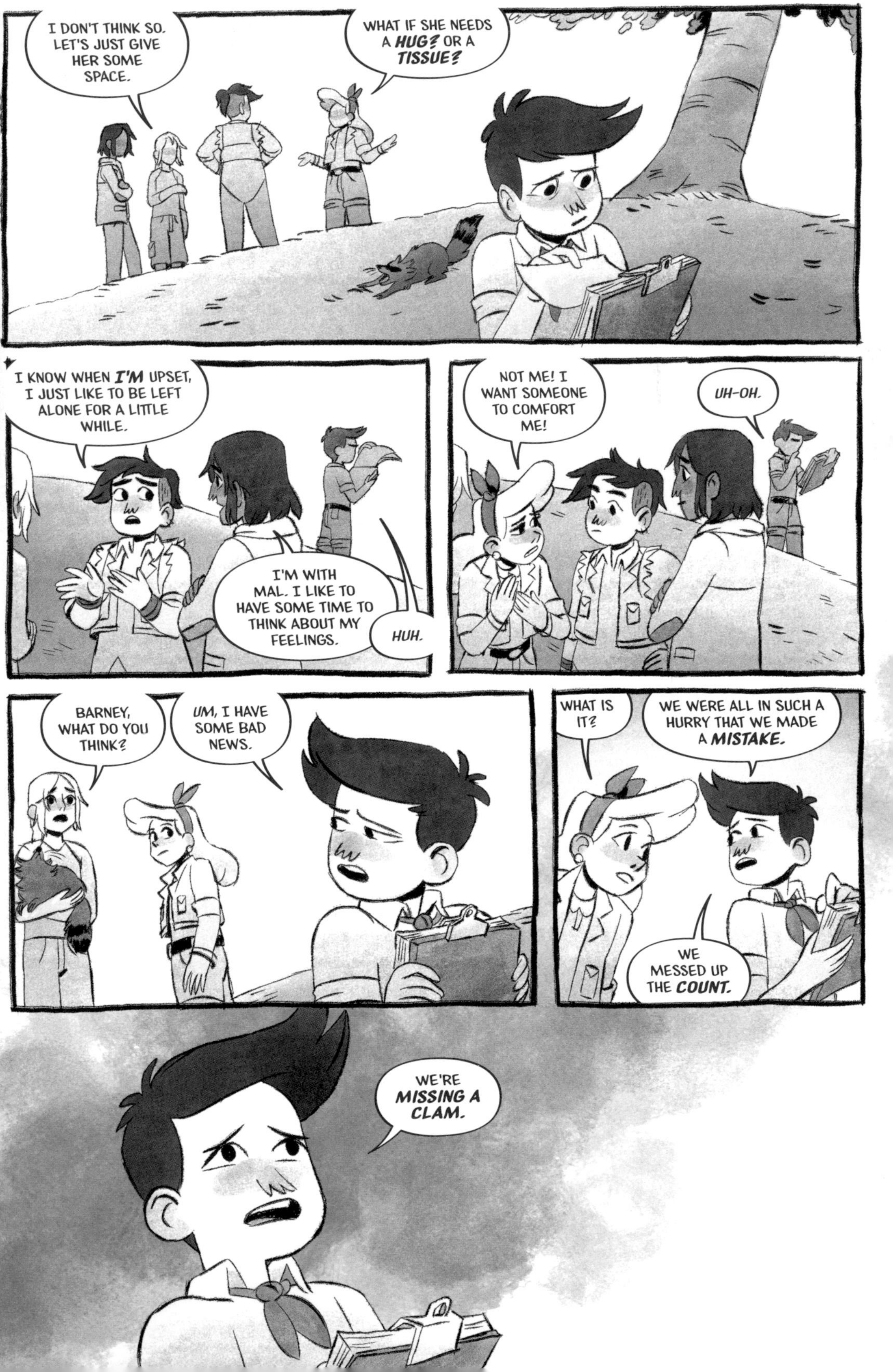

I DON'T THINK SO. LET'S JUST GIVE HER SOME SPACE.
WHAT IF SHE NEEDS A HUG? OR A TISSUE?
I KNOW WHEN I'M UPSET, I JUST LIKE TO BE LEFT ALONE FOR A LITTLE WHILE.
I'M WITH MAL. I LIKE TO HAVE SOME TIME TO THINK ABOUT MY FEELINGS.
HUH.
NOT ME! I WANT SOMEONE TO COMFORT ME!
UH-OH.
BARNEY, WHAT DO YOU THINK?
UM, I HAVE SOME BAD NEWS.
WHAT IS IT?
WE WERE ALL IN SUCH A HURRY THAT WE MADE A MISTAKE.
WE MESSED UP THE COUNT.
WE'RE MISSING A CLAM.

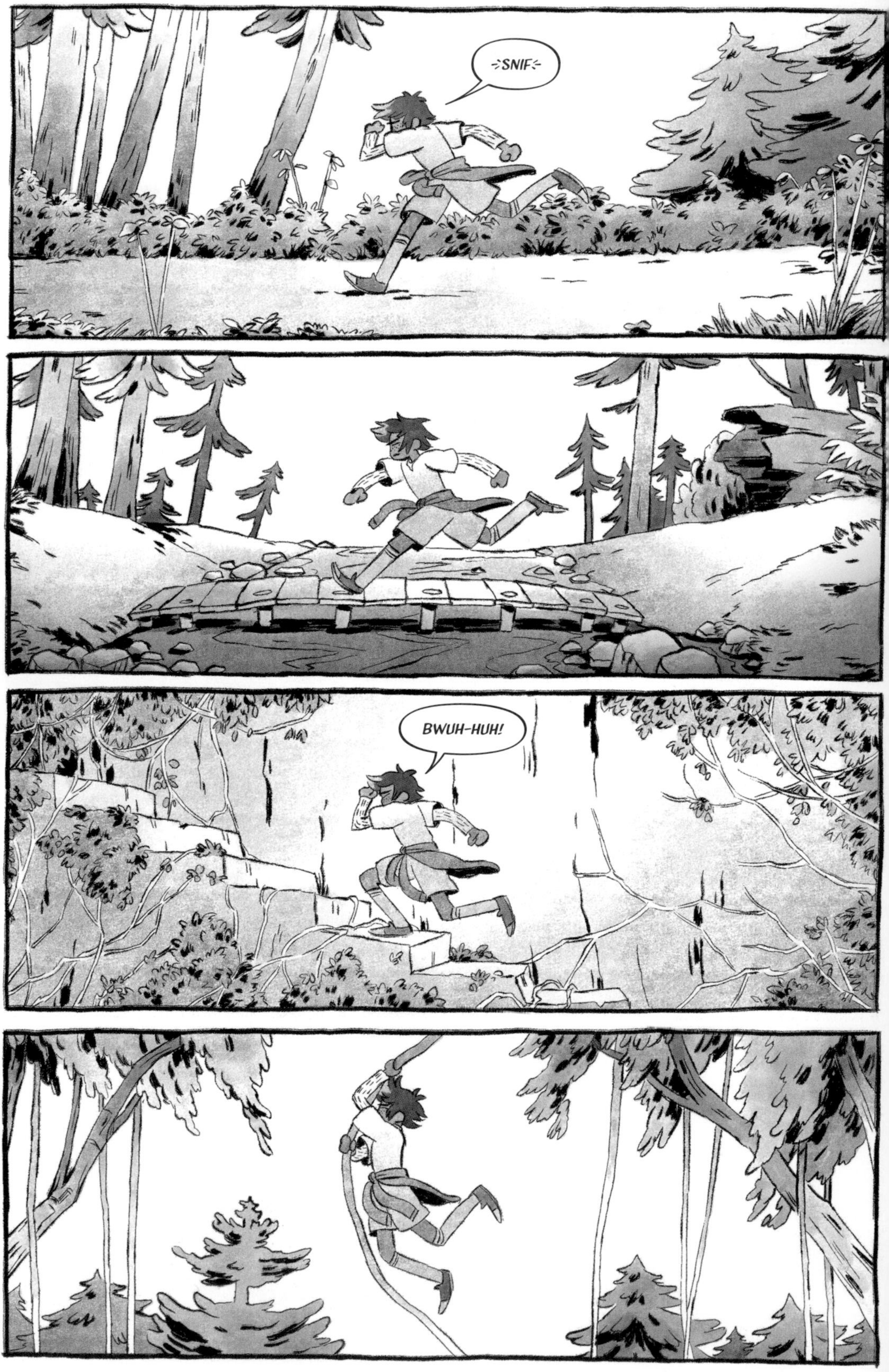
SNIF
BWUH-HUH!

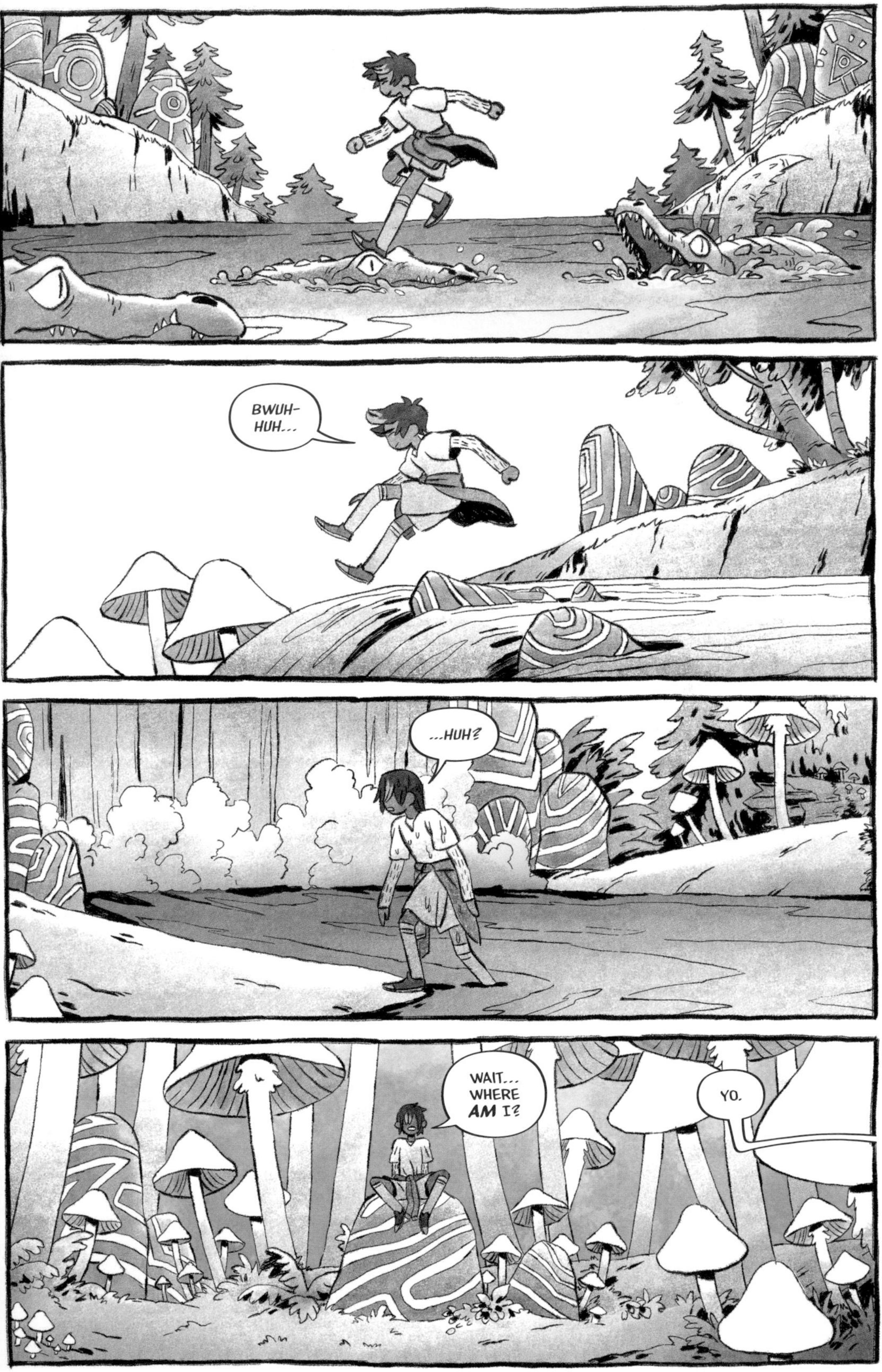
BWUH-HUH...
...HUH?
WAIT... WHERE AM I?
YO.

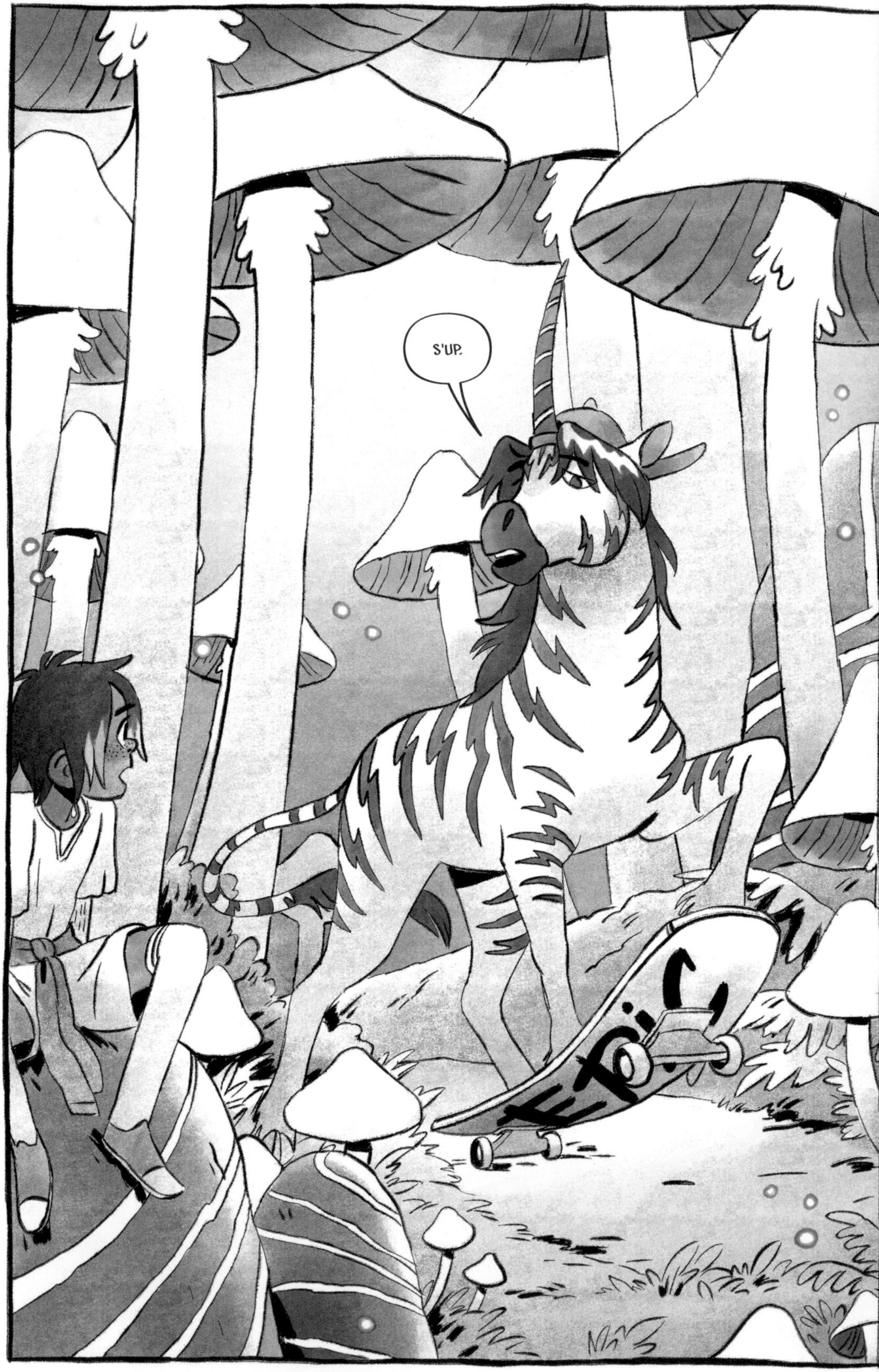
S'UP.

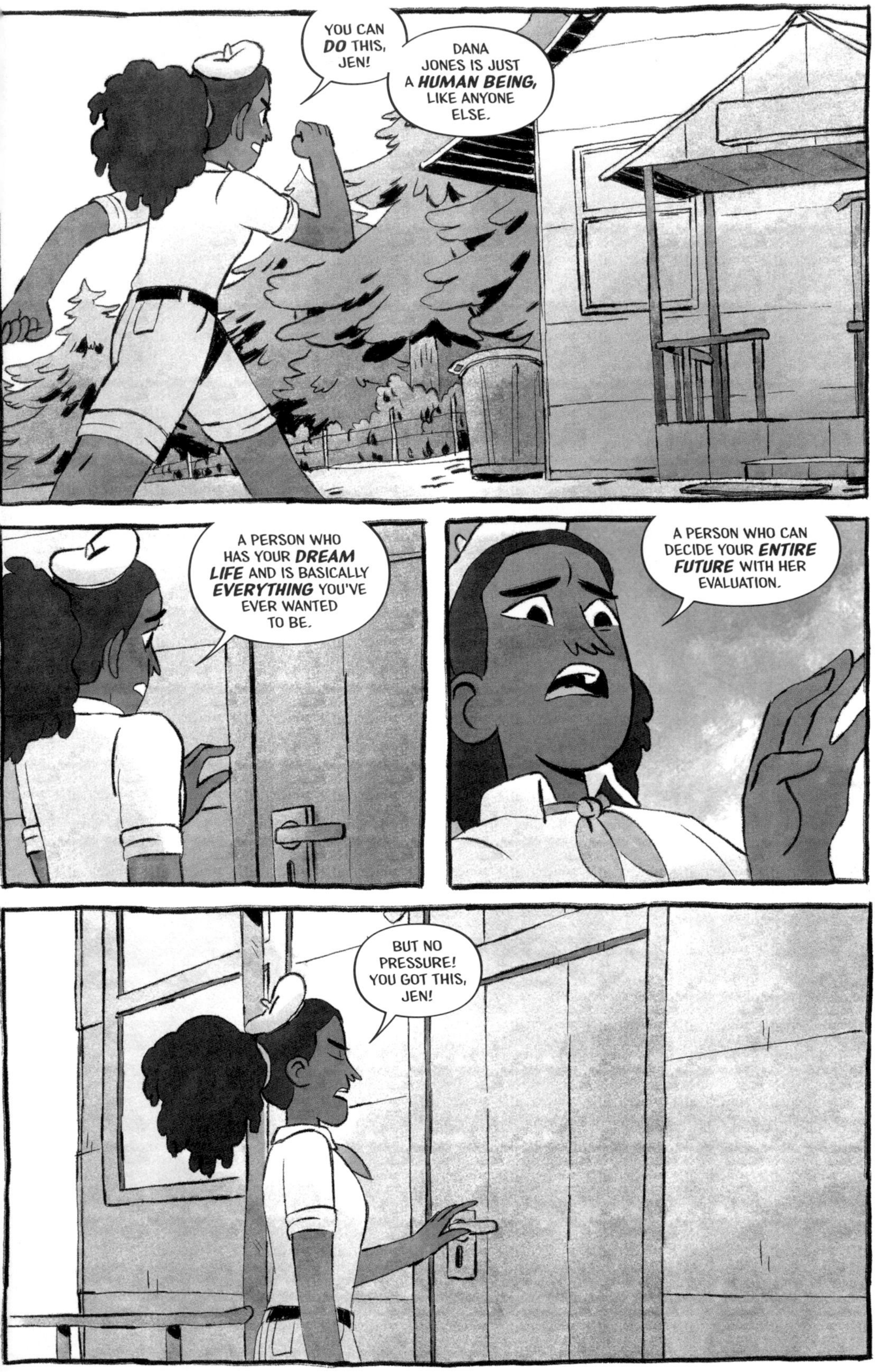
YOU CAN DO THIS, JEN!
DANA JONES IS JUST A HUMAN BEING, LIKE ANYONE ELSE.
A PERSON WHO HAS YOUR DREAM LIFE AND IS BASICALLY EVERYTHING YOU'VE EVER WANTED TO BE.
A PERSON WHO CAN DECIDE YOUR ENTIRE FUTURE WITH HER EVALUATION.
BUT NO PRESSURE! YOU GOT THIS, JEN!

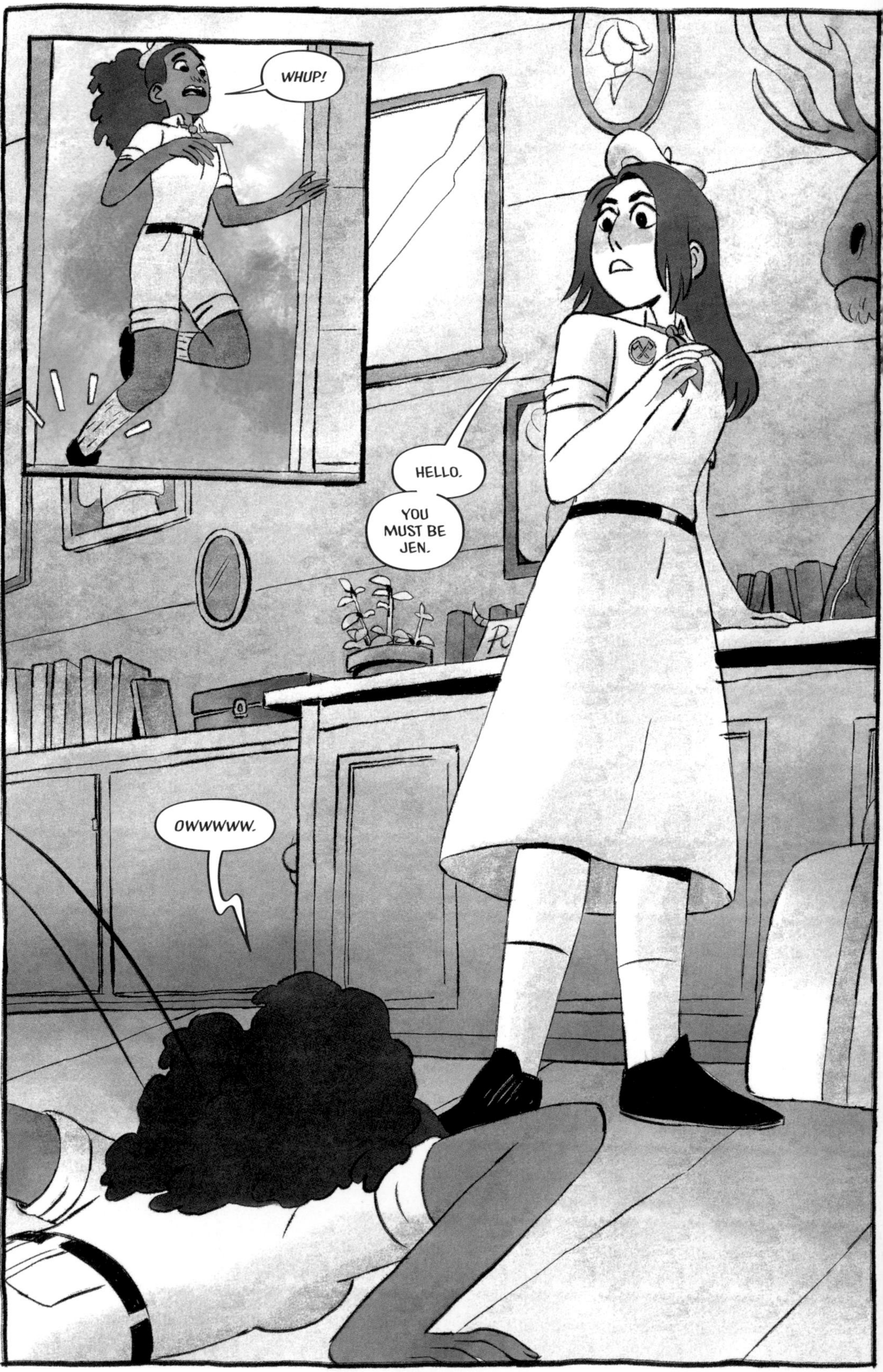
WHUP!
HELLO.
YOU MUST BE JEN.
OWWWWW.

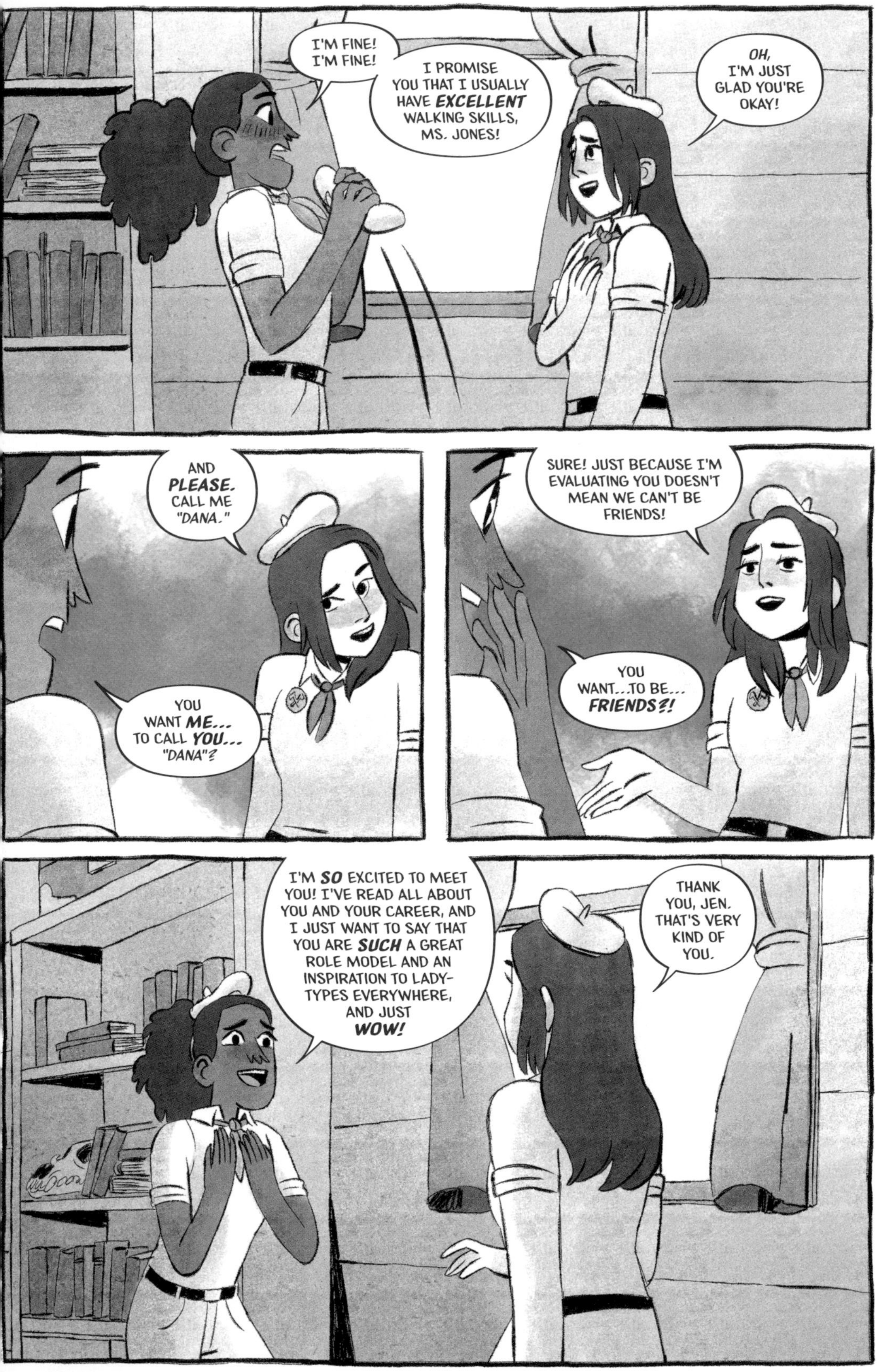
I'M FINE! I'M FINE!
I PROMISE YOU THAT I USUALLY HAVE EXCELLENT WALKING SKILLS, MS. JONES!
OH, I'M JUST GLAD YOU'RE OKAY!
AND PLEASE. CALL ME "DANA."
YOU WANT ME... TO CALL YOU... "DANA"?
SURE! JUST BECAUSE I'M EVALUATING YOU DOESN'T MEAN WE CAN'T BE FRIENDS!
YOU WANT...TO BE... FRIENDS?!
I'M SO EXCITED TO MEET YOU! I'VE READ ALL ABOUT YOU AND YOUR CAREER, AND I JUST WANT TO SAY THAT YOU ARE SUCH A GREAT ROLE MODEL AND AN INSPIRATION TO LADY-TYPES EVERYWHERE, AND JUST WOW!
THANK YOU, JEN. THAT'S VERY KIND OF YOU.

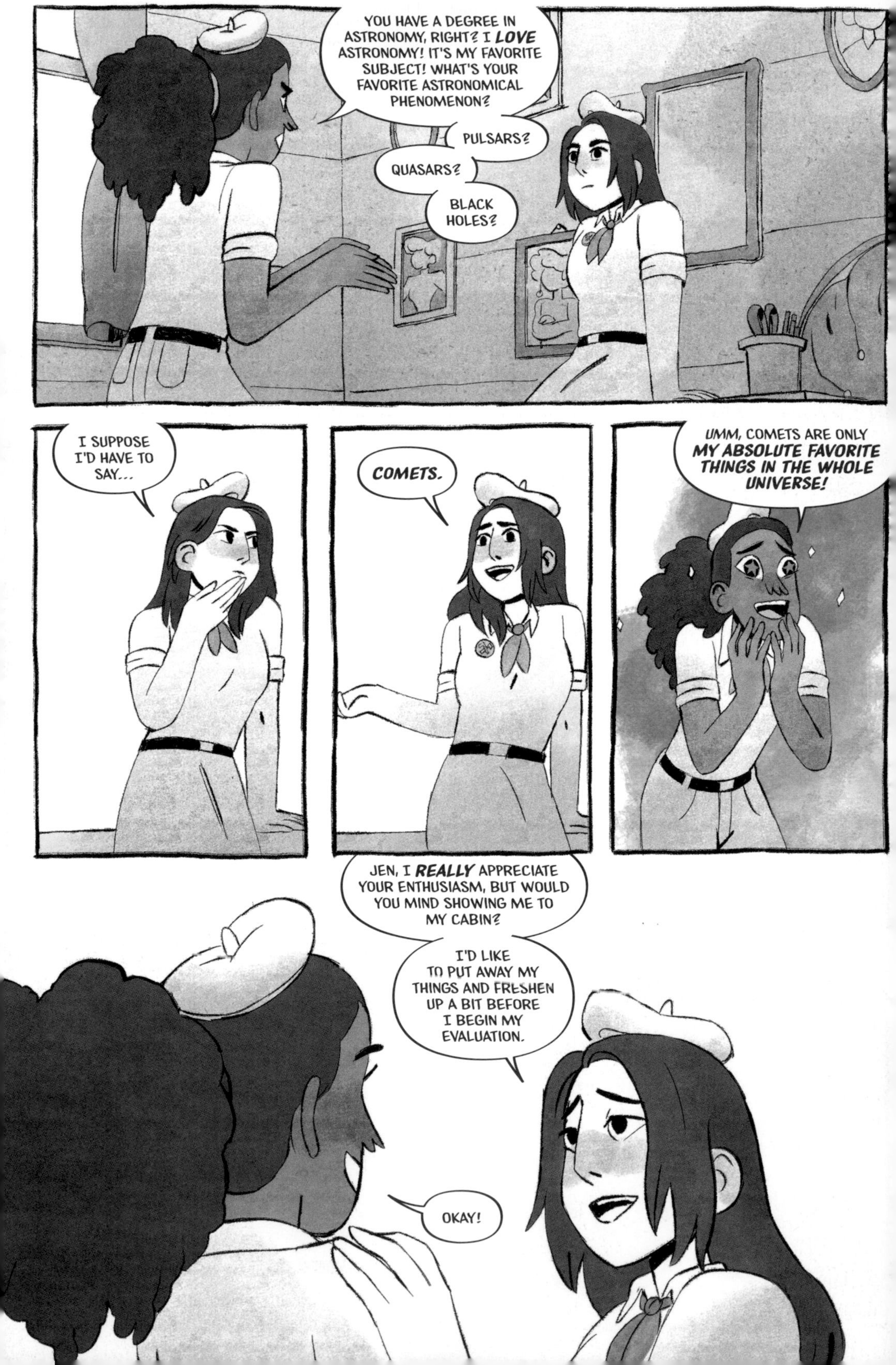
YOU HAVE A DEGREE IN ASTRONOMY, RIGHT? I LOVE ASTRONOMY! IT'S MY FAVORITE SUBJECT! WHAT'S YOUR FAVORITE ASTRONOMICAL PHENOMENON?
PULSARS?
QUASARS?
BLACK HOLES?
I SUPPOSE I'D HAVE TO SAY...
COMETS.
UMM, COMETS ARE ONLY MY ABSOLUTE FAVORITE THINGS IN THE WHOLE UNIVERSE!
JEN, I REALLY APPRECIATE YOUR ENTHUSIASM, BUT WOULD YOU MIND SHOWING ME TO MY CABIN?
I'D LIKE TO PUT AWAY MY THINGS AND FRESHEN UP A BIT BEFORE I BEGIN MY EVALUATION.
OKAY!

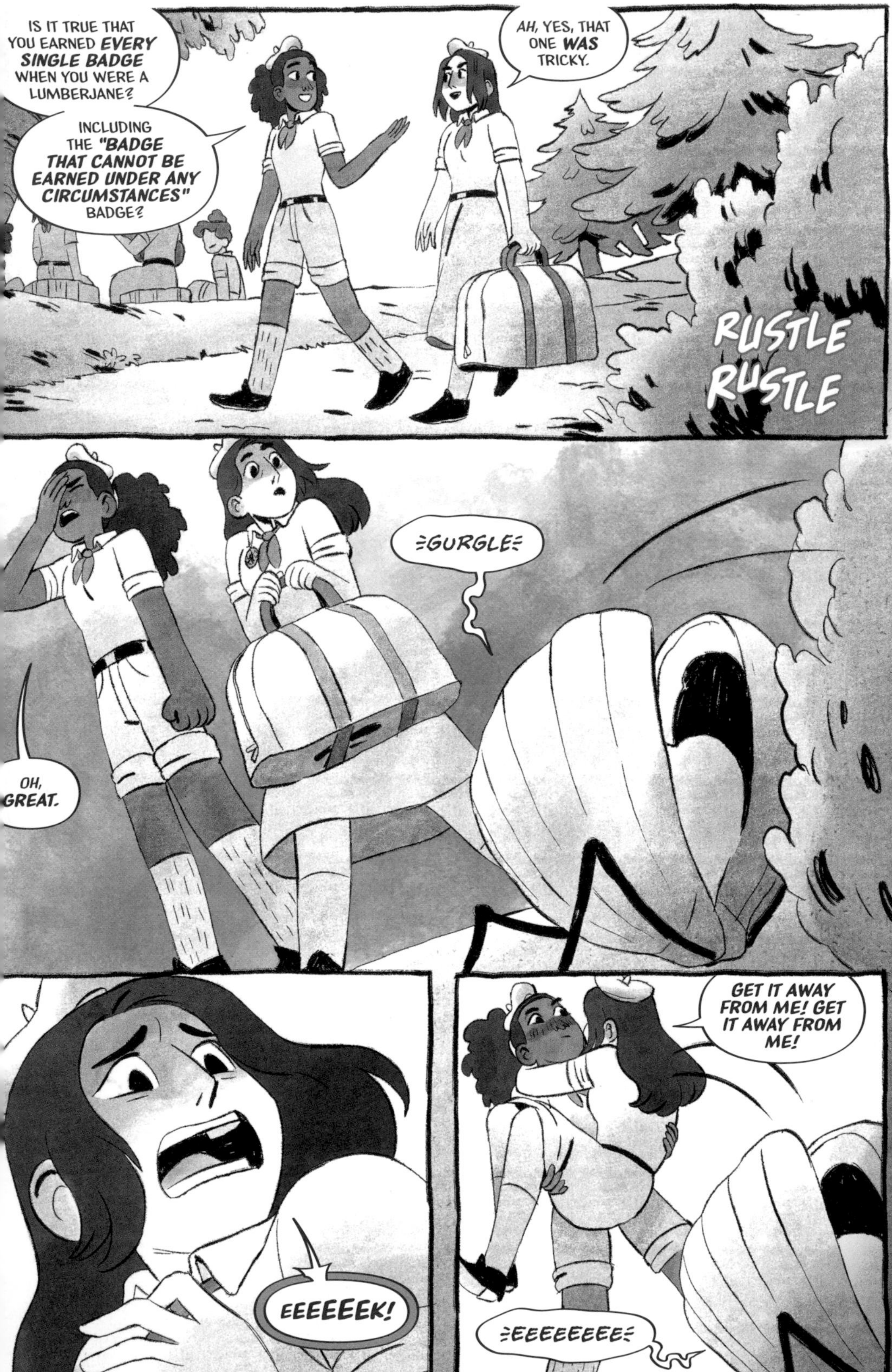
IS IT TRUE THAT YOU EARNED EVERY SINGLE BADGE WHEN YOU WERE A LUMBERJANE?
INCLUDING THE "BADGE THAT CANNOT BE EARNED UNDER ANY CIRCUMSTANCES" BADGE?
AH, YES, THAT ONE WAS TRICKY.
RUSTLE RUSTLE
GURGLE
OH, GREAT.
EEEEEEK!
GET IT AWAY FROM ME! GET IT AWAY FROM ME!
EEEEEEEE

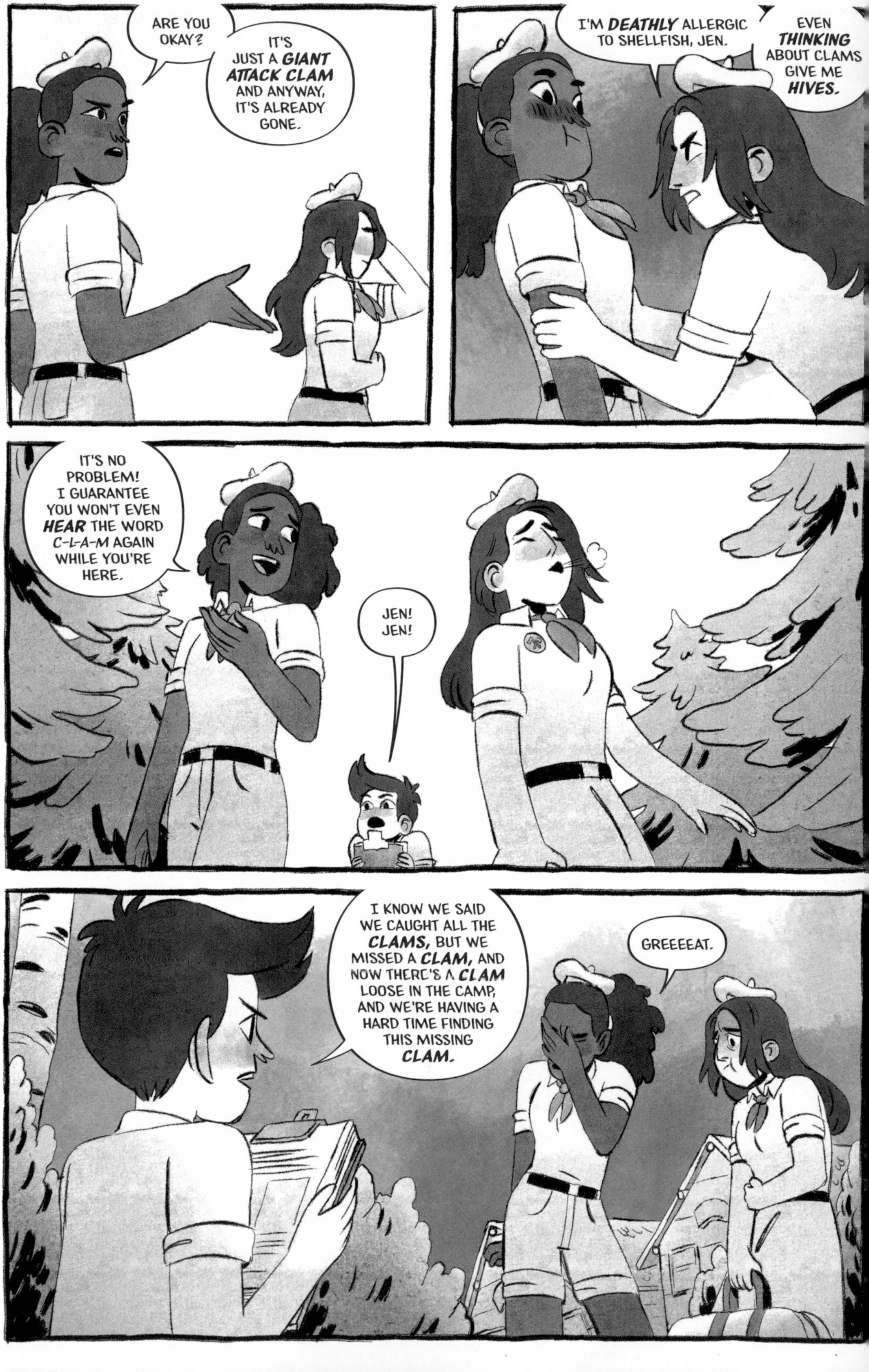
ARE YOU OKAY?
IT'S JUST A GIANT ATTACK CLAM AND ANYWAY, IT'S ALREADY GONE.
I'M DEATHLY ALLERGIC TO SHELLFISH, JEN.
EVEN THINKING ABOUT CLAMS GIVE ME HIVES.
IT'S NO PROBLEM! I GUARANTEE YOU WON'T EVEN HEAR THE WORD C-L-A-M AGAIN WHILE YOU'RE HERE.
JEN! JEN!
I KNOW WE SAID WE CAUGHT ALL THE CLAMS, BUT WE MISSED A CLAM, AND NOW THERE'S A CLAM LOOSE IN THE CAMP, AND WE'RE HAVING A HARD TIME FINDING THIS MISSING CLAM.
GREEEEAT.

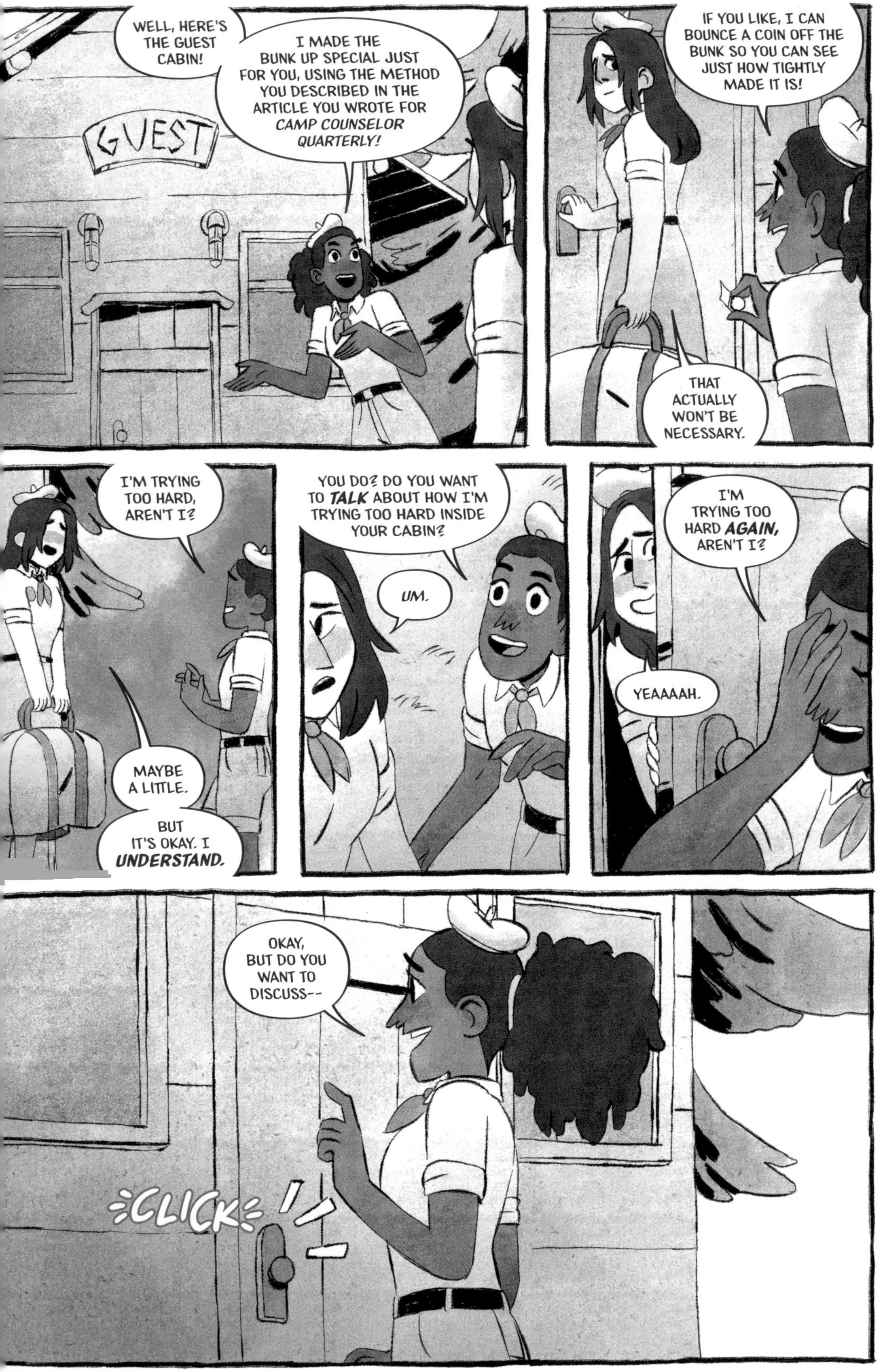
WELL, HERE'S THE GUEST CABIN!
I MADE THE BUNK UP SPECIAL JUST FOR YOU, USING THE METHOD YOU DESCRIBED IN THE ARTICLE YOU WROTE FOR *CAMP COUNSELOR QUARTERLY!*
GUEST
IF YOU LIKE, I CAN BOUNCE A COIN OFF THE BUNK SO YOU CAN SEE JUST HOW TIGHTLY MADE IT IS!
THAT ACTUALLY WON'T BE NECESSARY.
I'M TRYING TOO HARD, AREN'T I?
MAYBE A LITTLE.
BUT IT'S OKAY. I ***UNDERSTAND.***
YOU DO? DO YOU WANT TO ***TALK*** ABOUT HOW I'M TRYING TOO HARD INSIDE YOUR CABIN?
UM.
I'M TRYING TOO HARD ***AGAIN,*** AREN'T I?
YEAAAAH.
OKAY, BUT DO YOU WANT TO DISCUSS--
CLICK

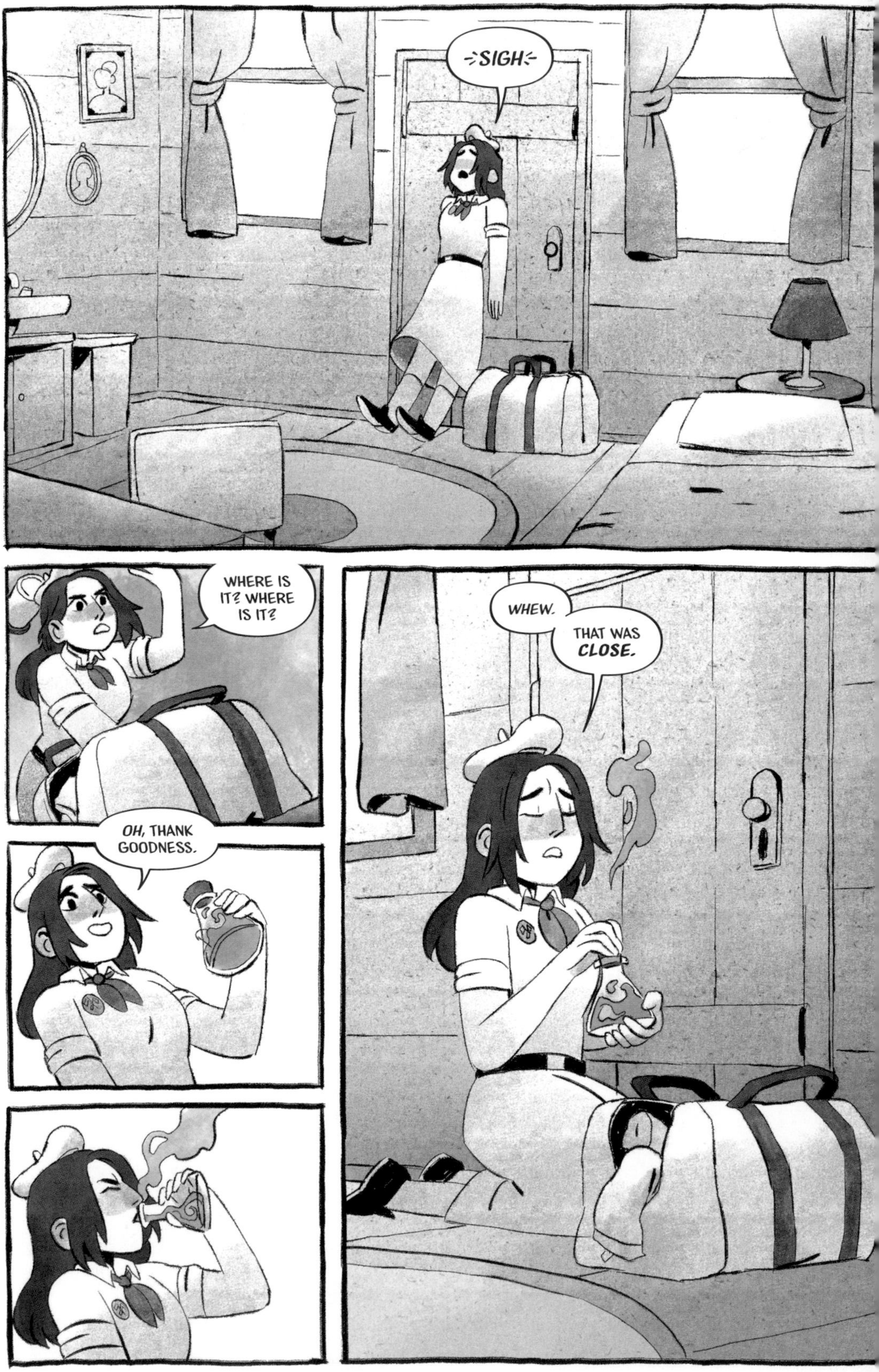
SIGH
WHERE IS IT? WHERE IS IT?
OH, THANK GOODNESS.
WHEW.
THAT WAS *CLOSE.*

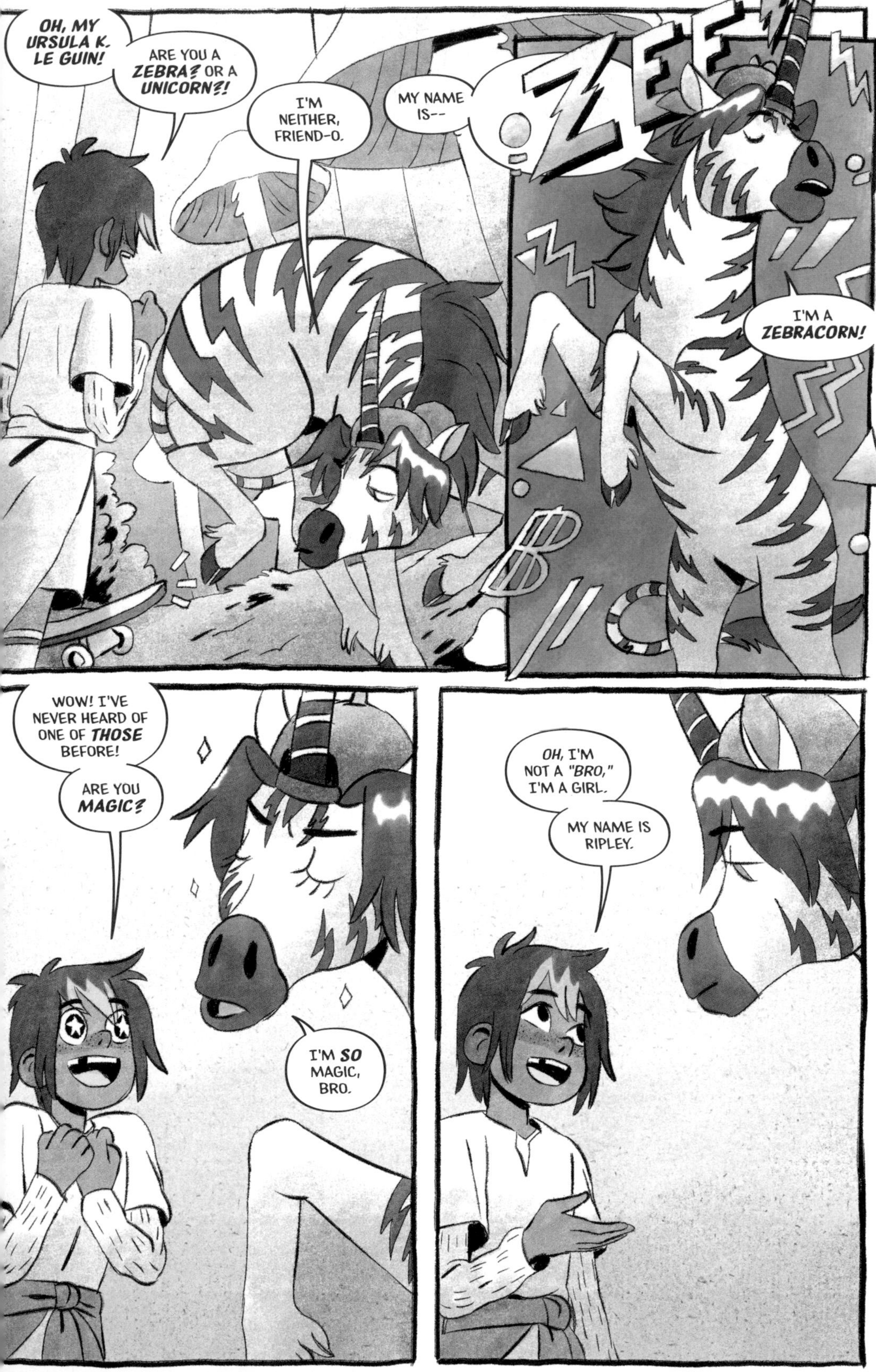
OH, MY URSULA K. LE GUIN!
ARE YOU A ZEBRA? OR A UNICORN?!
I'M NEITHER, FRIEND-O.
MY NAME IS--
ZEE!
I'M A ZEBRACORN!
WOW! I'VE NEVER HEARD OF ONE OF THOSE BEFORE!
ARE YOU MAGIC?
I'M SO MAGIC, BRO.
OH, I'M NOT A "BRO," I'M A GIRL.
MY NAME IS RIPLEY.

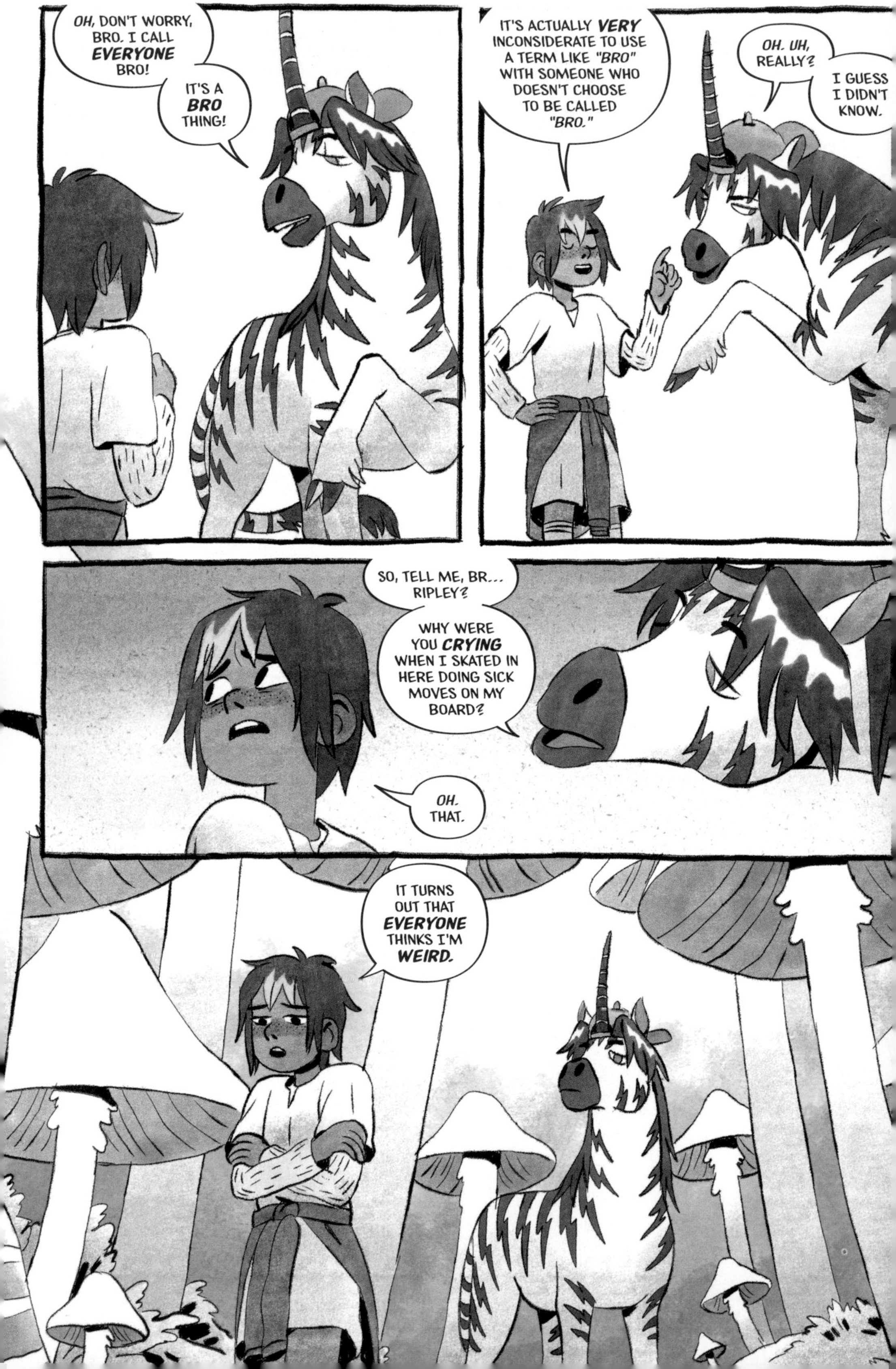
OH, DON'T WORRY, BRO. I CALL EVERYONE BRO!
IT'S A BRO THING!
IT'S ACTUALLY VERY INCONSIDERATE TO USE A TERM LIKE "BRO" WITH SOMEONE WHO DOESN'T CHOOSE TO BE CALLED "BRO."
OH. UH, REALLY?
I GUESS I DIDN'T KNOW.
SO, TELL ME, BR... RIPLEY?
WHY WERE YOU CRYING WHEN I SKATED IN HERE DOING SICK MOVES ON MY BOARD?
OH. THAT.
IT TURNS OUT THAT EVERYONE THINKS I'M WEIRD.

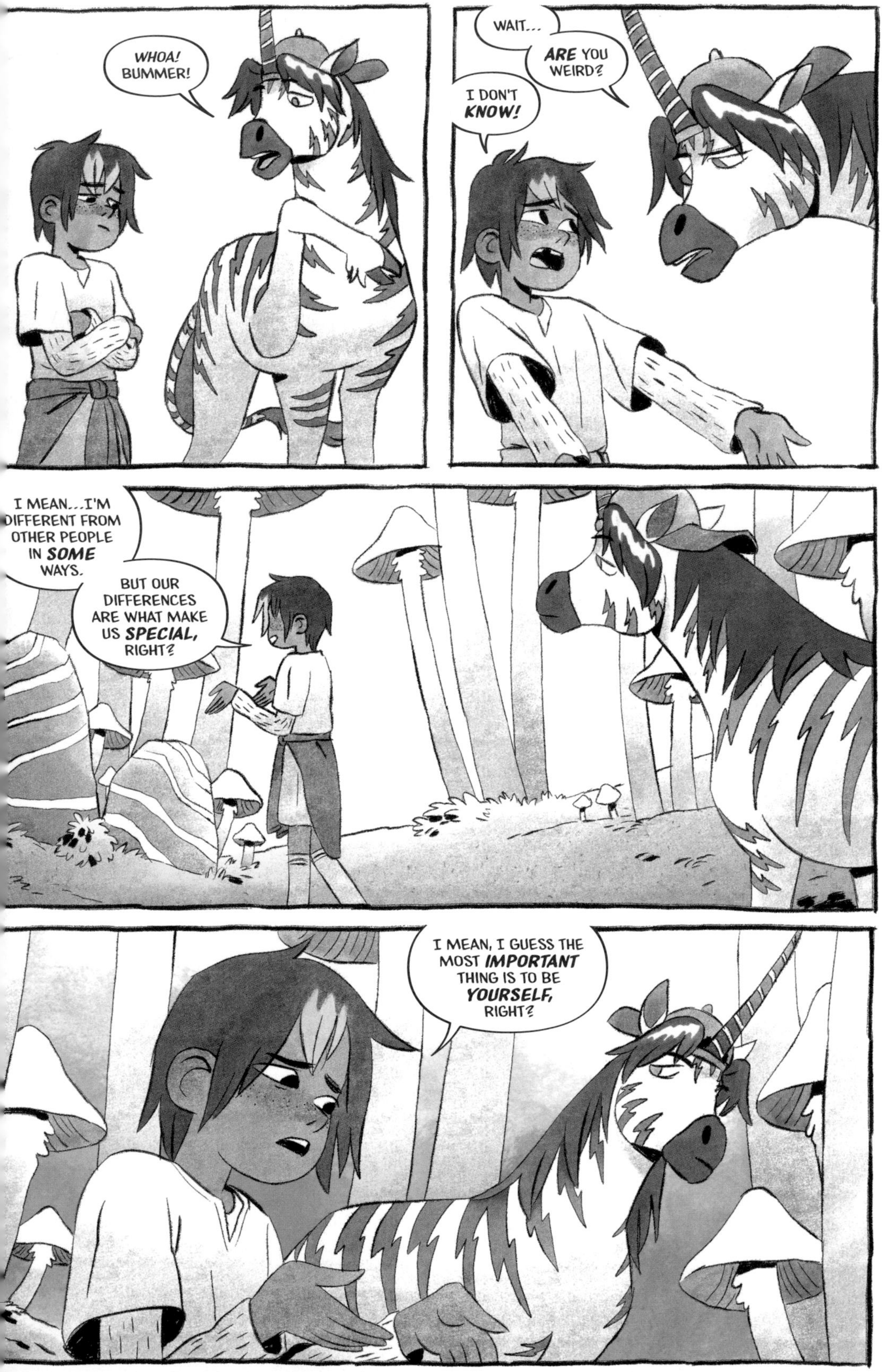
WHOA! BUMMER!
WAIT...
ARE YOU WEIRD?
I DON'T KNOW!
I MEAN...I'M DIFFERENT FROM OTHER PEOPLE IN SOME WAYS.
BUT OUR DIFFERENCES ARE WHAT MAKE US SPECIAL, RIGHT?
I MEAN, I GUESS THE MOST IMPORTANT THING IS TO BE YOURSELF, RIGHT?

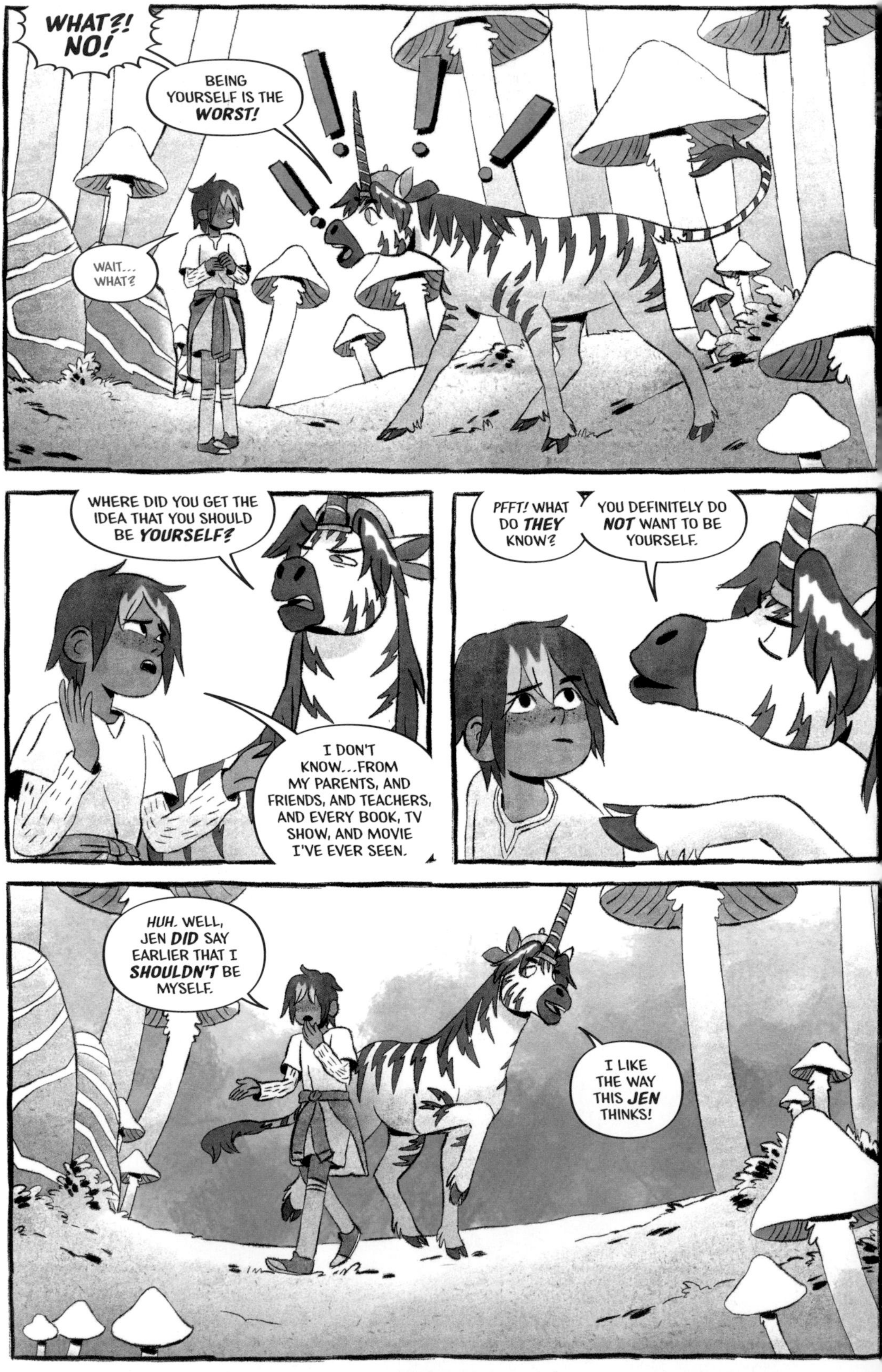
WHAT?! NO!
BEING YOURSELF IS THE *WORST!*
WAIT... WHAT?
WHERE DID YOU GET THE IDEA THAT YOU SHOULD BE *YOURSELF?*
I DON'T KNOW...FROM MY PARENTS, AND FRIENDS, AND TEACHERS, AND EVERY BOOK, TV SHOW, AND MOVIE I'VE EVER SEEN.
PFFT! WHAT DO *THEY* KNOW?
YOU DEFINITELY DO *NOT* WANT TO BE YOURSELF.
HUH. WELL, JEN *DID* SAY EARLIER THAT I *SHOULDN'T* BE MYSELF.
I LIKE THE WAY THIS *JEN* THINKS!

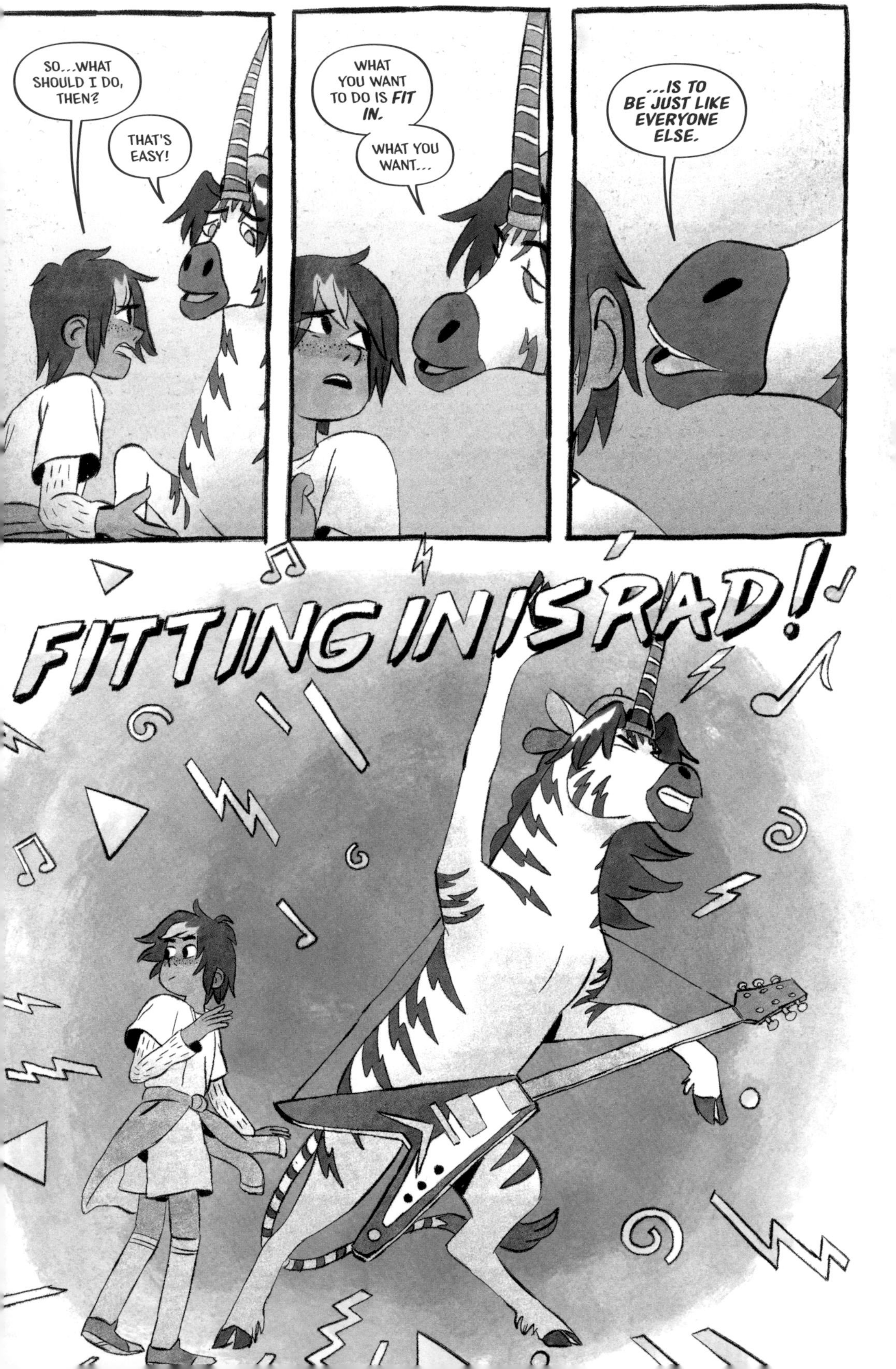
SO...WHAT SHOULD I DO, THEN?
THAT'S EASY!
WHAT YOU WANT TO DO IS FIT IN.
WHAT YOU WANT...
...IS TO BE JUST LIKE EVERYONE ELSE.
FITTING IN IS RAD!

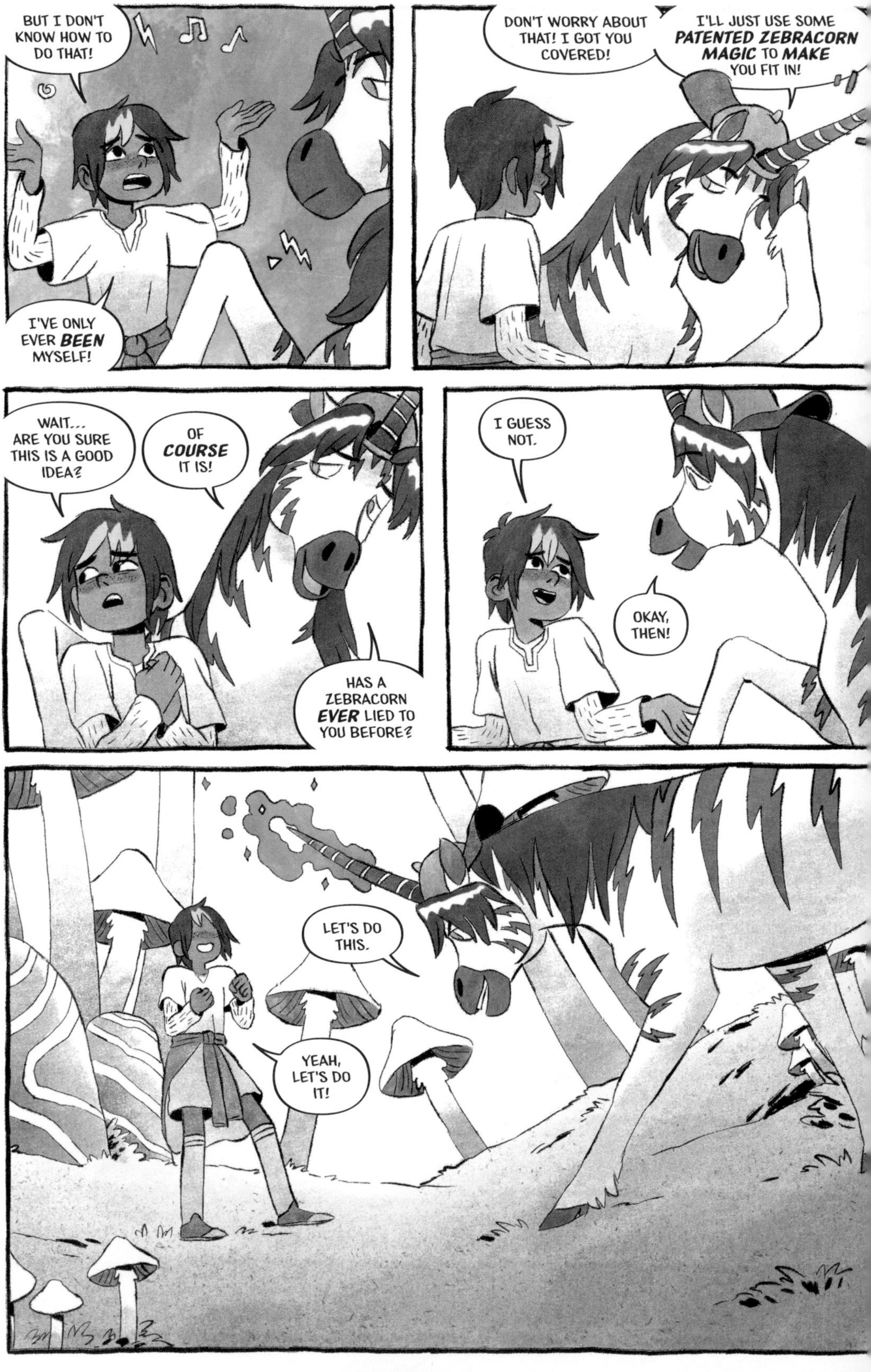
BUT I DON'T KNOW HOW TO DO THAT!
I'VE ONLY EVER **BEEN** MYSELF!
DON'T WORRY ABOUT THAT! I GOT YOU COVERED!
I'LL JUST USE SOME ***PATENTED ZEBRACORN MAGIC*** TO ***MAKE*** YOU FIT IN!
WAIT... ARE YOU SURE THIS IS A GOOD IDEA?
OF ***COURSE*** IT IS!
HAS A ZEBRACORN ***EVER*** LIED TO YOU BEFORE?
I GUESS NOT.
OKAY, THEN!
LET'S DO THIS.
YEAH, LET'S DO IT!

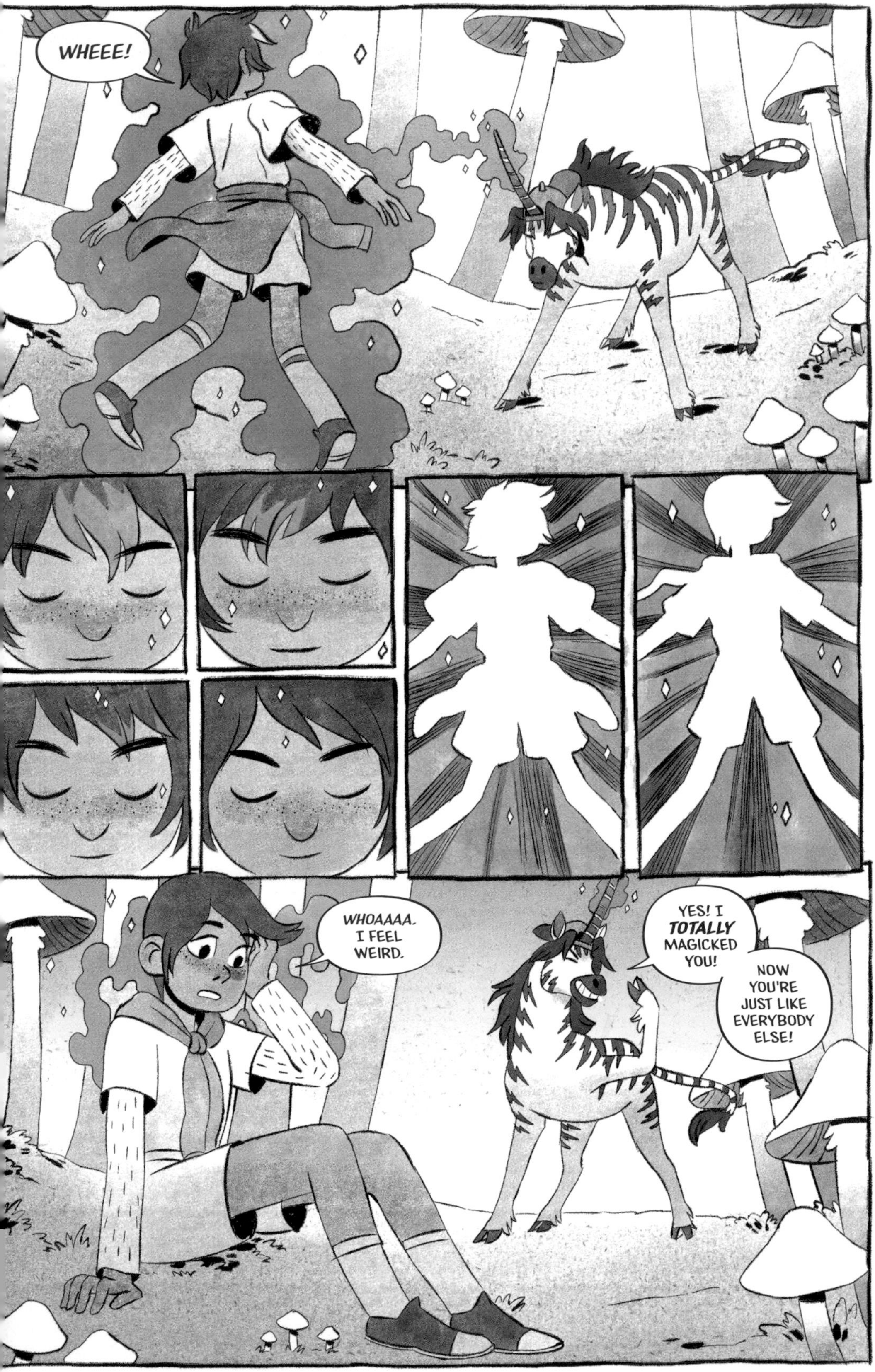
WHEEE!
WHOAAAA. I FEEL WEIRD.
YES! I TOTALLY MAGICKED YOU!
NOW YOU'RE JUST LIKE EVERYBODY ELSE!

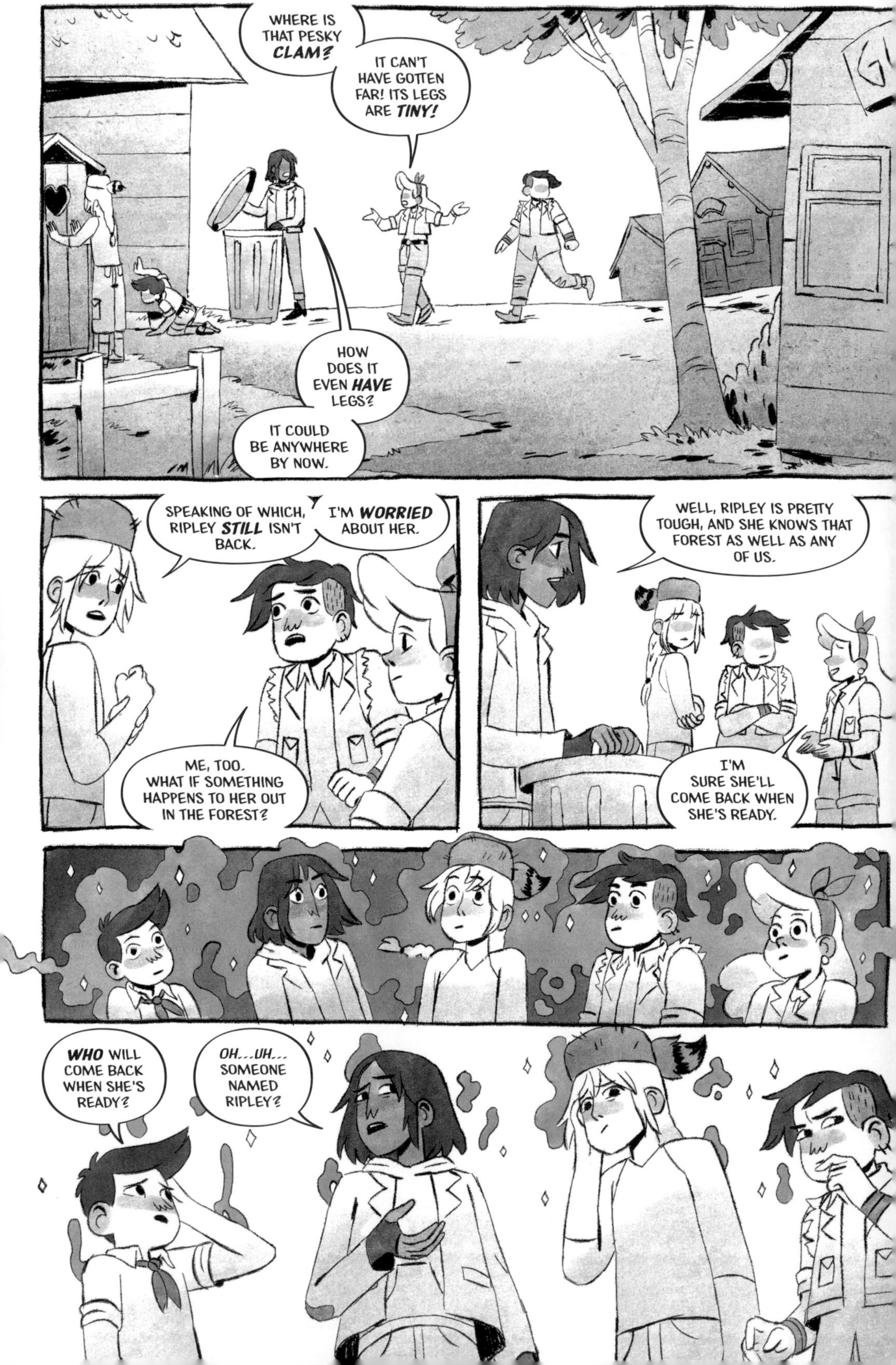
WHERE IS THAT PESKY *CLAM?*
IT CAN'T HAVE GOTTEN FAR! ITS LEGS ARE *TINY!*
HOW DOES IT EVEN *HAVE* LEGS?
IT COULD BE ANYWHERE BY NOW.
SPEAKING OF WHICH, RIPLEY *STILL* ISN'T BACK.
I'M *WORRIED* ABOUT HER.
ME, TOO. WHAT IF SOMETHING HAPPENS TO HER OUT IN THE FOREST?
WELL, RIPLEY IS PRETTY TOUGH, AND SHE KNOWS THAT FOREST AS WELL AS ANY OF US.
I'M SURE SHE'LL COME BACK WHEN SHE'S READY.
WHO WILL COME BACK WHEN SHE'S READY?
OH...UH... SOMEONE NAMED RIPLEY?

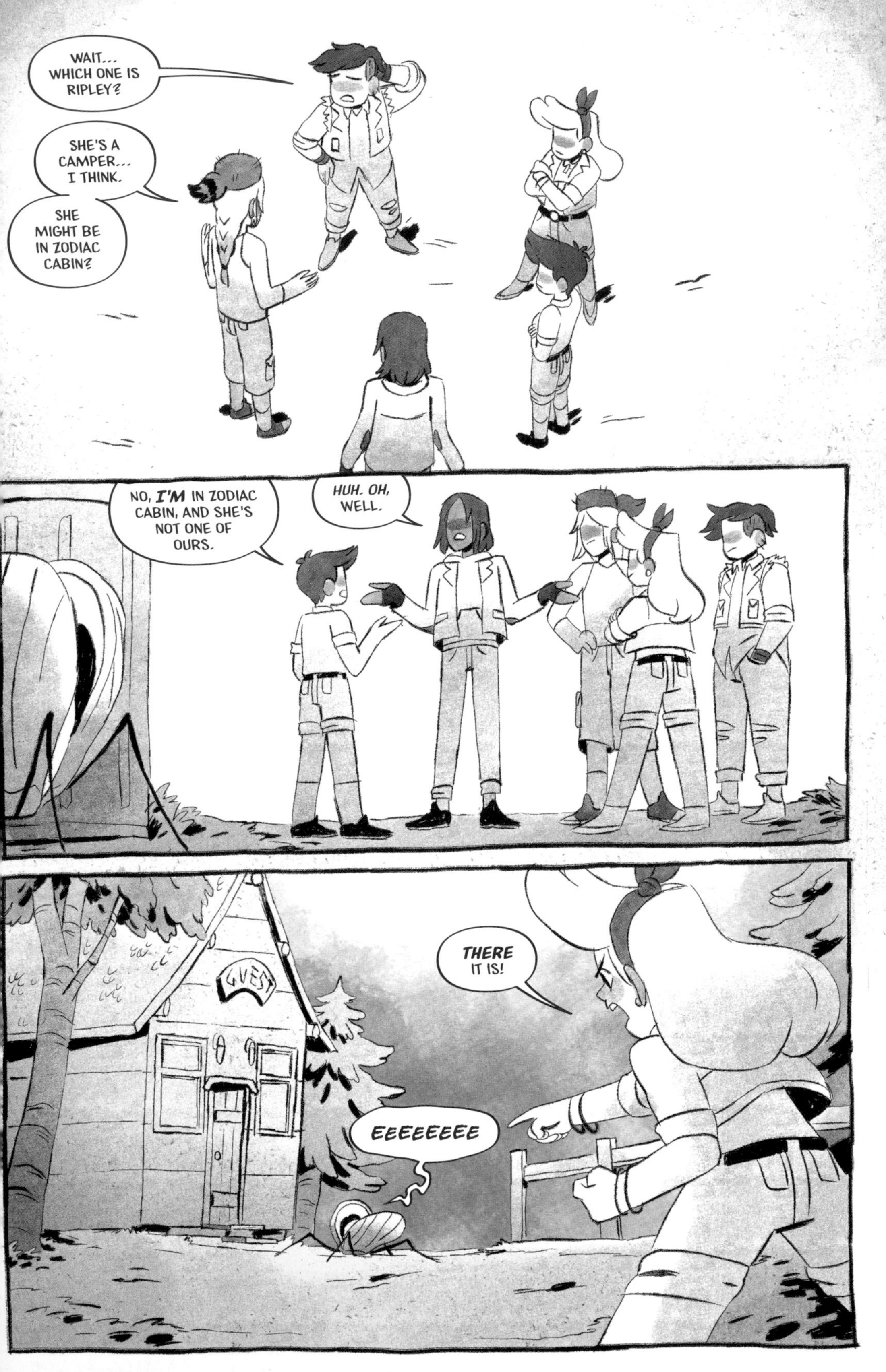
WAIT... WHICH ONE IS RIPLEY?
SHE'S A CAMPER... I THINK.
SHE MIGHT BE IN ZODIAC CABIN?
NO, I'M IN ZODIAC CABIN, AND SHE'S NOT ONE OF OURS.
HUH. OH, WELL.
GUEST
THERE IT IS!
EEEEEEEE

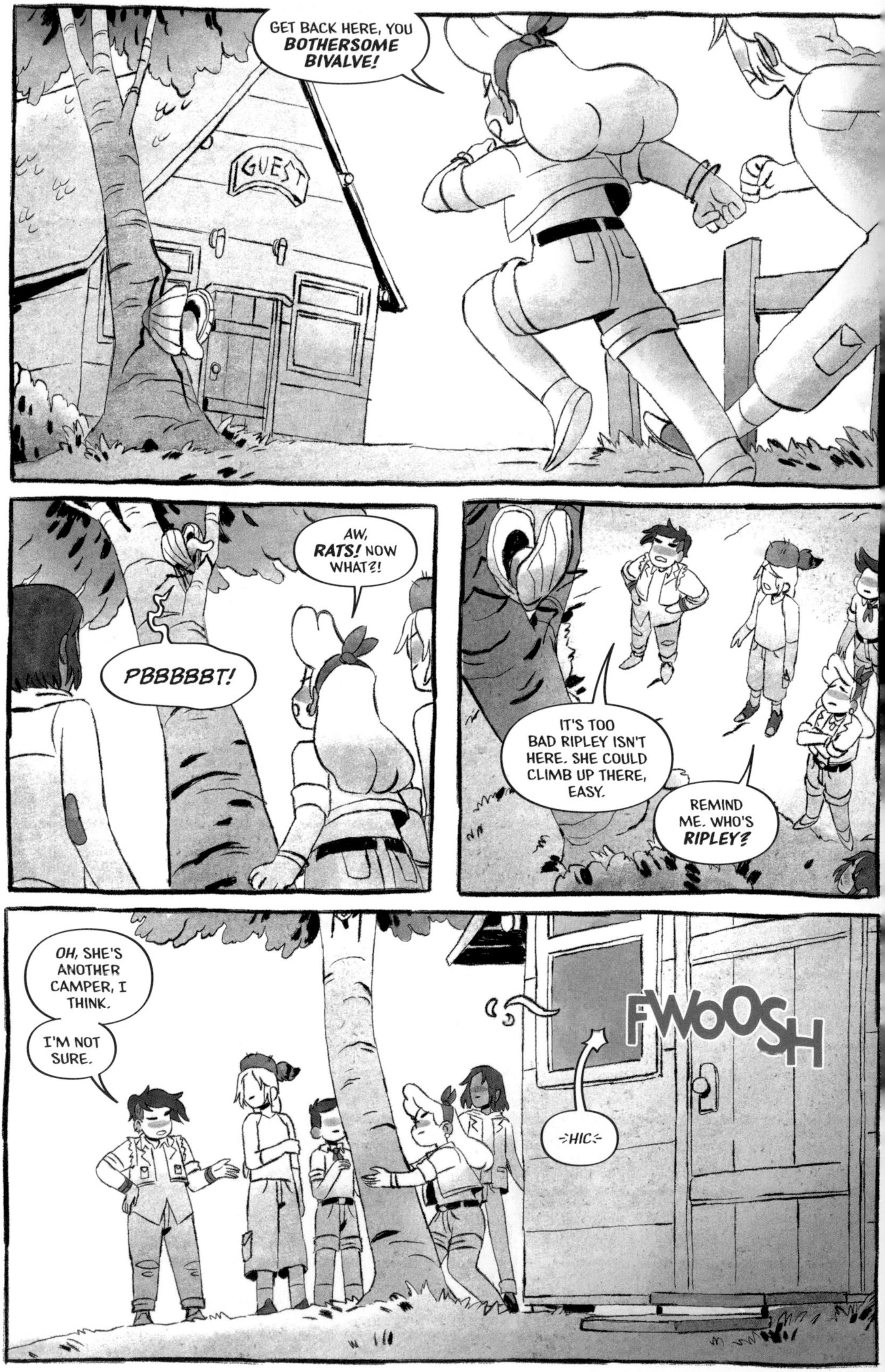
GET BACK HERE, YOU BOTHERSOME BIVALVE!
GUEST
AW, RATS! NOW WHAT?!
PBBBBBT!
IT'S TOO BAD RIPLEY ISN'T HERE. SHE COULD CLIMB UP THERE, EASY.
REMIND ME. WHO'S RIPLEY?
OH, SHE'S ANOTHER CAMPER, I THINK.
I'M NOT SURE.
FWOOSH
HIC

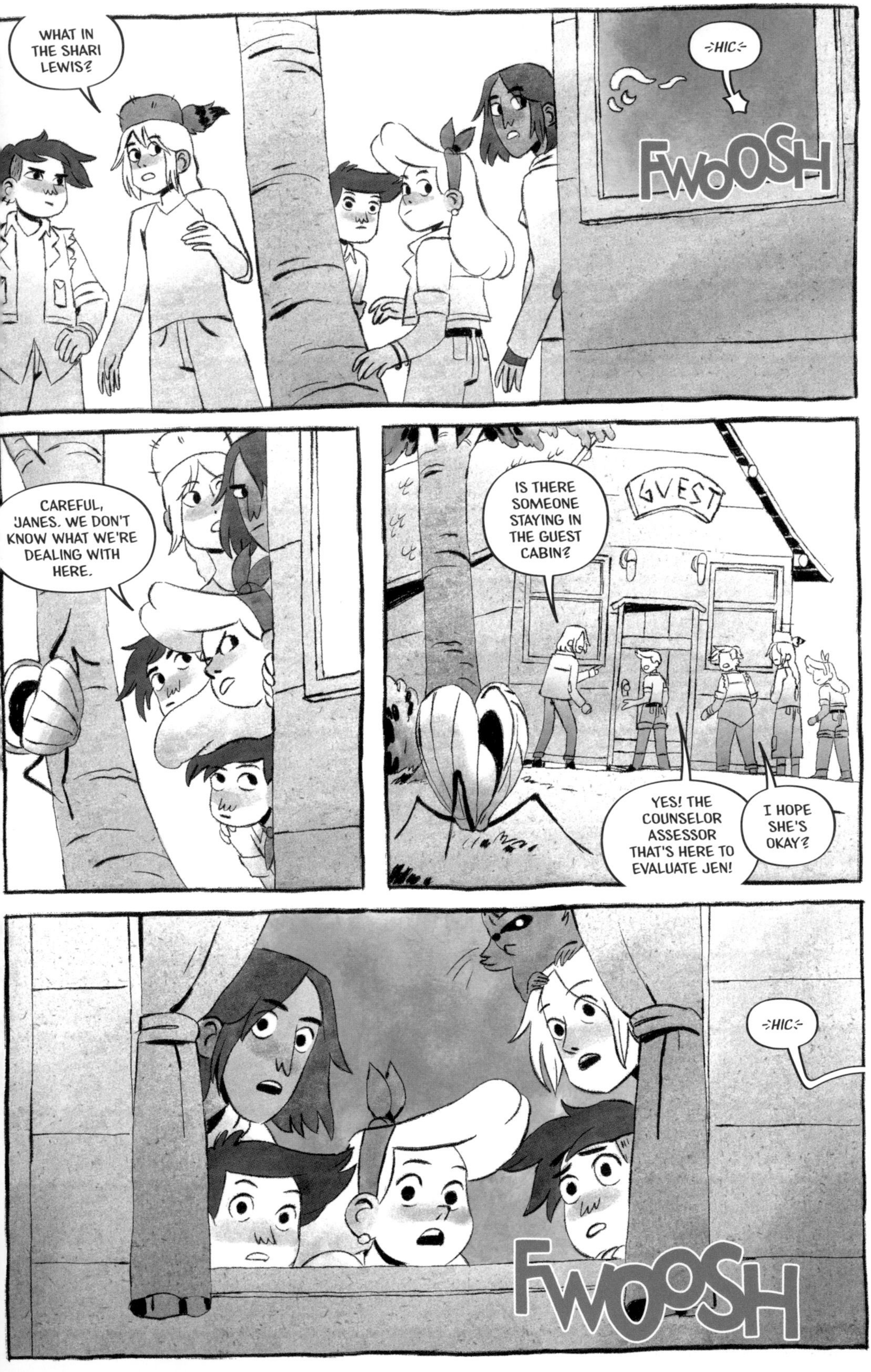
WHAT IN THE SHARI LEWIS?
HIC
FWOOSH
CAREFUL, JANES. WE DON'T KNOW WHAT WE'RE DEALING WITH HERE.
GUEST
IS THERE SOMEONE STAYING IN THE GUEST CABIN?
YES! THE COUNSELOR ASSESSOR THAT'S HERE TO EVALUATE JEN!
I HOPE SHE'S OKAY?
HIC
FWOOSH

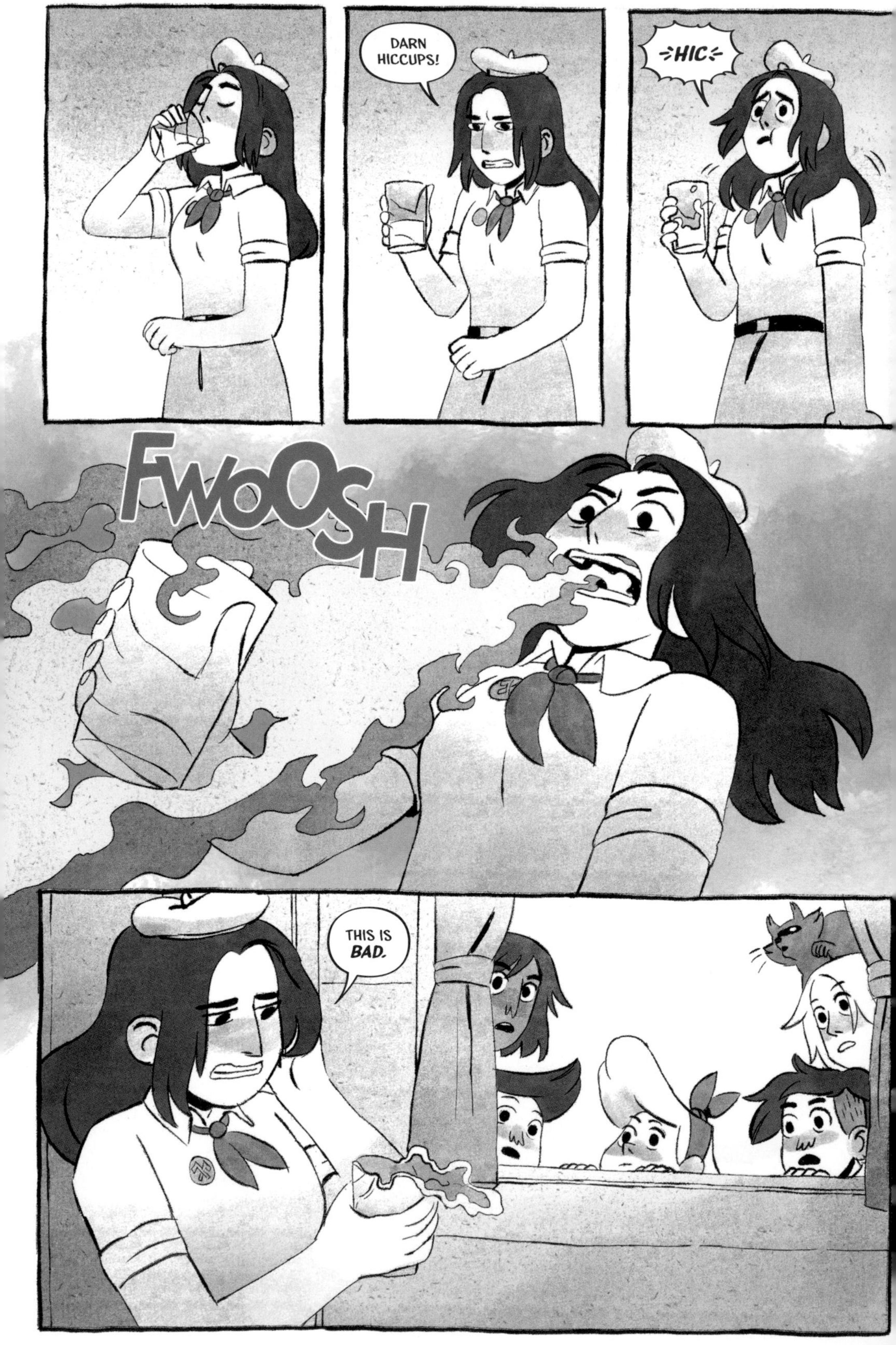
DARN HICCUPS!
HIC
FWOOSH
THIS IS BAD.

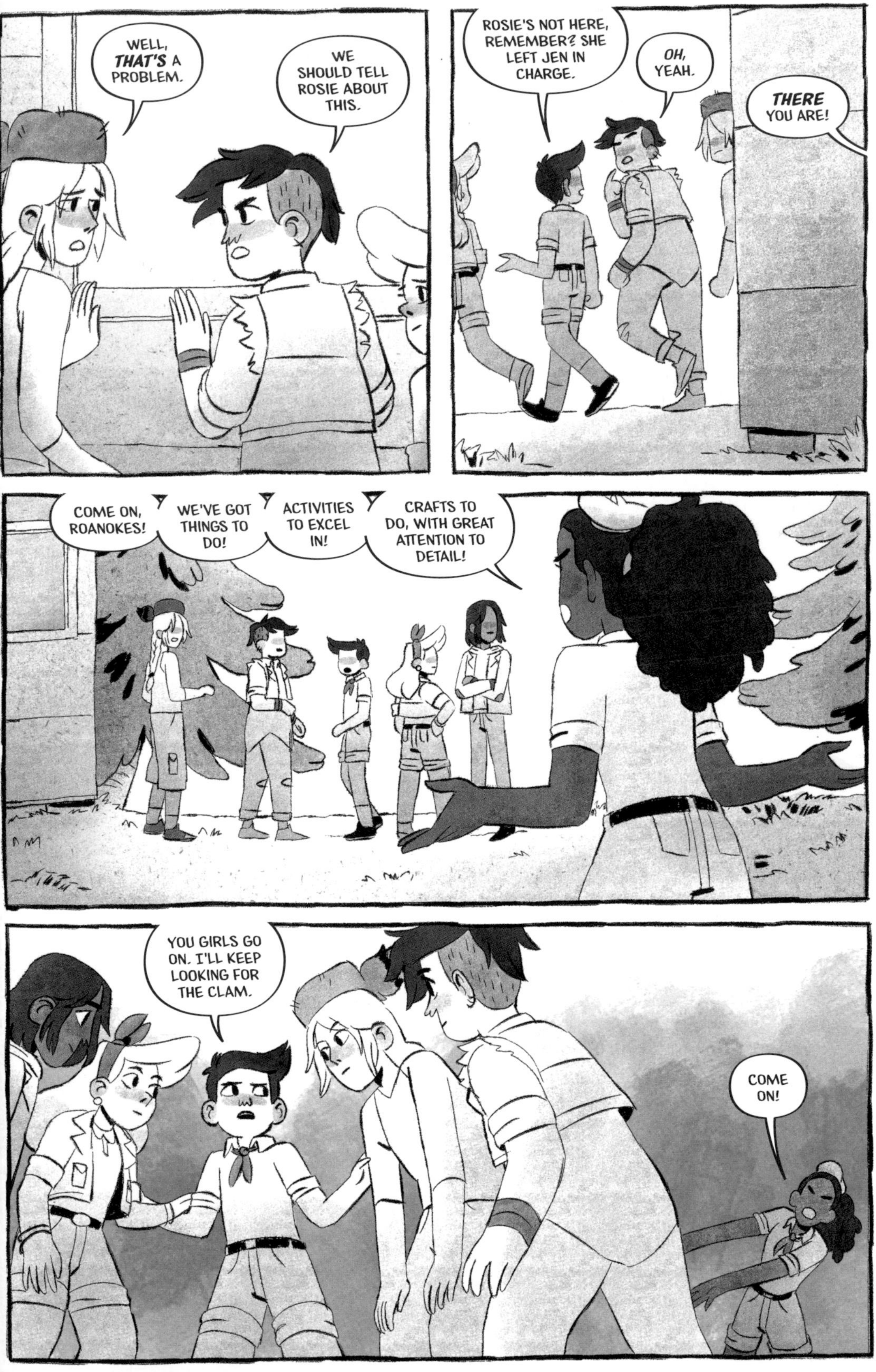
WELL, ***THAT'S*** A PROBLEM.
WE SHOULD TELL ROSIE ABOUT THIS.
ROSIE'S NOT HERE, REMEMBER? SHE LEFT JEN IN CHARGE.
OH, YEAH.
THERE YOU ARE!
COME ON, ROANOKES!
WE'VE GOT THINGS TO DO!
ACTIVITIES TO EXCEL IN!
CRAFTS TO DO, WITH GREAT ATTENTION TO DETAIL!
YOU GIRLS GO ON. I'LL KEEP LOOKING FOR THE CLAM.
COME ON!

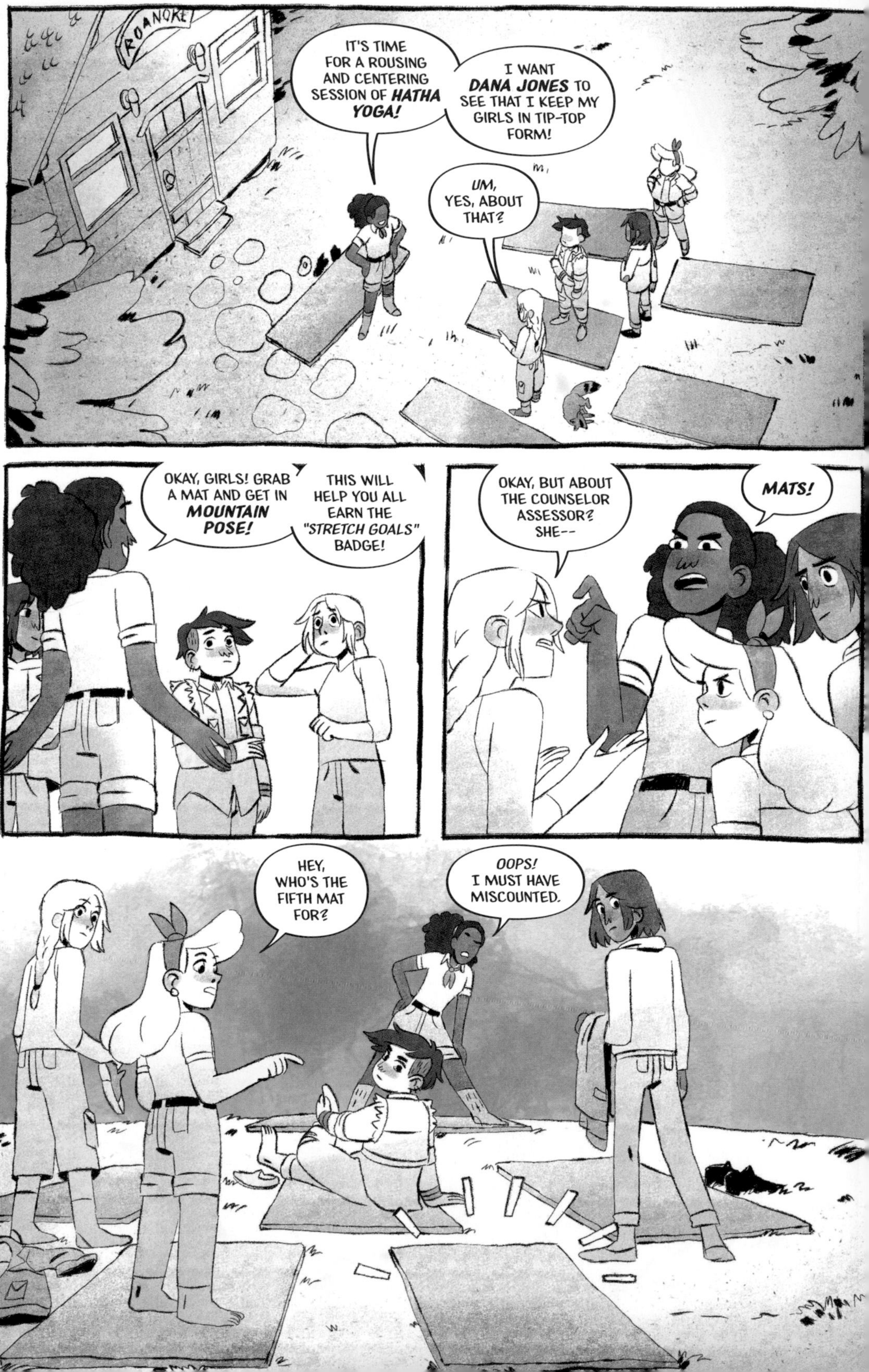

ROANOKE
IT'S TIME FOR A ROUSING AND CENTERING SESSION OF HATHA YOGA!
I WANT DANA JONES TO SEE THAT I KEEP MY GIRLS IN TIP-TOP FORM!
UM, YES, ABOUT THAT?
OKAY, GIRLS! GRAB A MAT AND GET IN MOUNTAIN POSE!
THIS WILL HELP YOU ALL EARN THE "STRETCH GOALS" BADGE!
OKAY, BUT ABOUT THE COUNSELOR ASSESSOR? SHE--
MATS!
HEY, WHO'S THE FIFTH MAT FOR?
OOPS! I MUST HAVE MISCOUNTED.

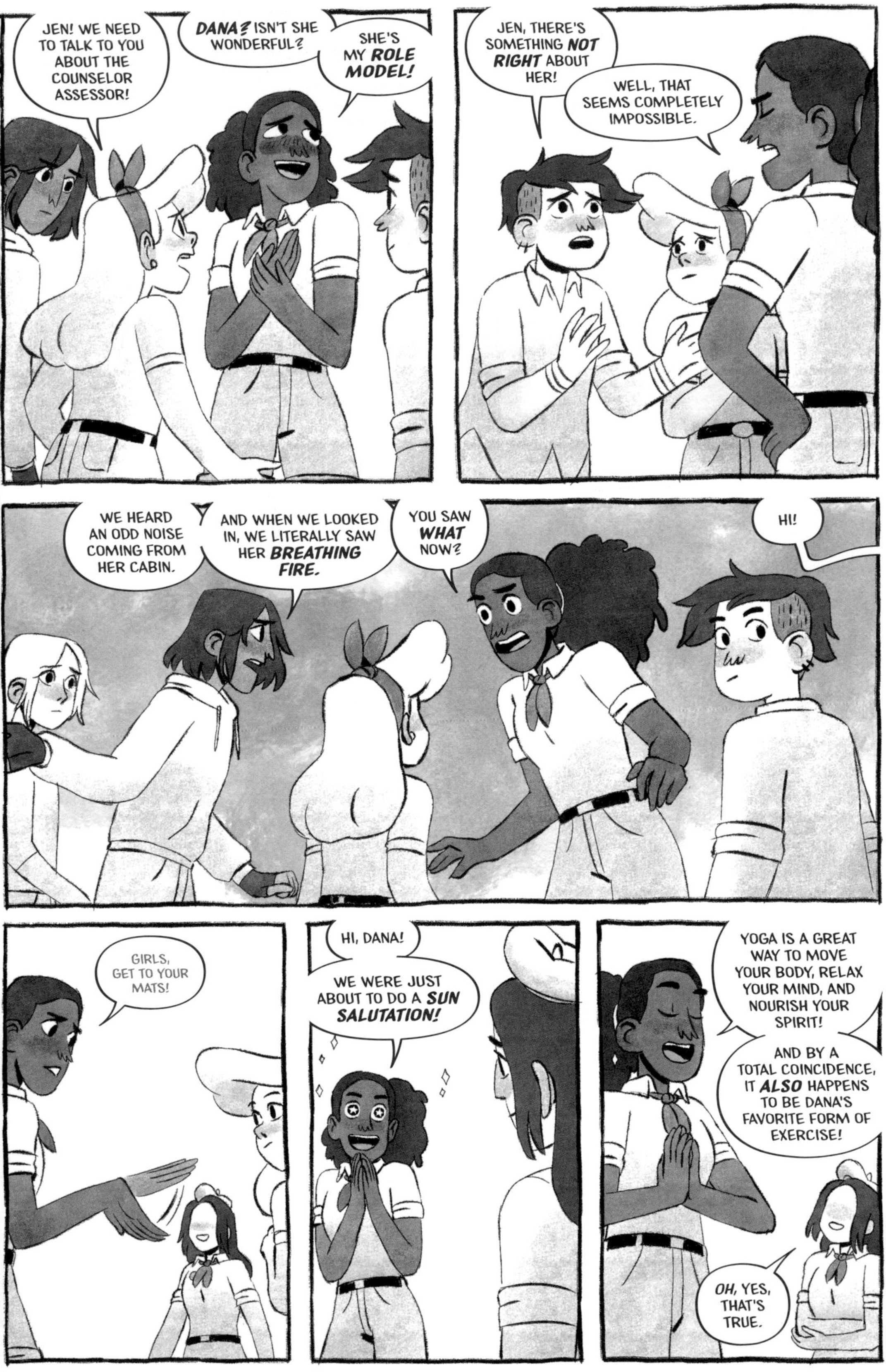
JEN! WE NEED TO TALK TO YOU ABOUT THE COUNSELOR ASSESSOR!
DANA? ISN'T SHE WONDERFUL?
SHE'S MY ROLE MODEL!
JEN, THERE'S SOMETHING NOT RIGHT ABOUT HER!
WELL, THAT SEEMS COMPLETELY IMPOSSIBLE.
WE HEARD AN ODD NOISE COMING FROM HER CABIN.
AND WHEN WE LOOKED IN, WE LITERALLY SAW HER BREATHING FIRE.
YOU SAW WHAT NOW?
HI!
GIRLS, GET TO YOUR MATS!
HI, DANA!
WE WERE JUST ABOUT TO DO A SUN SALUTATION!
YOGA IS A GREAT WAY TO MOVE YOUR BODY, RELAX YOUR MIND, AND NOURISH YOUR SPIRIT!
AND BY A TOTAL COINCIDENCE, IT ALSO HAPPENS TO BE DANA'S FAVORITE FORM OF EXERCISE!
OH, YES, THAT'S TRUE.

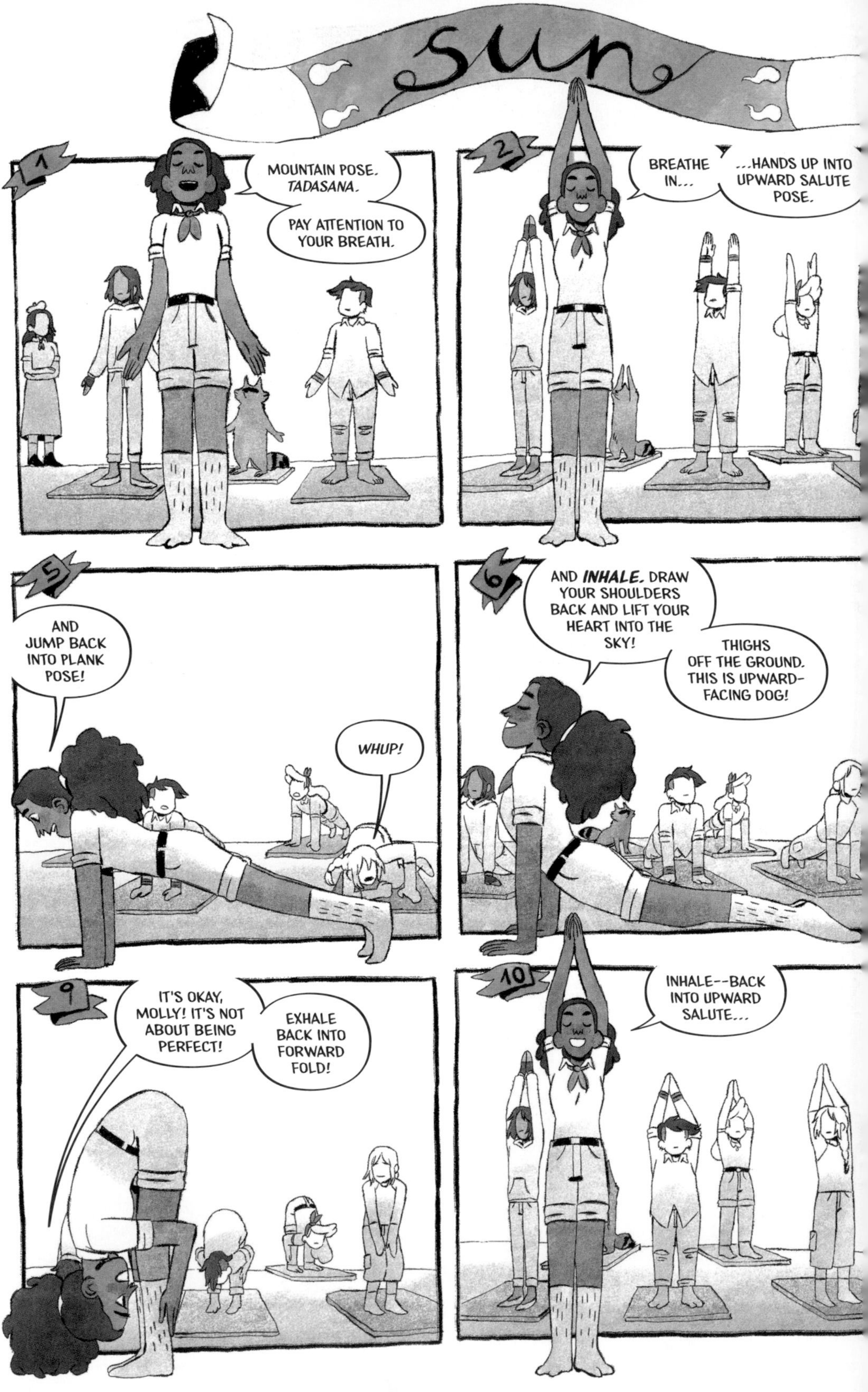
SUN
1
MOUNTAIN POSE. TADASANA.
PAY ATTENTION TO YOUR BREATH.
2
BREATHE IN...
...HANDS UP INTO UPWARD SALUTE POSE.
5
AND JUMP BACK INTO PLANK POSE!
WHUP!
6
AND INHALE. DRAW YOUR SHOULDERS BACK AND LIFT YOUR HEART INTO THE SKY!
THIGHS OFF THE GROUND. THIS IS UPWARD-FACING DOG!
9
IT'S OKAY, MOLLY! IT'S NOT ABOUT BEING PERFECT!
EXHALE BACK INTO FORWARD FOLD!
10
INHALE--BACK INTO UPWARD SALUTE...

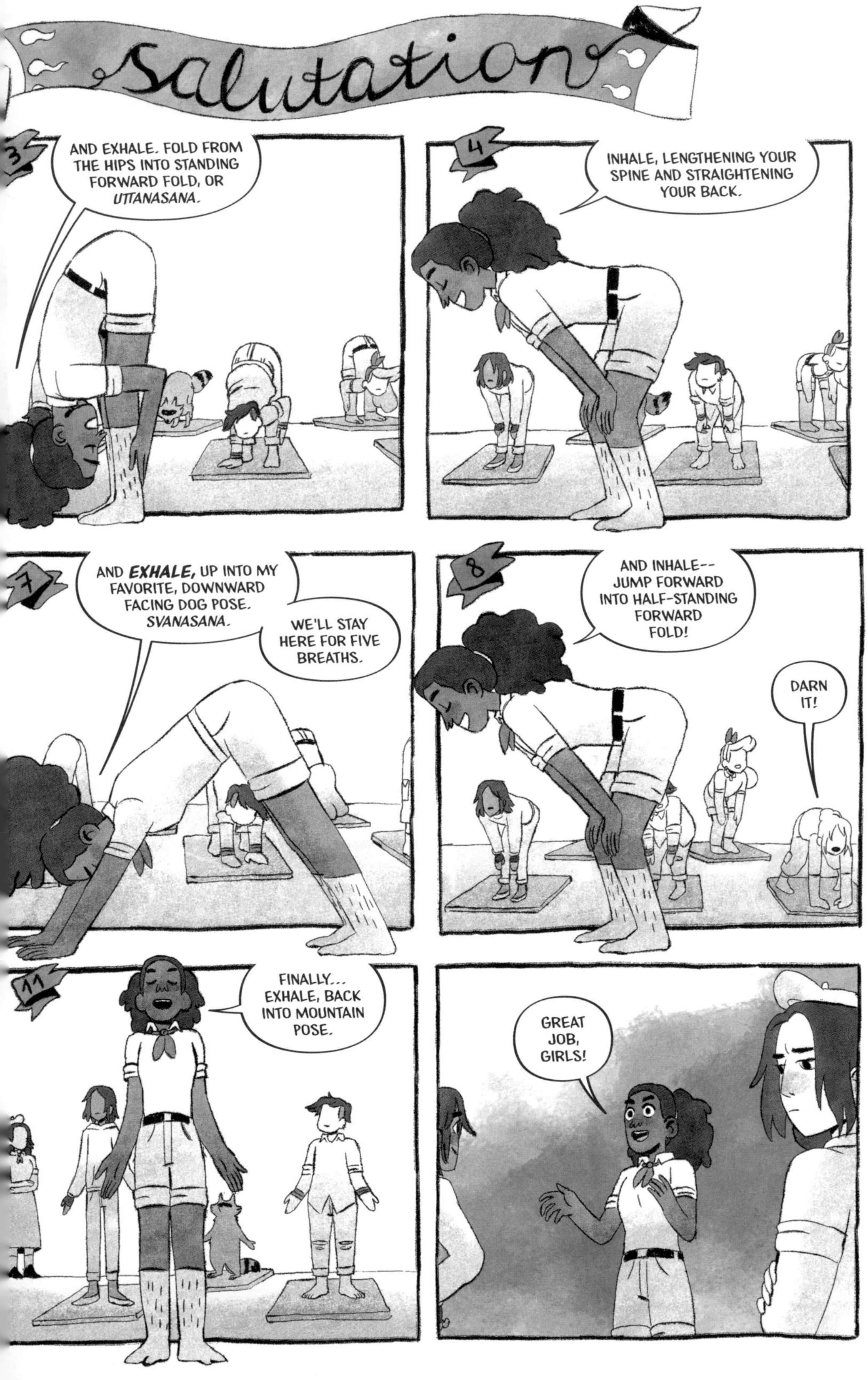

Salutation
3
AND EXHALE. FOLD FROM THE HIPS INTO STANDING FORWARD FOLD, OR *UTTANASANA.*
4
INHALE, LENGTHENING YOUR SPINE AND STRAIGHTENING YOUR BACK.
7
AND **EXHALE,** UP INTO MY FAVORITE, DOWNWARD FACING DOG POSE. *SVANASANA.*
WE'LL STAY HERE FOR FIVE BREATHS.
8
AND INHALE-- JUMP FORWARD INTO HALF-STANDING FORWARD FOLD!
DARN IT!
11
FINALLY... EXHALE, BACK INTO MOUNTAIN POSE.
GREAT JOB, GIRLS!

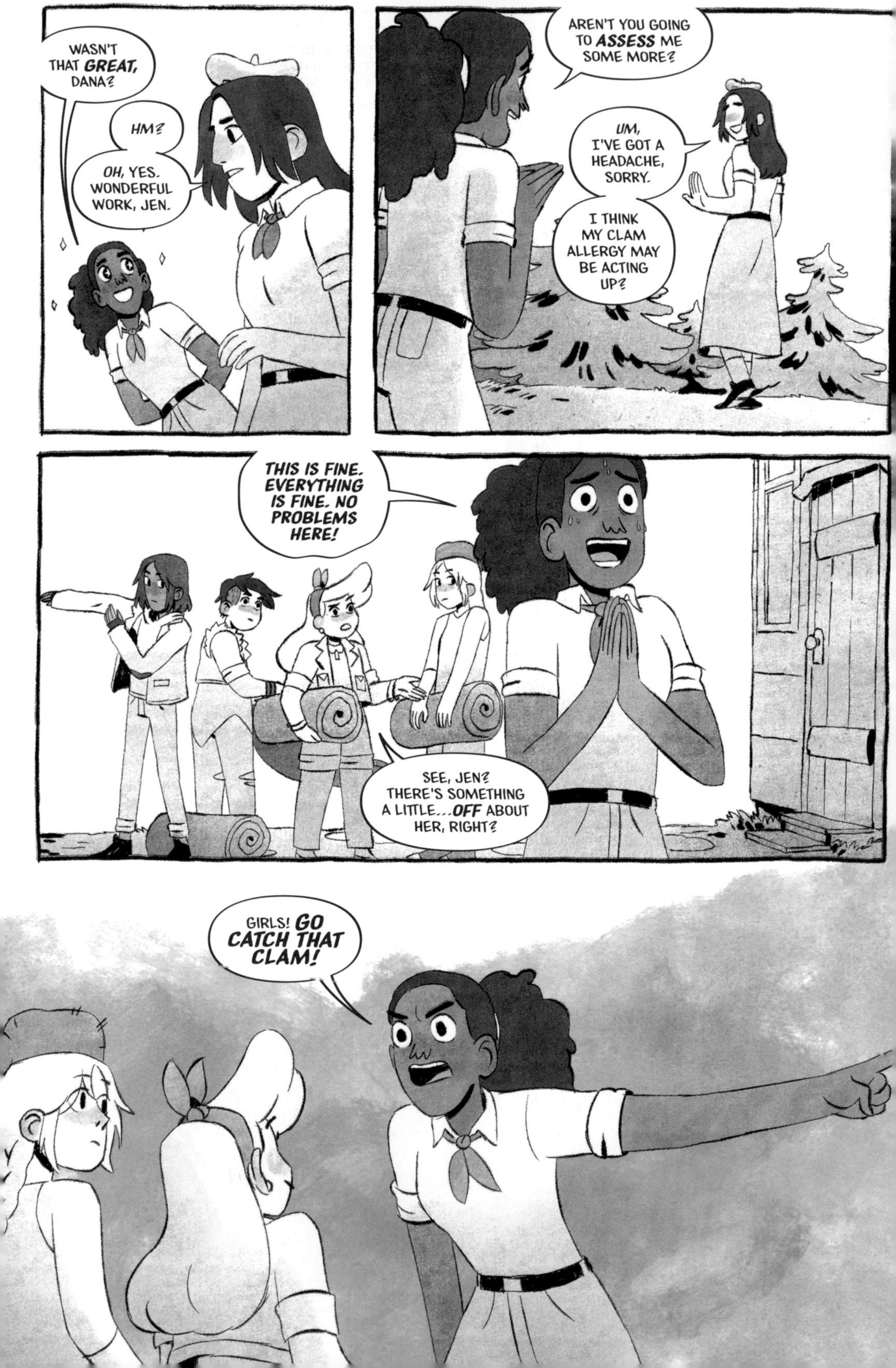
WASN'T THAT GREAT, DANA?
HM?
OH, YES. WONDERFUL WORK, JEN.
AREN'T YOU GOING TO ASSESS ME SOME MORE?
UM, I'VE GOT A HEADACHE, SORRY.
I THINK MY CLAM ALLERGY MAY BE ACTING UP?
THIS IS FINE. EVERYTHING IS FINE. NO PROBLEMS HERE!
SEE, JEN? THERE'S SOMETHING A LITTLE...OFF ABOUT HER, RIGHT?
GIRLS! GO CATCH THAT CLAM!

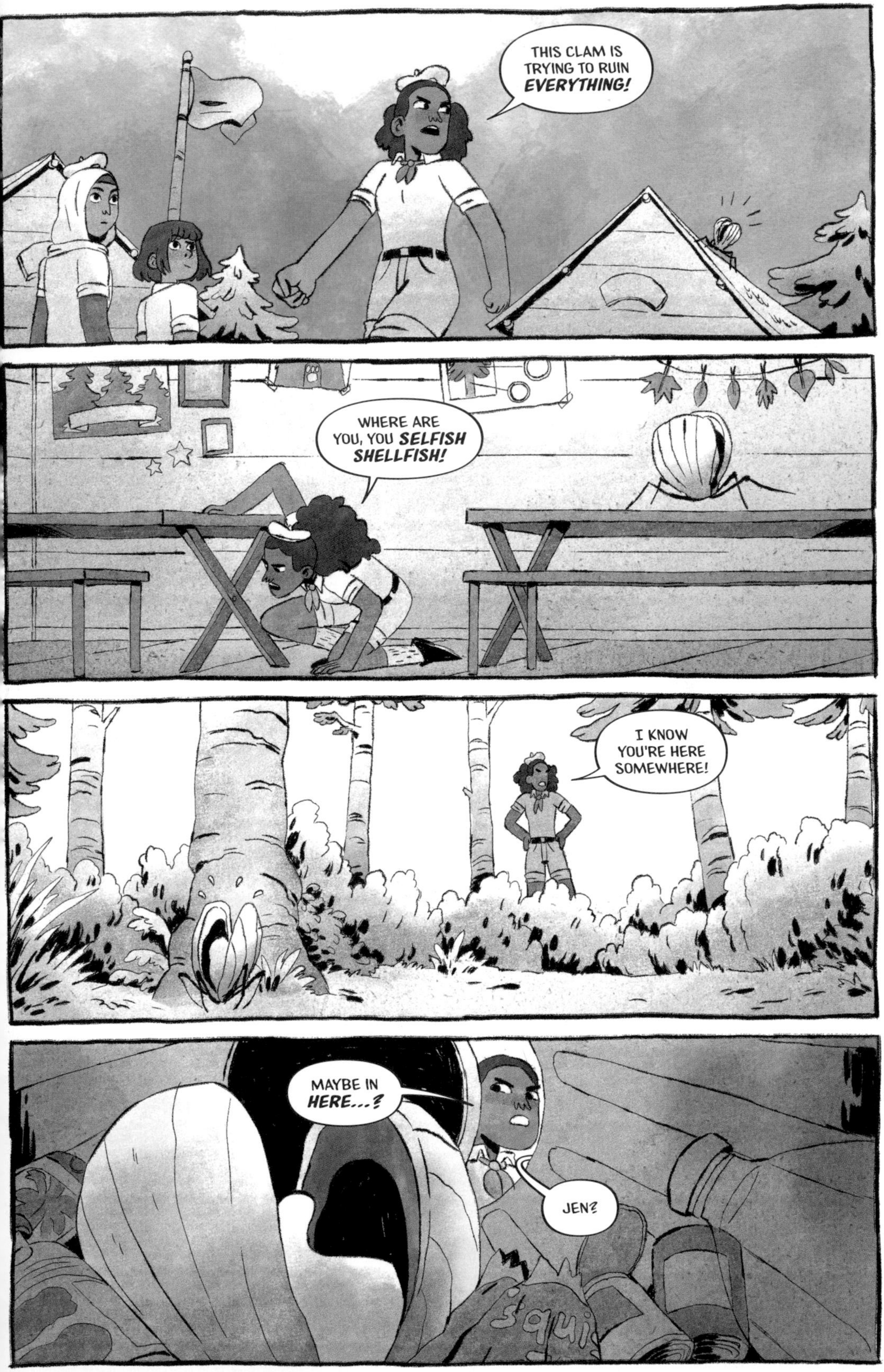
THIS CLAM IS TRYING TO RUIN EVERYTHING!
WHERE ARE YOU, YOU SELFISH SHELLFISH!
I KNOW YOU'RE HERE SOMEWHERE!
MAYBE IN HERE...?
JEN?

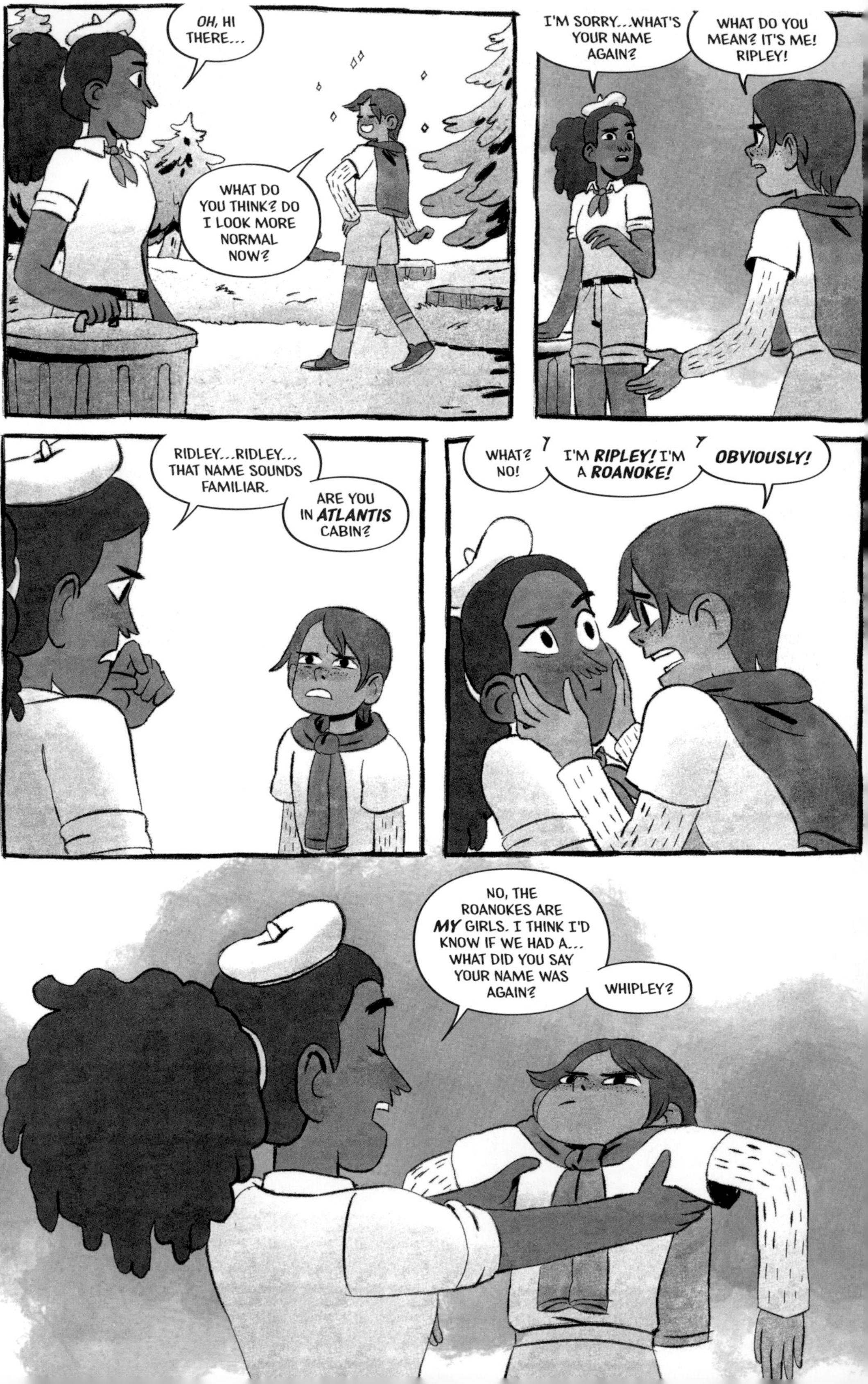

OH, HI THERE...
WHAT DO YOU THINK? DO I LOOK MORE NORMAL NOW?
I'M SORRY... WHAT'S YOUR NAME AGAIN?
WHAT DO YOU MEAN? IT'S ME! RIPLEY!
RIDLEY... RIDLEY... THAT NAME SOUNDS FAMILIAR.
ARE YOU IN ATLANTIS CABIN?
WHAT? NO!
I'M RIPLEY! I'M A ROANOKE!
OBVIOUSLY!
NO, THE ROANOKES ARE MY GIRLS. I THINK I'D KNOW IF WE HAD A... WHAT DID YOU SAY YOUR NAME WAS AGAIN?
WHIPLEY?

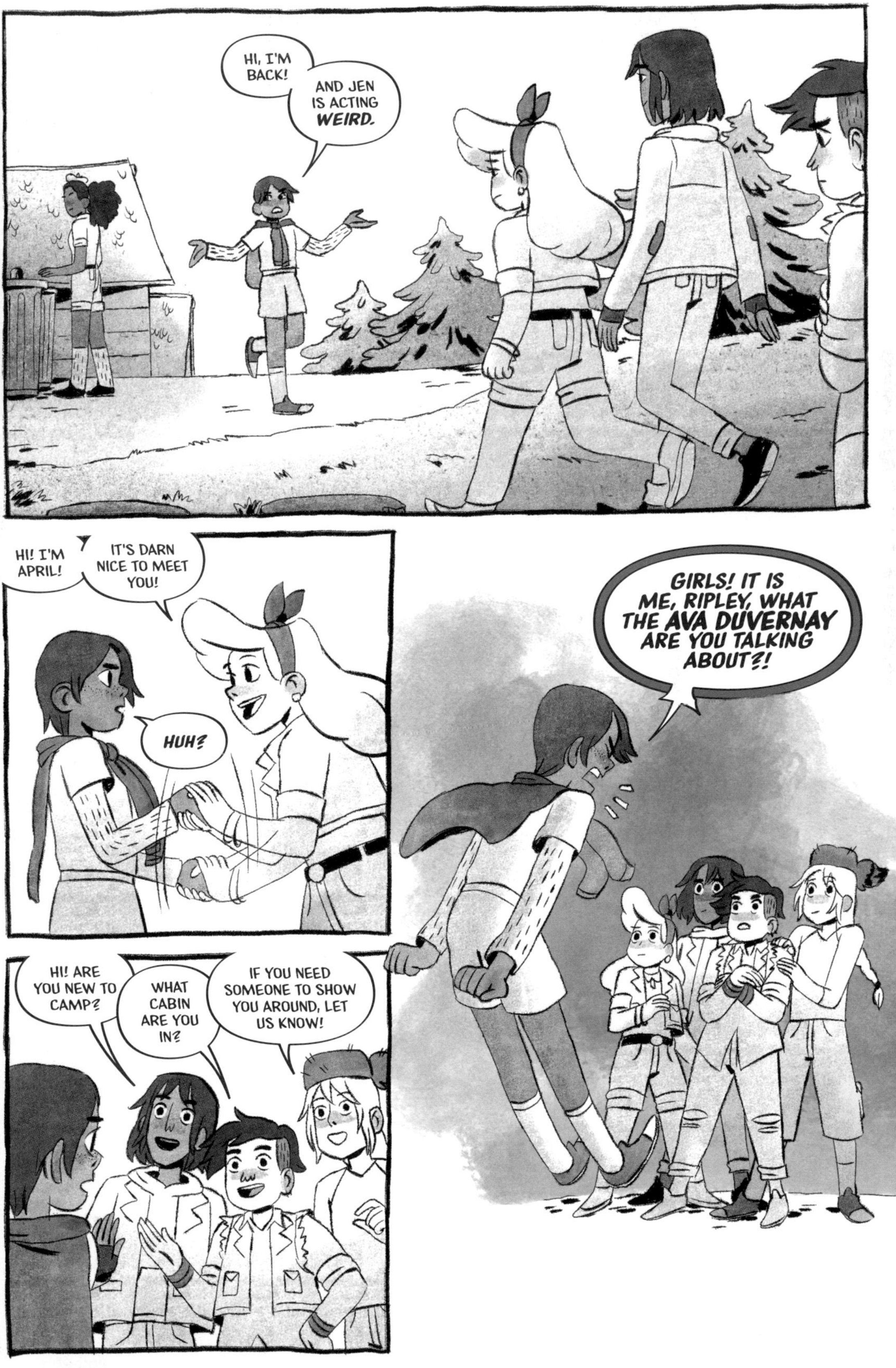
HI, I'M BACK!
AND JEN IS ACTING WEIRD.
HI! I'M APRIL!
IT'S DARN NICE TO MEET YOU!
HUH?
HI! ARE YOU NEW TO CAMP?
WHAT CABIN ARE YOU IN?
IF YOU NEED SOMEONE TO SHOW YOU AROUND, LET US KNOW!
GIRLS! IT IS ME, RIPLEY, WHAT THE AVA DUVERNAY ARE YOU TALKING ABOUT?!

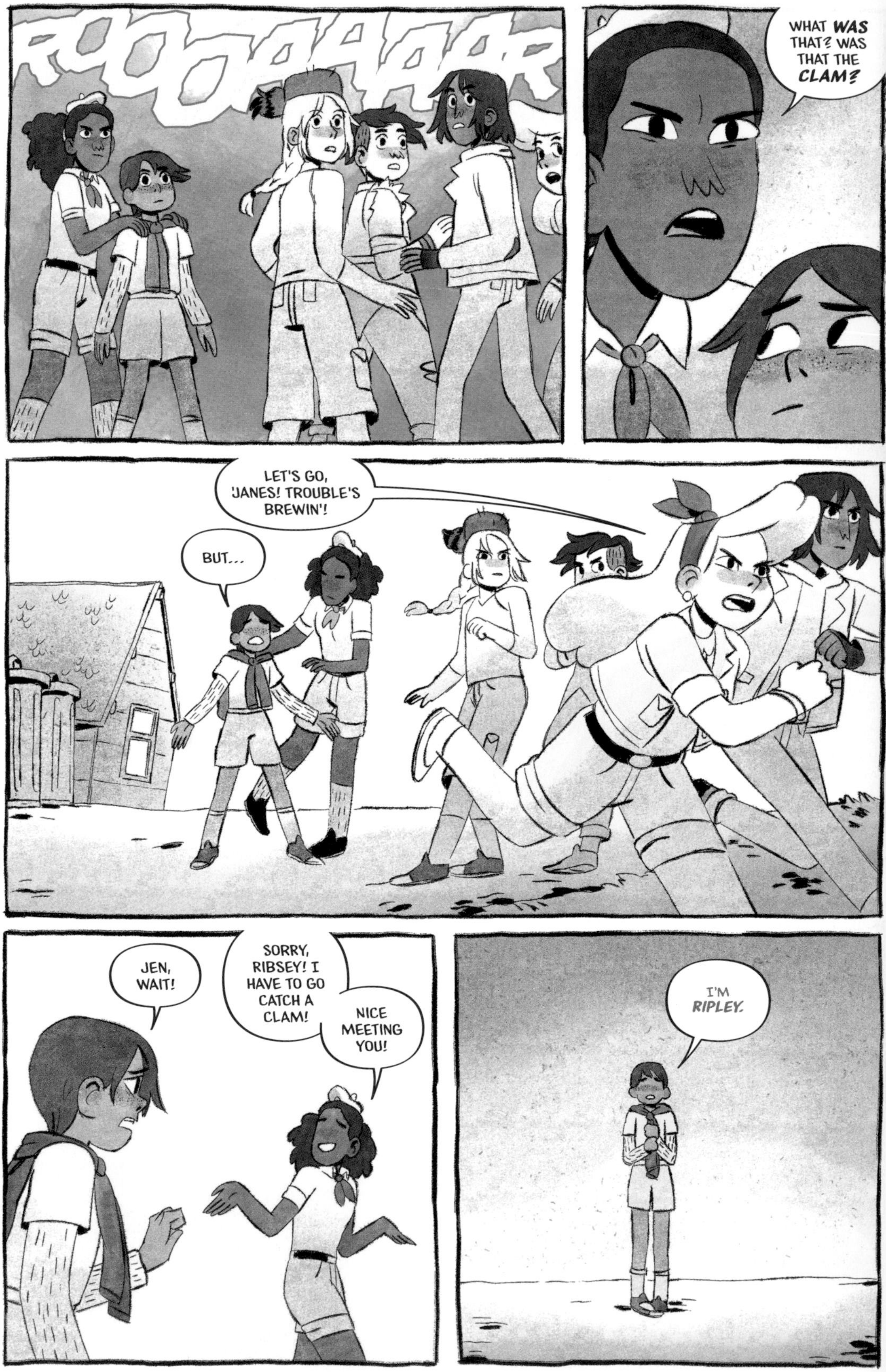
ROOOAAAAR
WHAT WAS THAT? WAS THAT THE CLAM?
LET'S GO, 'JANES! TROUBLE'S BREWIN'!
BUT...
JEN, WAIT!
SORRY, RIBSEY! I HAVE TO GO CATCH A CLAM!
NICE MEETING YOU!
I'M RIPLEY.

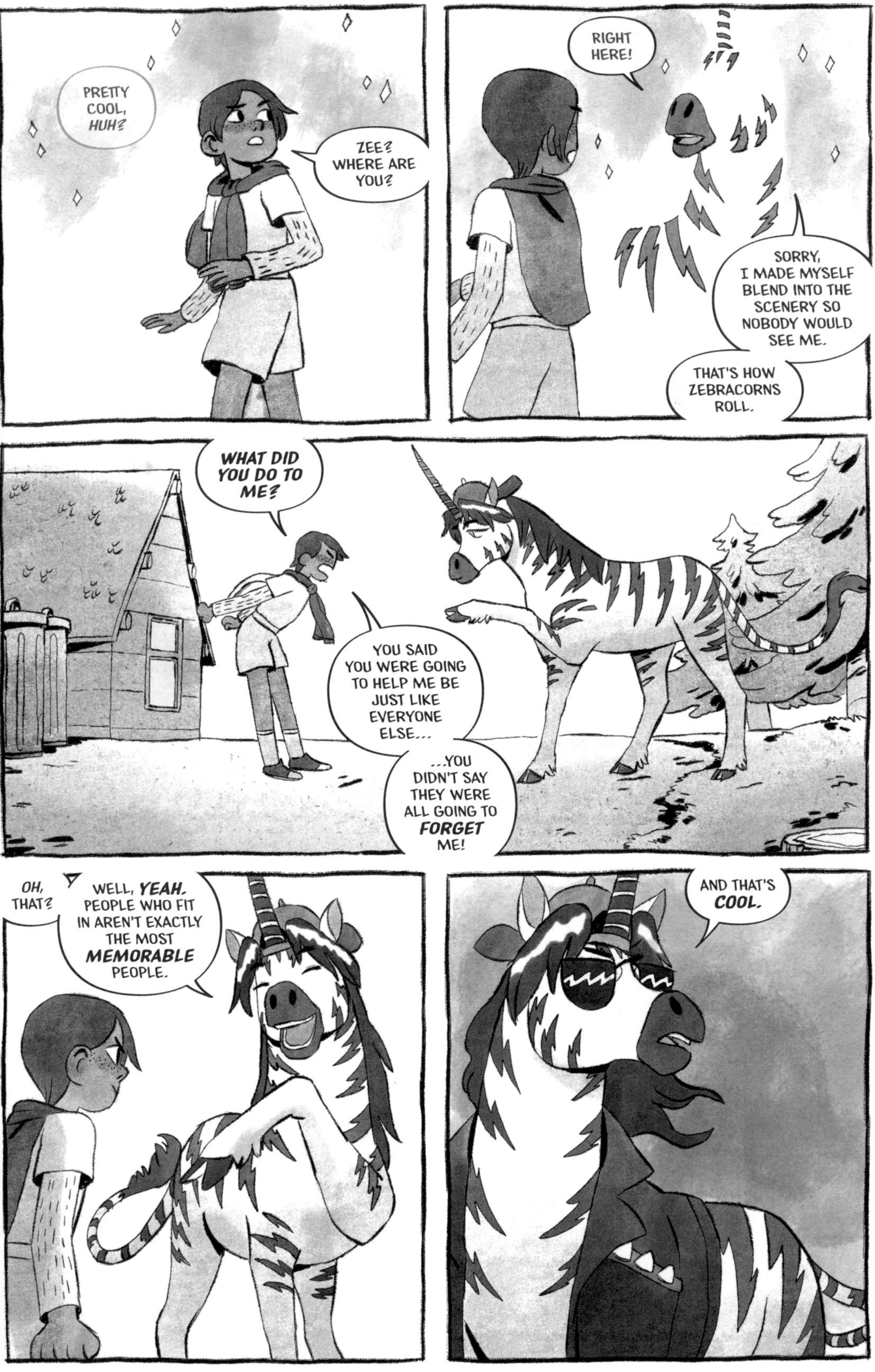
PRETTY COOL, HUH?
ZEE? WHERE ARE YOU?
RIGHT HERE!
SORRY, I MADE MYSELF BLEND INTO THE SCENERY SO NOBODY WOULD SEE ME.
THAT'S HOW ZEBRACORNS ROLL.
WHAT DID YOU DO TO ME?
YOU SAID YOU WERE GOING TO HELP ME BE JUST LIKE EVERYONE ELSE...
...YOU DIDN'T SAY THEY WERE ALL GOING TO FORGET ME!
OH, THAT?
WELL, YEAH. PEOPLE WHO FIT IN AREN'T EXACTLY THE MOST MEMORABLE PEOPLE.
AND THAT'S COOL.

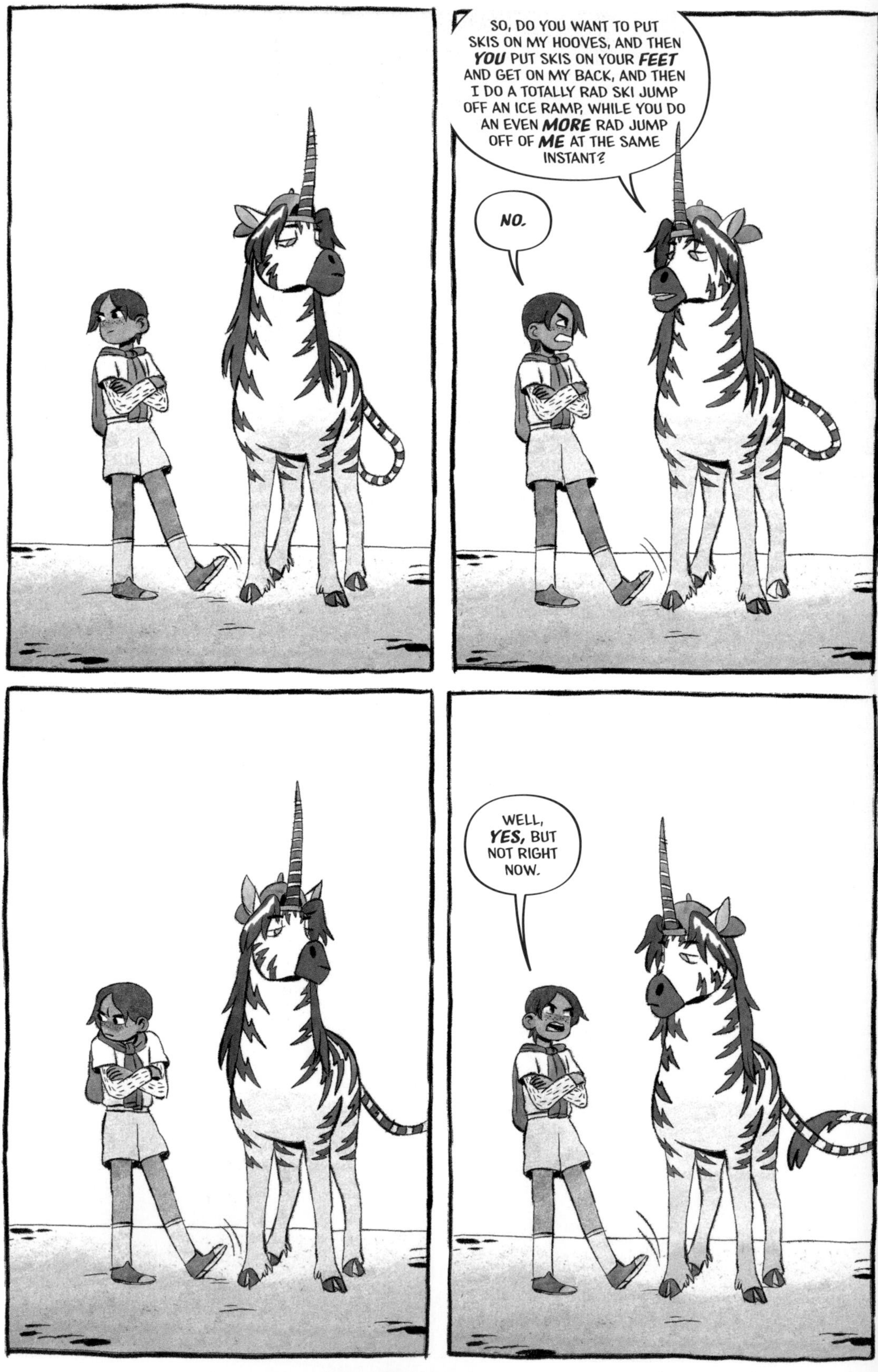
SO, DO YOU WANT TO PUT SKIS ON MY HOOVES, AND THEN *YOU* PUT SKIS ON YOUR *FEET* AND GET ON MY BACK, AND THEN I DO A TOTALLY RAD SKI JUMP OFF AN ICE RAMP, WHILE YOU DO AN EVEN *MORE* RAD JUMP OFF OF *ME* AT THE SAME INSTANT?
NO.
WELL, *YES,* BUT NOT RIGHT NOW.

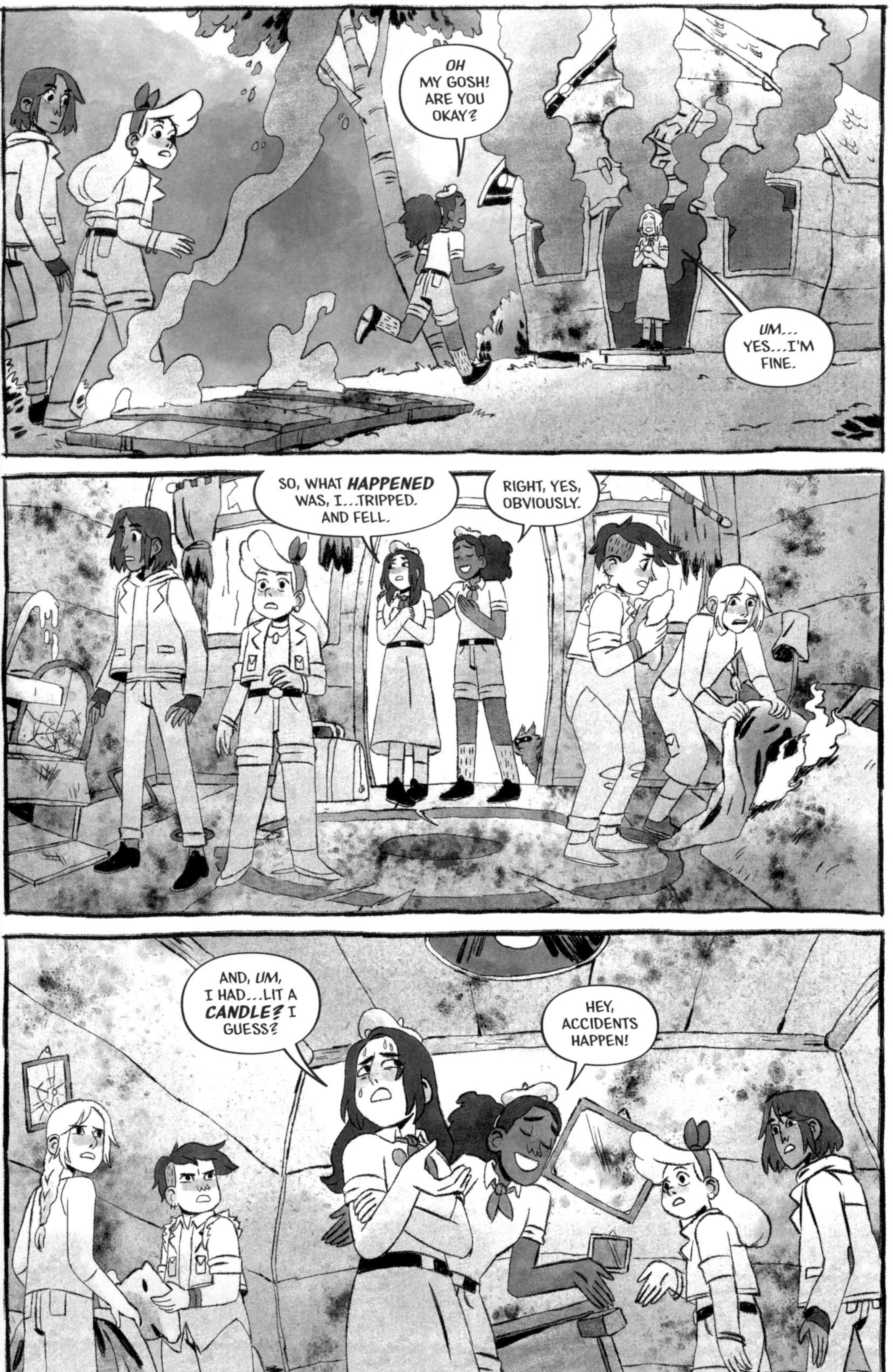

OH MY GOSH! ARE YOU OKAY?
UM... YES...I'M FINE.
SO, WHAT HAPPENED WAS, I...TRIPPED. AND FELL.
RIGHT, YES, OBVIOUSLY.
AND, UM, I HAD...LIT A CANDLE? I GUESS?
HEY, ACCIDENTS HAPPEN!

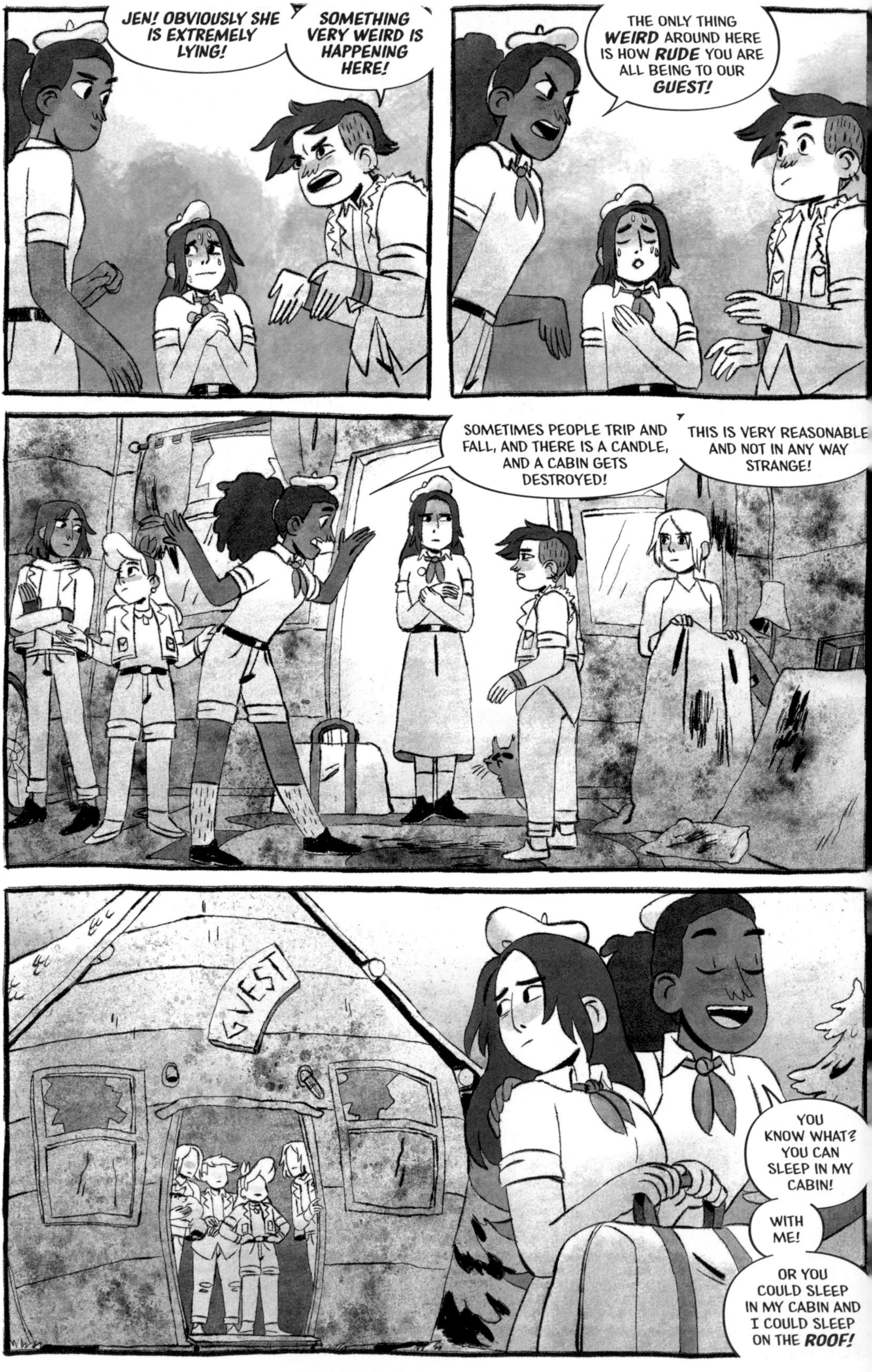
JEN! OBVIOUSLY SHE IS EXTREMELY LYING!
SOMETHING VERY WEIRD IS HAPPENING HERE!
THE ONLY THING WEIRD AROUND HERE IS HOW RUDE YOU ARE ALL BEING TO OUR GUEST!
SOMETIMES PEOPLE TRIP AND FALL, AND THERE IS A CANDLE, AND A CABIN GETS DESTROYED!
THIS IS VERY REASONABLE AND NOT IN ANY WAY STRANGE!
GUEST
YOU KNOW WHAT? YOU CAN SLEEP IN MY CABIN!
WITH ME!
OR YOU COULD SLEEP IN MY CABIN AND I COULD SLEEP ON THE ROOF!

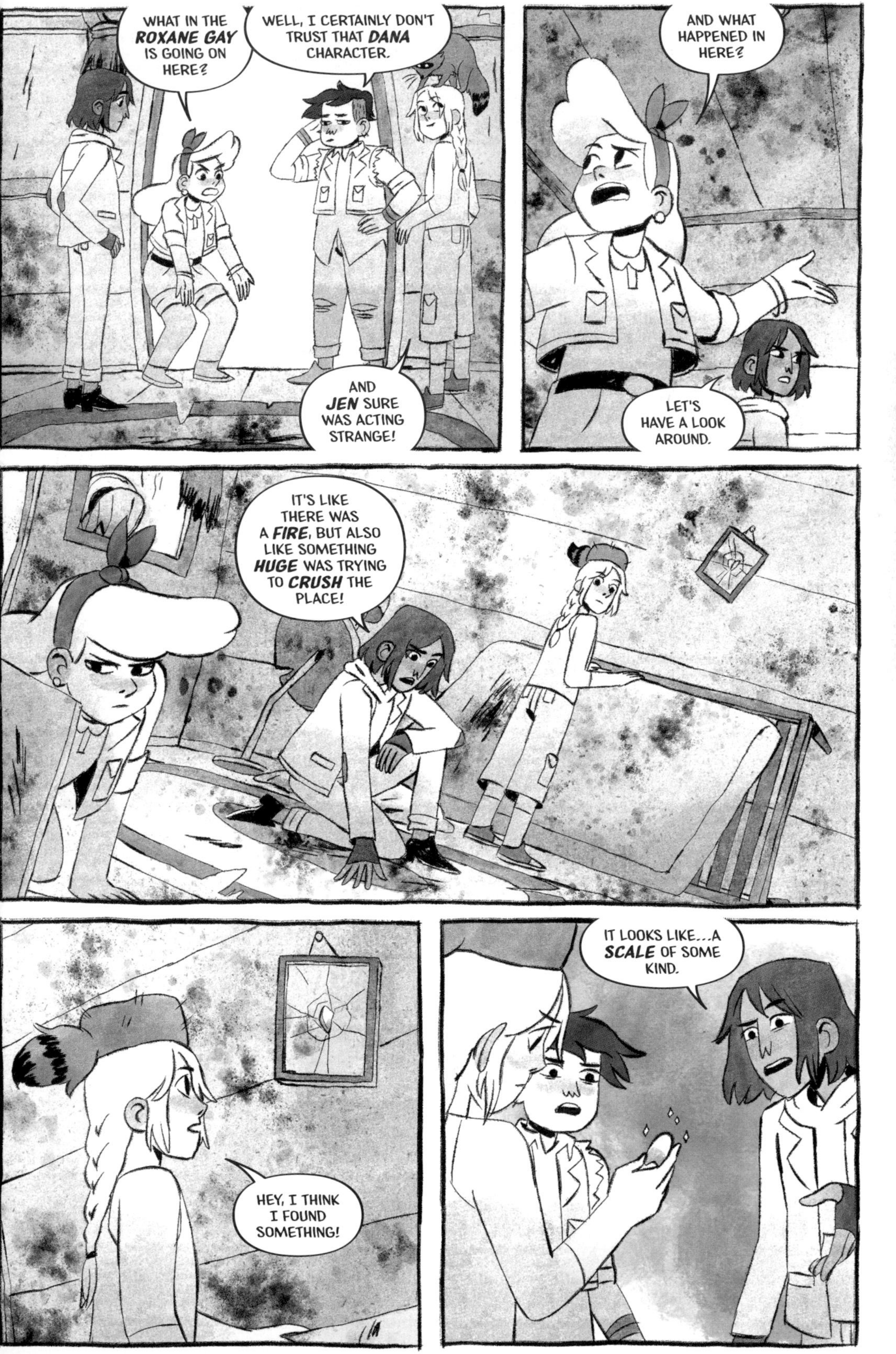
WHAT IN THE ROXANE GAY IS GOING ON HERE?
WELL, I CERTAINLY DON'T TRUST THAT DANA CHARACTER.
AND JEN SURE WAS ACTING STRANGE!
AND WHAT HAPPENED IN HERE?
LET'S HAVE A LOOK AROUND.
IT'S LIKE THERE WAS A FIRE, BUT ALSO LIKE SOMETHING HUGE WAS TRYING TO CRUSH THE PLACE!
HEY, I THINK I FOUND SOMETHING!
IT LOOKS LIKE...A SCALE OF SOME KIND.

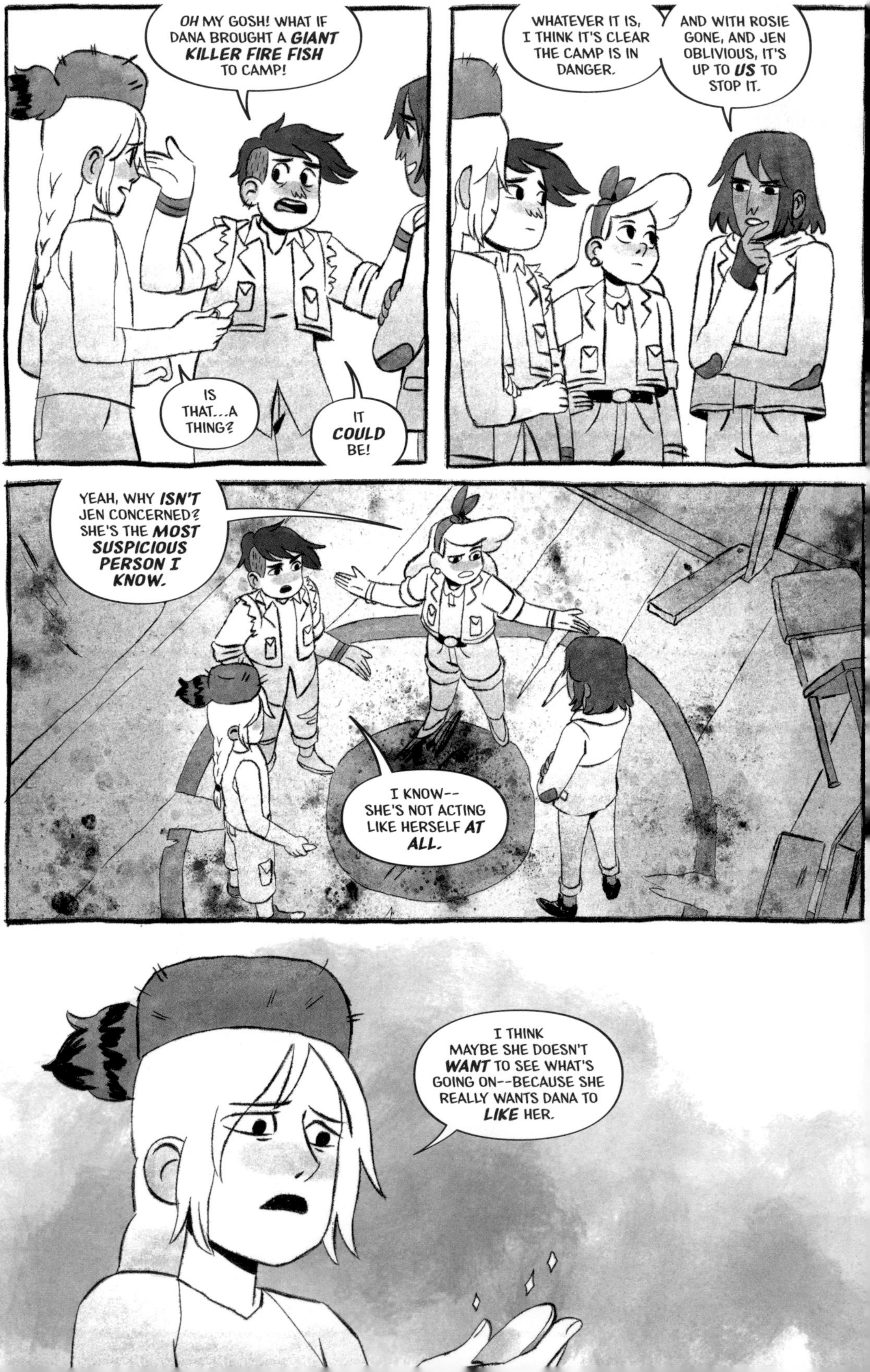
OH MY GOSH! WHAT IF DANA BROUGHT A GIANT KILLER FIRE FISH TO CAMP!
IS THAT...A THING?
IT COULD BE!
WHATEVER IT IS, I THINK IT'S CLEAR THE CAMP IS IN DANGER.
AND WITH ROSIE GONE, AND JEN OBLIVIOUS, IT'S UP TO US TO STOP IT.
YEAH, WHY ISN'T JEN CONCERNED? SHE'S THE MOST SUSPICIOUS PERSON I KNOW.
I KNOW--SHE'S NOT ACTING LIKE HERSELF AT ALL.
I THINK MAYBE SHE DOESN'T WANT TO SEE WHAT'S GOING ON--BECAUSE SHE REALLY WANTS DANA TO LIKE HER.

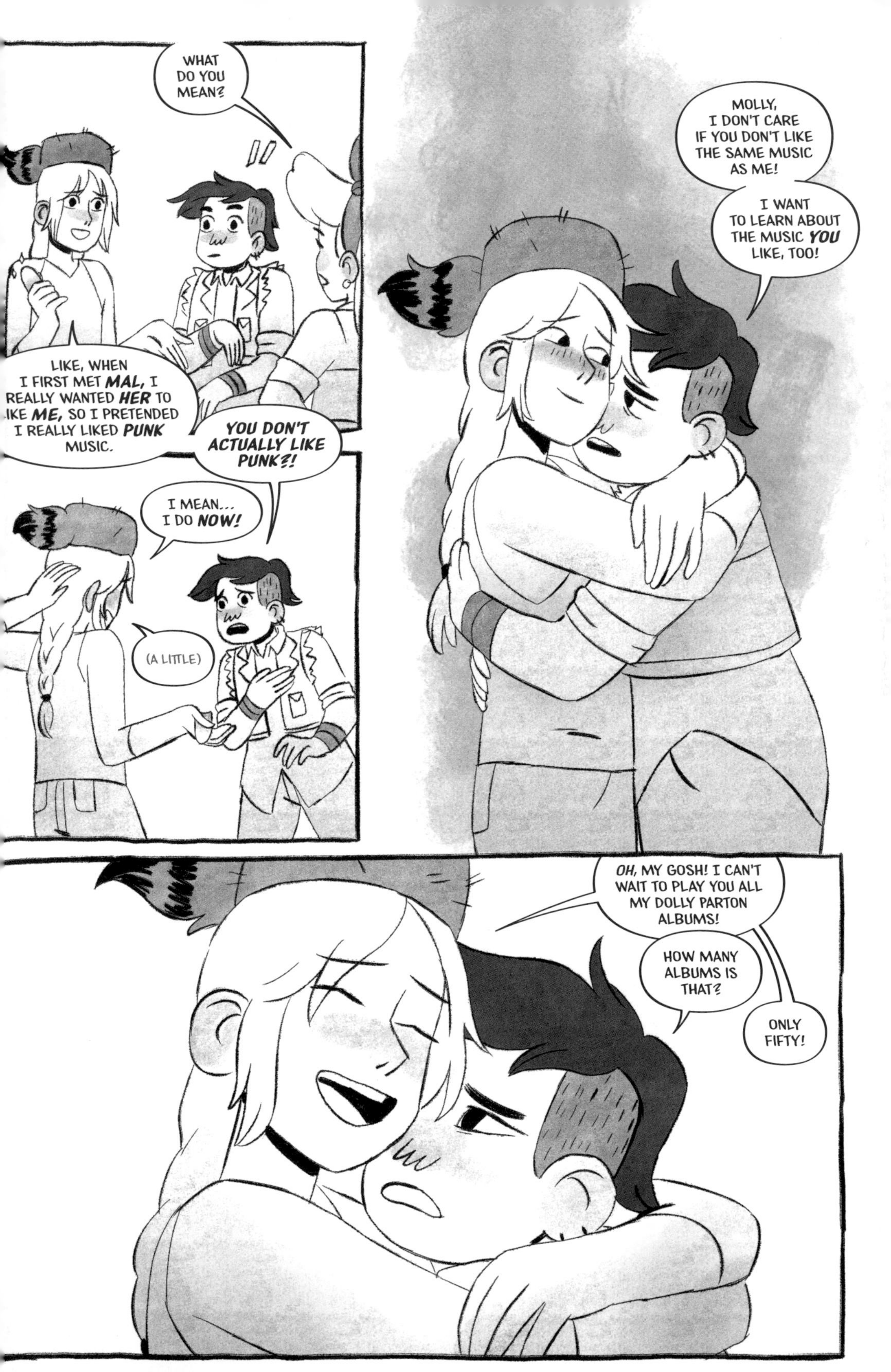
WHAT DO YOU MEAN?
LIKE, WHEN I FIRST MET MAL, I REALLY WANTED HER TO LIKE ME, SO I PRETENDED I REALLY LIKED PUNK MUSIC.
YOU DON'T ACTUALLY LIKE PUNK?!
I MEAN... I DO NOW!
(A LITTLE)
MOLLY, I DON'T CARE IF YOU DON'T LIKE THE SAME MUSIC AS ME!
I WANT TO LEARN ABOUT THE MUSIC YOU LIKE, TOO!
OH, MY GOSH! I CAN'T WAIT TO PLAY YOU ALL MY DOLLY PARTON ALBUMS!
HOW MANY ALBUMS IS THAT?
ONLY FIFTY!

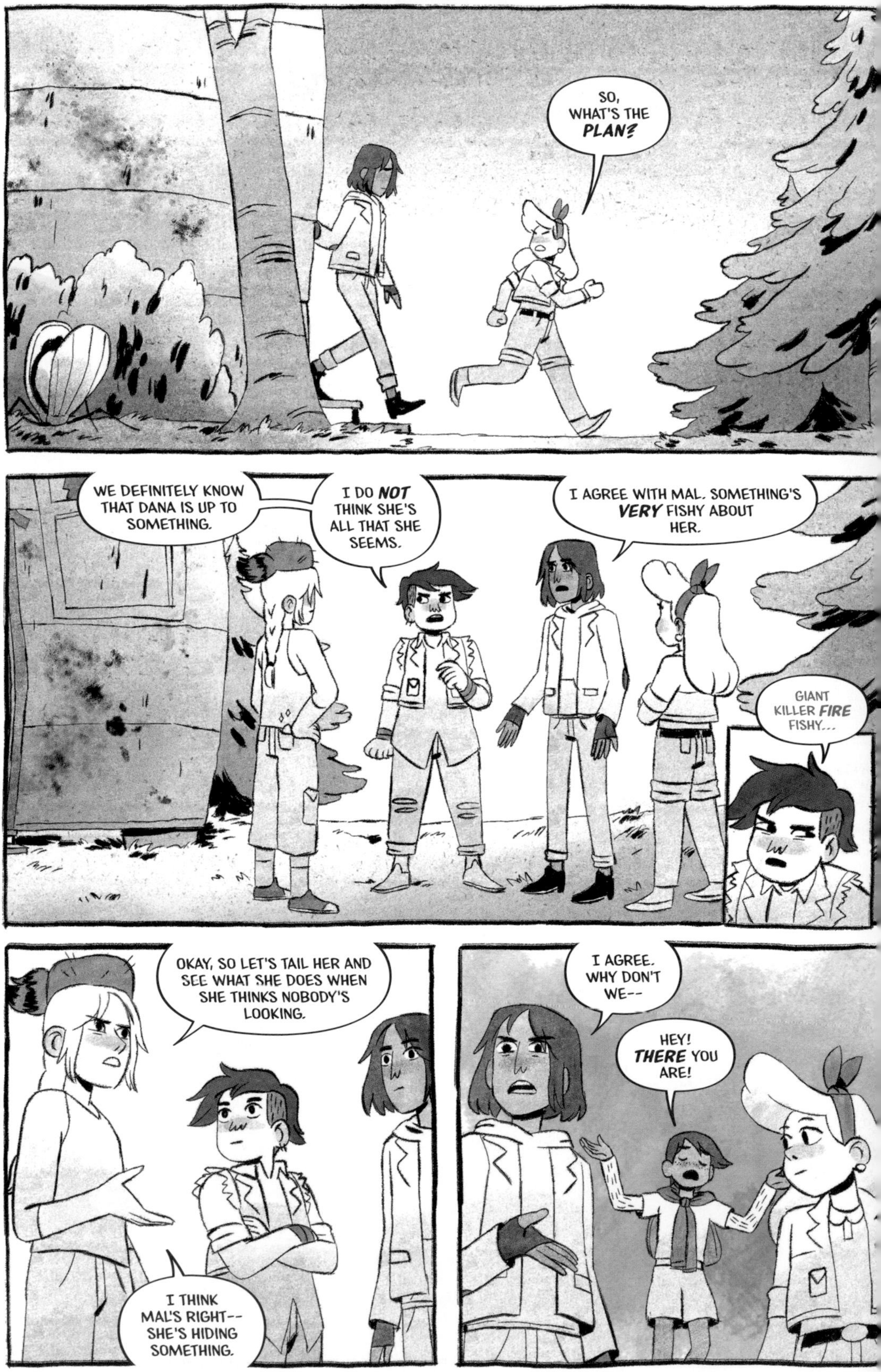
SO, WHAT'S THE PLAN?
WE DEFINITELY KNOW THAT DANA IS UP TO SOMETHING.
I DO NOT THINK SHE'S ALL THAT SHE SEEMS.
I AGREE WITH MAL. SOMETHING'S VERY FISHY ABOUT HER.
GIANT KILLER FIRE FISHY...
OKAY, SO LET'S TAIL HER AND SEE WHAT SHE DOES WHEN SHE THINKS NOBODY'S LOOKING.
I THINK MAL'S RIGHT-- SHE'S HIDING SOMETHING.
I AGREE. WHY DON'T WE--
HEY! THERE YOU ARE!

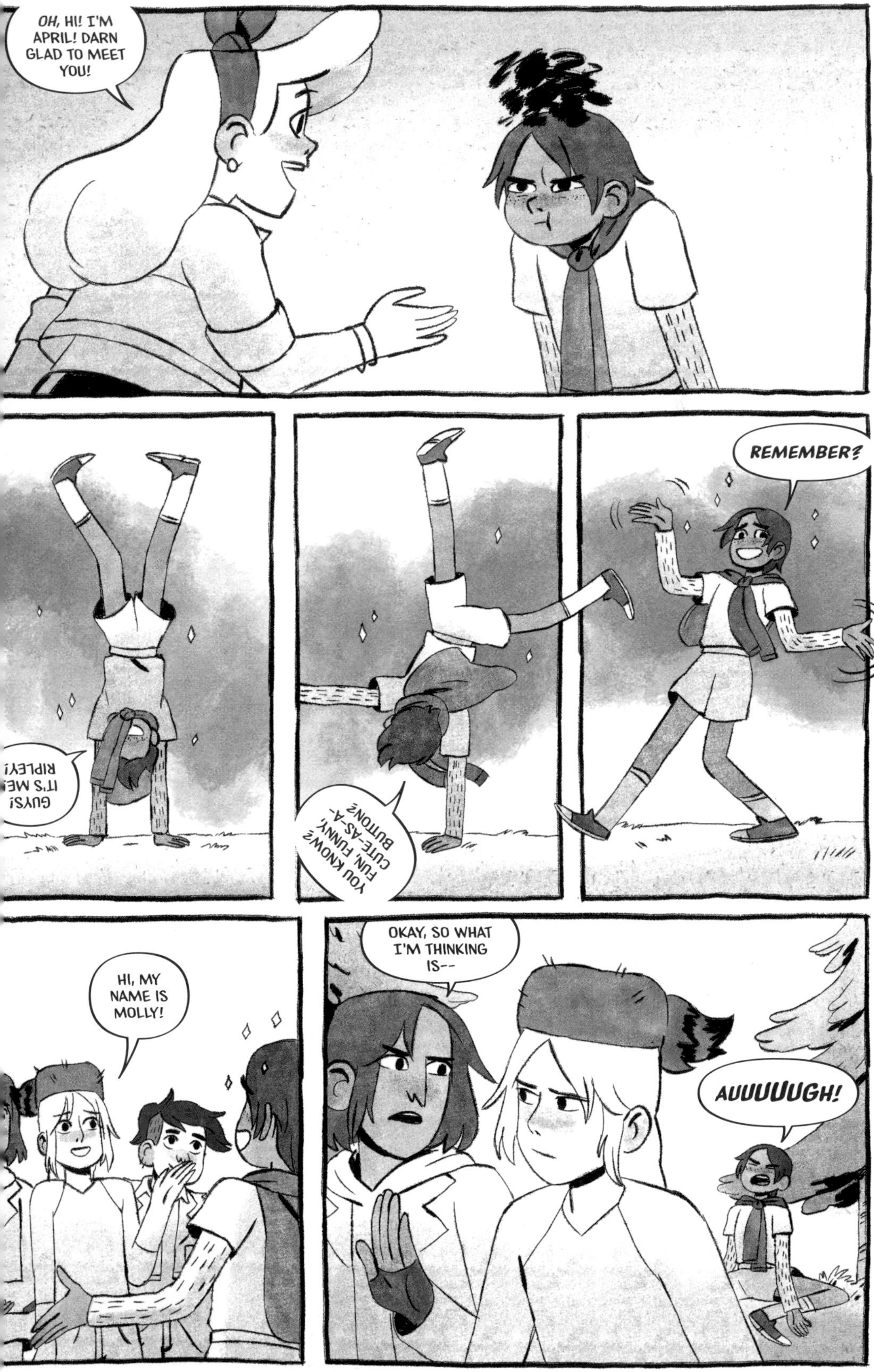
OH, HI! I'M APRIL! DARN GLAD TO MEET YOU!
GUYS! IT'S ME! RIPLEY!
YOU KNOW? FUN, FUNNY, CUTE-AS-A-BUTTON?
REMEMBER?
HI, MY NAME IS MOLLY!
OKAY, SO WHAT I'M THINKING IS--
AUUUUUGH!

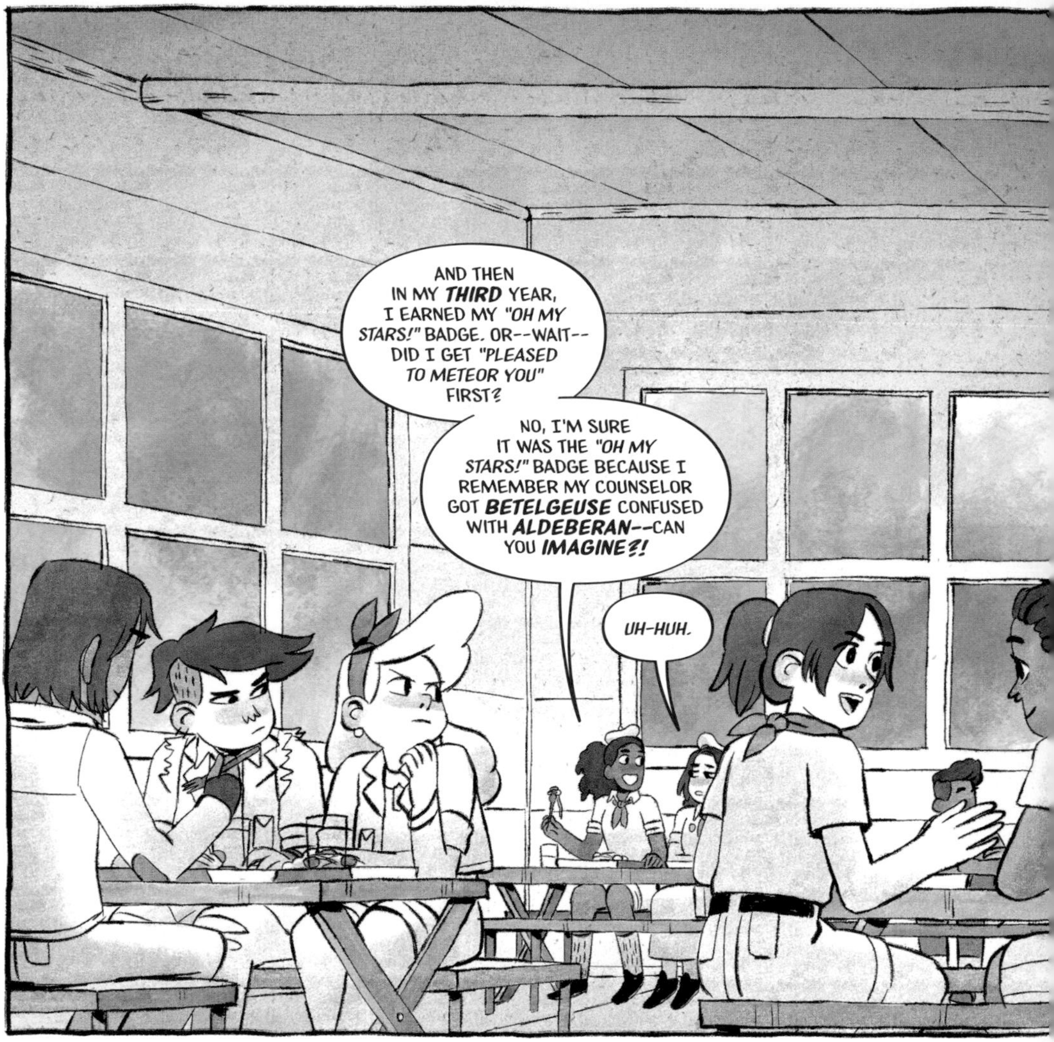
AND THEN IN MY THIRD YEAR, I EARNED MY "OH MY STARS!" BADGE. OR--WAIT--DID I GET "PLEASED TO METEOR YOU" FIRST?
NO, I'M SURE IT WAS THE "OH MY STARS!" BADGE BECAUSE I REMEMBER MY COUNSELOR GOT BETELGEUSE CONFUSED WITH ALDEBERAN--CAN YOU IMAGINE?!
UH-HUH.

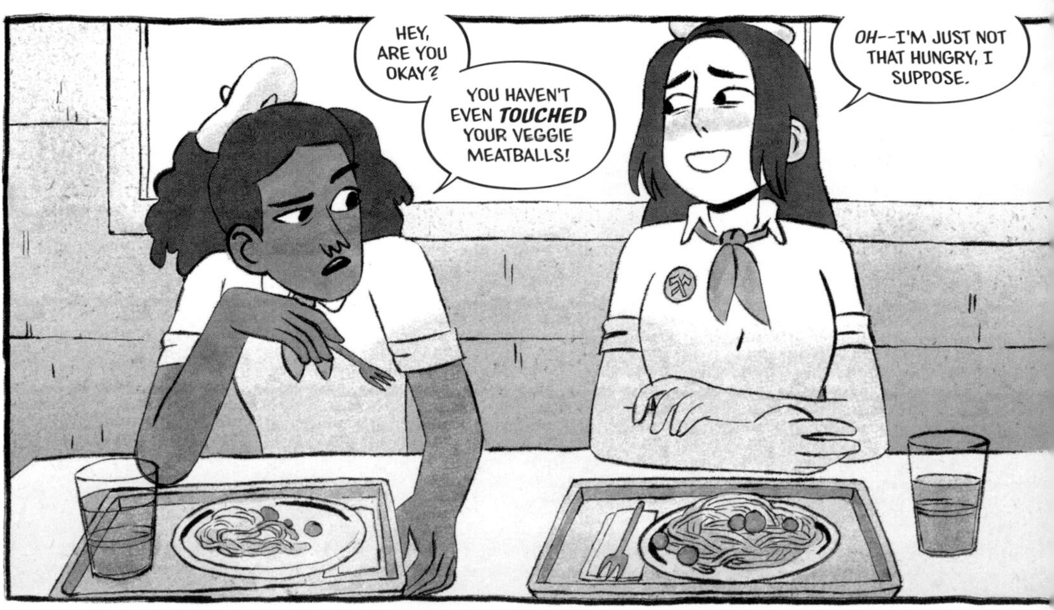
HEY, ARE YOU OKAY?
YOU HAVEN'T EVEN TOUCHED YOUR VEGGIE MEATBALLS!
OH--I'M JUST NOT THAT HUNGRY, I SUPPOSE.

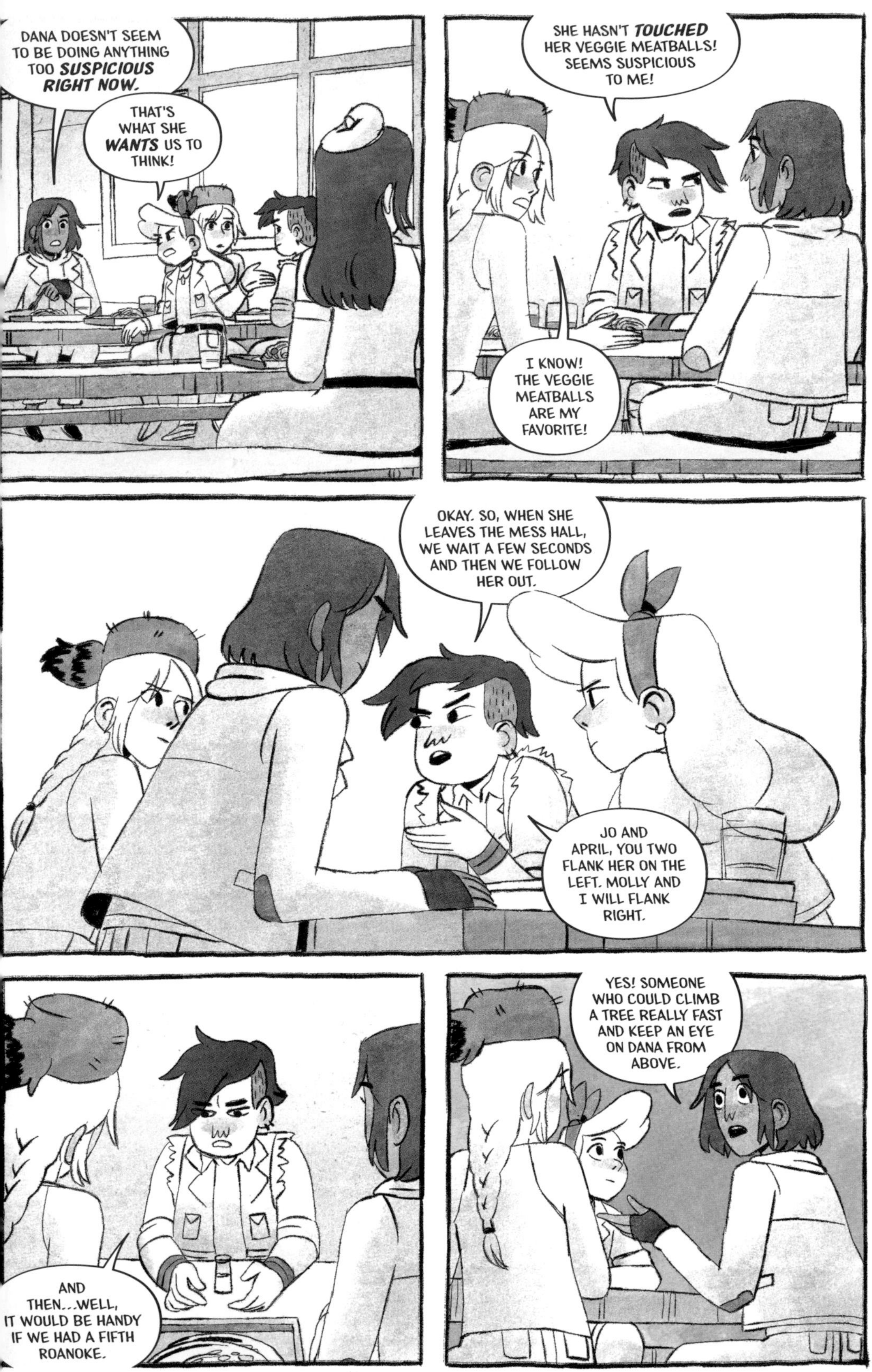
DANA DOESN'T SEEM TO BE DOING ANYTHING TOO **SUSPICIOUS RIGHT NOW.**
THAT'S WHAT SHE **WANTS** US TO THINK!
SHE HASN'T **TOUCHED** HER VEGGIE MEATBALLS! SEEMS SUSPICIOUS TO ME!
I KNOW! THE VEGGIE MEATBALLS ARE MY FAVORITE!
OKAY. SO, WHEN SHE LEAVES THE MESS HALL, WE WAIT A FEW SECONDS AND THEN WE FOLLOW HER OUT.
JO AND APRIL, YOU TWO FLANK HER ON THE LEFT. MOLLY AND I WILL FLANK RIGHT.
AND THEN...WELL, IT WOULD BE HANDY IF WE HAD A FIFTH ROANOKE.
YES! SOMEONE WHO COULD CLIMB A TREE REALLY FAST AND KEEP AN EYE ON DANA FROM ABOVE.

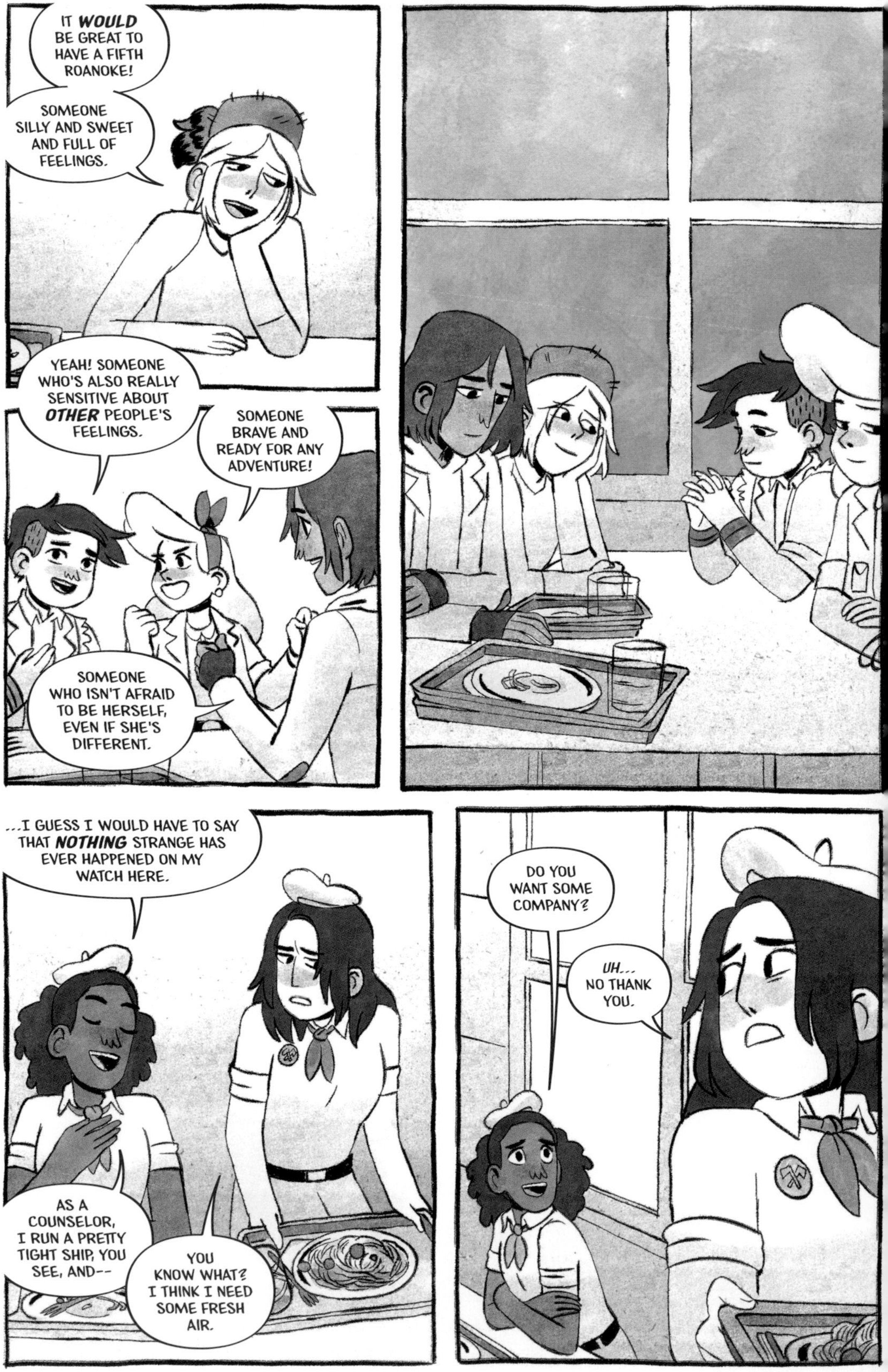
IT *WOULD* BE GREAT TO HAVE A FIFTH ROANOKE!
SOMEONE SILLY AND SWEET AND FULL OF FEELINGS.
YEAH! SOMEONE WHO'S ALSO REALLY SENSITIVE ABOUT *OTHER* PEOPLE'S FEELINGS.
SOMEONE BRAVE AND READY FOR ANY ADVENTURE!
SOMEONE WHO ISN'T AFRAID TO BE HERSELF, EVEN IF SHE'S DIFFERENT.
...I GUESS I WOULD HAVE TO SAY THAT *NOTHING* STRANGE HAS EVER HAPPENED ON MY WATCH HERE.
AS A COUNSELOR, I RUN A PRETTY TIGHT SHIP, YOU SEE, AND--
YOU KNOW WHAT? I THINK I NEED SOME FRESH AIR.
DO YOU WANT SOME COMPANY?
UH... NO THANK YOU.

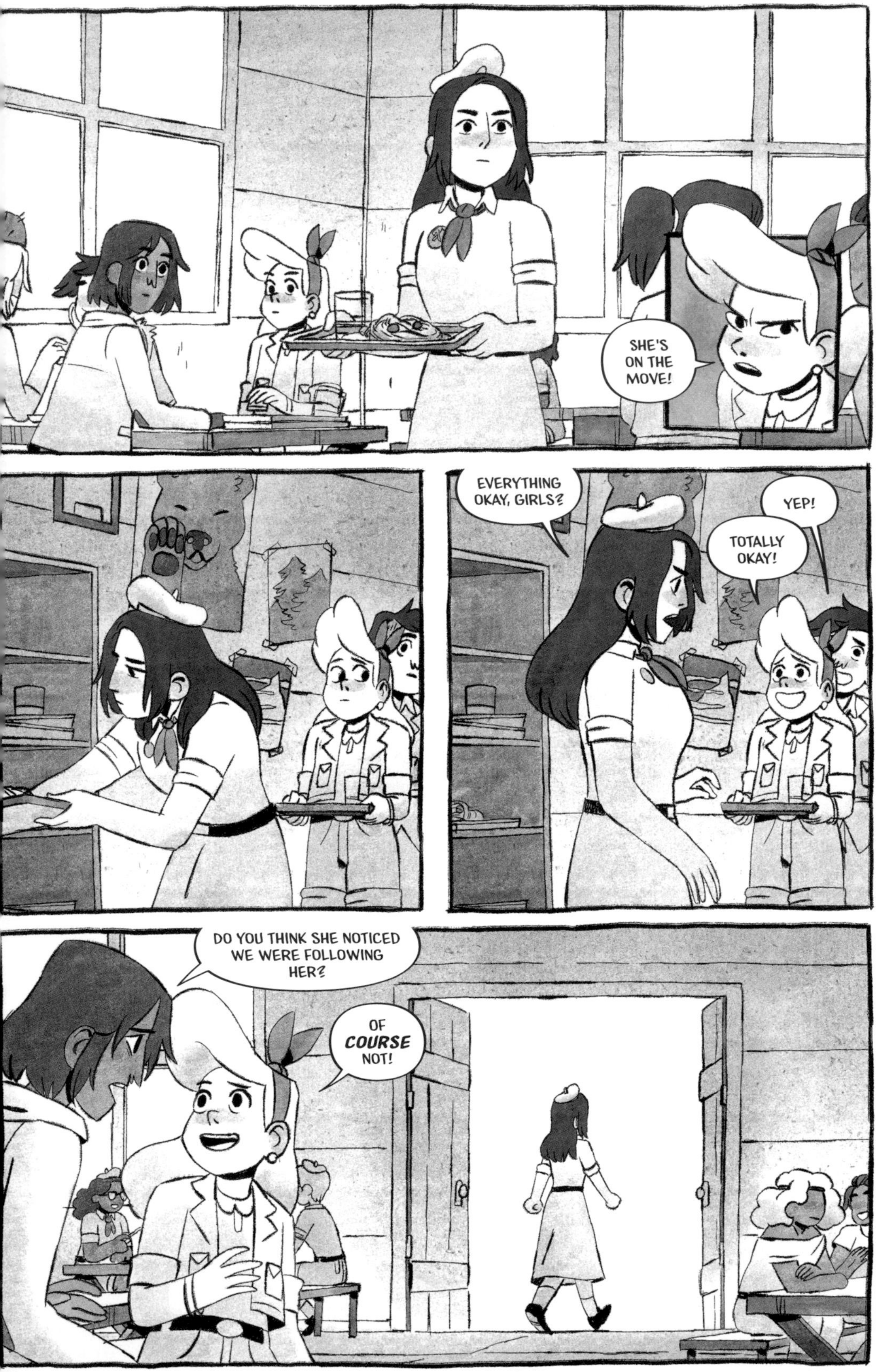
SHE'S ON THE MOVE!
EVERYTHING OKAY, GIRLS?
YEP!
TOTALLY OKAY!
DO YOU THINK SHE NOTICED WE WERE FOLLOWING HER?
OF *COURSE* NOT!

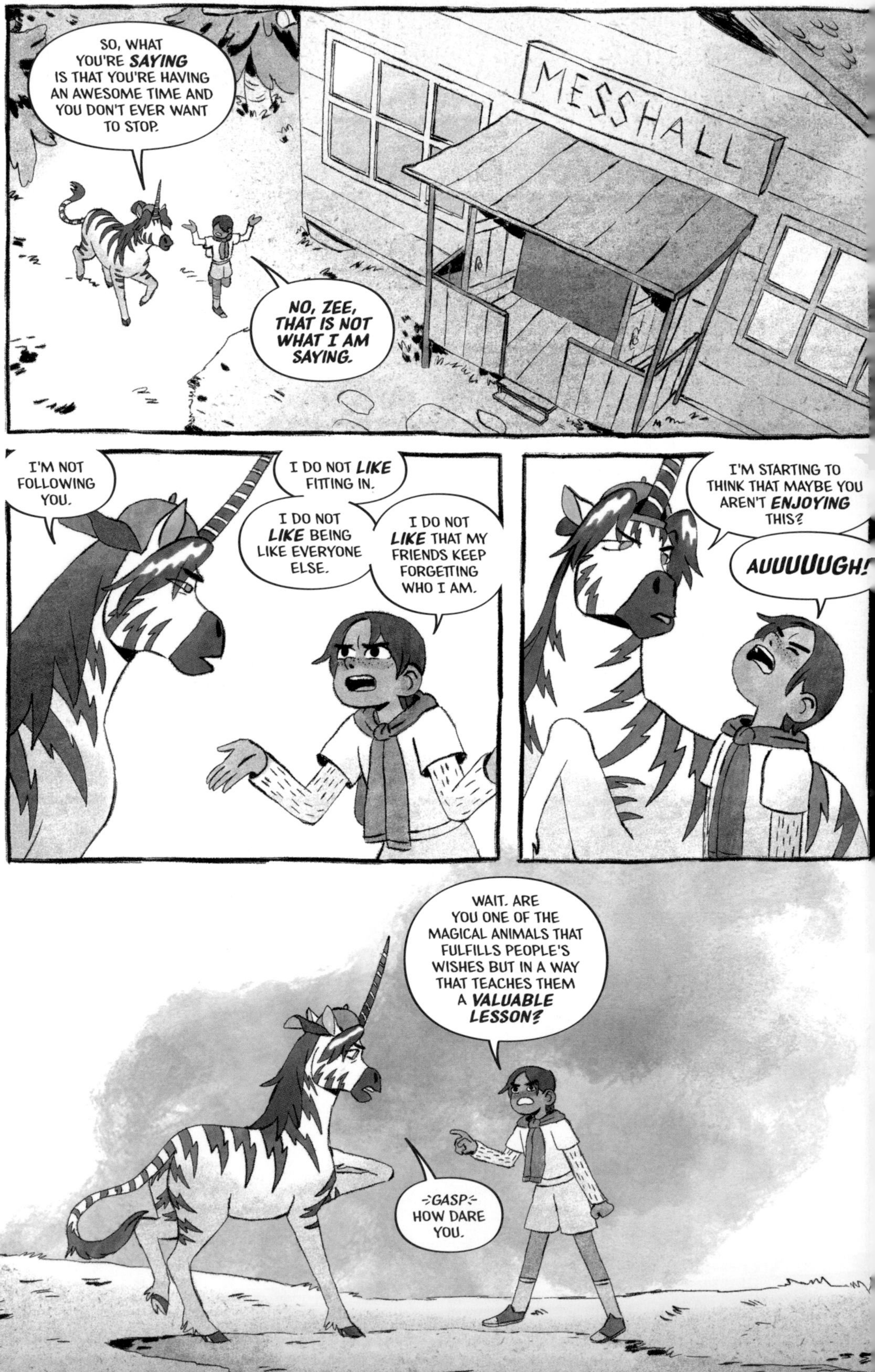
SO, WHAT YOU'RE SAYING IS THAT YOU'RE HAVING AN AWESOME TIME AND YOU DON'T EVER WANT TO STOP.
MESSHALL
NO, ZEE, THAT IS NOT WHAT I AM SAYING.
I'M NOT FOLLOWING YOU.
I DO NOT LIKE FITTING IN.
I DO NOT LIKE BEING LIKE EVERYONE ELSE.
I DO NOT LIKE THAT MY FRIENDS KEEP FORGETTING WHO I AM.
I'M STARTING TO THINK THAT MAYBE YOU AREN'T ENJOYING THIS?
AUUUUUGH!
WAIT. ARE YOU ONE OF THE MAGICAL ANIMALS THAT FULFILLS PEOPLE'S WISHES BUT IN A WAY THAT TEACHES THEM A VALUABLE LESSON?
GASP HOW DARE YOU.

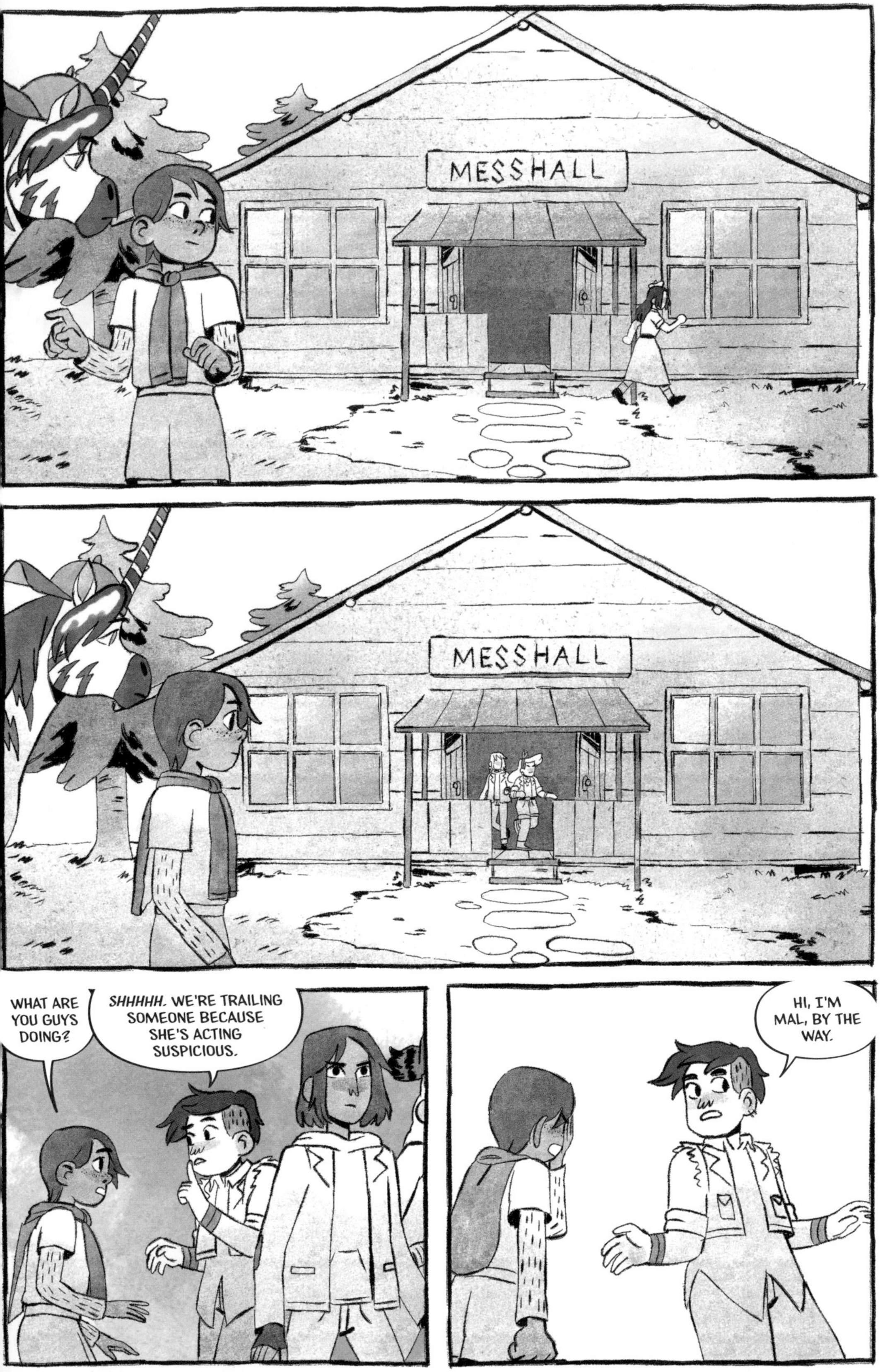
MESSHALL
MESSHALL
WHAT ARE YOU GUYS DOING?
SHHHHH. WE'RE TRAILING SOMEONE BECAUSE SHE'S ACTING SUSPICIOUS.
HI, I'M MAL, BY THE WAY.

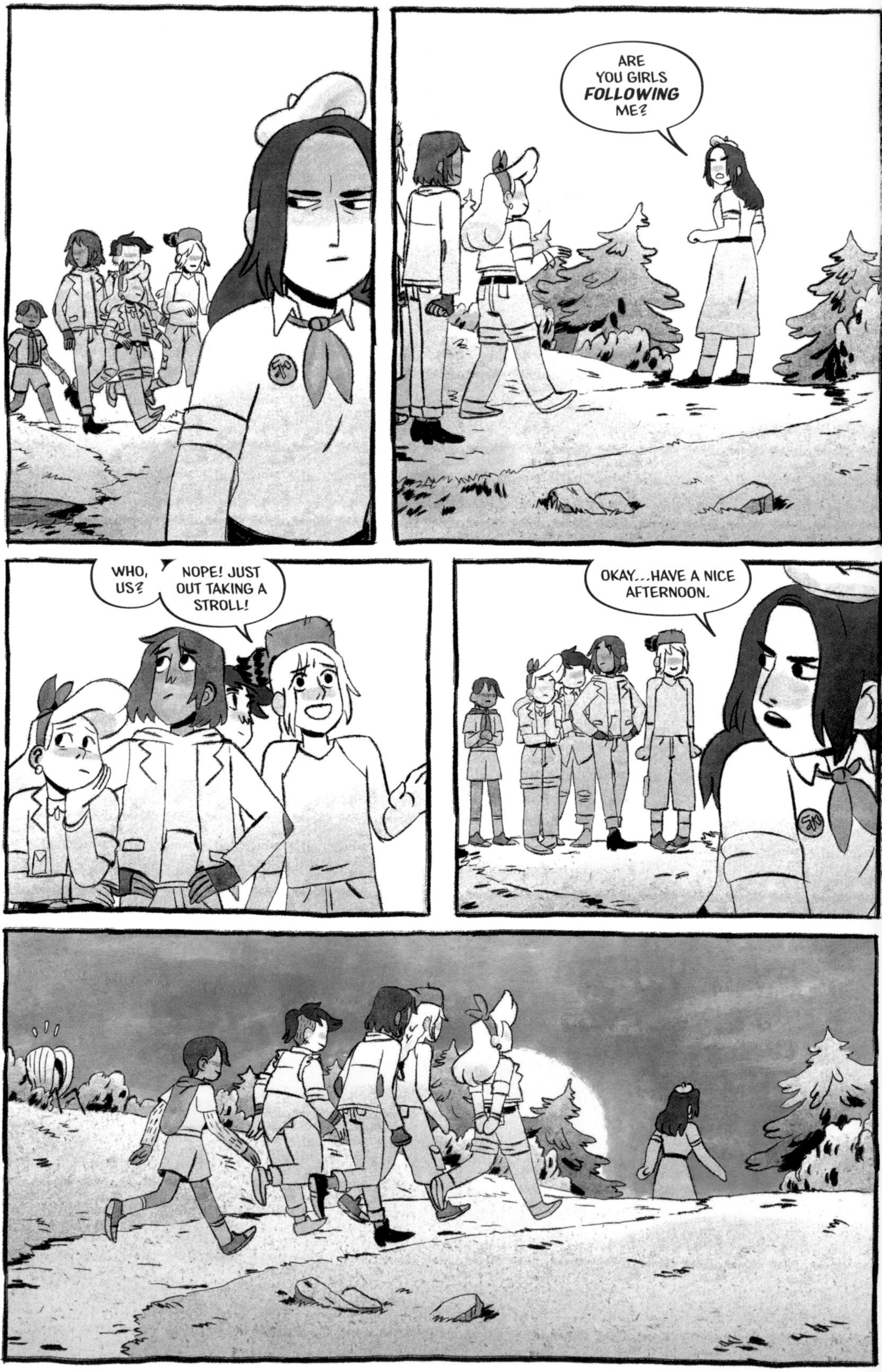
ARE YOU GIRLS FOLLOWING ME?
WHO, US?
NOPE! JUST OUT TAKING A STROLL!
OKAY...HAVE A NICE AFTERNOON.

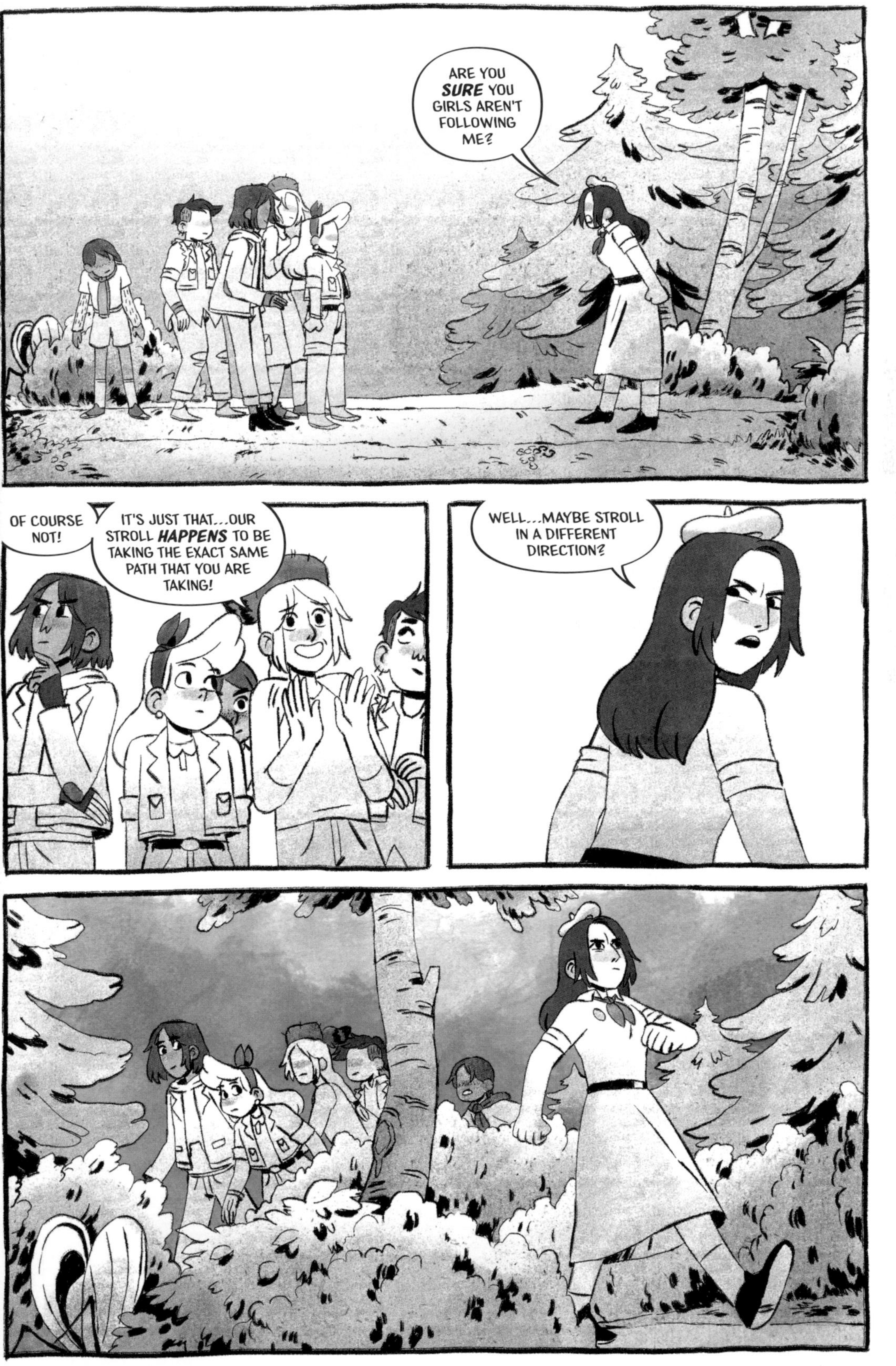

ARE YOU *SURE* YOU GIRLS AREN'T FOLLOWING ME?
OF COURSE NOT!
IT'S JUST THAT...OUR STROLL *HAPPENS* TO BE TAKING THE EXACT SAME PATH THAT YOU ARE TAKING!
WELL...MAYBE STROLL IN A DIFFERENT DIRECTION?

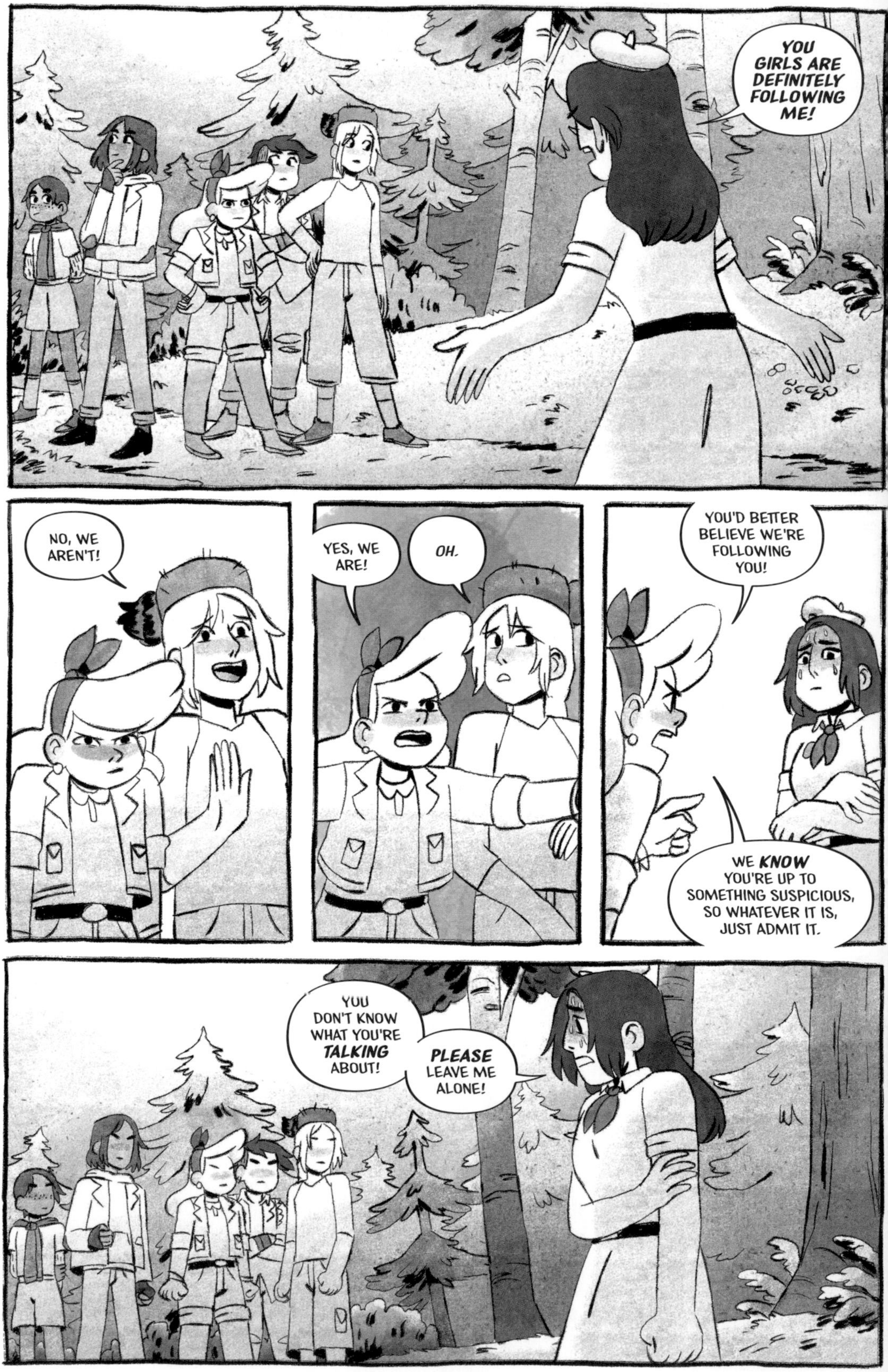
YOU GIRLS ARE DEFINITELY FOLLOWING ME!
NO, WE AREN'T!
YES, WE ARE!
OH.
YOU'D BETTER BELIEVE WE'RE FOLLOWING YOU!
WE KNOW YOU'RE UP TO SOMETHING SUSPICIOUS, SO WHATEVER IT IS, JUST ADMIT IT.
YOU DON'T KNOW WHAT YOU'RE TALKING ABOUT!
PLEASE LEAVE ME ALONE!

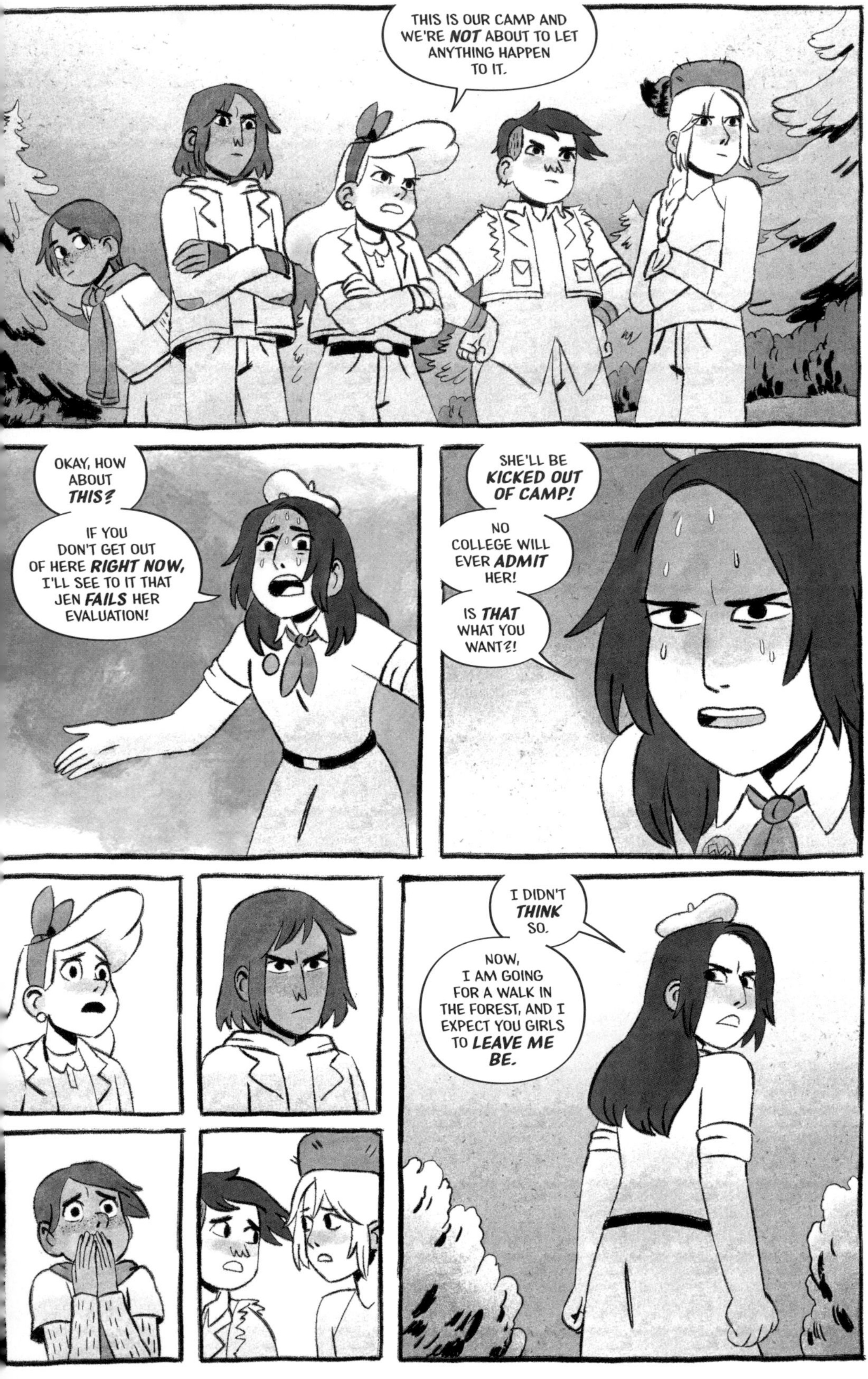
THIS IS OUR CAMP AND WE'RE NOT ABOUT TO LET ANYTHING HAPPEN TO IT.
OKAY, HOW ABOUT THIS?
IF YOU DON'T GET OUT OF HERE RIGHT NOW, I'LL SEE TO IT THAT JEN FAILS HER EVALUATION!
SHE'LL BE KICKED OUT OF CAMP!
NO COLLEGE WILL EVER ADMIT HER!
IS THAT WHAT YOU WANT?!
I DIDN'T THINK SO.
NOW, I AM GOING FOR A WALK IN THE FOREST, AND I EXPECT YOU GIRLS TO LEAVE ME BE.

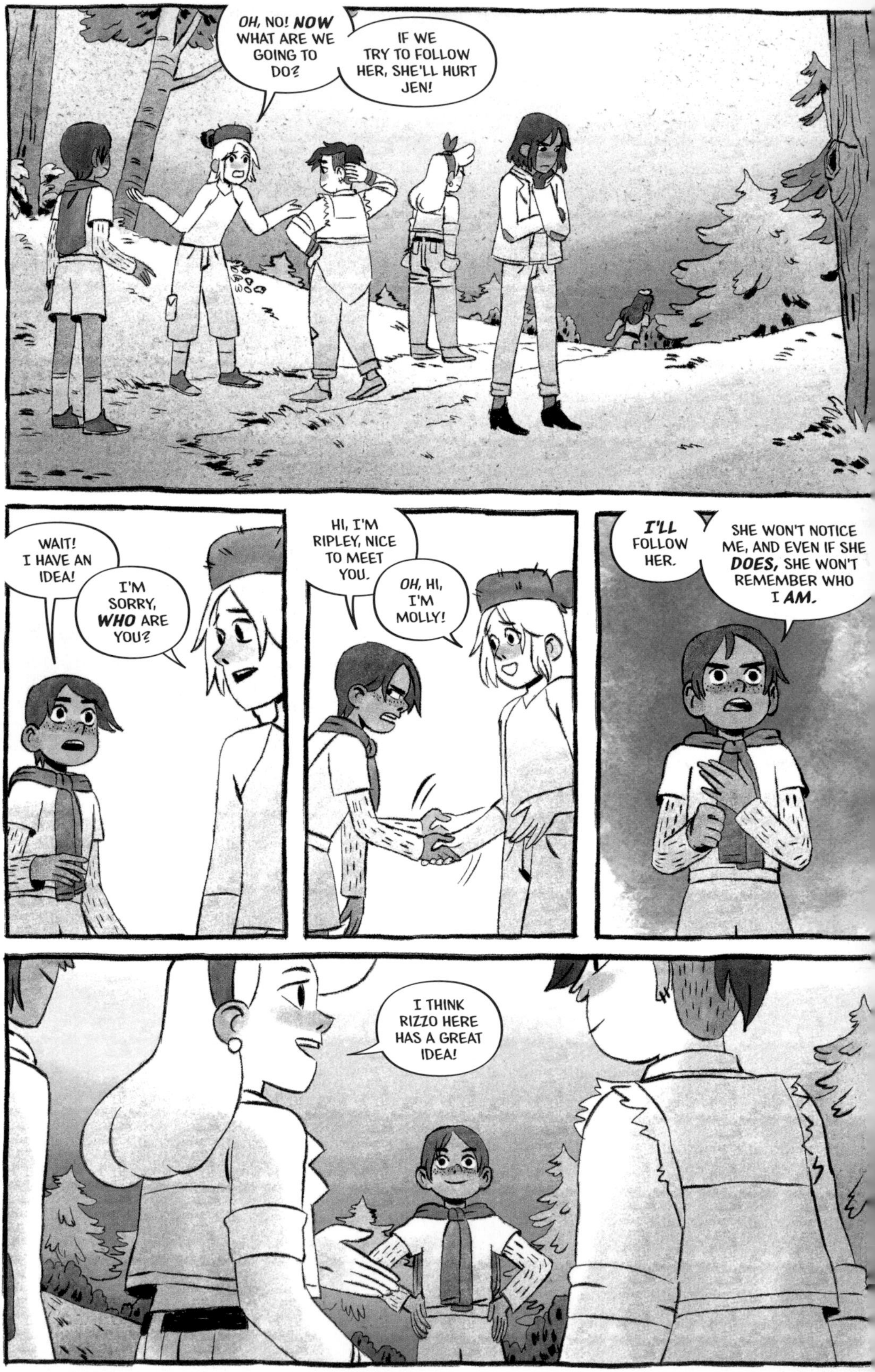
OH, NO! NOW WHAT ARE WE GOING TO DO?
IF WE TRY TO FOLLOW HER, SHE'LL HURT JEN!
WAIT! I HAVE AN IDEA!
I'M SORRY, WHO ARE YOU?
HI, I'M RIPLEY, NICE TO MEET YOU.
OH, HI, I'M MOLLY!
I'LL FOLLOW HER.
SHE WON'T NOTICE ME, AND EVEN IF SHE DOES, SHE WON'T REMEMBER WHO I AM.
I THINK RIZZO HERE HAS A GREAT IDEA!

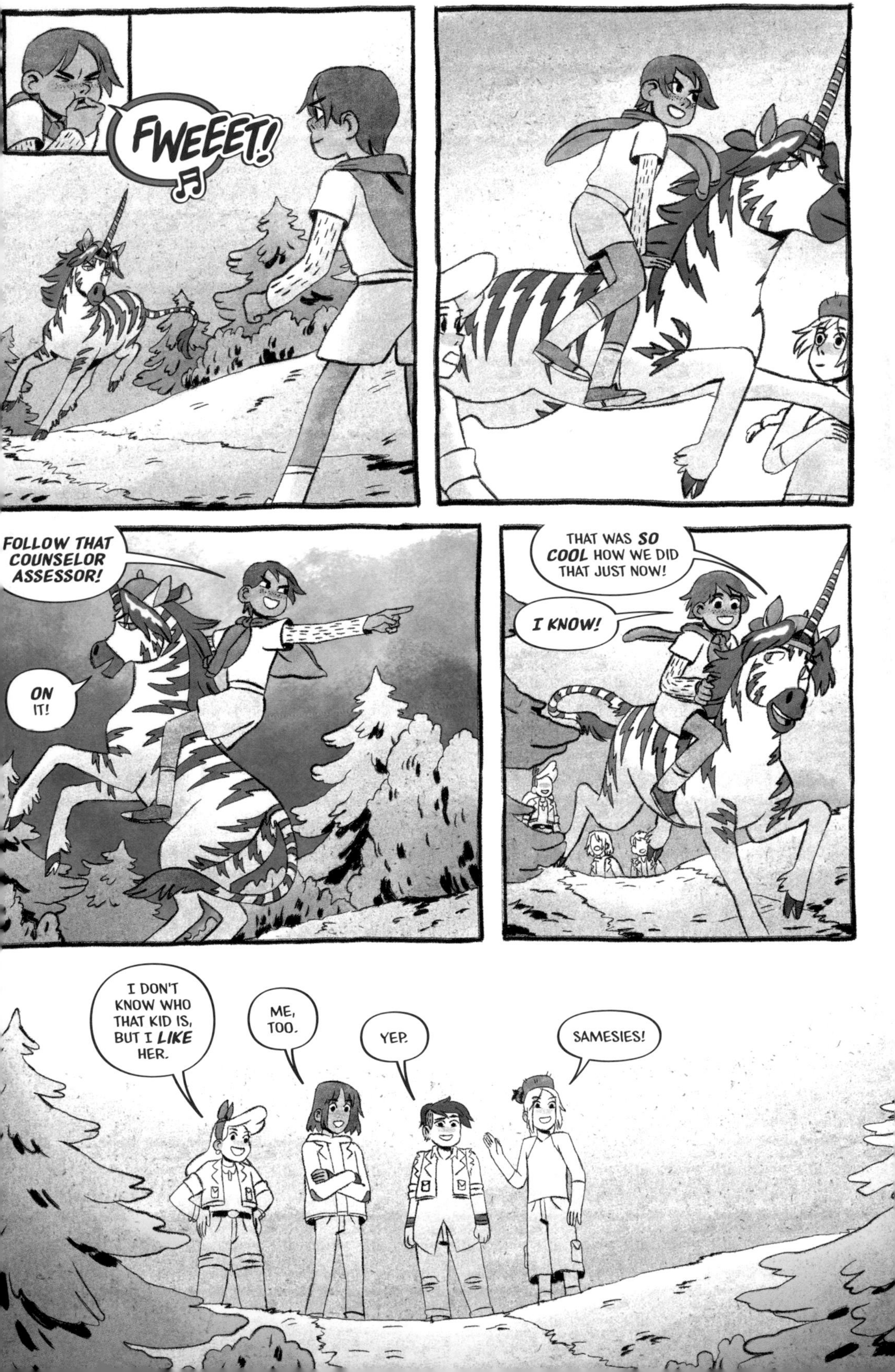

FWEEET!
FOLLOW THAT COUNSELOR ASSESSOR!
ON IT!
THAT WAS SO COOL HOW WE DID THAT JUST NOW!
I KNOW!
I DON'T KNOW WHO THAT KID IS, BUT I LIKE HER.
ME, TOO.
YEP.
SAMESIES!

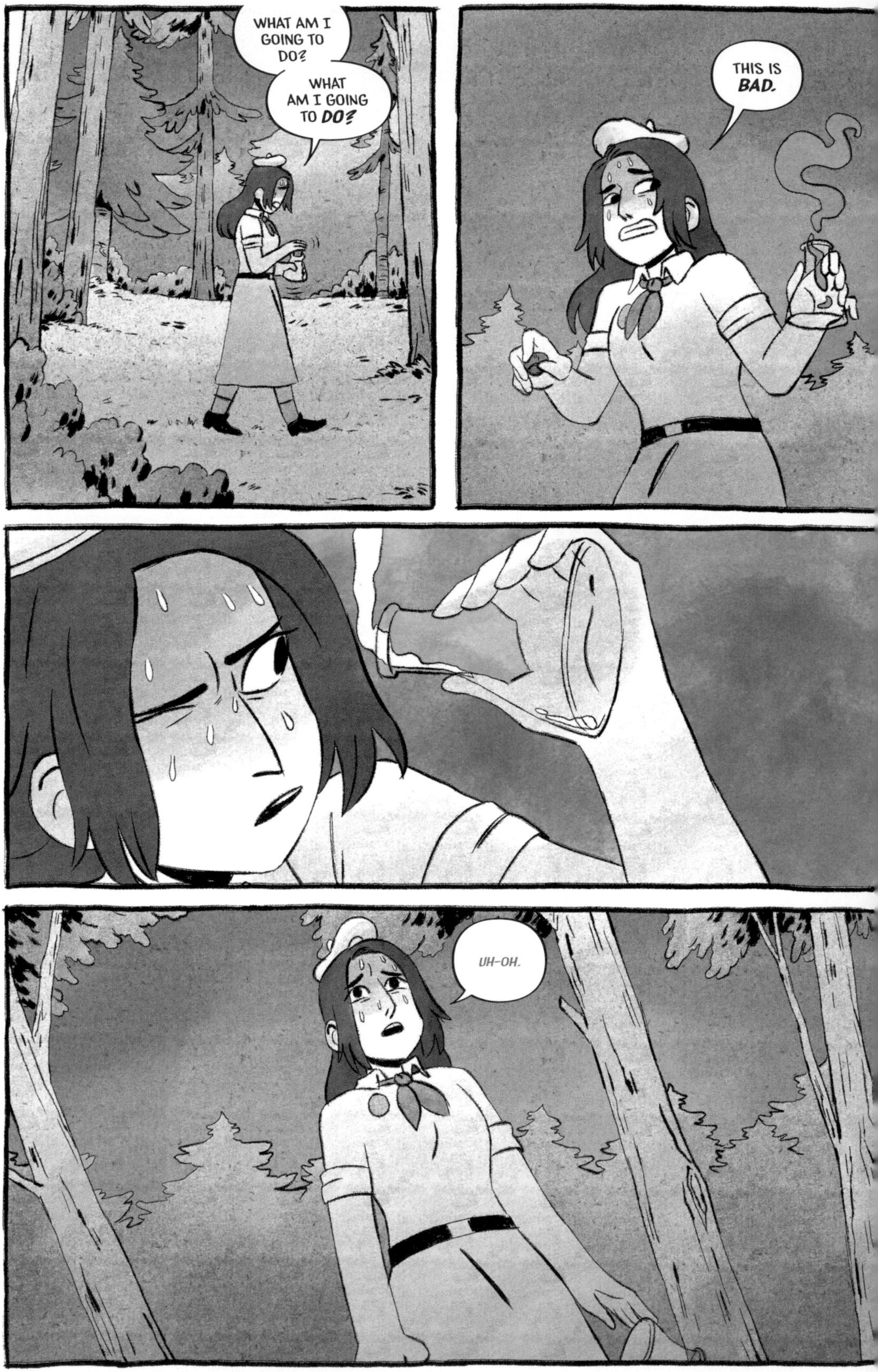
WHAT AM I GOING TO DO?
WHAT AM I GOING TO DO?
THIS IS BAD.
UH-OH.

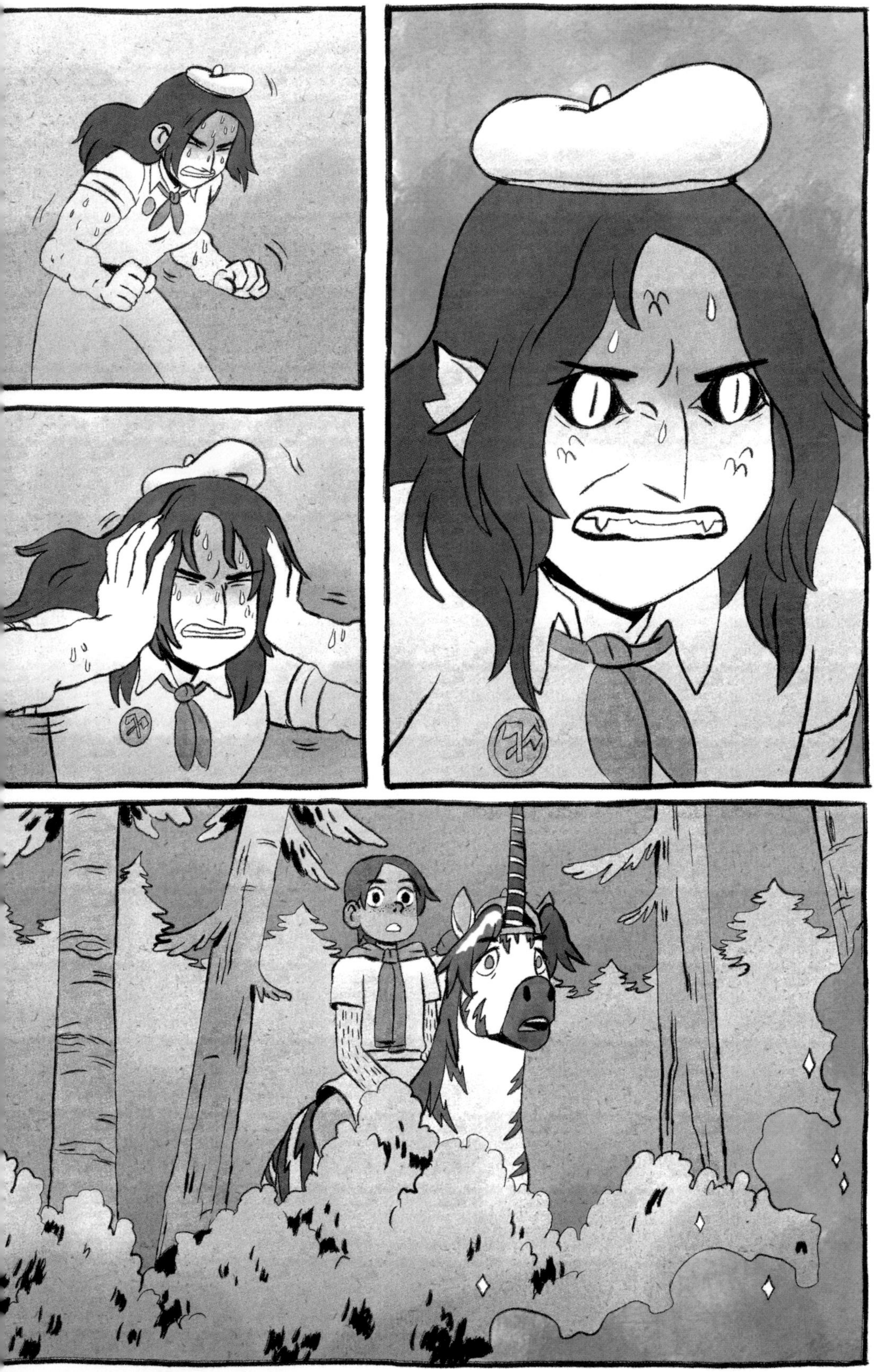

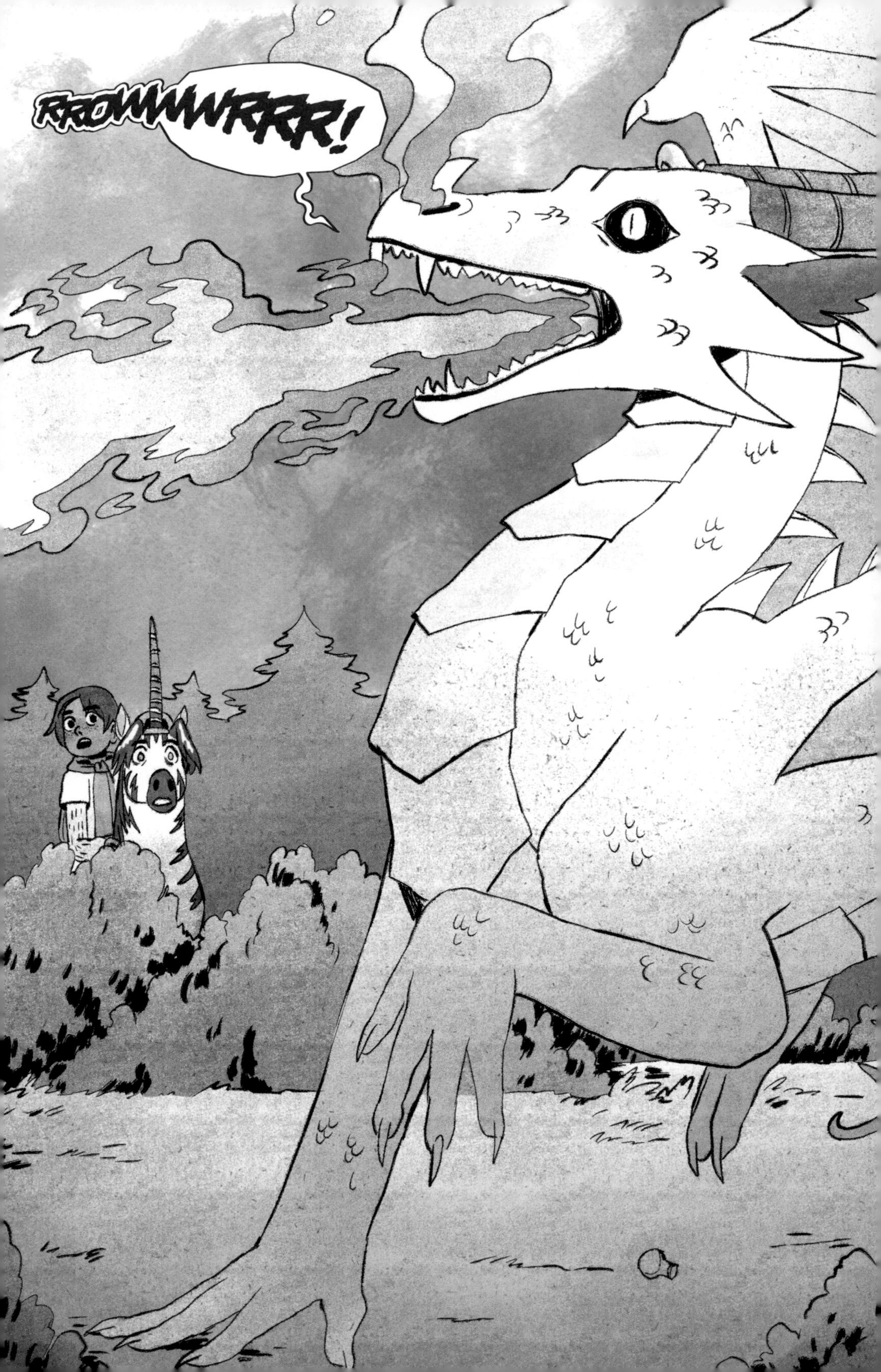
RRROWWWRRR!

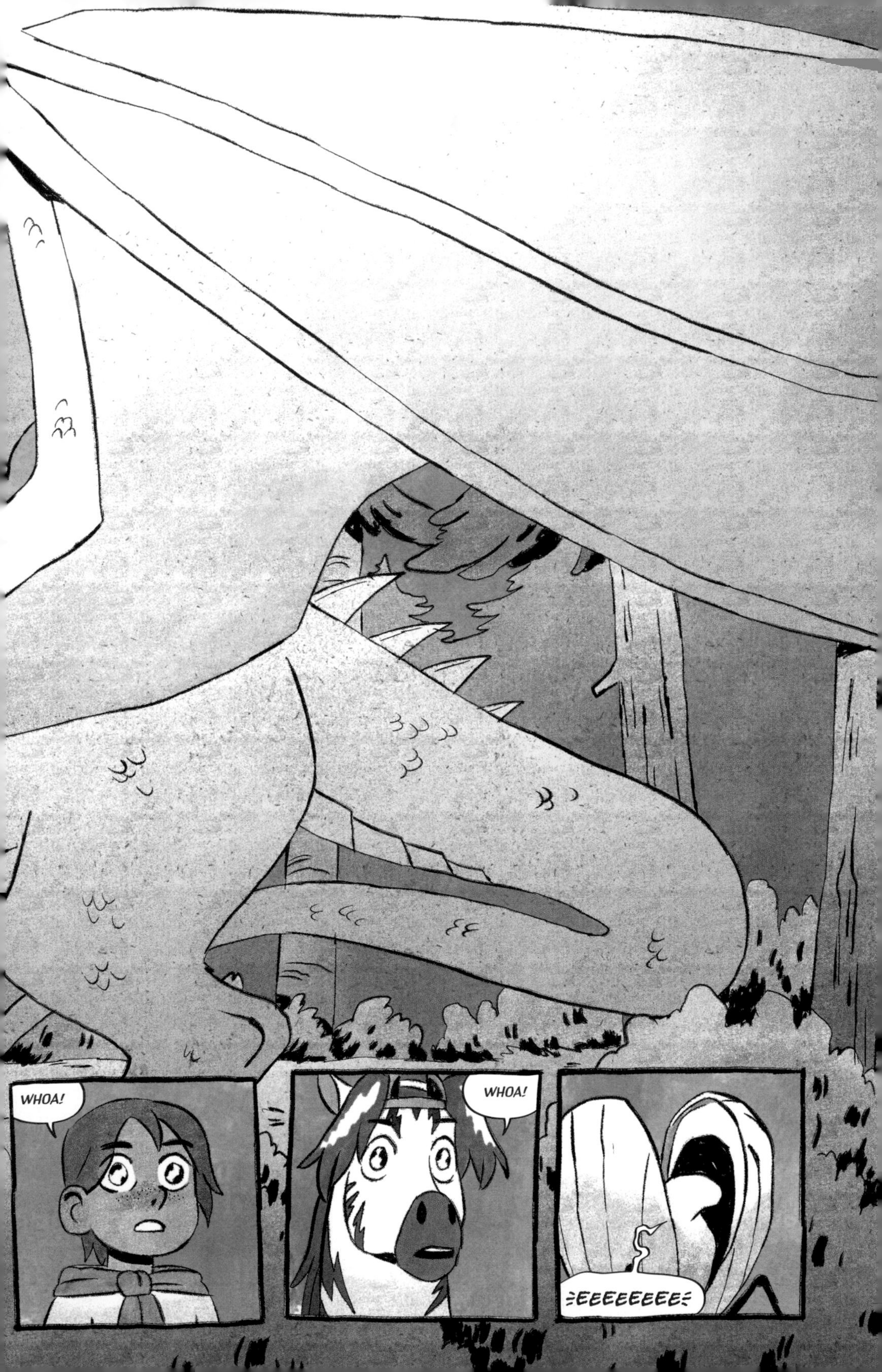
WHOA!
WHOA!
EEEEEEEEE

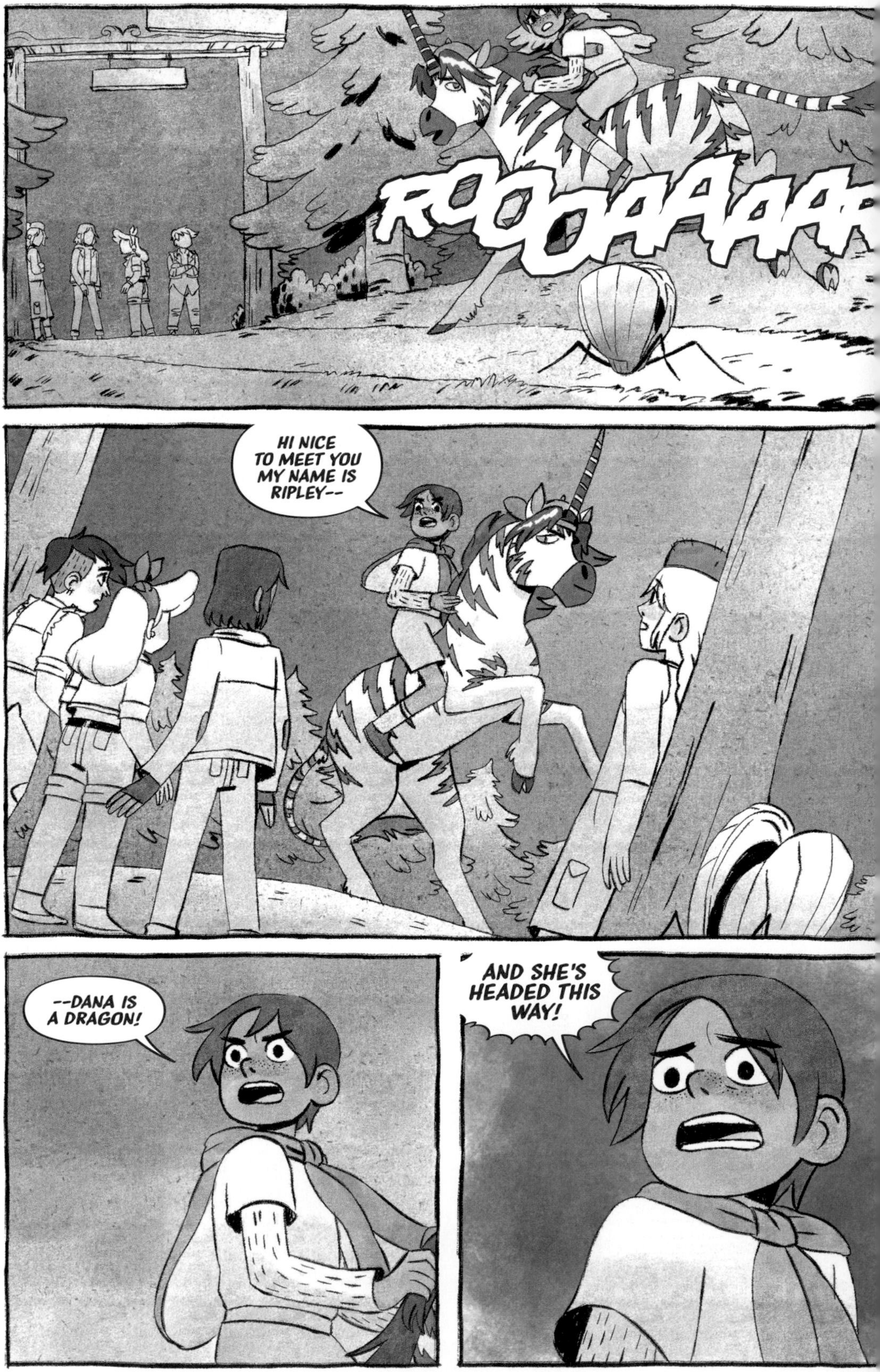
ROOOAAAAR
HI NICE TO MEET YOU MY NAME IS RIPLEY--
--DANA IS A DRAGON!
AND SHE'S HEADED THIS WAY!

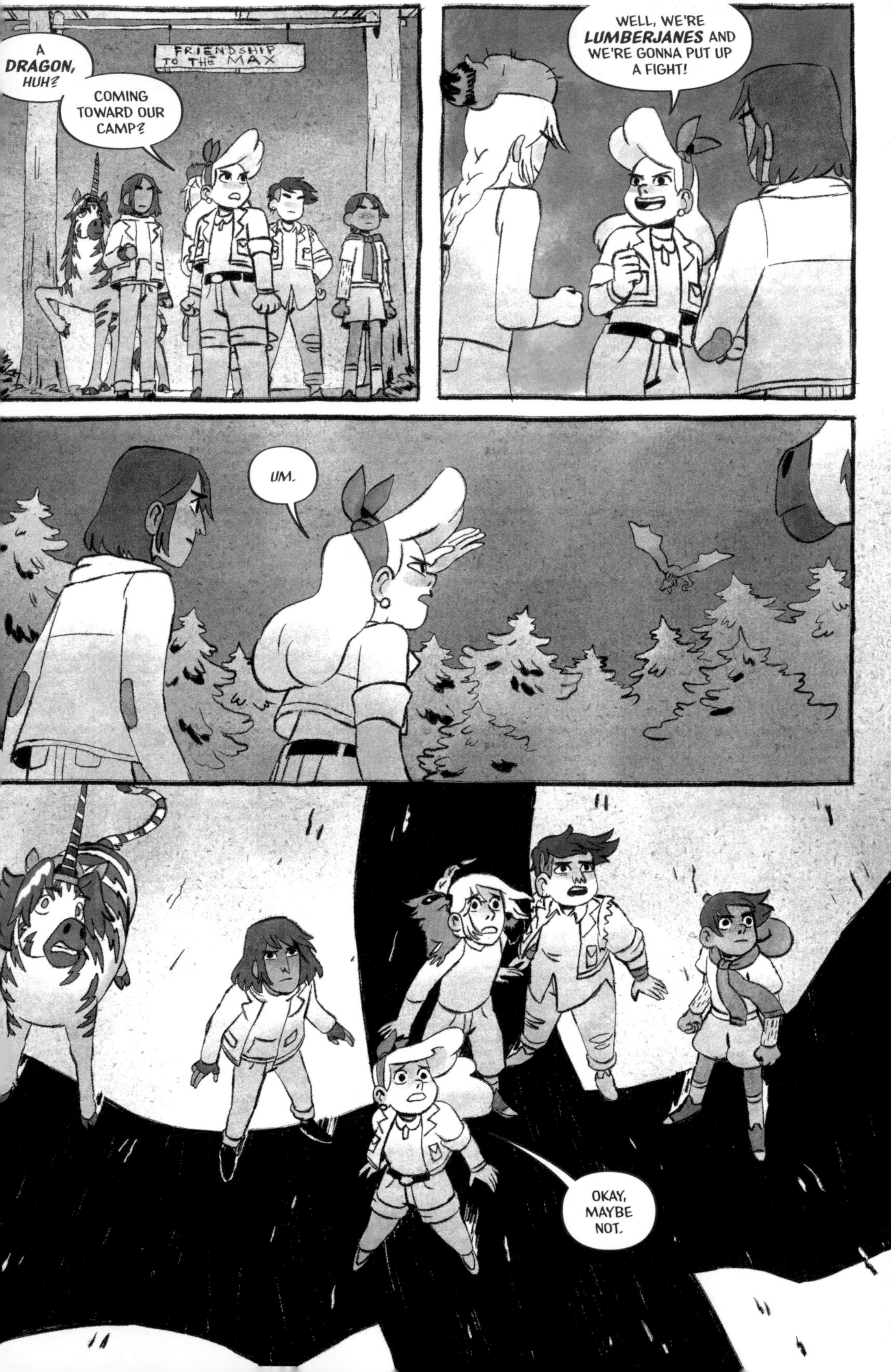
FRIENDSHIP TO THE MAX
A DRAGON, HUH?
COMING TOWARD OUR CAMP?
WELL, WE'RE LUMBERJANES AND WE'RE GONNA PUT UP A FIGHT!
UM.
OKAY, MAYBE NOT.

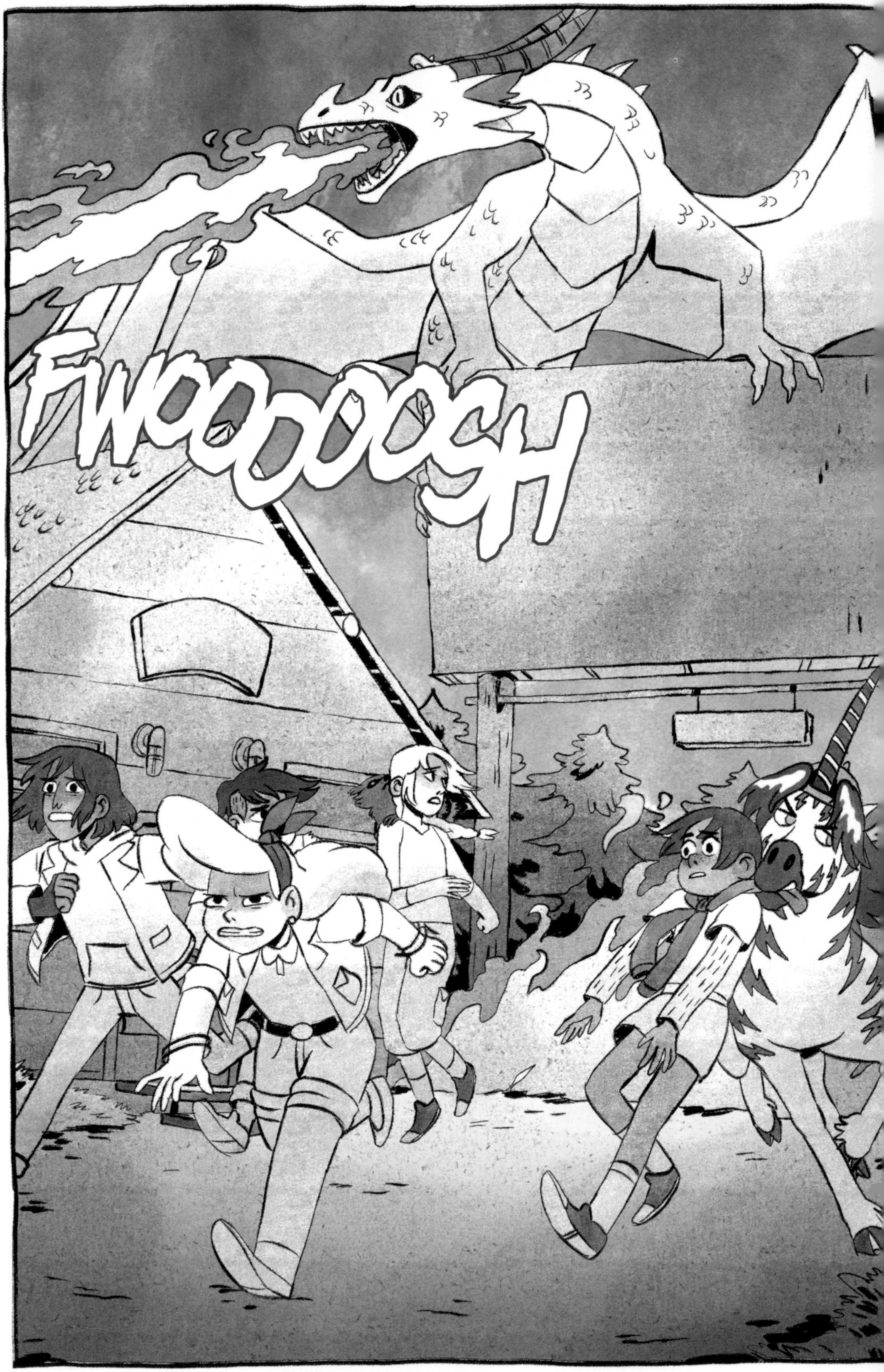
FWOOOOOSH

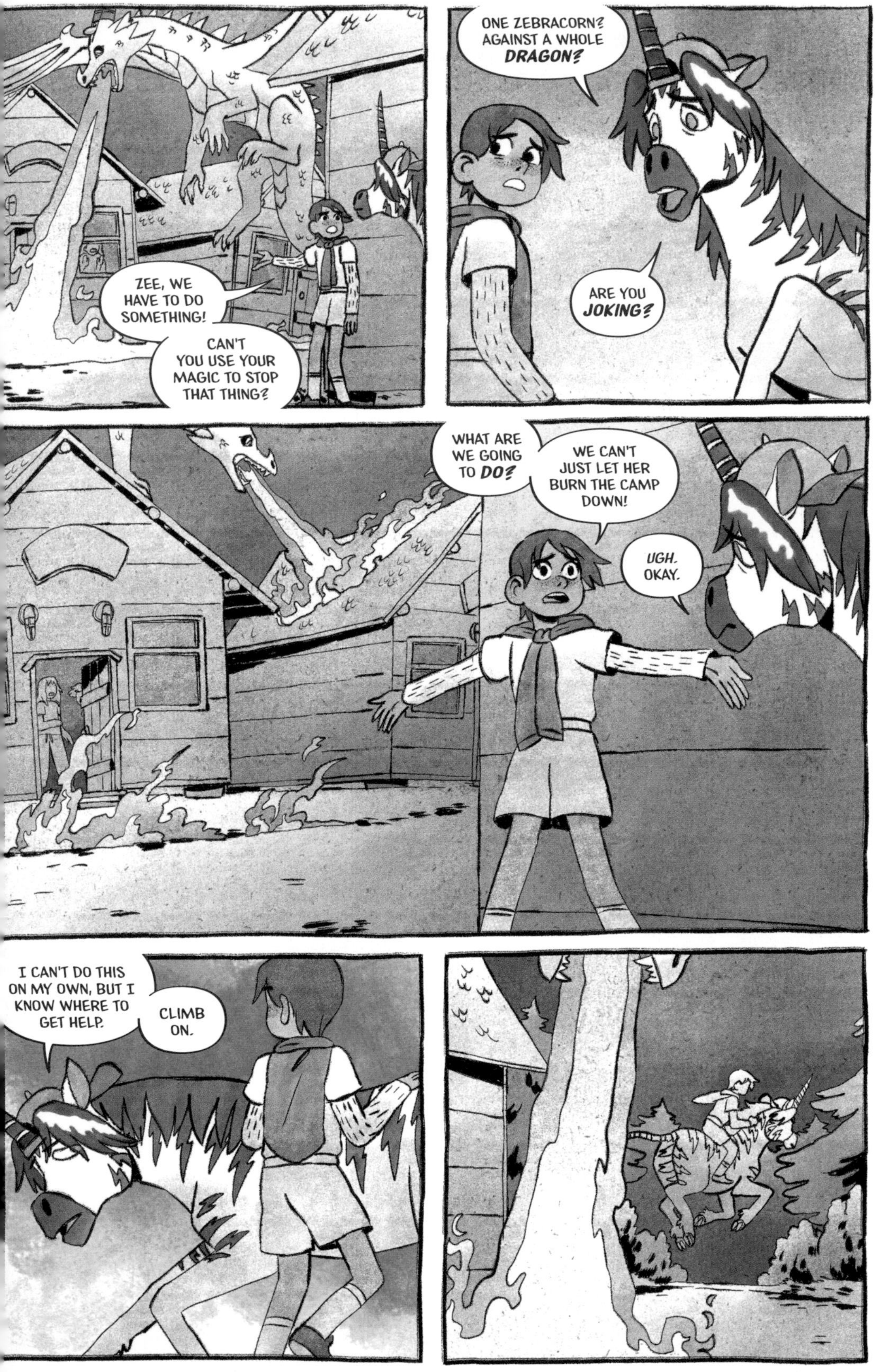
ZEE, WE HAVE TO DO SOMETHING!
CAN'T YOU USE YOUR MAGIC TO STOP THAT THING?
ONE ZEBRACORN? AGAINST A WHOLE DRAGON?
ARE YOU JOKING?
WHAT ARE WE GOING TO DO?
WE CAN'T JUST LET HER BURN THE CAMP DOWN!
UGH. OKAY.
I CAN'T DO THIS ON MY OWN, BUT I KNOW WHERE TO GET HELP.
CLIMB ON.

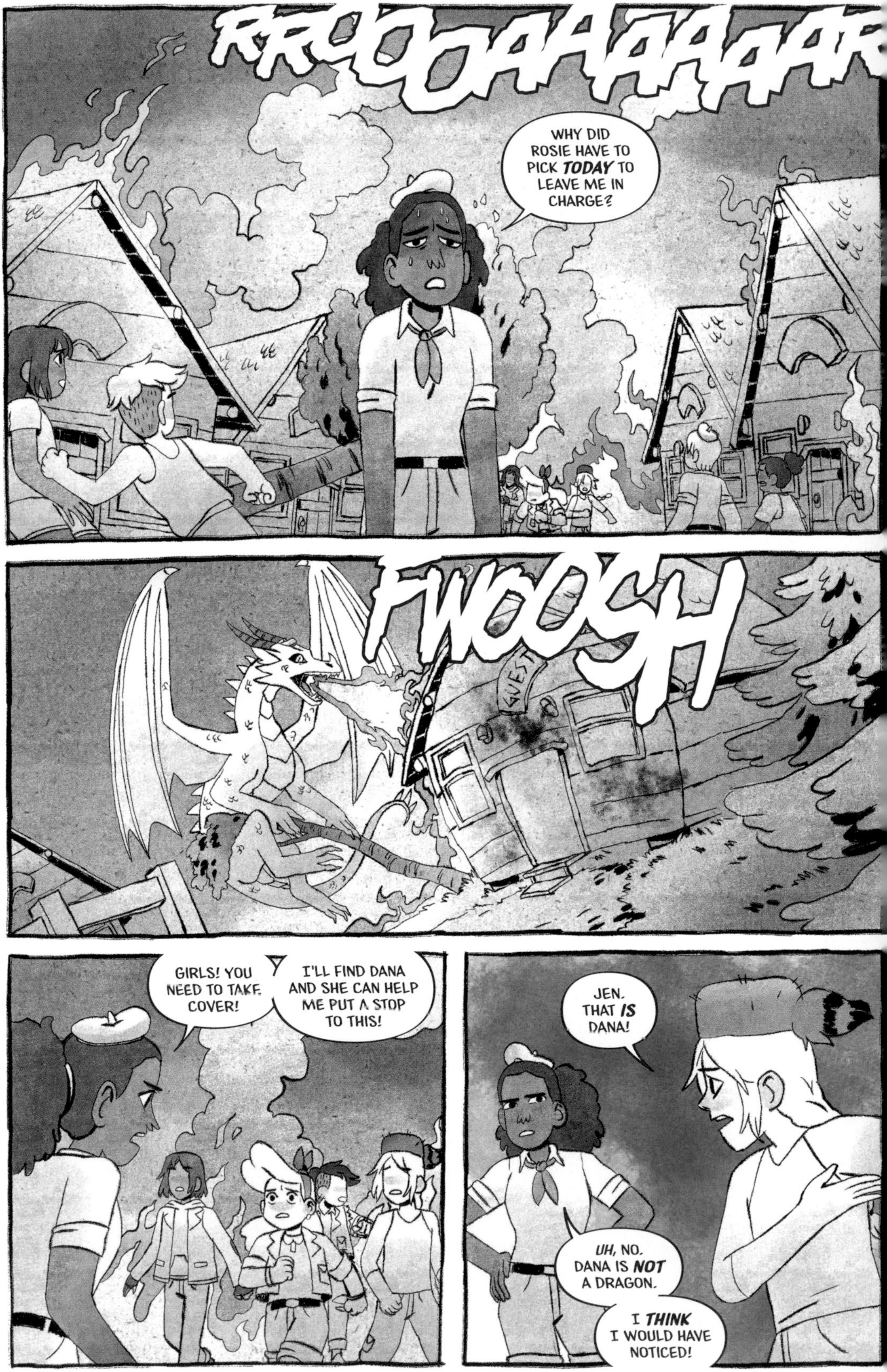
RRROOOAAAAAAAR
WHY DID ROSIE HAVE TO PICK TODAY TO LEAVE ME IN CHARGE?
FWOOSH
GUEST
GIRLS! YOU NEED TO TAKE COVER!
I'LL FIND DANA AND SHE CAN HELP ME PUT A STOP TO THIS!
JEN. THAT IS DANA!
UH, NO. DANA IS NOT A DRAGON.
I THINK I WOULD HAVE NOTICED!

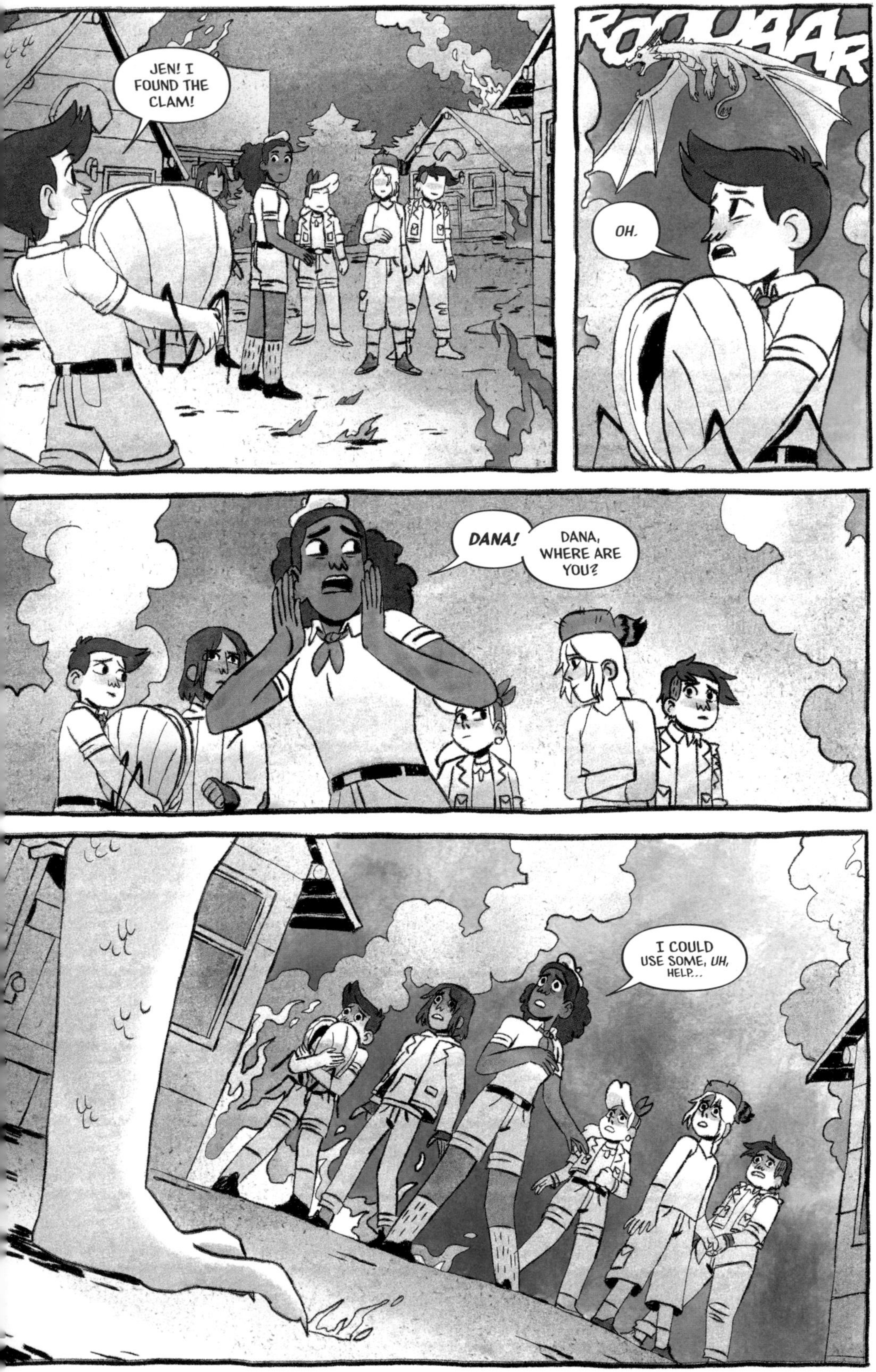
JEN! I FOUND THE CLAM!
ROOUAAR
OH.
DANA!
DANA, WHERE ARE YOU?
I COULD USE SOME, UH, HELP...

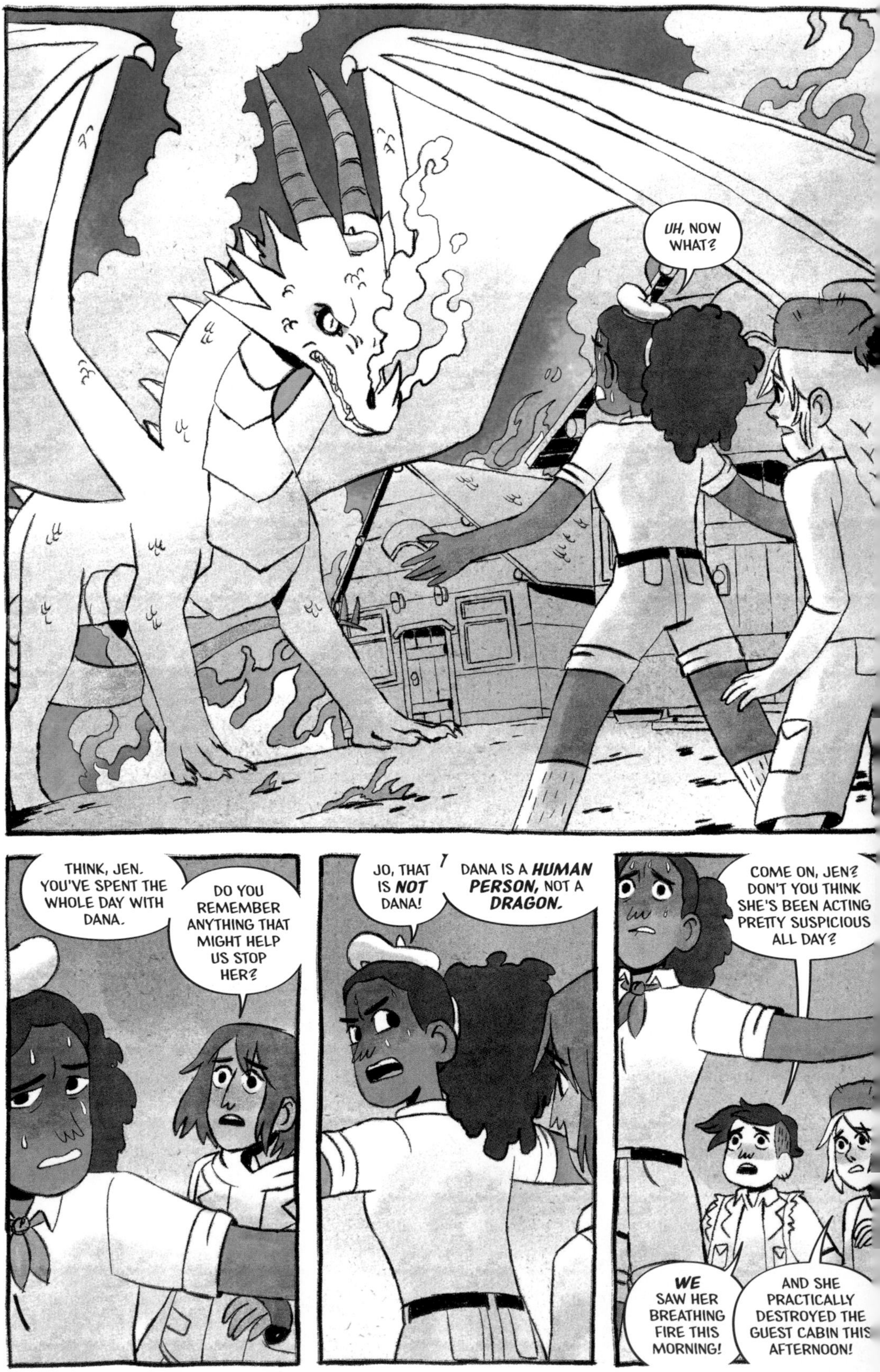
UH, NOW WHAT?
THINK, JEN. YOU'VE SPENT THE WHOLE DAY WITH DANA.
DO YOU REMEMBER ANYTHING THAT MIGHT HELP US STOP HER?
JO, THAT IS NOT DANA!
DANA IS A HUMAN PERSON, NOT A DRAGON.
COME ON, JEN? DON'T YOU THINK SHE'S BEEN ACTING PRETTY SUSPICIOUS ALL DAY?
WE SAW HER BREATHING FIRE THIS MORNING!
AND SHE PRACTICALLY DESTROYED THE GUEST CABIN THIS AFTERNOON!

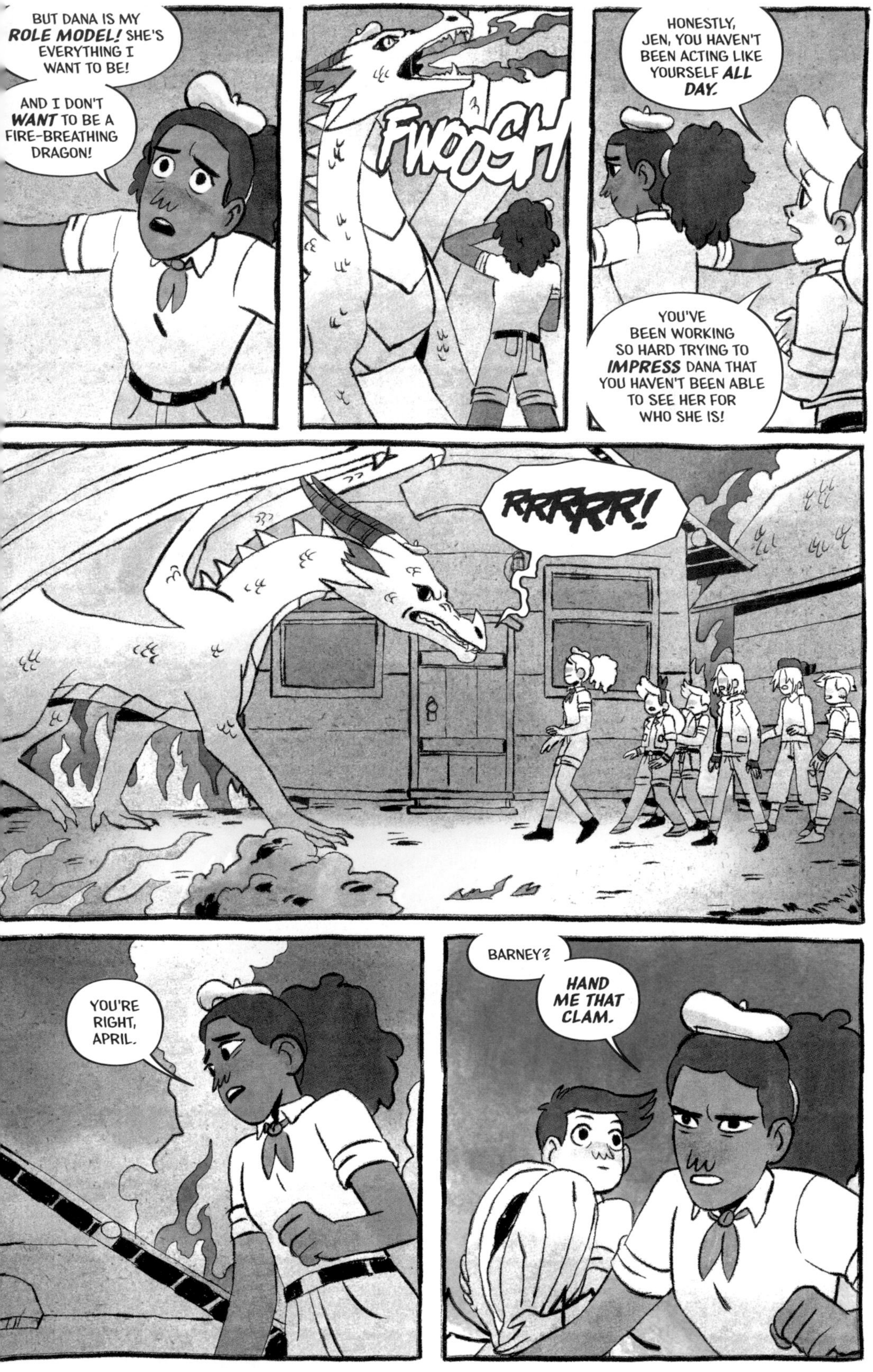

BUT DANA IS MY ROLE MODEL! SHE'S EVERYTHING I WANT TO BE!
AND I DON'T WANT TO BE A FIRE-BREATHING DRAGON!
FWOOSH
HONESTLY, JEN, YOU HAVEN'T BEEN ACTING LIKE YOURSELF ALL DAY.
YOU'VE BEEN WORKING SO HARD TRYING TO IMPRESS DANA THAT YOU HAVEN'T BEEN ABLE TO SEE HER FOR WHO SHE IS!
RRRRR!
YOU'RE RIGHT, APRIL.
BARNEY?
HAND ME THAT CLAM.

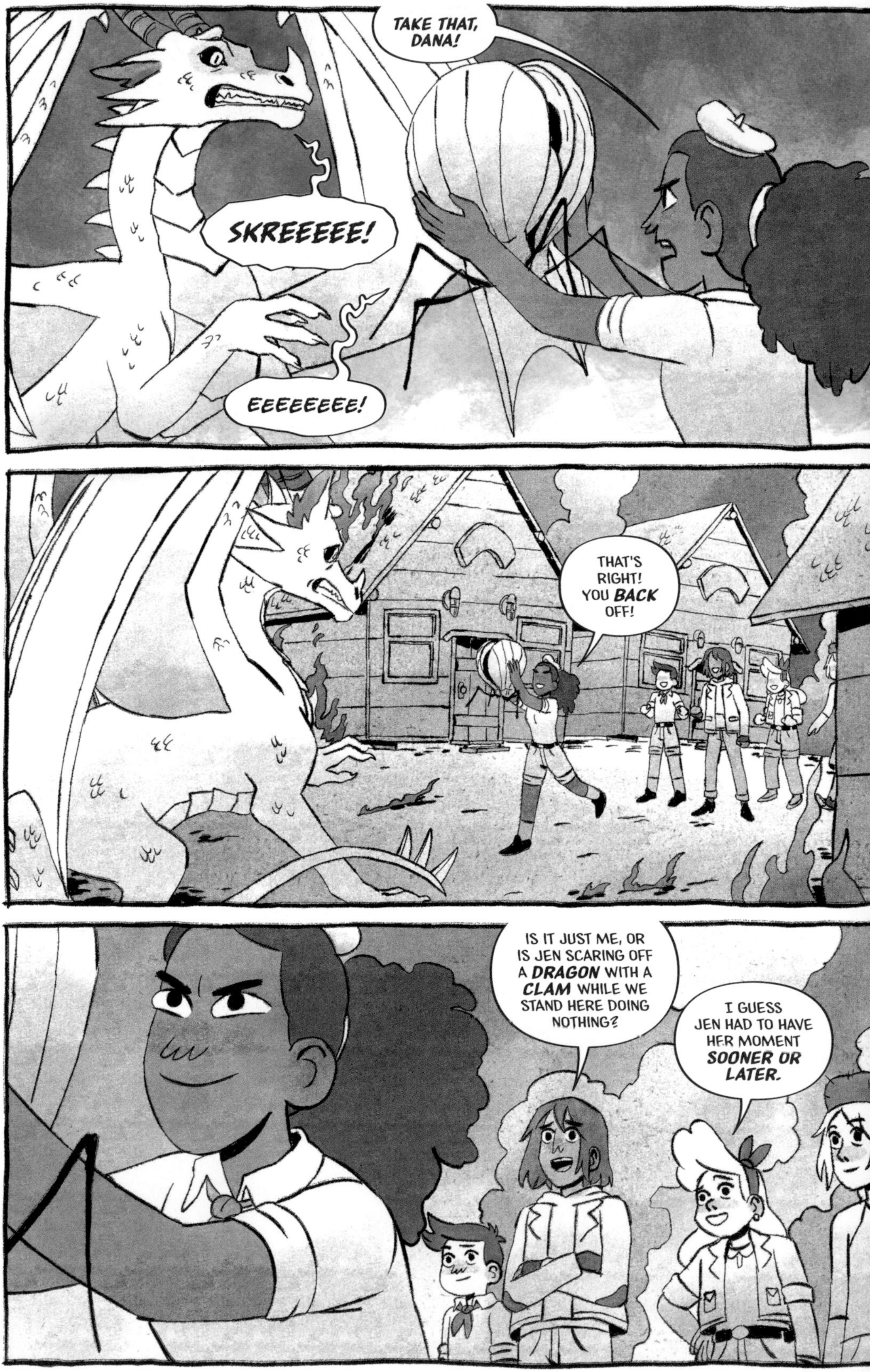
TAKE THAT, DANA!
SKREEEEE!
EEEEEEEE!
THAT'S RIGHT! YOU BACK OFF!
IS IT JUST ME, OR IS JEN SCARING OFF A DRAGON WITH A CLAM WHILE WE STAND HERE DOING NOTHING?
I GUESS JEN HAD TO HAVE HER MOMENT SOONER OR LATER.

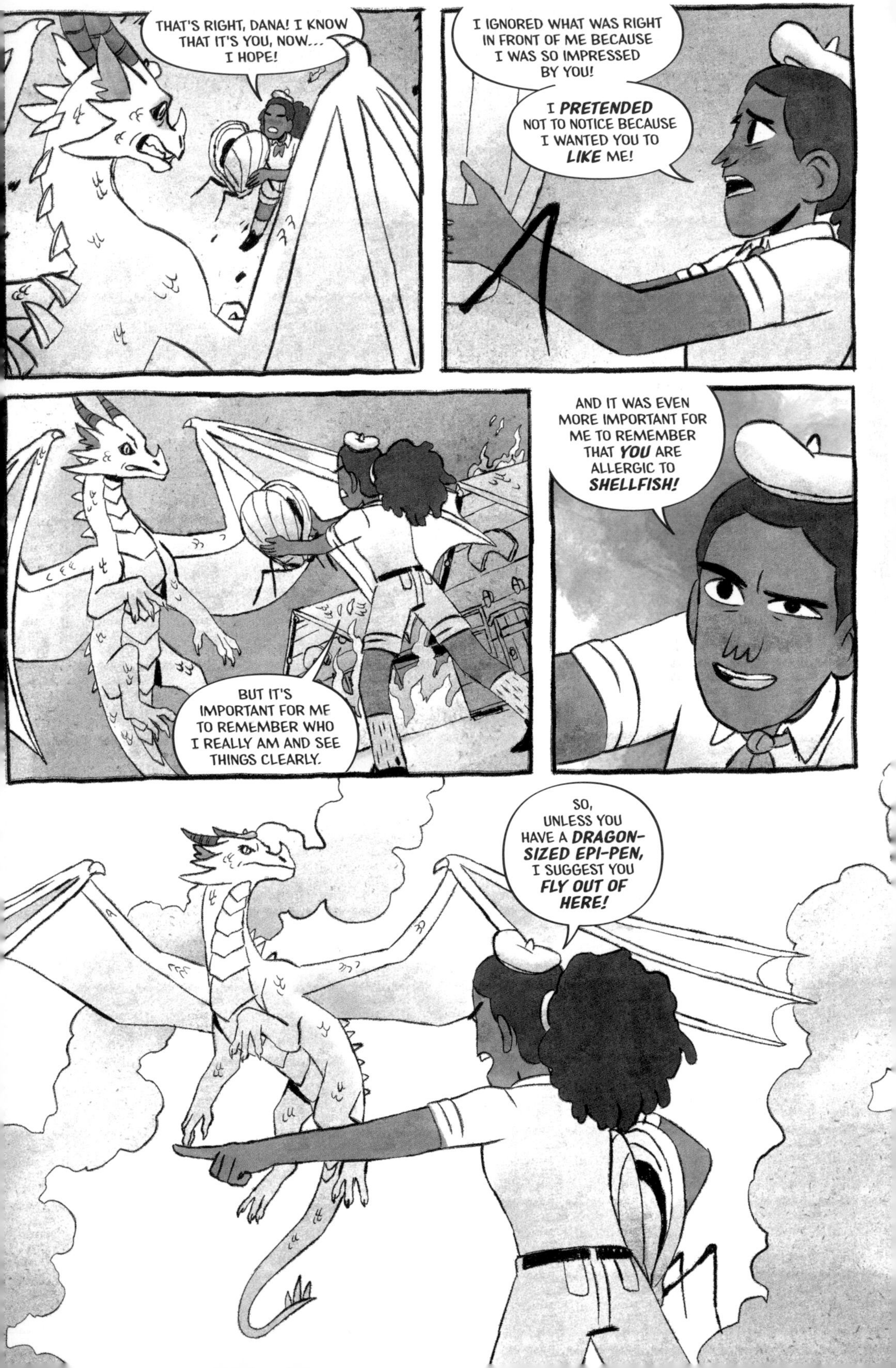
THAT'S RIGHT, DANA! I KNOW THAT IT'S YOU, NOW... I HOPE!
I IGNORED WHAT WAS RIGHT IN FRONT OF ME BECAUSE I WAS SO IMPRESSED BY YOU!
I PRETENDED NOT TO NOTICE BECAUSE I WANTED YOU TO LIKE ME!
BUT IT'S IMPORTANT FOR ME TO REMEMBER WHO I REALLY AM AND SEE THINGS CLEARLY.
AND IT WAS EVEN MORE IMPORTANT FOR ME TO REMEMBER THAT YOU ARE ALLERGIC TO SHELLFISH!
SO, UNLESS YOU HAVE A DRAGON-SIZED EPI-PEN, I SUGGEST YOU FLY OUT OF HERE!

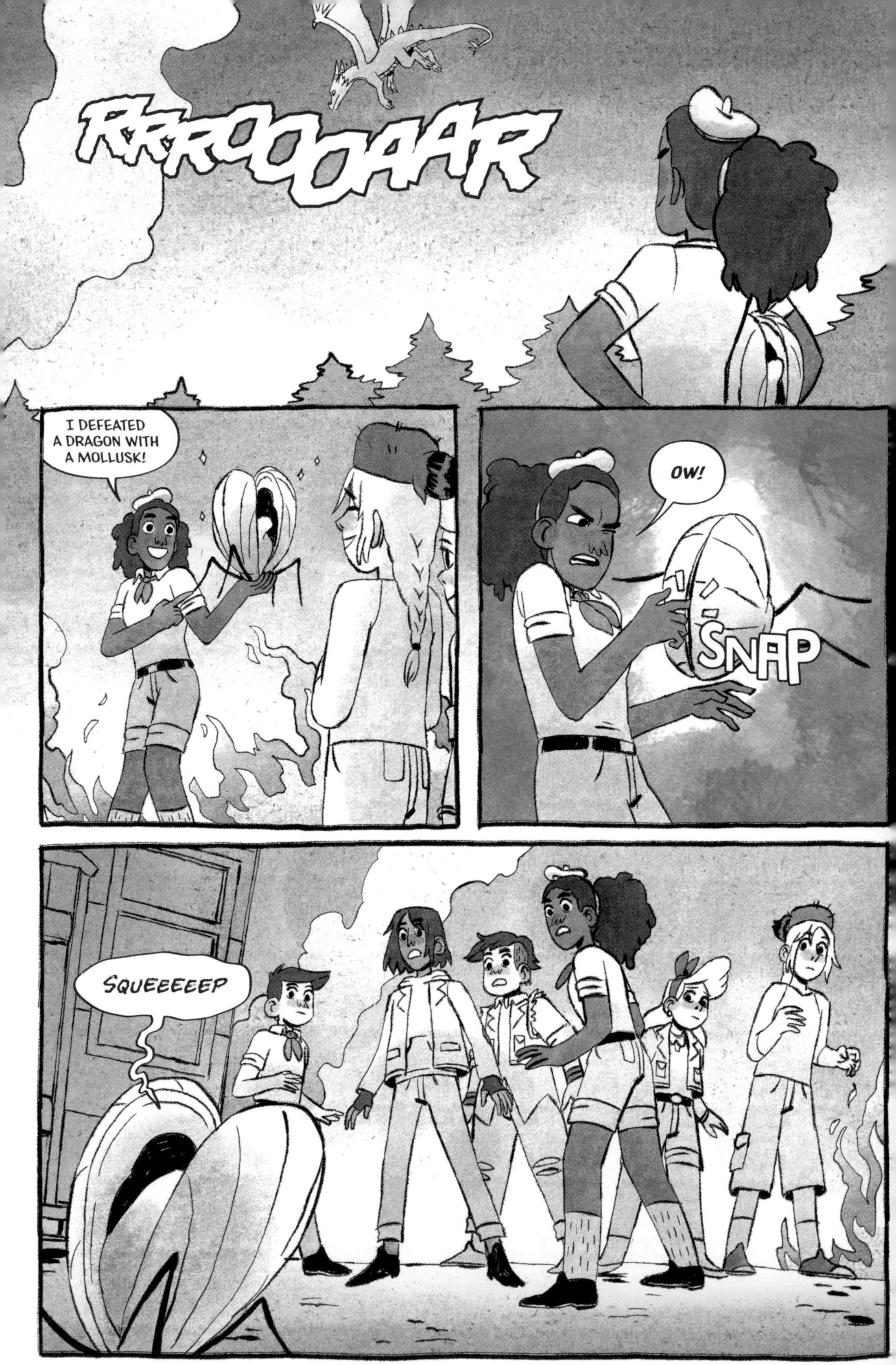
RRRROOOOAAAR
I DEFEATED A DRAGON WITH A MOLLUSK!
OW!
SNAP
SQUEEEEEP

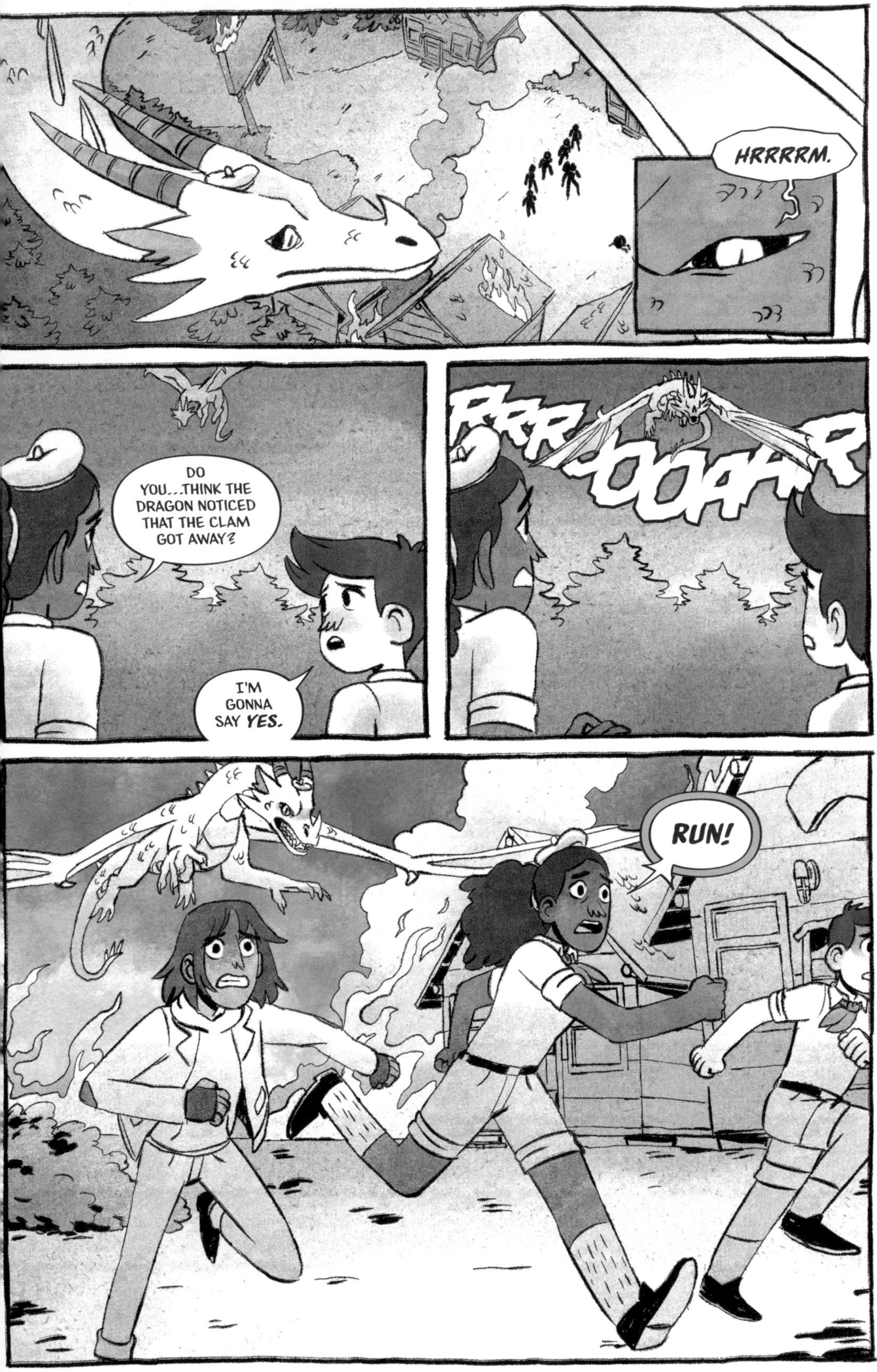
HRRRRM.
DO YOU...THINK THE DRAGON NOTICED THAT THE CLAM GOT AWAY?
I'M GONNA SAY YES.
RUN!

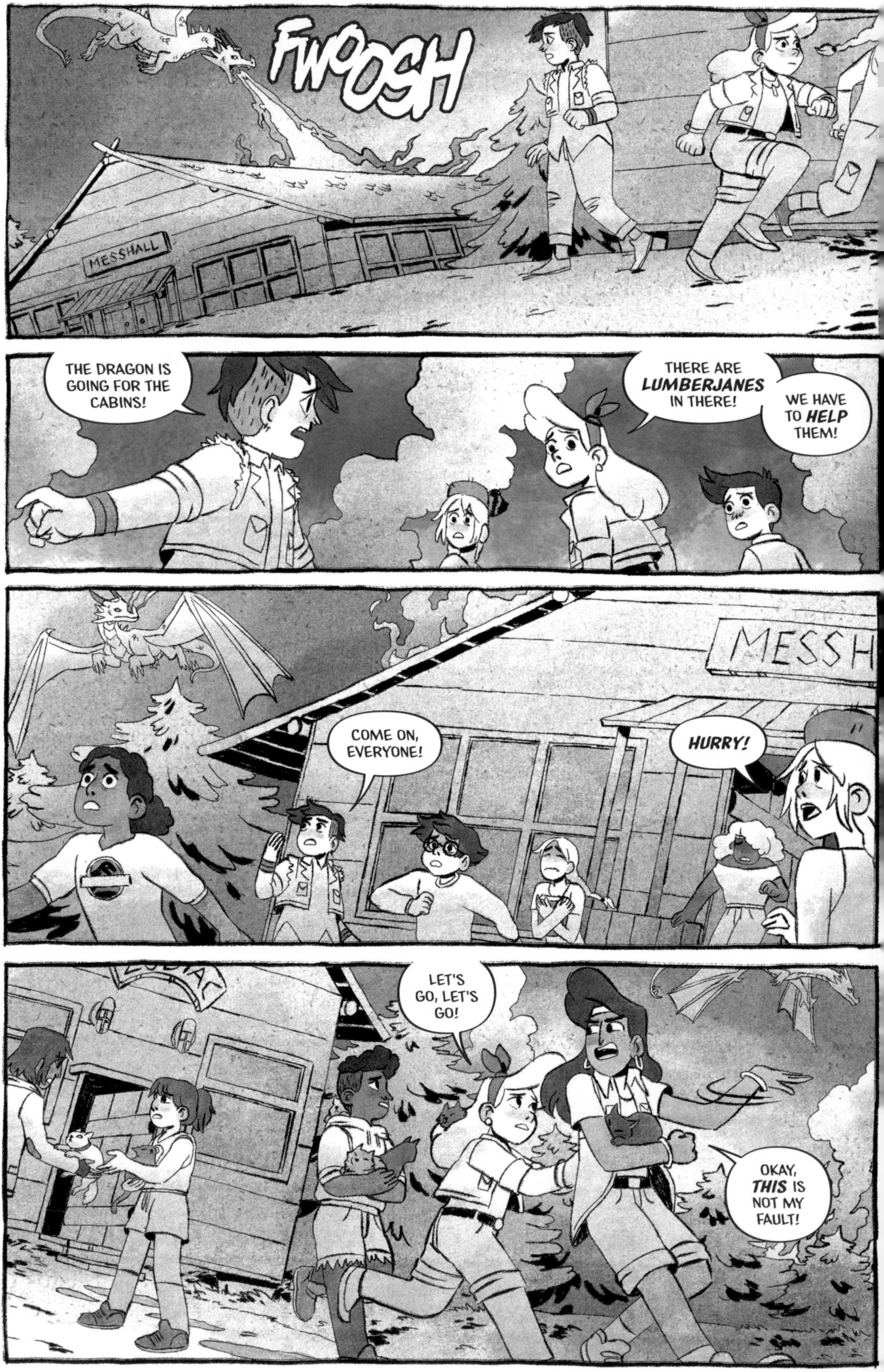
FWOOSH
MESSHALL
THE DRAGON IS GOING FOR THE CABINS!
THERE ARE LUMBERJANES IN THERE!
WE HAVE TO HELP THEM!
MESSH
COME ON, EVERYONE!
HURRY!
LET'S GO, LET'S GO!
OKAY, THIS IS NOT MY FAULT!

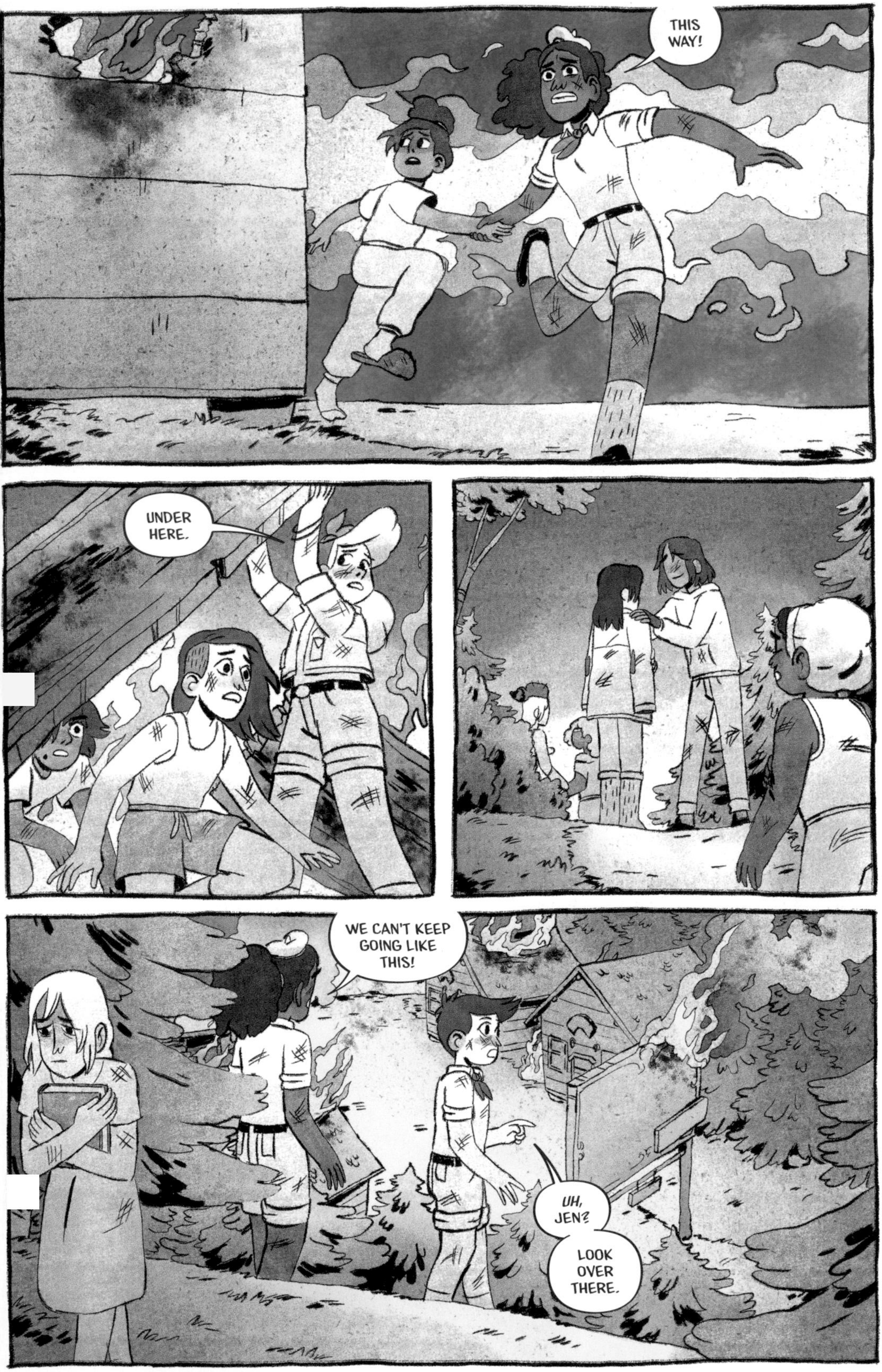
THIS WAY!
UNDER HERE.
WE CAN'T KEEP GOING LIKE THIS!
UH, JEN?
LOOK OVER THERE.

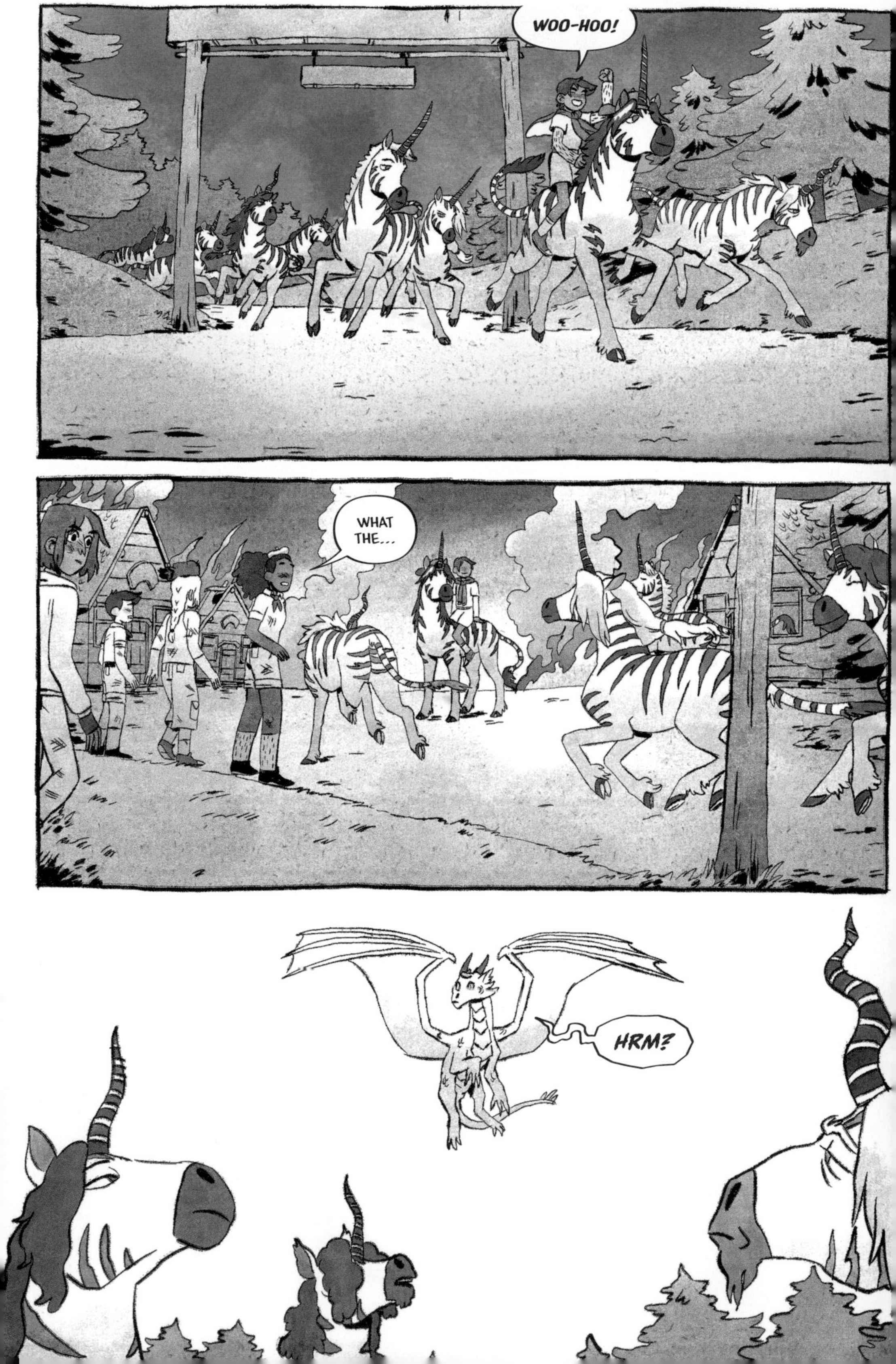
WOO-HOO!
WHAT THE...
HRM?

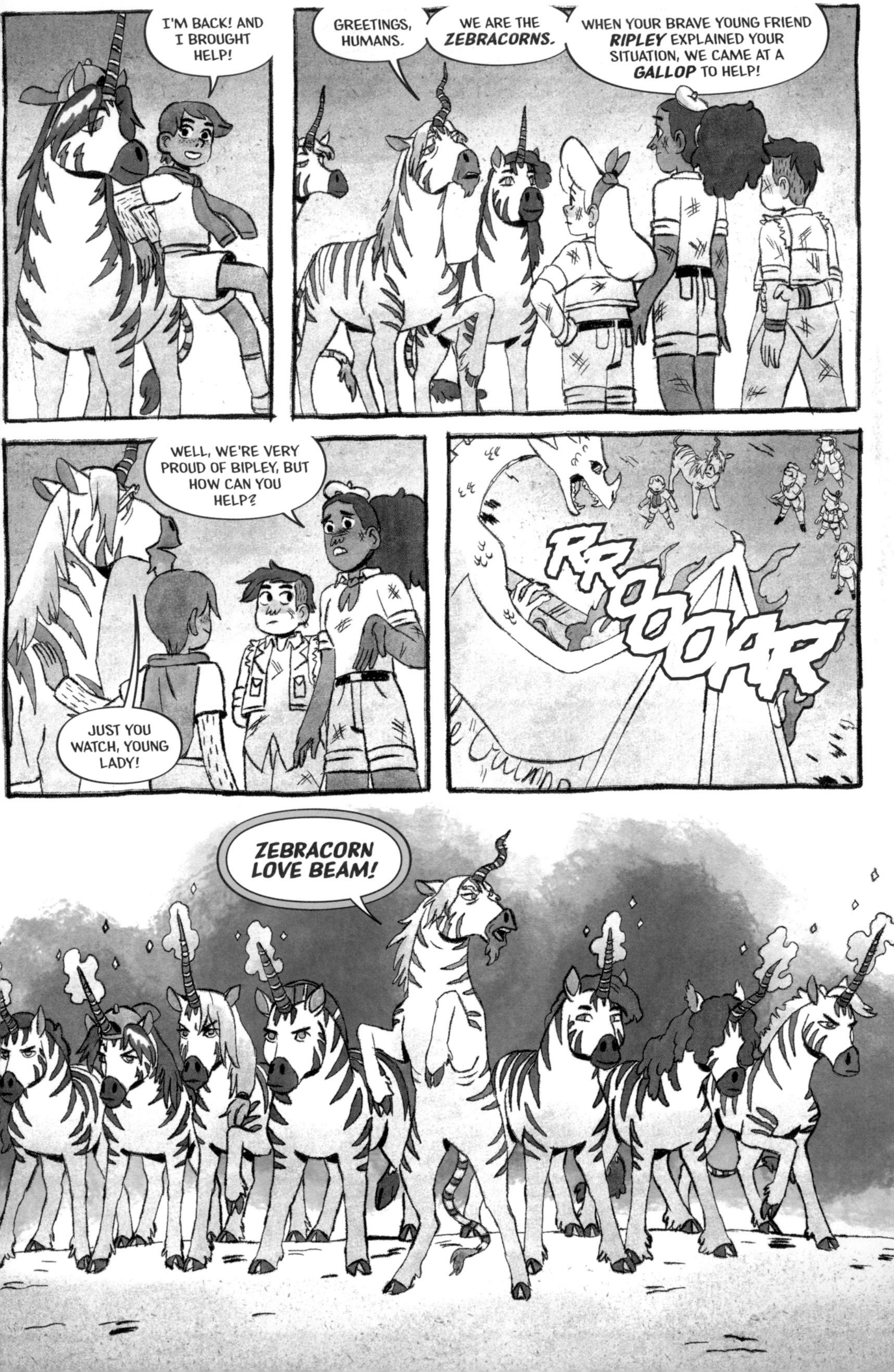
I'M BACK! AND I BROUGHT HELP!
GREETINGS, HUMANS.
WE ARE THE ZEBRACORNS.
WHEN YOUR BRAVE YOUNG FRIEND RIPLEY EXPLAINED YOUR SITUATION, WE CAME AT A GALLOP TO HELP!
WELL, WE'RE VERY PROUD OF BIPLEY, BUT HOW CAN YOU HELP?
JUST YOU WATCH, YOUNG LADY!
RROOOAR
ZEBRACORN LOVE BEAM!

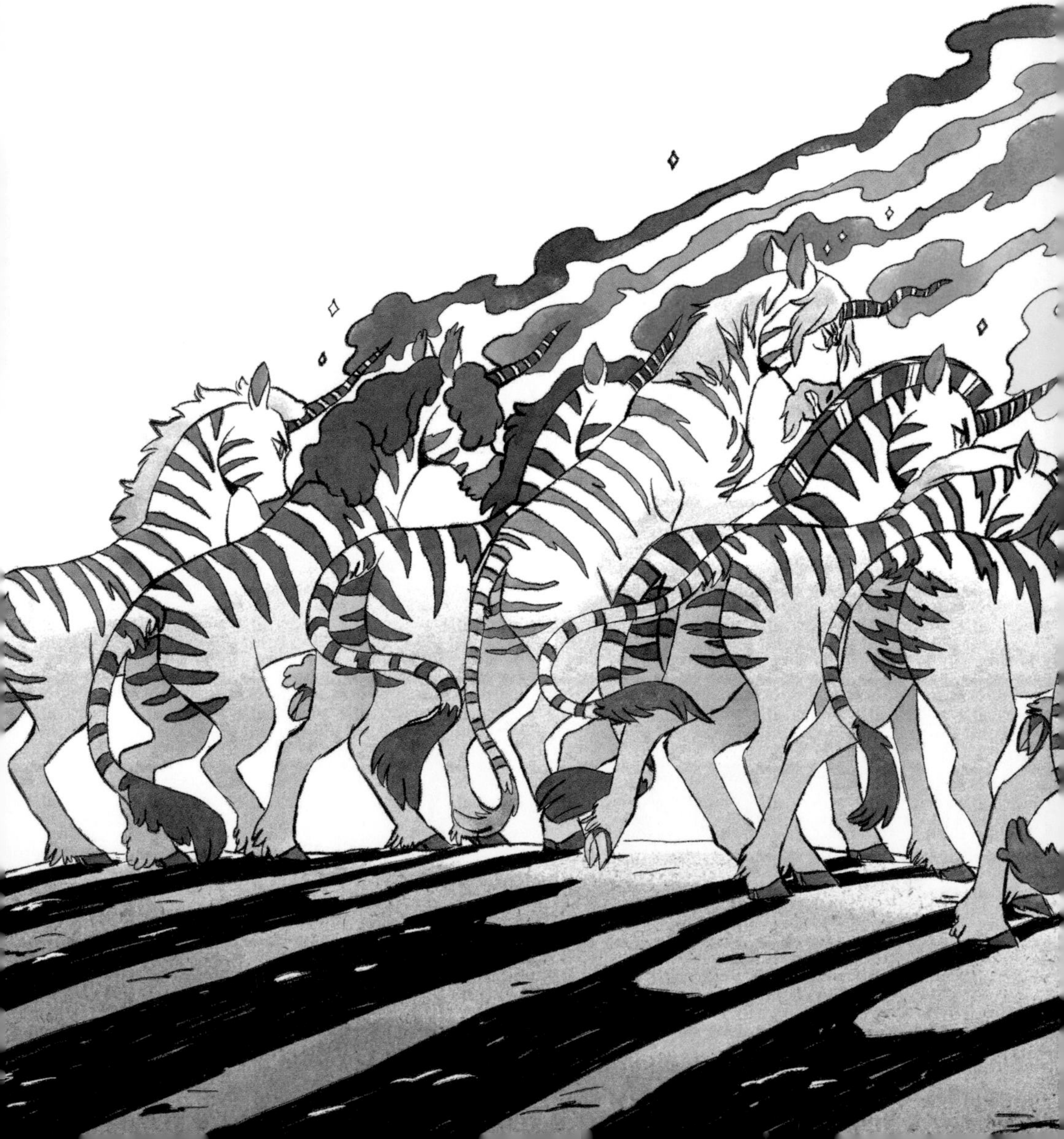

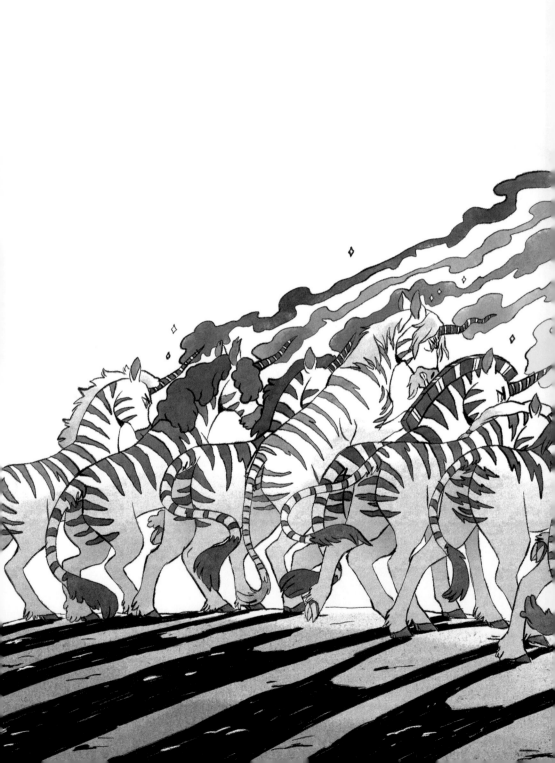

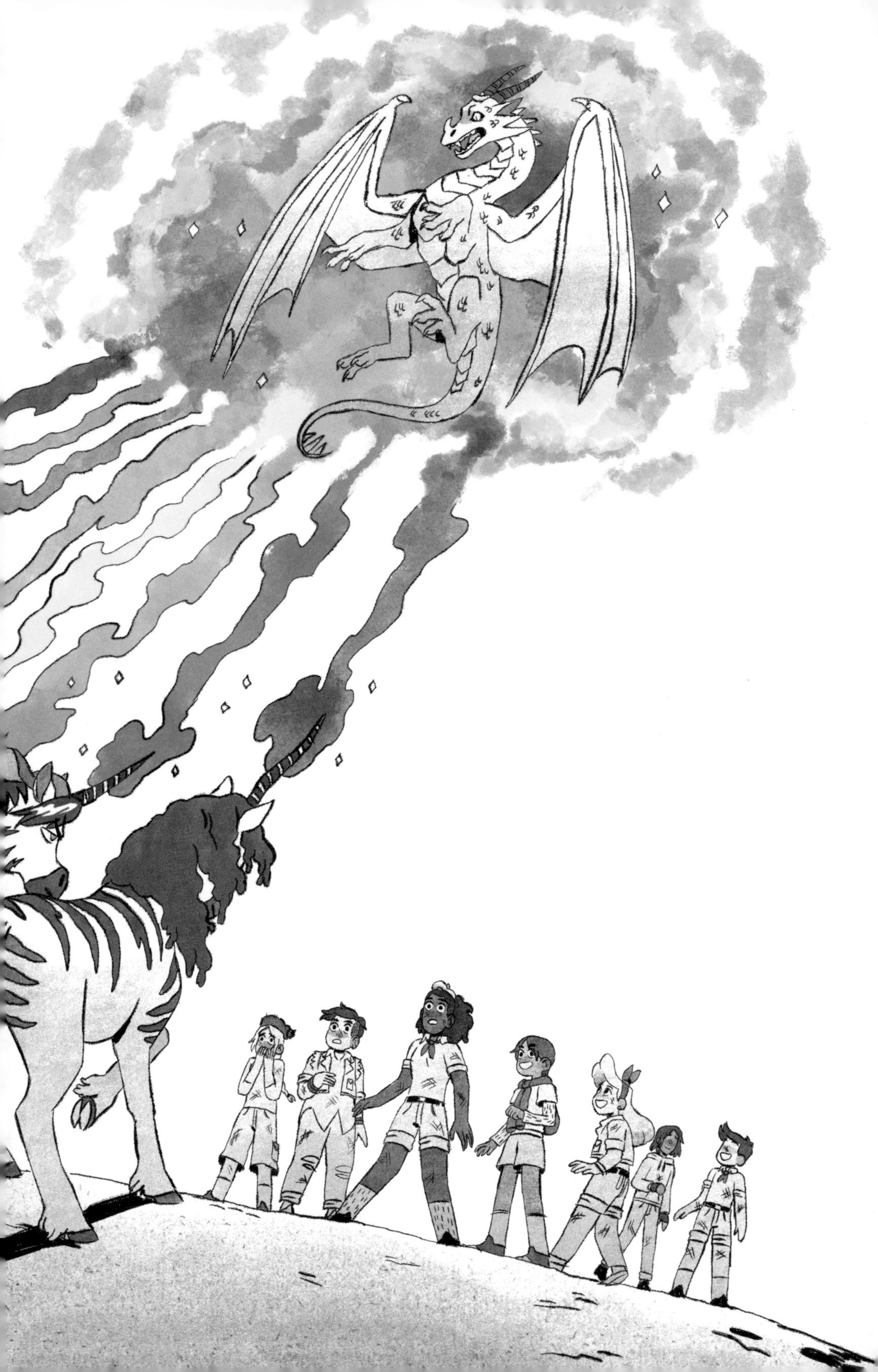

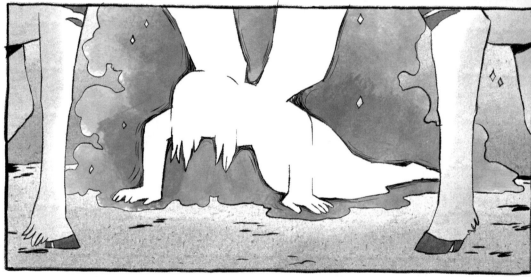

I'VE GOT YOU, DANA!

JEN?

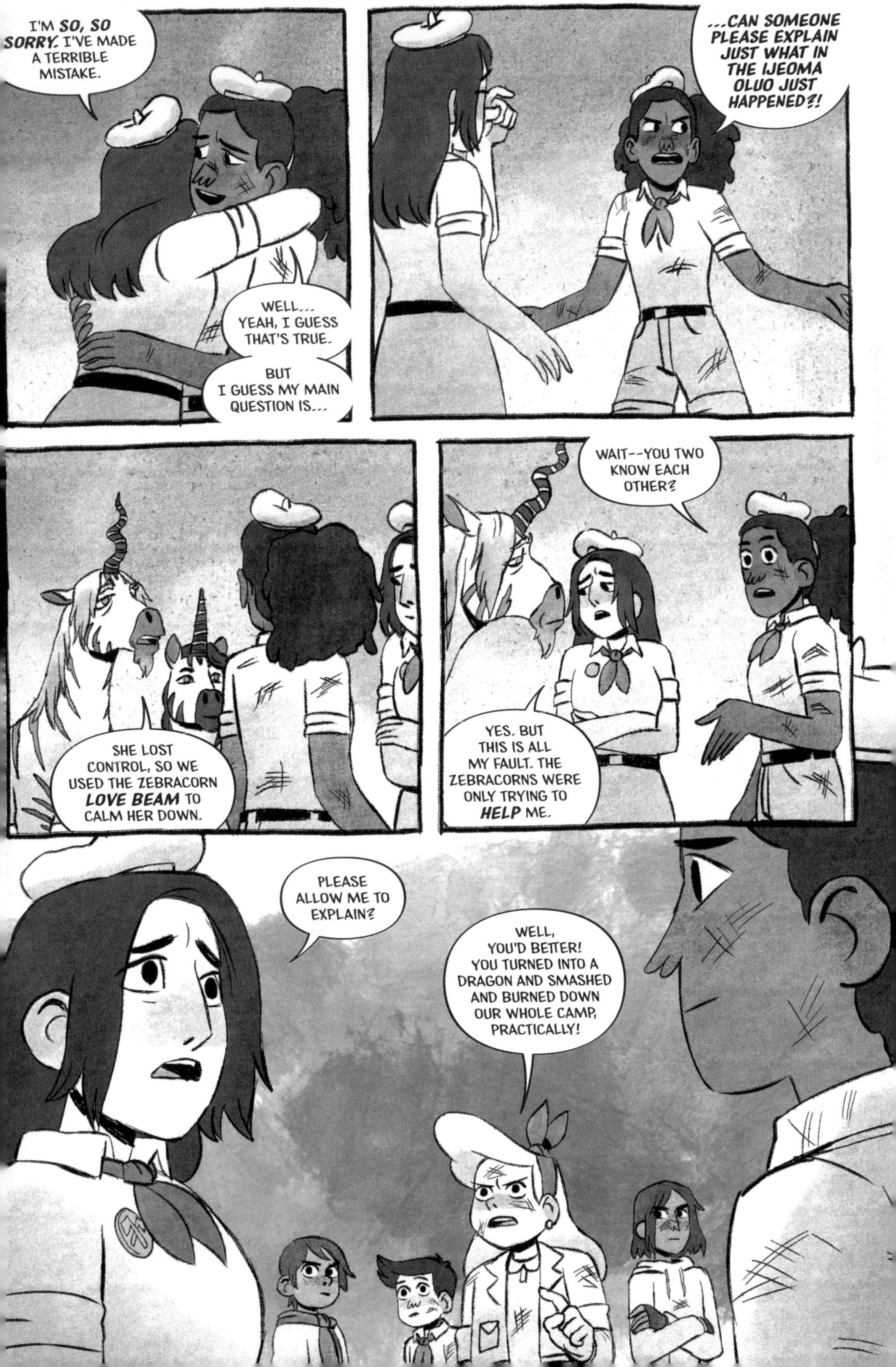
I'M SO, SO SORRY. I'VE MADE A TERRIBLE MISTAKE.
WELL... YEAH, I GUESS THAT'S TRUE.
BUT I GUESS MY MAIN QUESTION IS...
...CAN SOMEONE PLEASE EXPLAIN JUST WHAT IN THE IJEOMA OLUO JUST HAPPENED?!
SHE LOST CONTROL, SO WE USED THE ZEBRACORN LOVE BEAM TO CALM HER DOWN.
WAIT--YOU TWO KNOW EACH OTHER?
YES. BUT THIS IS ALL MY FAULT. THE ZEBRACORNS WERE ONLY TRYING TO HELP ME.
PLEASE ALLOW ME TO EXPLAIN?
WELL, YOU'D BETTER! YOU TURNED INTO A DRAGON AND SMASHED AND BURNED DOWN OUR WHOLE CAMP, PRACTICALLY!

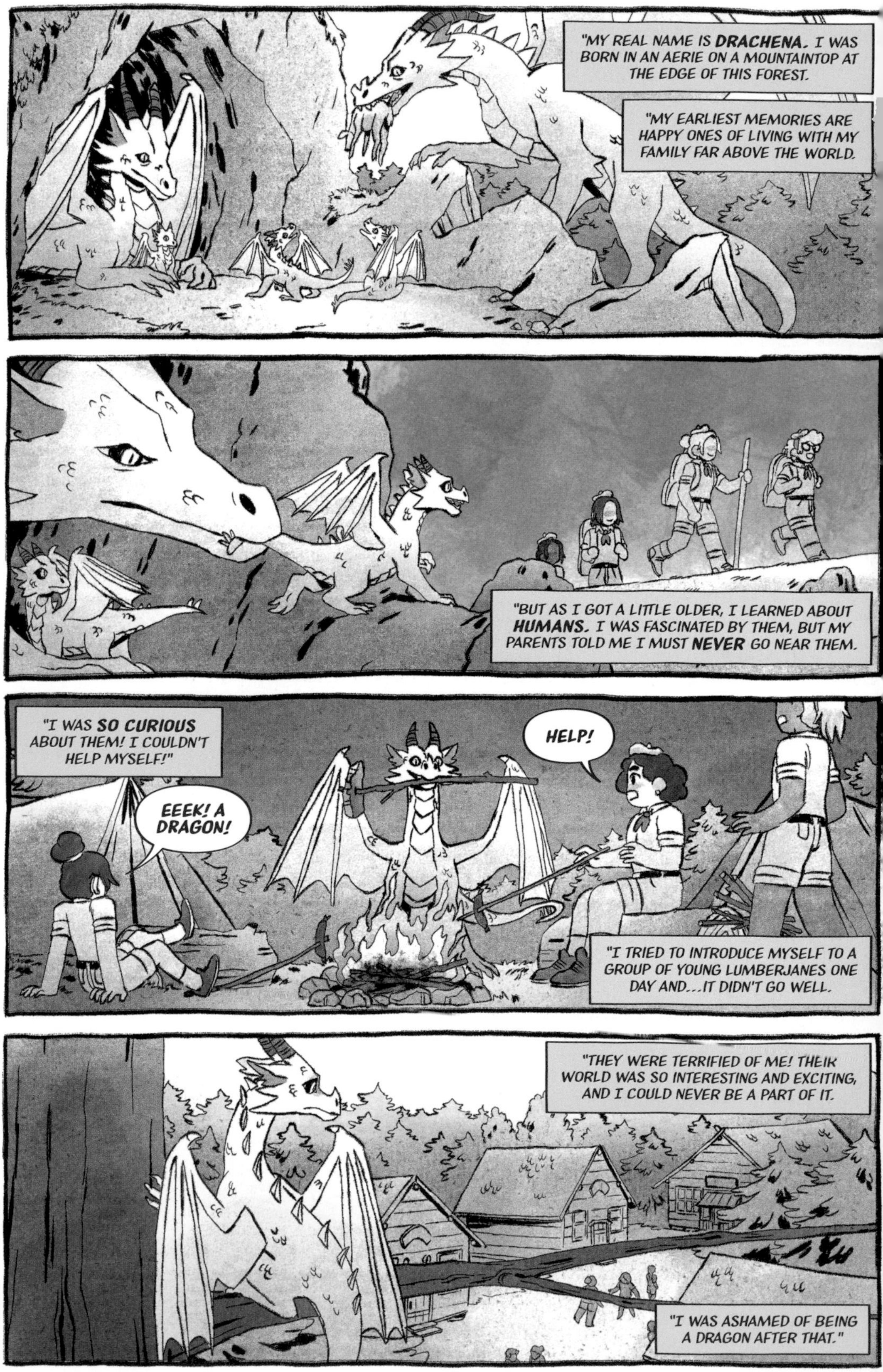

"MY REAL NAME IS **DRACHENA.** I WAS BORN IN AN AERIE ON A MOUNTAINTOP AT THE EDGE OF THIS FOREST.
"MY EARLIEST MEMORIES ARE HAPPY ONES OF LIVING WITH MY FAMILY FAR ABOVE THE WORLD.
"BUT AS I GOT A LITTLE OLDER, I LEARNED ABOUT **HUMANS.** I WAS FASCINATED BY THEM, BUT MY PARENTS TOLD ME I MUST **NEVER** GO NEAR THEM.
"I WAS **SO CURIOUS** ABOUT THEM! I COULDN'T HELP MYSELF!"
EEEK! A DRAGON!
HELP!
"I TRIED TO INTRODUCE MYSELF TO A GROUP OF YOUNG LUMBERJANES ONE DAY AND...IT DIDN'T GO WELL.
"THEY WERE TERRIFIED OF ME! THEIR WORLD WAS SO INTERESTING AND EXCITING, AND I COULD NEVER BE A PART OF IT.
"I WAS ASHAMED OF BEING A DRAGON AFTER THAT."

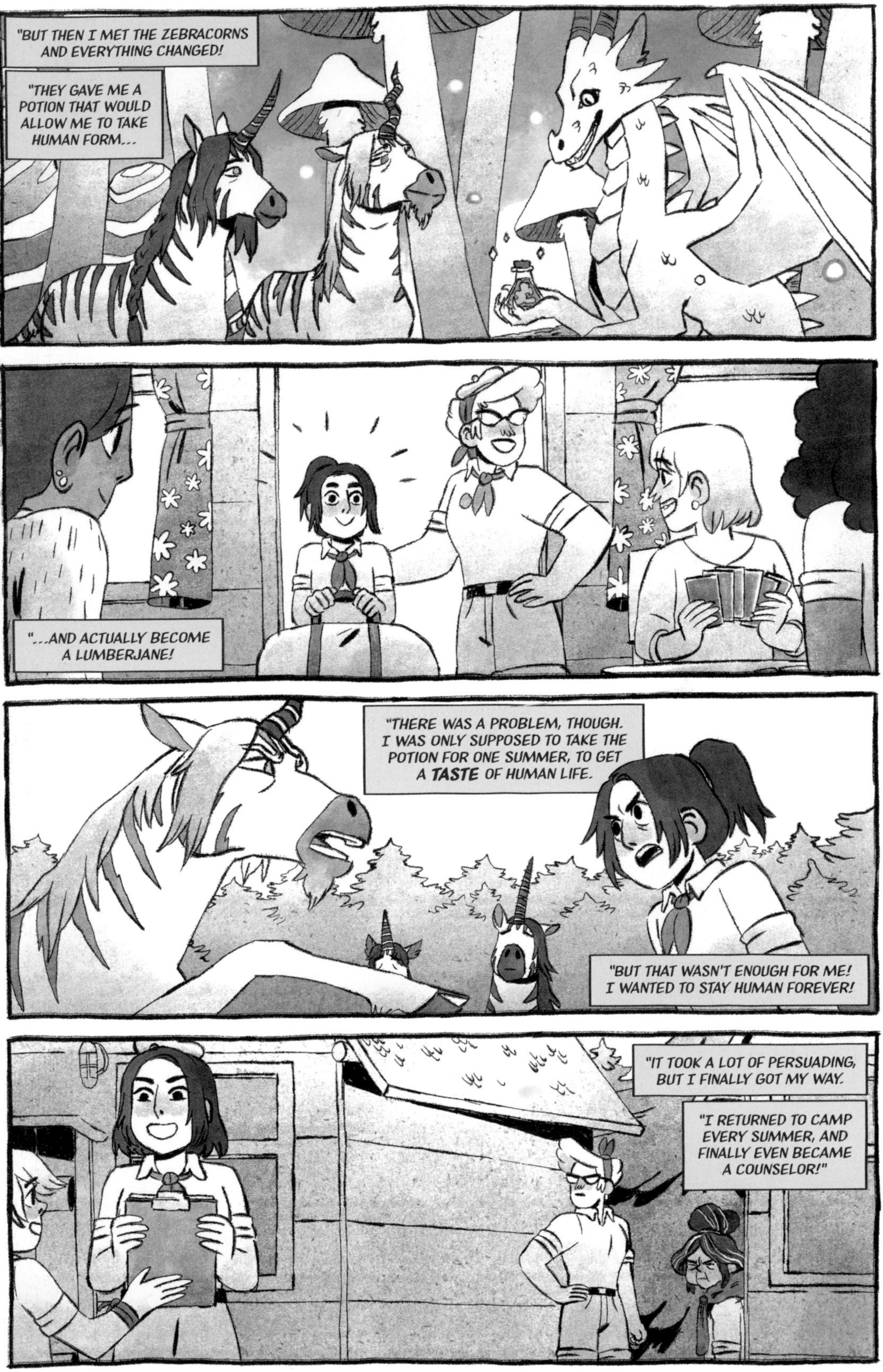
"BUT THEN I MET THE ZEBRACORNS AND EVERYTHING CHANGED!
"THEY GAVE ME A POTION THAT WOULD ALLOW ME TO TAKE HUMAN FORM...
"...AND ACTUALLY BECOME A LUMBERJANE!
"THERE WAS A PROBLEM, THOUGH. I WAS ONLY SUPPOSED TO TAKE THE POTION FOR ONE SUMMER, TO GET A TASTE OF HUMAN LIFE.
"BUT THAT WASN'T ENOUGH FOR ME! I WANTED TO STAY HUMAN FOREVER!
"IT TOOK A LOT OF PERSUADING, BUT I FINALLY GOT MY WAY.
"I RETURNED TO CAMP EVERY SUMMER, AND FINALLY EVEN BECAME A COUNSELOR!"

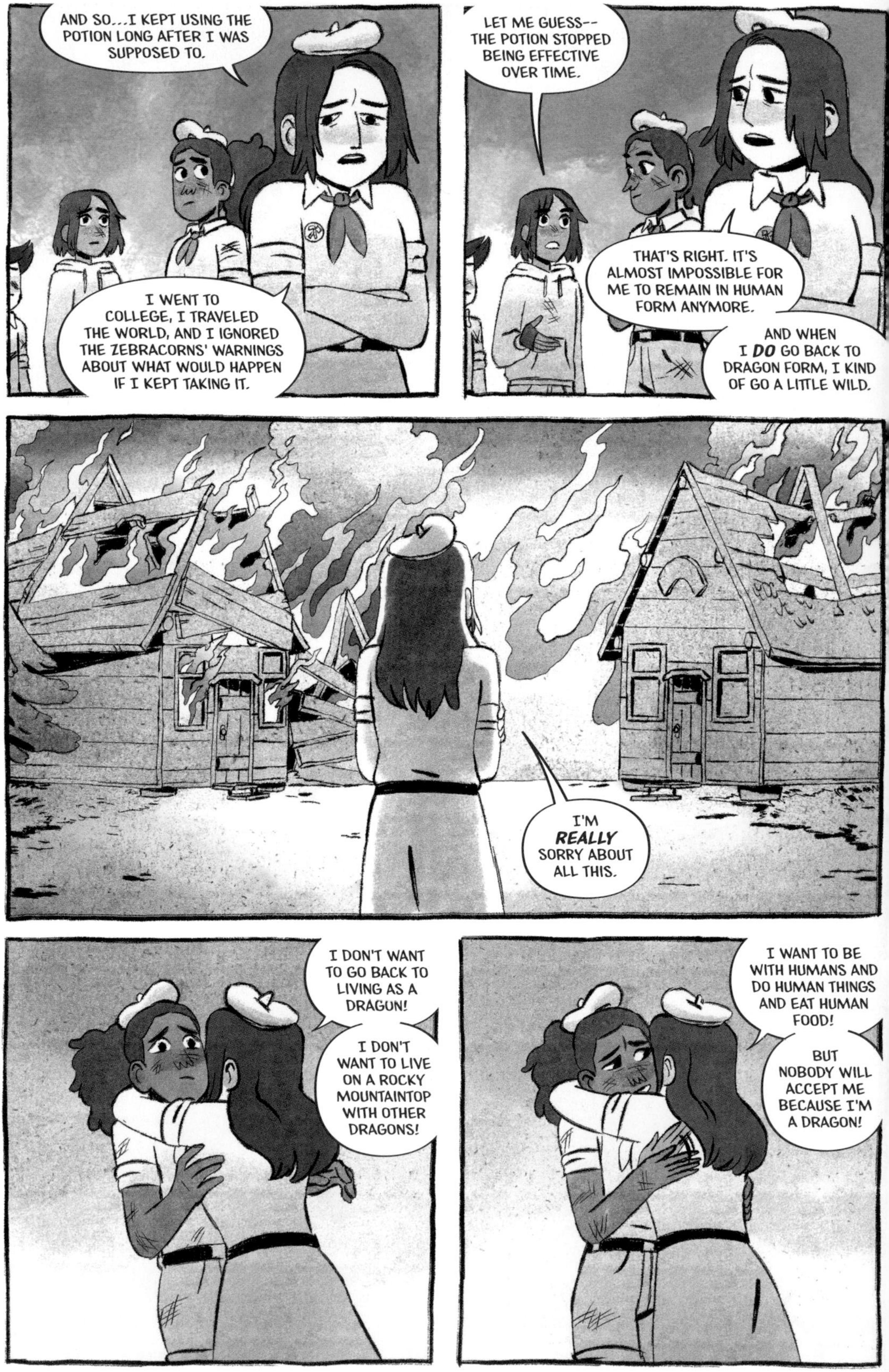
AND SO...I KEPT USING THE POTION LONG AFTER I WAS SUPPOSED TO.
I WENT TO COLLEGE, I TRAVELED THE WORLD, AND I IGNORED THE ZEBRACORNS' WARNINGS ABOUT WHAT WOULD HAPPEN IF I KEPT TAKING IT.
LET ME GUESS-- THE POTION STOPPED BEING EFFECTIVE OVER TIME.
THAT'S RIGHT. IT'S ALMOST IMPOSSIBLE FOR ME TO REMAIN IN HUMAN FORM ANYMORE.
AND WHEN I DO GO BACK TO DRAGON FORM, I KIND OF GO A LITTLE WILD.
I'M REALLY SORRY ABOUT ALL THIS.
I DON'T WANT TO GO BACK TO LIVING AS A DRAGON!
I DON'T WANT TO LIVE ON A ROCKY MOUNTAINTOP WITH OTHER DRAGONS!
I WANT TO BE WITH HUMANS AND DO HUMAN THINGS AND EAT HUMAN FOOD!
BUT NOBODY WILL ACCEPT ME BECAUSE I'M A DRAGON!

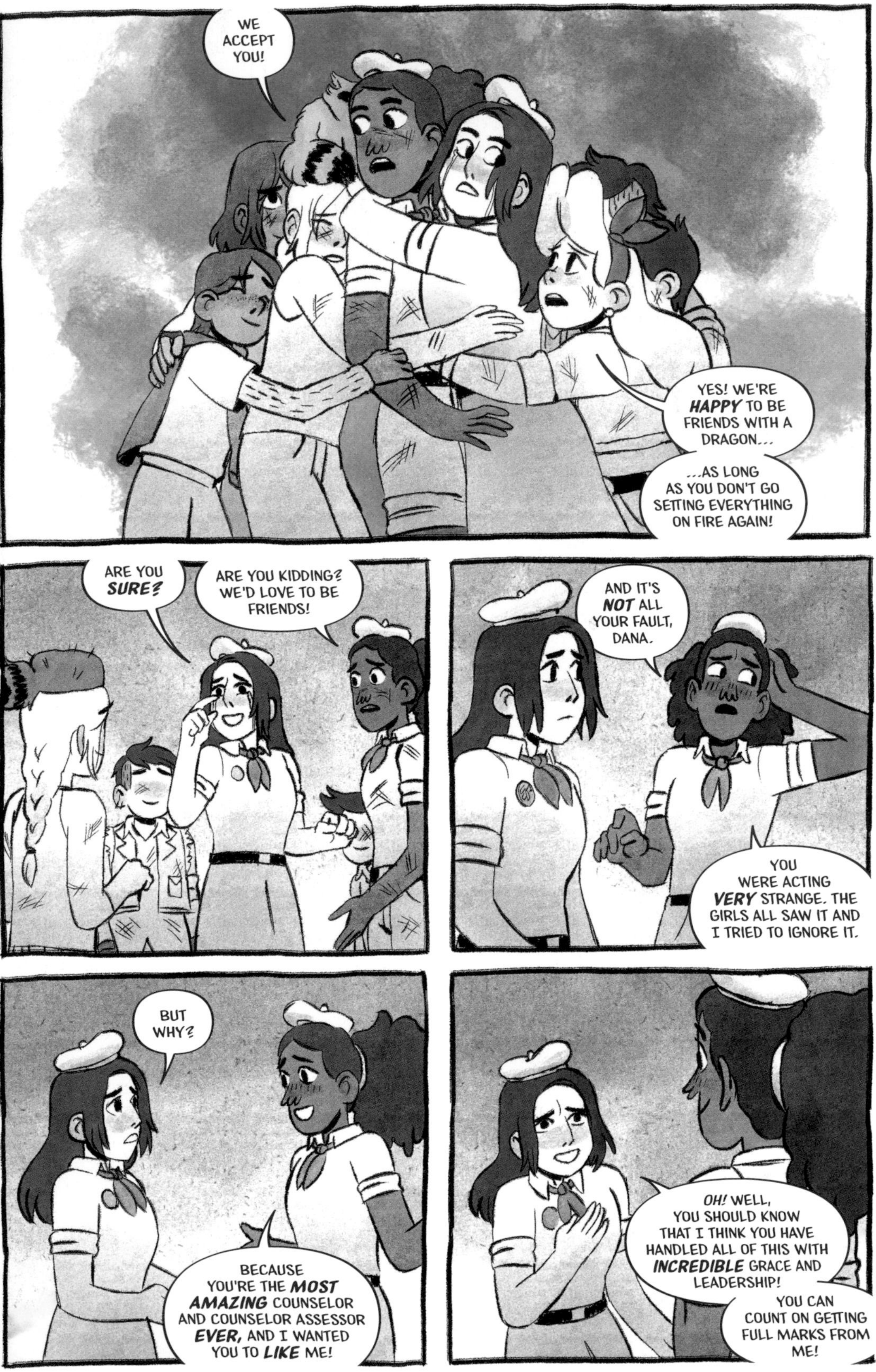
WE ACCEPT YOU!
YES! WE'RE *HAPPY* TO BE FRIENDS WITH A DRAGON...
...AS LONG AS YOU DON'T GO SETTING EVERYTHING ON FIRE AGAIN!
ARE YOU *SURE?*
ARE YOU KIDDING? WE'D LOVE TO BE FRIENDS!
AND IT'S *NOT* ALL YOUR FAULT, DANA.
YOU WERE ACTING *VERY* STRANGE. THE GIRLS ALL SAW IT AND I TRIED TO IGNORE IT.
BUT WHY?
BECAUSE YOU'RE THE *MOST AMAZING* COUNSELOR AND COUNSELOR ASSESSOR *EVER,* AND I WANTED YOU TO *LIKE* ME!
OH! WELL, YOU SHOULD KNOW THAT I THINK YOU HAVE HANDLED ALL OF THIS WITH *INCREDIBLE* GRACE AND LEADERSHIP!
YOU CAN COUNT ON GETTING FULL MARKS FROM ME!

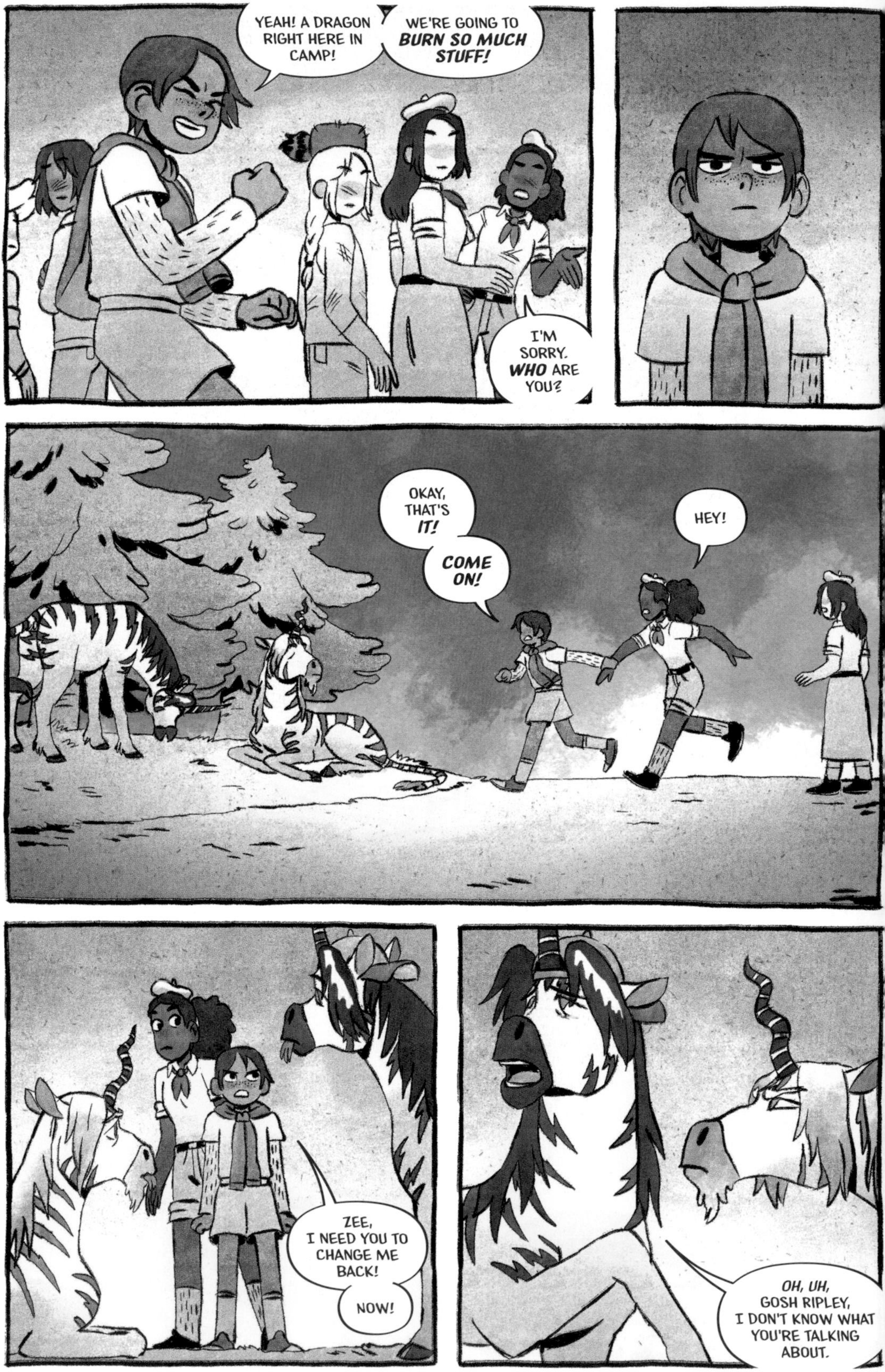
YEAH! A DRAGON RIGHT HERE IN CAMP!
WE'RE GOING TO BURN SO MUCH STUFF!
I'M SORRY. WHO ARE YOU?
OKAY, THAT'S IT!
COME ON!
HEY!
ZEE, I NEED YOU TO CHANGE ME BACK!
NOW!
OH, UH, GOSH RIPLEY, I DON'T KNOW WHAT YOU'RE TALKING ABOUT.

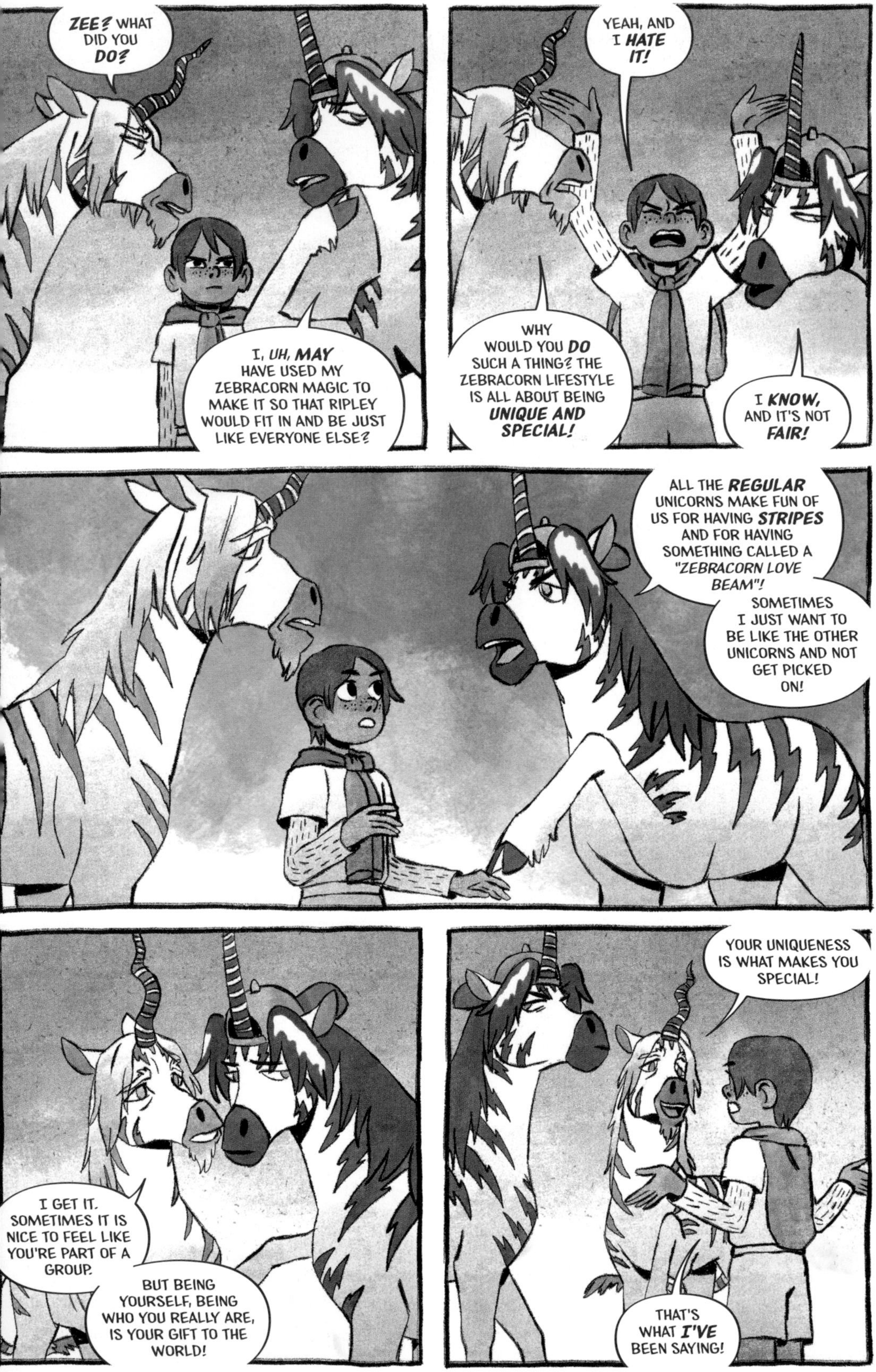

ZEE? WHAT DID YOU DO?
I, UH, MAY HAVE USED MY ZEBRACORN MAGIC TO MAKE IT SO THAT RIPLEY WOULD FIT IN AND BE JUST LIKE EVERYONE ELSE?
YEAH, AND I HATE IT!
WHY WOULD YOU DO SUCH A THING? THE ZEBRACORN LIFESTYLE IS ALL ABOUT BEING UNIQUE AND SPECIAL!
I KNOW, AND IT'S NOT FAIR!
ALL THE REGULAR UNICORNS MAKE FUN OF US FOR HAVING STRIPES AND FOR HAVING SOMETHING CALLED A "ZEBRACORN LOVE BEAM"!
SOMETIMES I JUST WANT TO BE LIKE THE OTHER UNICORNS AND NOT GET PICKED ON!
I GET IT. SOMETIMES IT IS NICE TO FEEL LIKE YOU'RE PART OF A GROUP.
BUT BEING YOURSELF, BEING WHO YOU REALLY ARE, IS YOUR GIFT TO THE WORLD!
YOUR UNIQUENESS IS WHAT MAKES YOU SPECIAL!
THAT'S WHAT I'VE BEEN SAYING!

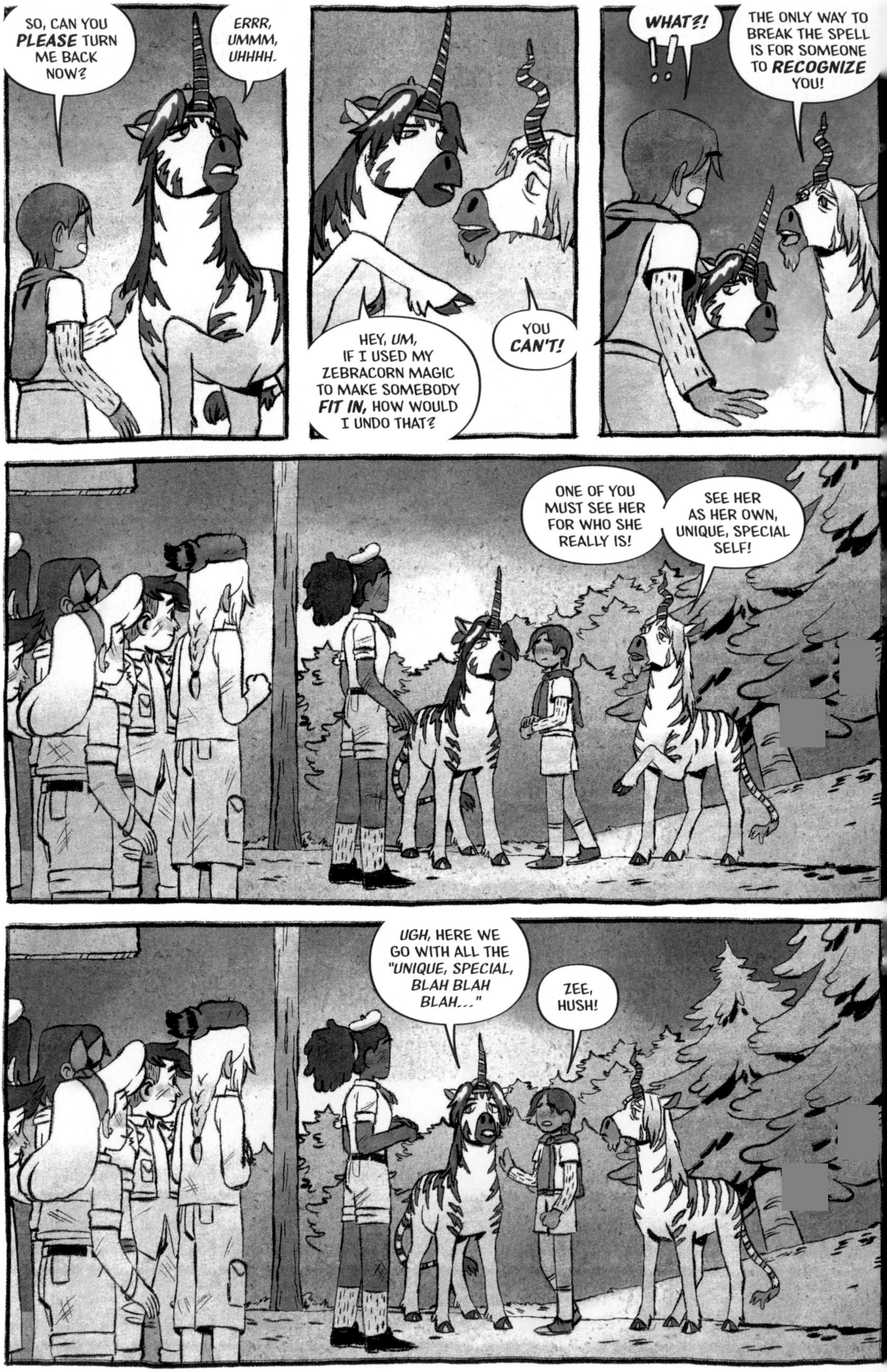
SO, CAN YOU PLEASE TURN ME BACK NOW?
ERRR, UMMM, UHHHH.
HEY, UM, IF I USED MY ZEBRACORN MAGIC TO MAKE SOMEBODY FIT IN, HOW WOULD I UNDO THAT?
YOU CAN'T!
WHAT?!
!!
THE ONLY WAY TO BREAK THE SPELL IS FOR SOMEONE TO RECOGNIZE YOU!
ONE OF YOU MUST SEE HER FOR WHO SHE REALLY IS!
SEE HER AS HER OWN, UNIQUE, SPECIAL SELF!
UGH, HERE WE GO WITH ALL THE "UNIQUE, SPECIAL, BLAH BLAH BLAH..."
ZEE, HUSH!

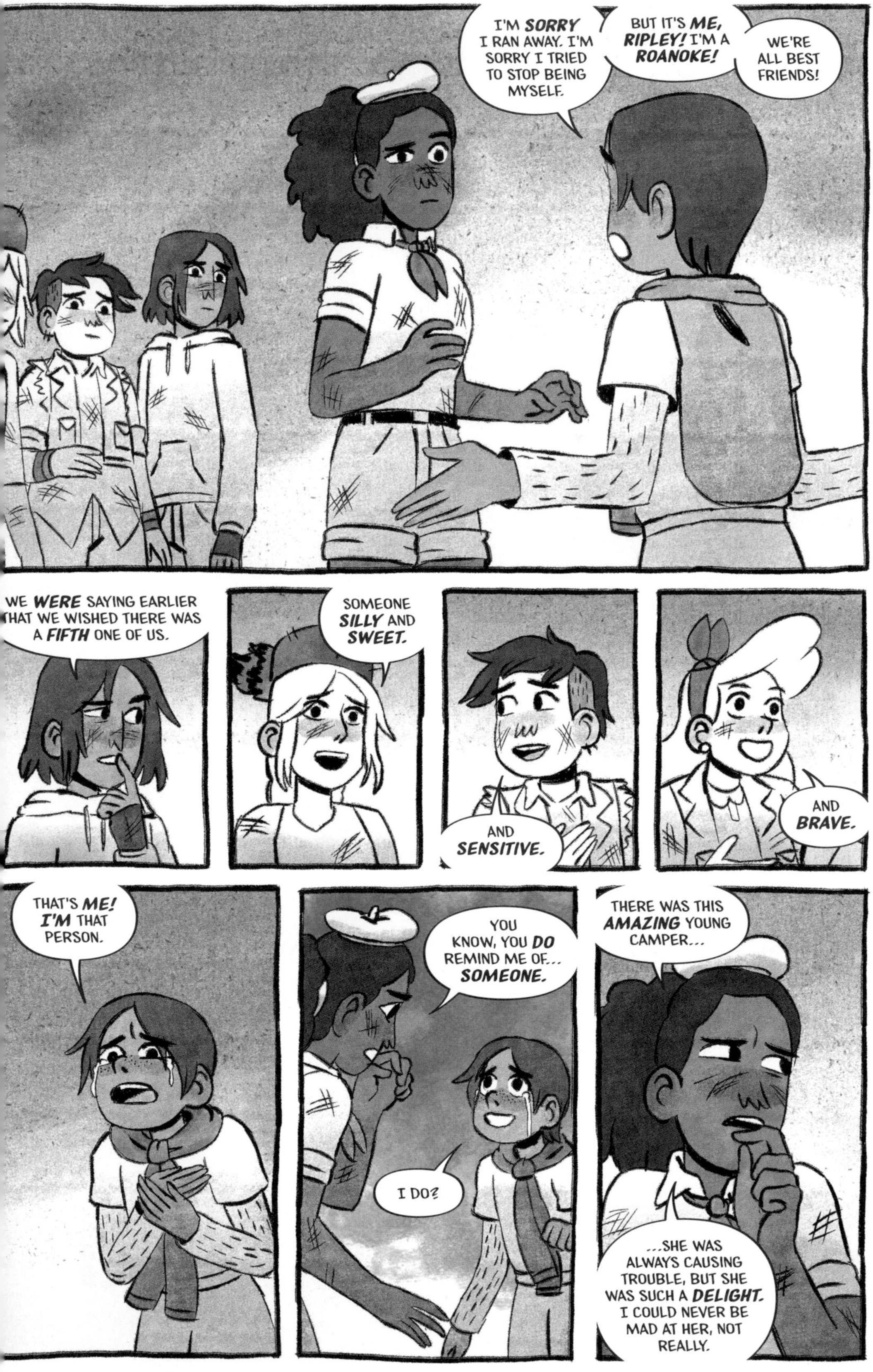

I'M SORRY I RAN AWAY. I'M SORRY I TRIED TO STOP BEING MYSELF.
BUT IT'S ME, RIPLEY! I'M A ROANOKE!
WE'RE ALL BEST FRIENDS!
WE WERE SAYING EARLIER THAT WE WISHED THERE WAS A FIFTH ONE OF US.
SOMEONE SILLY AND SWEET.
AND SENSITIVE.
AND BRAVE.
THAT'S ME! I'M THAT PERSON.
YOU KNOW, YOU DO REMIND ME OF... SOMEONE.
I DO?
THERE WAS THIS AMAZING YOUNG CAMPER...
...SHE WAS ALWAYS CAUSING TROUBLE, BUT SHE WAS SUCH A DELIGHT. I COULD NEVER BE MAD AT HER, NOT REALLY.

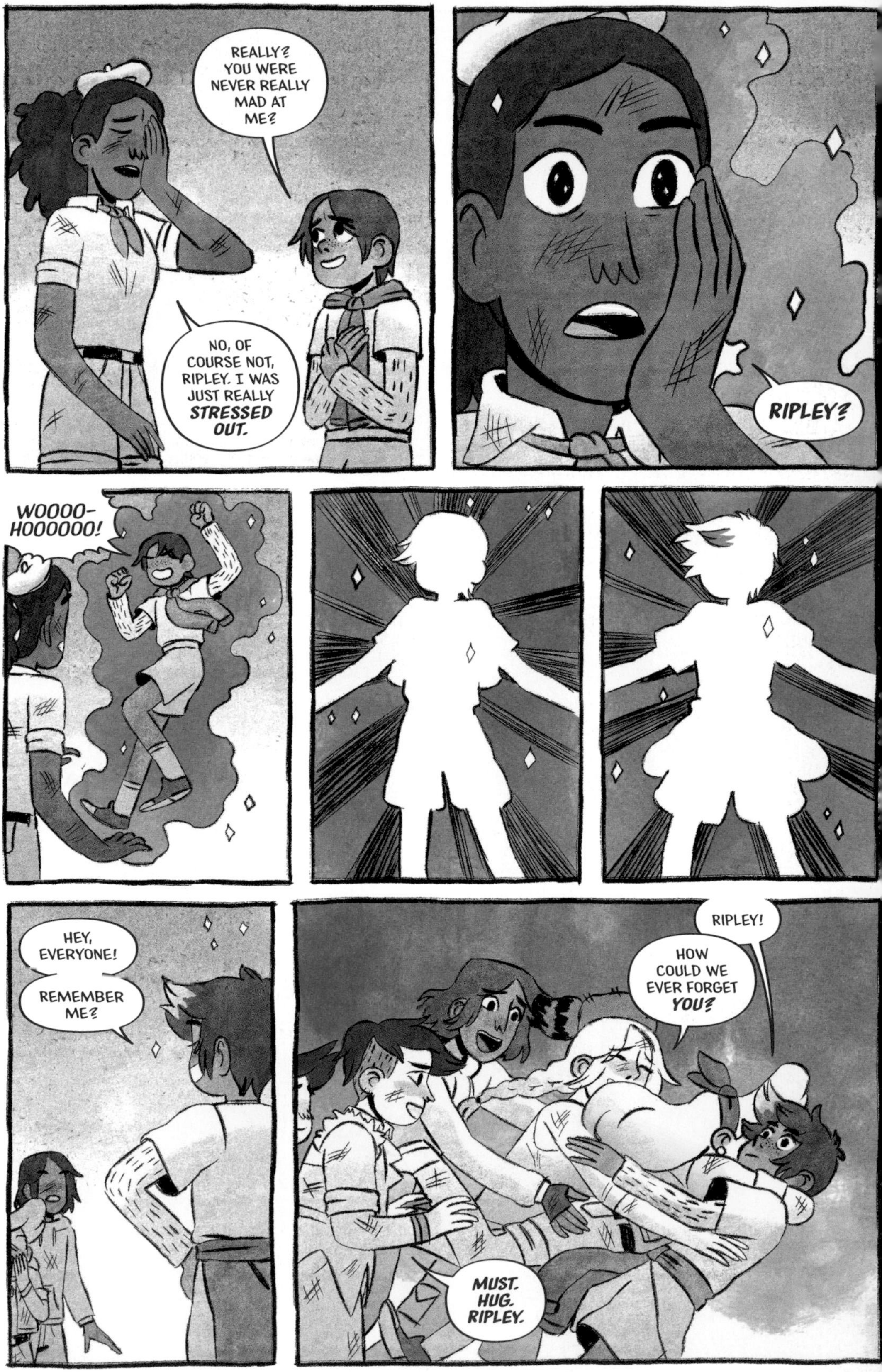
REALLY? YOU WERE NEVER REALLY MAD AT ME?
NO, OF COURSE NOT, RIPLEY. I WAS JUST REALLY STRESSED OUT.
RIPLEY?
WOOOO-HOOOOOO!
HEY, EVERYONE!
REMEMBER ME?
RIPLEY!
HOW COULD WE EVER FORGET YOU?
MUST. HUG. RIPLEY.

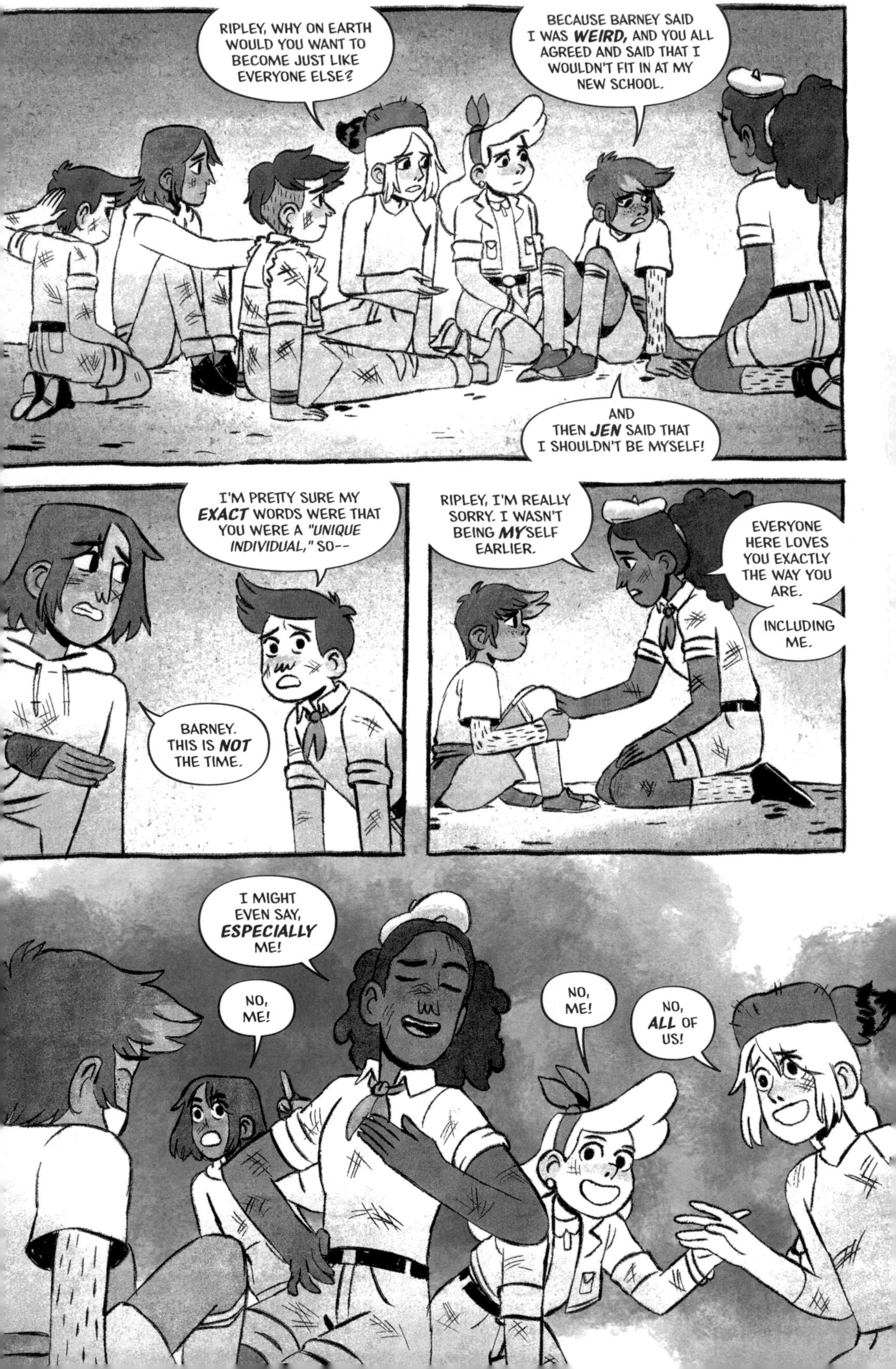
RIPLEY, WHY ON EARTH WOULD YOU WANT TO BECOME JUST LIKE EVERYONE ELSE?
BECAUSE BARNEY SAID I WAS WEIRD, AND YOU ALL AGREED AND SAID THAT I WOULDN'T FIT IN AT MY NEW SCHOOL.
AND THEN JEN SAID THAT I SHOULDN'T BE MYSELF!
I'M PRETTY SURE MY EXACT WORDS WERE THAT YOU WERE A "UNIQUE INDIVIDUAL," SO--
BARNEY. THIS IS NOT THE TIME.
RIPLEY, I'M REALLY SORRY. I WASN'T BEING MYSELF EARLIER.
EVERYONE HERE LOVES YOU EXACTLY THE WAY YOU ARE.
INCLUDING ME.
I MIGHT EVEN SAY, ESPECIALLY ME!
NO, ME!
NO, ME!
NO, ALL OF US!

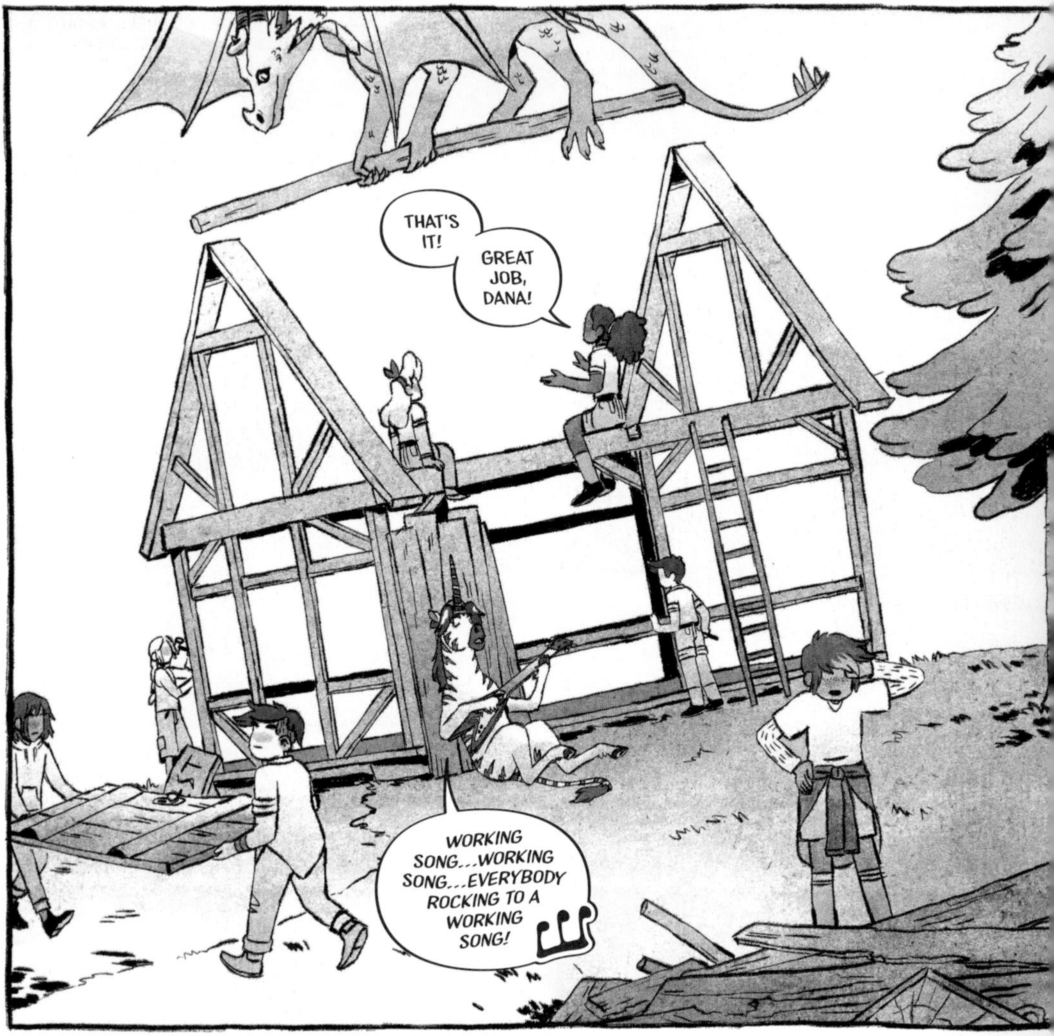
THAT'S IT!
GREAT JOB, DANA!
WORKING SONG...WORKING SONG...EVERYBODY ROCKING TO A WORKING SONG!

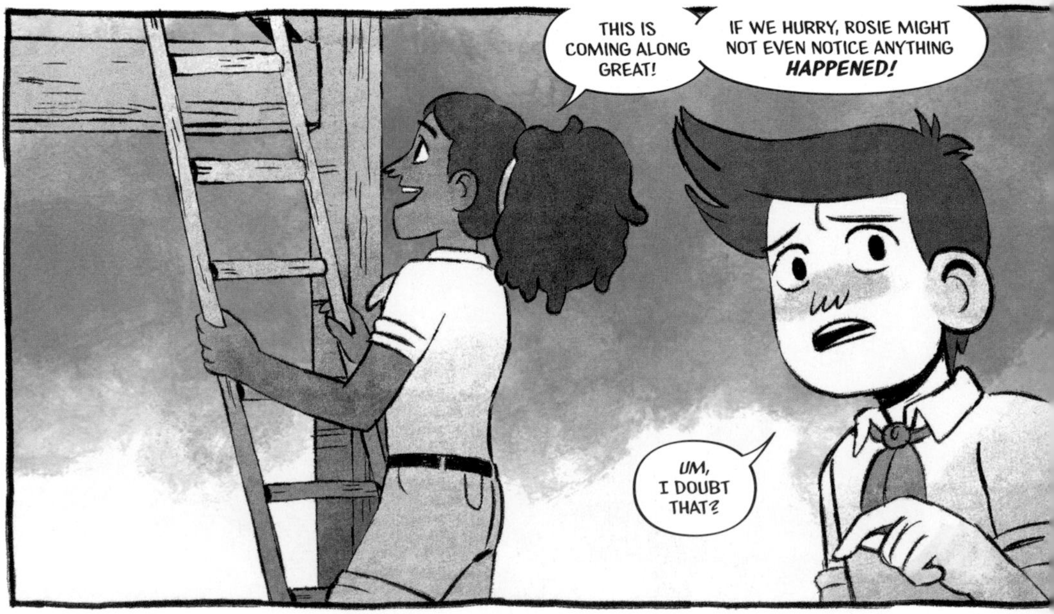
THIS IS COMING ALONG GREAT!
IF WE HURRY, ROSIE MIGHT NOT EVEN NOTICE ANYTHING HAPPENED!
UM, I DOUBT THAT?

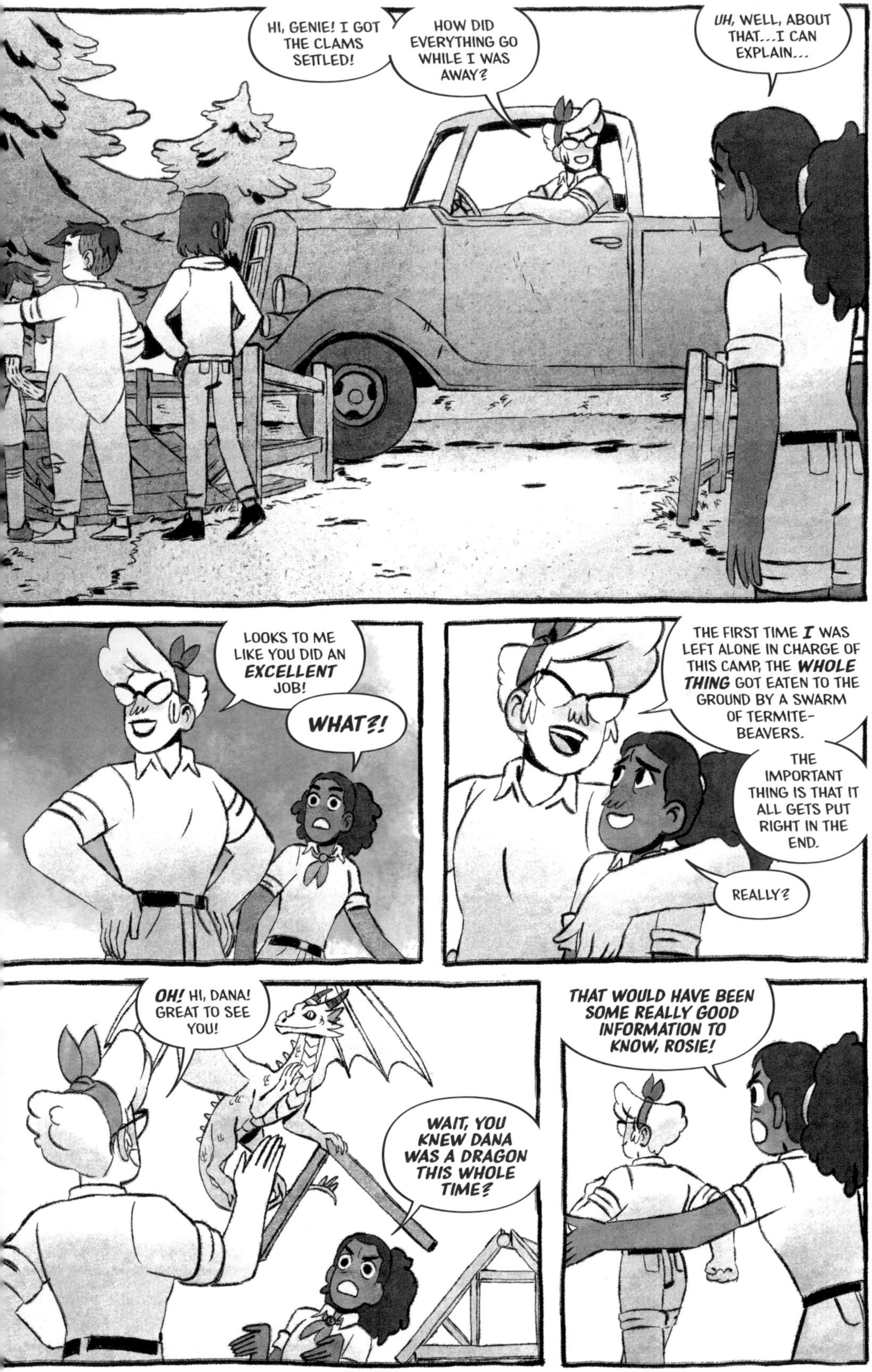
HI, GENIE! I GOT THE CLAMS SETTLED!
HOW DID EVERYTHING GO WHILE I WAS AWAY?
UH, WELL, ABOUT THAT... I CAN EXPLAIN...
LOOKS TO ME LIKE YOU DID AN EXCELLENT JOB!
WHAT?!
THE FIRST TIME I WAS LEFT ALONE IN CHARGE OF THIS CAMP, THE WHOLE THING GOT EATEN TO THE GROUND BY A SWARM OF TERMITE-BEAVERS.
THE IMPORTANT THING IS THAT IT ALL GETS PUT RIGHT IN THE END.
REALLY?
OH! HI, DANA! GREAT TO SEE YOU!
WAIT, YOU KNEW DANA WAS A DRAGON THIS WHOLE TIME?
THAT WOULD HAVE BEEN SOME REALLY GOOD INFORMATION TO KNOW, ROSIE!

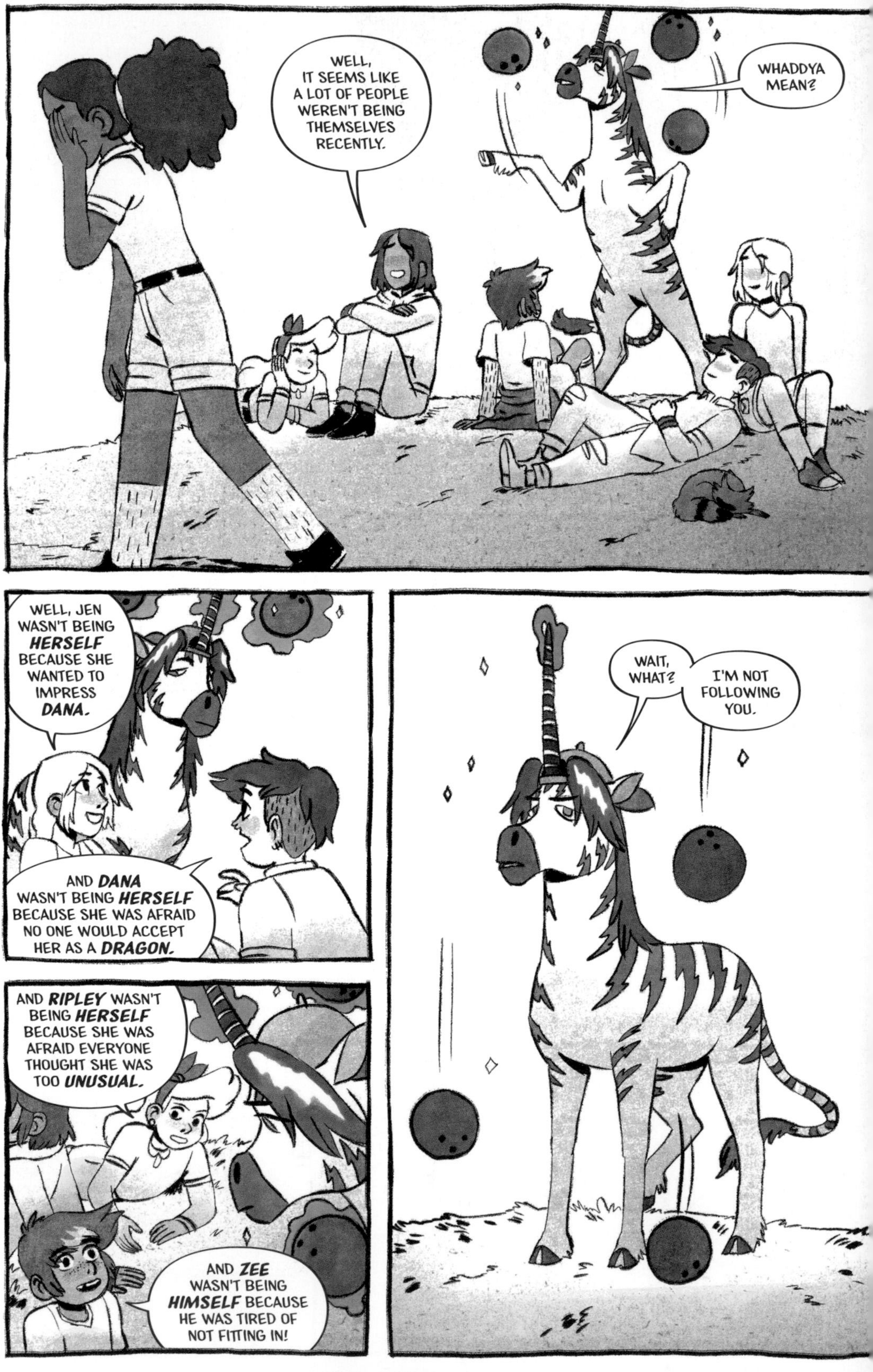
WELL, IT SEEMS LIKE A LOT OF PEOPLE WEREN'T BEING THEMSELVES RECENTLY.
WHADDYA MEAN?
WELL, JEN WASN'T BEING HERSELF BECAUSE SHE WANTED TO IMPRESS DANA.
AND DANA WASN'T BEING HERSELF BECAUSE SHE WAS AFRAID NO ONE WOULD ACCEPT HER AS A DRAGON.
AND RIPLEY WASN'T BEING HERSELF BECAUSE SHE WAS AFRAID EVERYONE THOUGHT SHE WAS TOO UNUSUAL.
AND ZEE WASN'T BEING HIMSELF BECAUSE HE WAS TIRED OF NOT FITTING IN!
WAIT, WHAT?
I'M NOT FOLLOWING YOU.

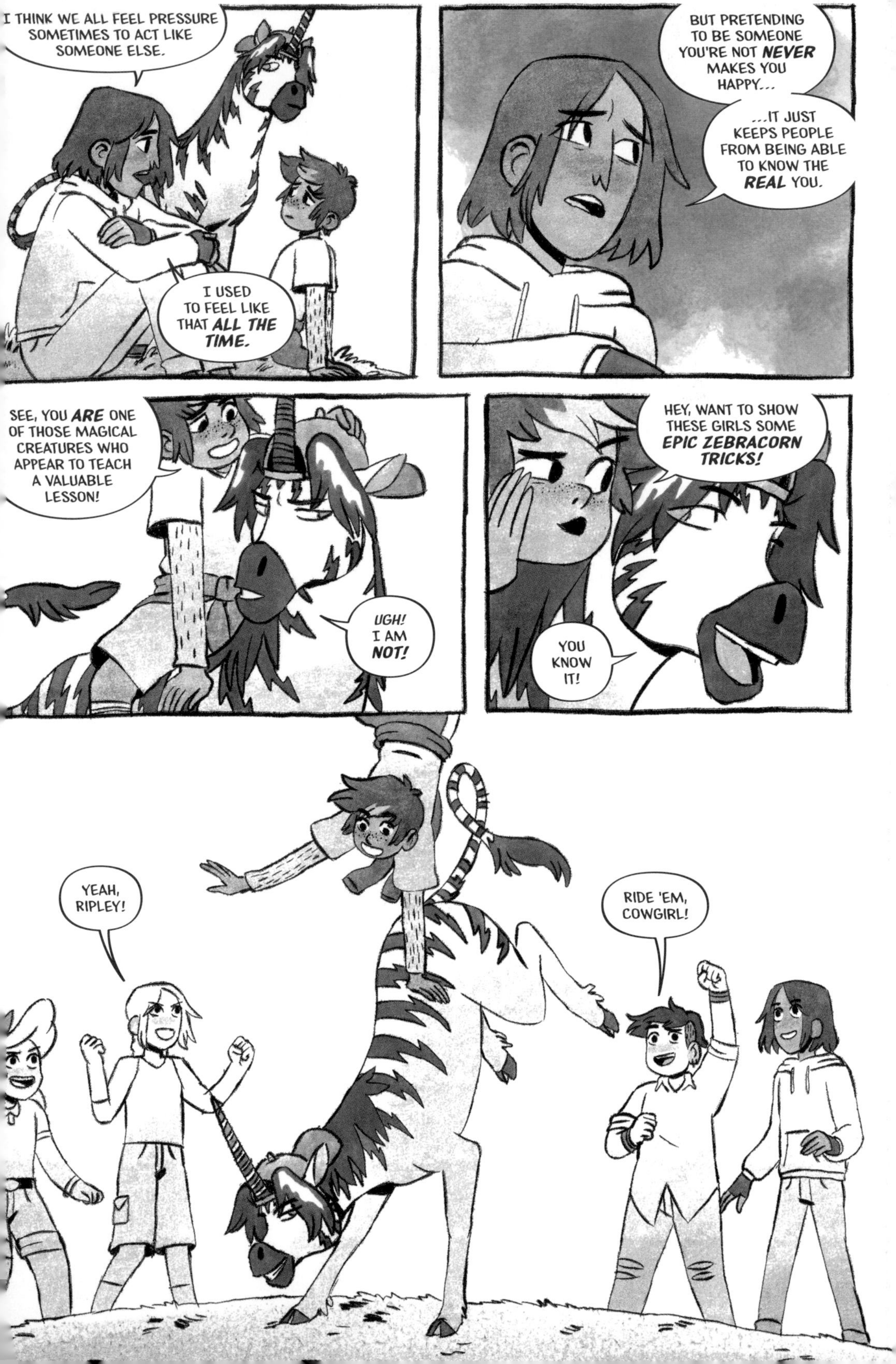
I THINK WE ALL FEEL PRESSURE SOMETIMES TO ACT LIKE SOMEONE ELSE.
I USED TO FEEL LIKE THAT ALL THE TIME.
BUT PRETENDING TO BE SOMEONE YOU'RE NOT NEVER MAKES YOU HAPPY...
...IT JUST KEEPS PEOPLE FROM BEING ABLE TO KNOW THE REAL YOU.
SEE, YOU ARE ONE OF THOSE MAGICAL CREATURES WHO APPEAR TO TEACH A VALUABLE LESSON!
UGH! I AM NOT!
HEY, WANT TO SHOW THESE GIRLS SOME EPIC ZEBRACORN TRICKS!
YOU KNOW IT!
YEAH, RIPLEY!
RIDE 'EM, COWGIRL!

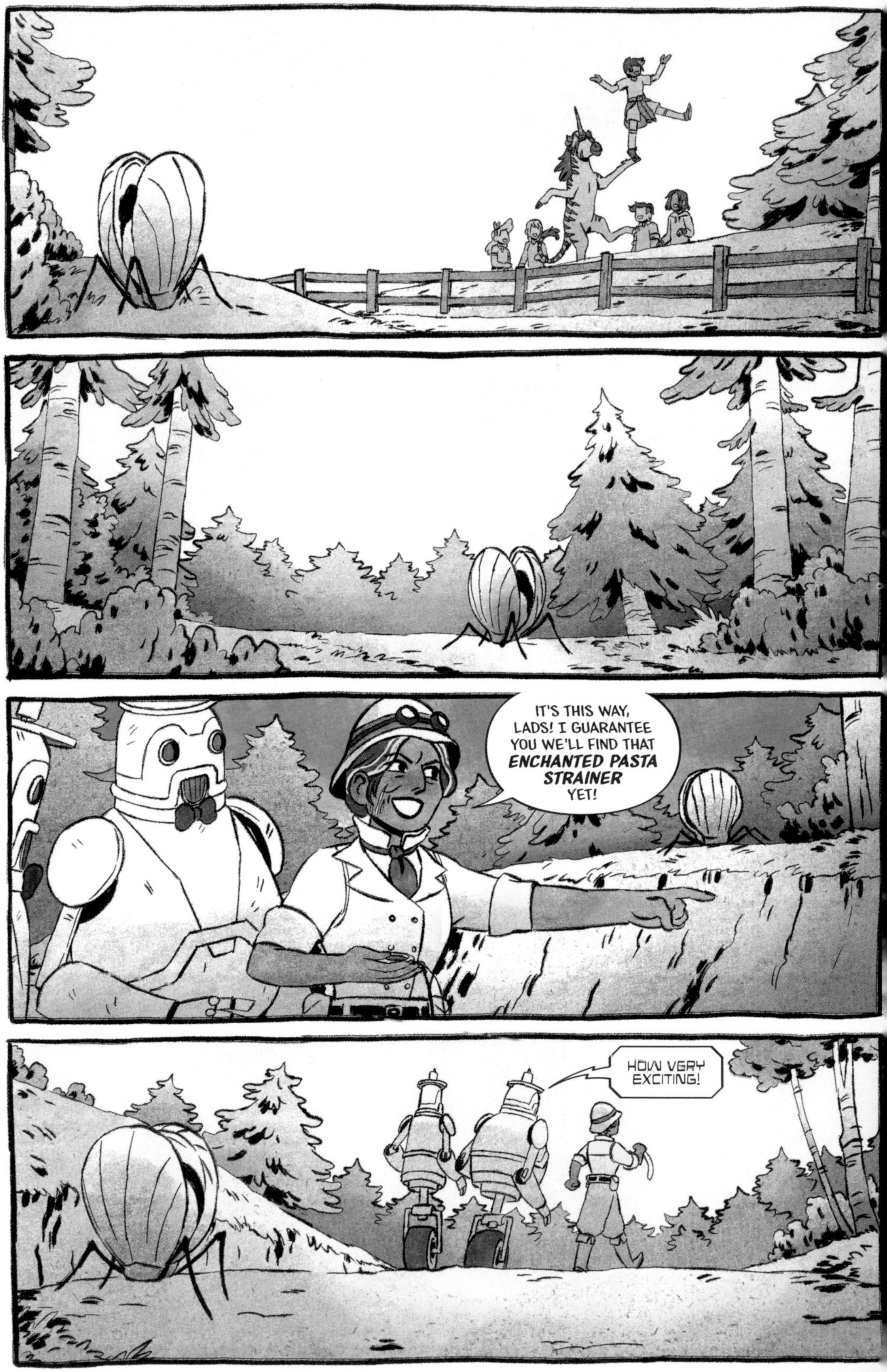
IT'S THIS WAY, LADS! I GUARANTEE YOU WE'LL FIND THAT ENCHANTED PASTA STRAINER YET!
HOW VERY EXCITING!

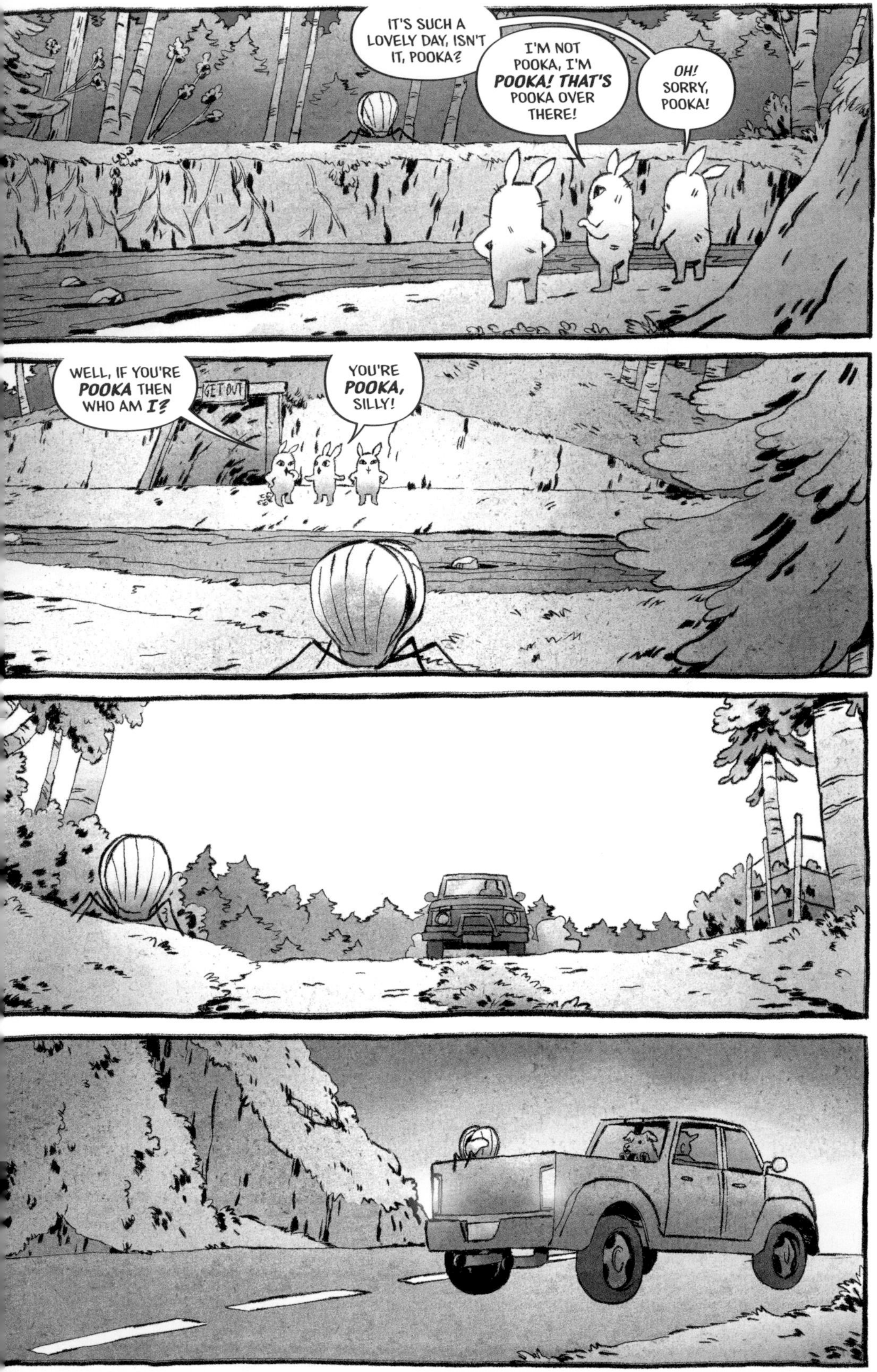
IT'S SUCH A LOVELY DAY, ISN'T IT, POOKA?
I'M NOT POOKA, I'M **POOKA! THAT'S** POOKA OVER THERE!
OH! SORRY, POOKA!
GET OUT
WELL, IF YOU'RE **POOKA** THEN WHO AM ***I?***
YOU'RE **POOKA,** SILLY!

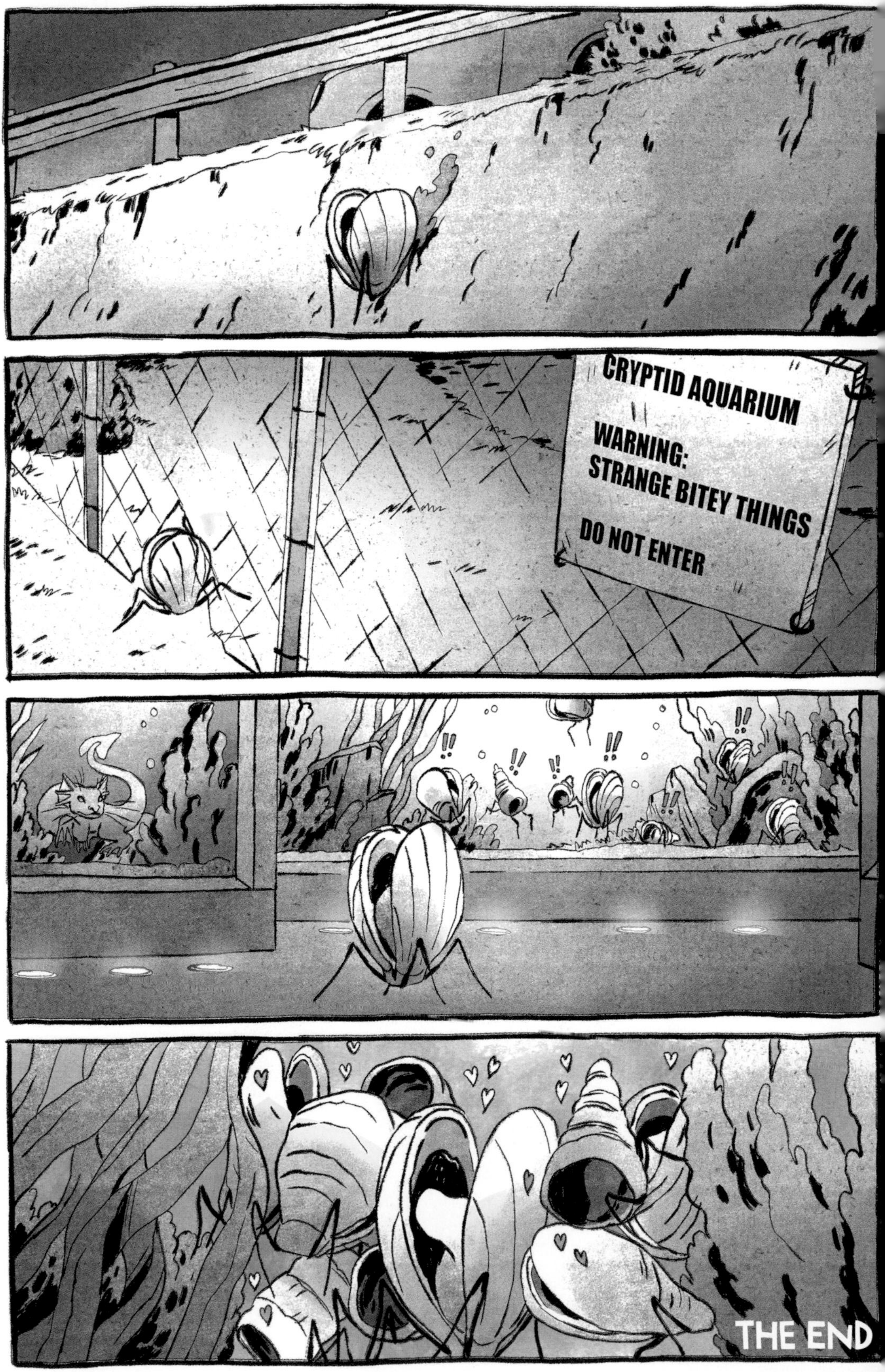
CRYPTID AQUARIUM
WARNING:
STRANGE BITEY THINGS
DO NOT ENTER
!!
!!
!!
!!
!!
!!
!!
THE END

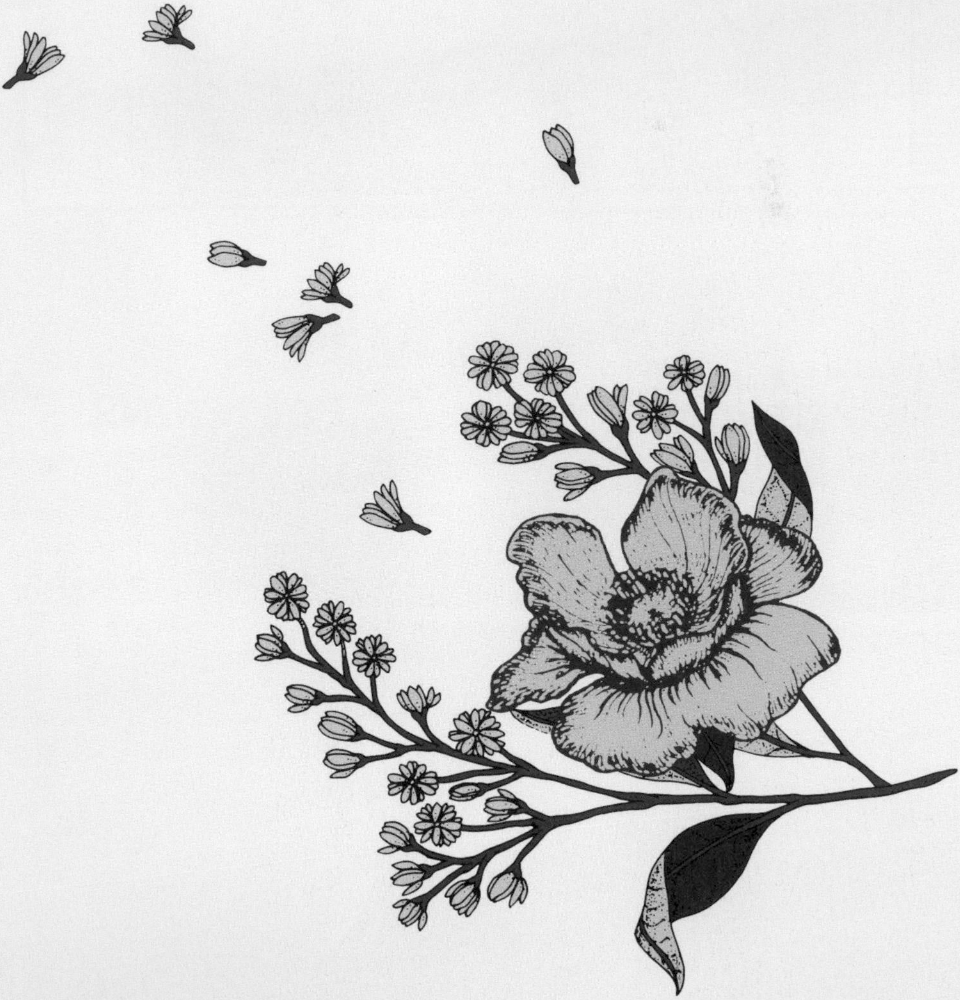

LILAH STURGES

Lilah Sturges has been writing comics for over a decade and believes she is finally getting the hang of it. She lives in Austin, Texas with her two daughters and a cat named Greg.

POLTERINK

polterink (also sometimes referred to as Claudia Rinofner) is a freelance artist and professional tea-drinker from Austria. As a kid she really liked spending time in the woods, feeding squirrels and building little homes for fairies out of twigs and moss.

SHANNON WATTERS

Shannon Watters is an editor lady by day and the co-creator of *Lumberjanes*...also by day. She helped guide KaBOOM!—BOOM! Studios' all-ages imprint—to commercial and critical success, and oversees BOOM! Box, an experimental imprint created "for the love of it." She has a great love for all things indie and comics, which is something she's been passionate about since growing up in the wilds of Arizona. When she's not working on comics she can be found watching classic films and enjoying the local cuisine.

NOELLE STEVENSON

Noelle Stevenson is the *New York Times* bestselling author of *Nimona*. She's been nominated for Harvey Awards, and was awarded the Slate Cartoonist Studio Prize for Best Web Comic in 2012 for *Nimona*. A graduate of the Maryland Institute College of Art, Noelle has worked on Disney's *Wander Over Yonder* and *She-Ra*, she has written for Marvel and DC Comics. She lives in Los Angeles. In her spare time she can be found drawing superheroes and talking about bad TV.
www.gingerhaze.com

GRACE ELLIS

Grace Ellis is a writer and co-creator of *Lumberjanes*. She is currently writing *Moonstruck*, a comic about lesbian werewolf baristas, as well as scripts for the animated show *Bravest Warriors*. Grace lives in Columbus, Ohio, where she co-parents a preternaturally smart cat, even though she's usually more of a dog person.

BROOKLYN ALLEN

Brooklyn Allen is a co-creator and original artist for *Lumberjanes* and when he is not drawing, then he will most likely be found with a saw in his hand making something rad. Currently residing in the "for lovers" state of Virginia, he spends most of his time working on comics with his not-so-helpful assistant Linus...his dog.

Goldie Vance is on the case in

GOLDIE VANCE
LARCENY IN LA LA LAND

Jackie Ball • Mollie Rose • Natalia Nesterenko
GOLDIE VANCE
"A delight for readers of all ages."
—Newsarama
Larceny in La La Land

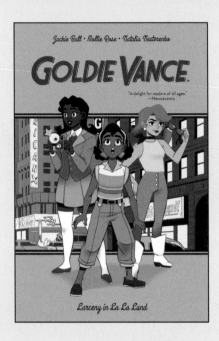

Created by
HOPE LARSON & BRITTNEY WILLIAMS

Written by
JACKIE BALL

Illustrated by
MOLLIE ROSE

Colored by
NATALIA NESTERENKO

Lettered by
JIM CAMPBELL

Cover by
BRITTNEY WILLIAMS

CATCH UP WITH ALL OF GOLDIE'S ADVENTURES!

Hope Larson • Brittney Williams • Sarah Stern
GOLDIE VANCE
Volume One

Hope Larson • Brittney Williams • Sarah Stern
GOLDIE VANCE
Volume Two

GOLDIE VANCE
Volume Three

GOLDIE VANCE
Volume Four

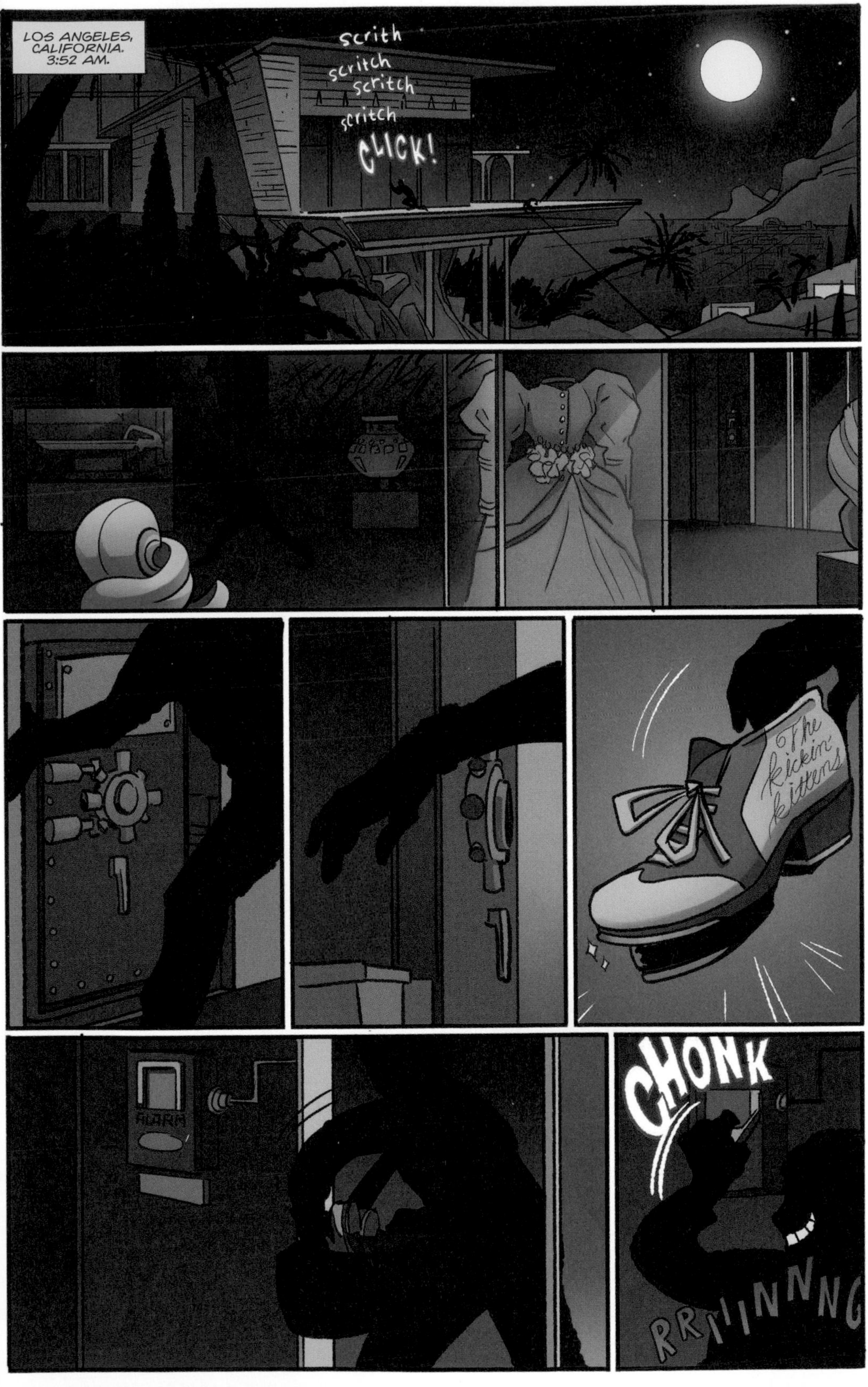
LOS ANGELES, CALIFORNIA. 3:52 AM.
scrith
scritch
scritch
scritch
CLICK!
The kickin' kittens
ALARM
CHONK
RRIIINNNG

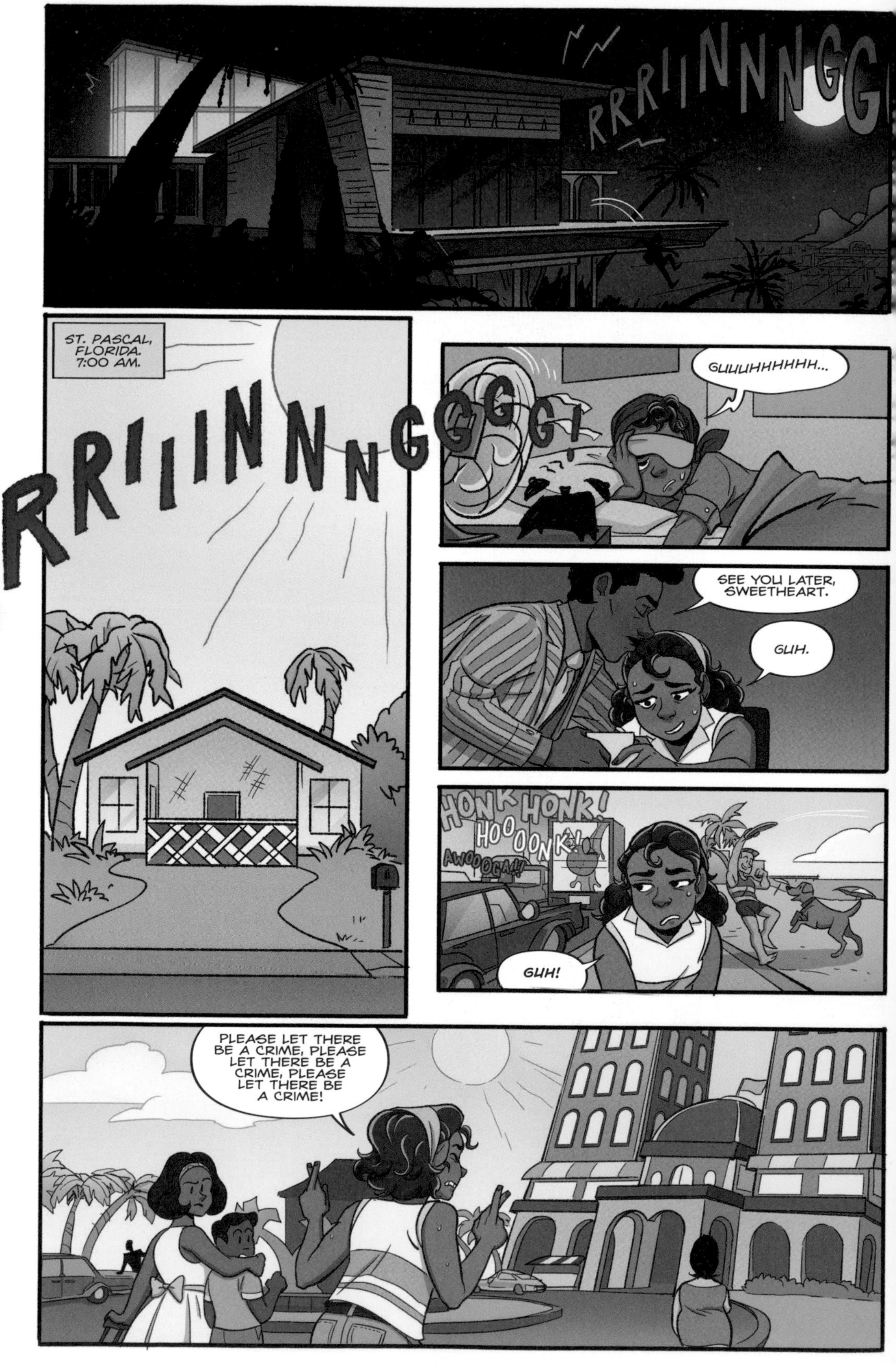
RRRIINNNNGGG
ST. PASCAL, FLORIDA. 7:00 AM.
RRIIINNNNGGGG!
GUUUHHHHHH...
SEE YOU LATER, SWEETHEART.
GUH.
HONK HONK!
HOOOONK!
AWOOOGA!!
GUH!
PLEASE LET THERE BE A CRIME, PLEASE LET THERE BE A CRIME, PLEASE LET THERE BE A CRIME!

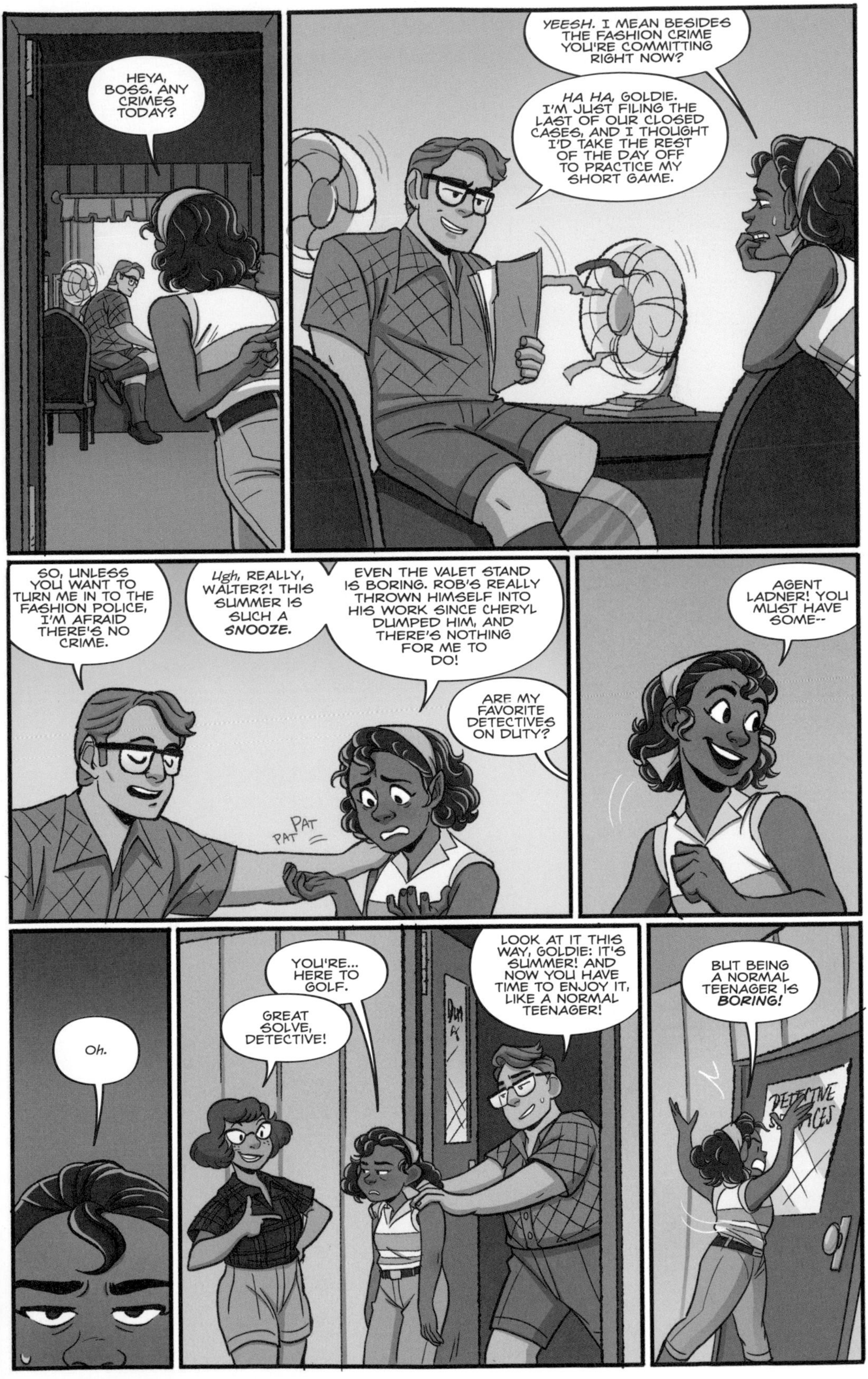
HEYA, BOSS. ANY CRIMES TODAY?
YEESH. I MEAN BESIDES THE FASHION CRIME YOU'RE COMMITTING RIGHT NOW?
HA HA, GOLDIE. I'M JUST FILING THE LAST OF OUR CLOSED CASES, AND I THOUGHT I'D TAKE THE REST OF THE DAY OFF TO PRACTICE MY SHORT GAME.
SO, UNLESS YOU WANT TO TURN ME IN TO THE FASHION POLICE, I'M AFRAID THERE'S NO CRIME.
Ugh, REALLY, WALTER?! THIS SUMMER IS SUCH A SNOOZE.
EVEN THE VALET STAND IS BORING. ROB'S REALLY THROWN HIMSELF INTO HIS WORK SINCE CHERYL DUMPED HIM, AND THERE'S NOTHING FOR ME TO DO!
PAT PAT
ARE MY FAVORITE DETECTIVES ON DUTY?
AGENT LADNER! YOU MUST HAVE SOME--
Oh.
YOU'RE... HERE TO GOLF.
GREAT SOLVE, DETECTIVE!
LOOK AT IT THIS WAY, GOLDIE: IT'S SUMMER! AND NOW YOU HAVE TIME TO ENJOY IT, LIKE A NORMAL TEENAGER!
BUT BEING A NORMAL TEENAGER IS BORING!
DETECTIVE SERVICES

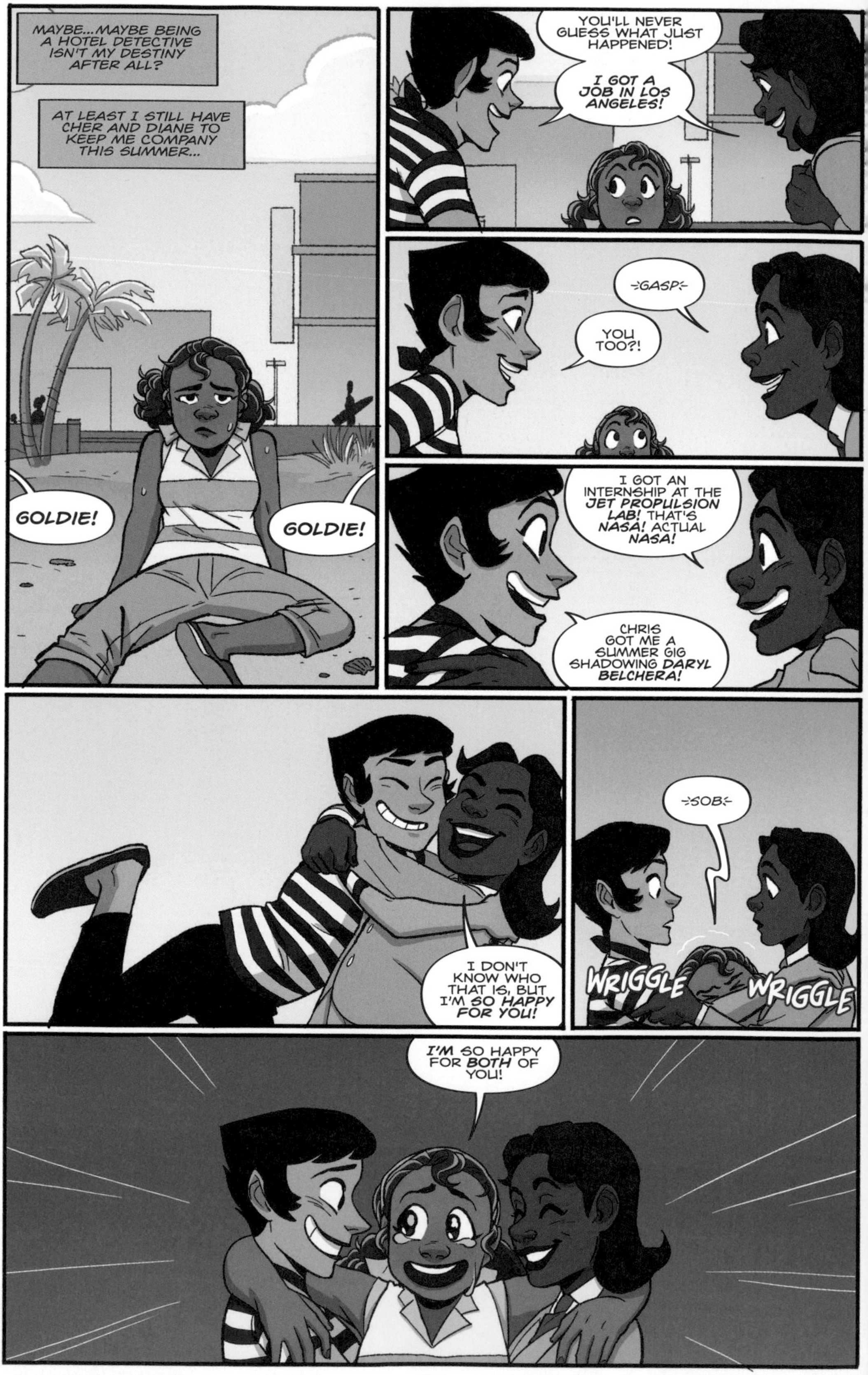
MAYBE...MAYBE BEING A HOTEL DETECTIVE ISN'T MY DESTINY AFTER ALL?
AT LEAST I STILL HAVE CHER AND DIANE TO KEEP ME COMPANY THIS SUMMER...
GOLDIE!
GOLDIE!
YOU'LL NEVER GUESS WHAT JUST HAPPENED!
I GOT A JOB IN LOS ANGELES!
-GASP-
YOU TOO?!
I GOT AN INTERNSHIP AT THE JET PROPULSION LAB! THAT'S NASA! ACTUAL NASA!
CHRIS GOT ME A SUMMER GIG SHADOWING DARYL BELCHERA!
I DON'T KNOW WHO THAT IS, BUT I'M SO HAPPY FOR YOU!
-SOB-
WRIGGLE
WRIGGLE
I'M SO HAPPY FOR BOTH OF YOU!

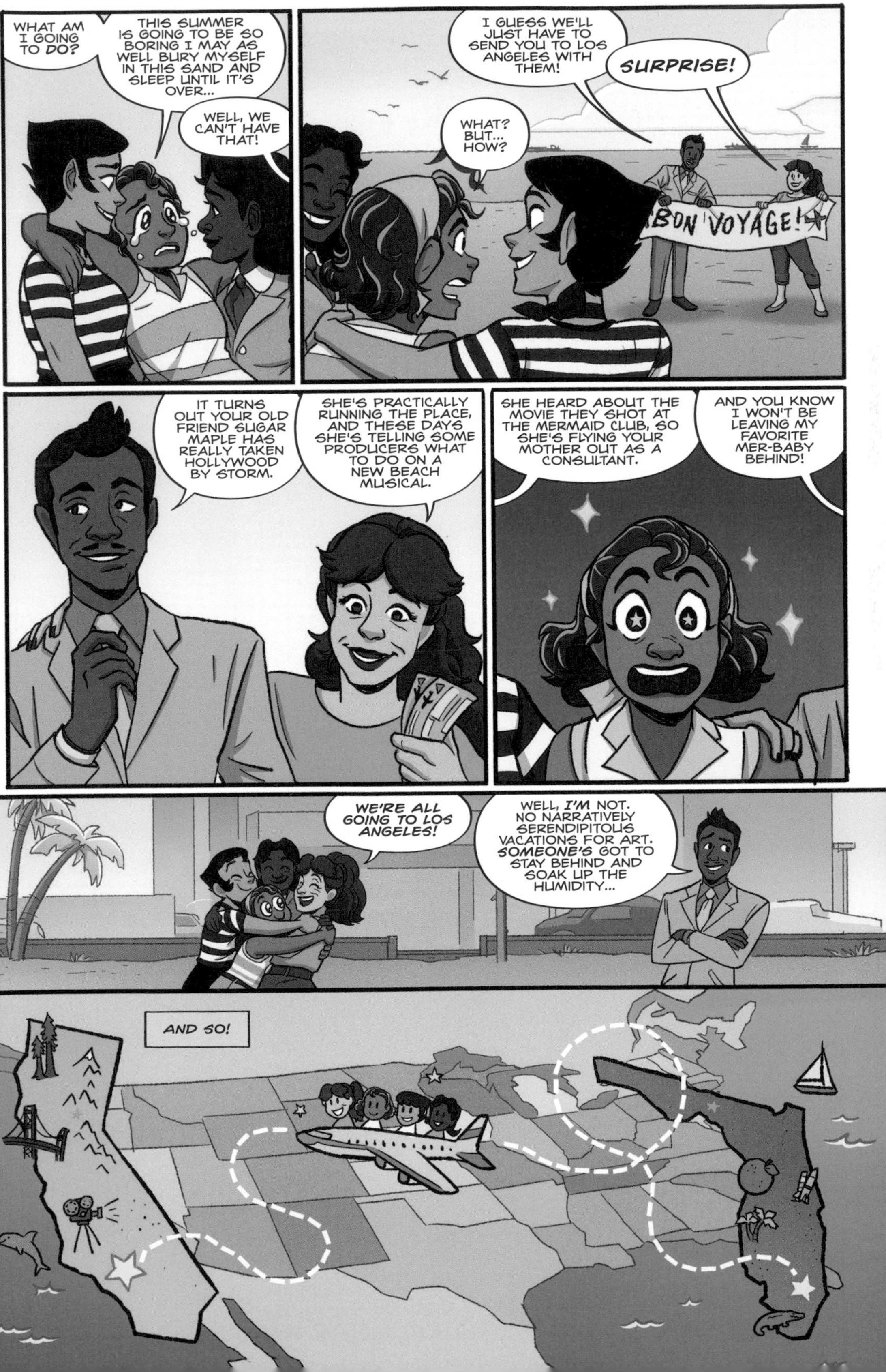

WHAT AM I GOING TO *DO*?
THIS SUMMER IS GOING TO BE SO BORING I MAY AS WELL BURY MYSELF IN THIS SAND AND SLEEP UNTIL IT'S OVER...
WELL, WE CAN'T HAVE THAT!
I GUESS WE'LL JUST HAVE TO SEND YOU TO LOS ANGELES WITH THEM!
SURPRISE!
WHAT? BUT... HOW?
BON VOYAGE!
IT TURNS OUT YOUR OLD FRIEND SUGAR MAPLE HAS REALLY TAKEN HOLLYWOOD BY STORM.
SHE'S PRACTICALLY RUNNING THE PLACE, AND THESE DAYS SHE'S TELLING SOME PRODUCERS WHAT TO DO ON A NEW BEACH MUSICAL.
SHE HEARD ABOUT THE MOVIE THEY SHOT AT THE MERMAID CLUB, SO SHE'S FLYING YOUR MOTHER OUT AS A CONSULTANT.
AND YOU KNOW I WON'T BE LEAVING MY FAVORITE MER-BABY BEHIND!
WE'RE ALL GOING TO LOS ANGELES!
WELL, *I'M* NOT. NO NARRATIVELY SERENDIPITOUS VACATIONS FOR ART. *SOMEONE'S* GOT TO STAY BEHIND AND SOAK UP THE HUMIDITY...
AND SO!

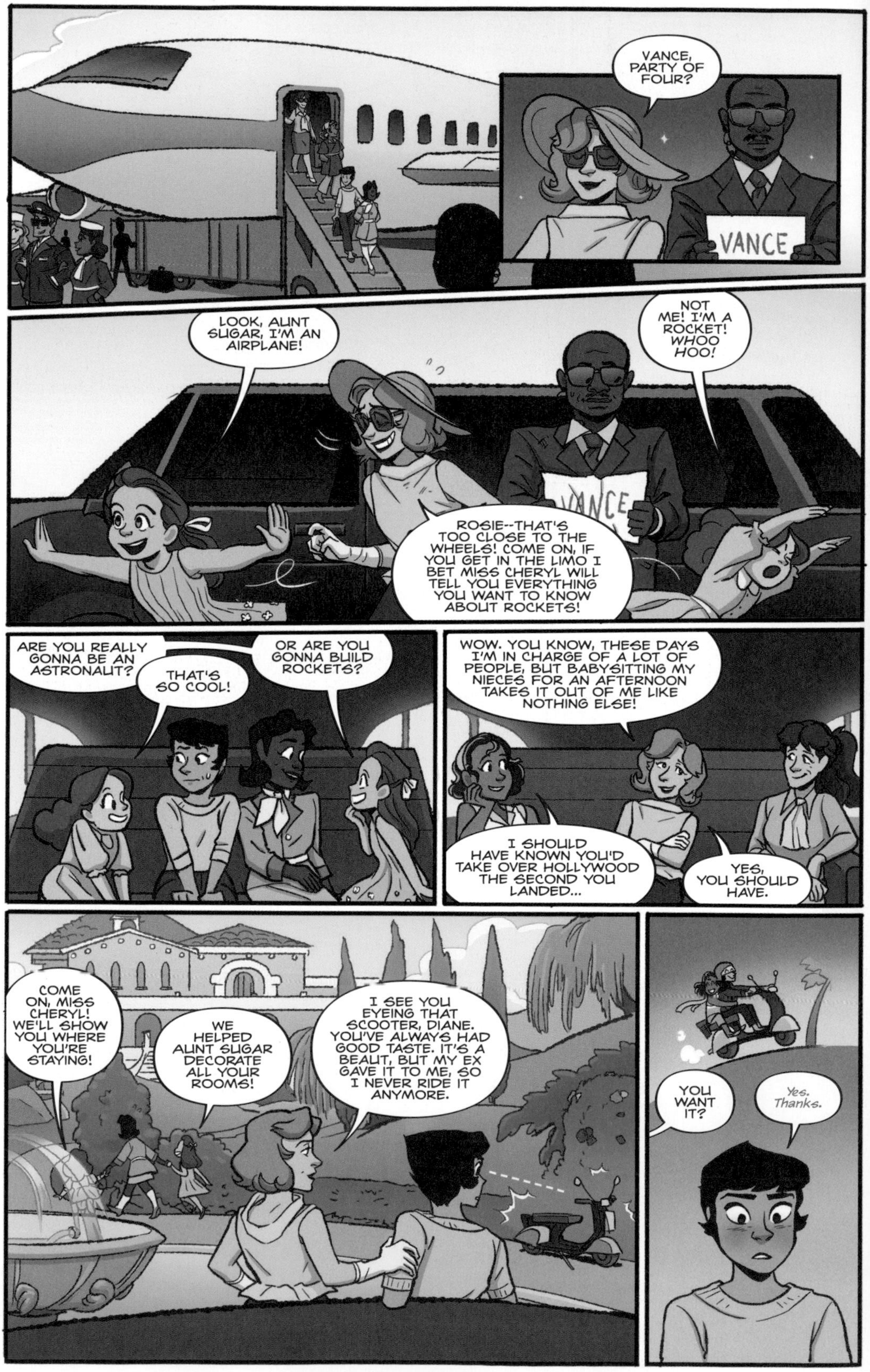
VANCE, PARTY OF FOUR?
VANCE
LOOK, AUNT SUGAR, I'M AN AIRPLANE!
NOT ME! I'M A ROCKET! WHOO HOO!
ROSIE--THAT'S TOO CLOSE TO THE WHEELS! COME ON, IF YOU GET IN THE LIMO I BET MISS CHERYL WILL TELL YOU EVERYTHING YOU WANT TO KNOW ABOUT ROCKETS!
ARE YOU REALLY GONNA BE AN ASTRONAUT?
OR ARE YOU GONNA BUILD ROCKETS?
THAT'S SO COOL!
WOW. YOU KNOW, THESE DAYS I'M IN CHARGE OF A LOT OF PEOPLE, BUT BABYSITTING MY NIECES FOR AN AFTERNOON TAKES IT OUT OF ME LIKE NOTHING ELSE!
I SHOULD HAVE KNOWN YOU'D TAKE OVER HOLLYWOOD THE SECOND YOU LANDED...
YES, YOU SHOULD HAVE.
COME ON, MISS CHERYL! WE'LL SHOW YOU WHERE YOU'RE STAYING!
WE HELPED AUNT SUGAR DECORATE ALL YOUR ROOMS!
I SEE YOU EYEING THAT SCOOTER, DIANE. YOU'VE ALWAYS HAD GOOD TASTE. IT'S A BEAUT, BUT MY EX GAVE IT TO ME, SO I NEVER RIDE IT ANYMORE.
YOU WANT IT?
Yes. Thanks.

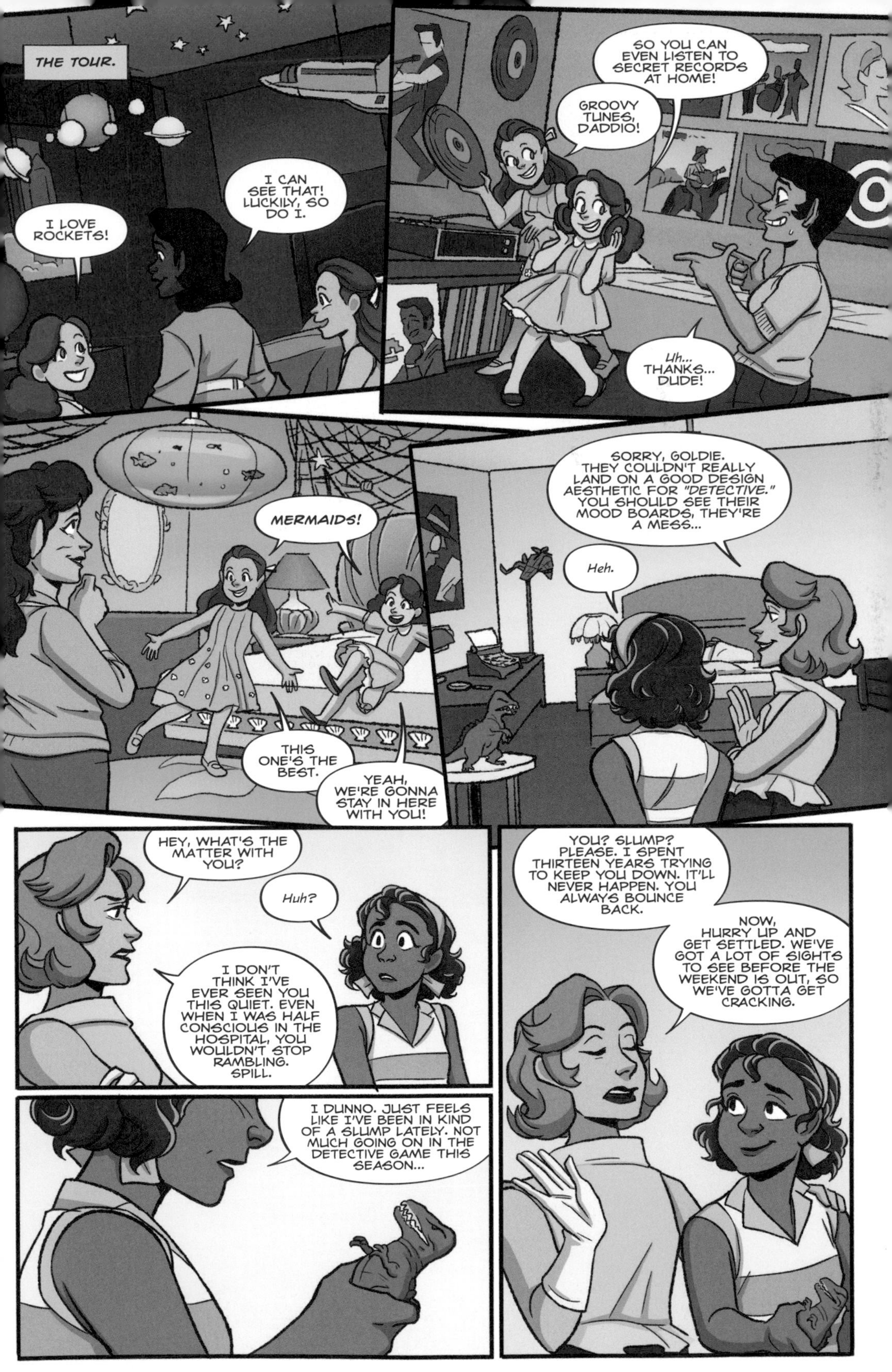
THE TOUR.
I LOVE ROCKETS!
I CAN SEE THAT! LUCKILY, SO DO I.
SO YOU CAN EVEN LISTEN TO SECRET RECORDS AT HOME!
GROOVY TUNES, DADDIO!
Uh... THANKS... DUDE!
MERMAIDS!
THIS ONE'S THE BEST.
YEAH, WE'RE GONNA STAY IN HERE WITH YOU!
SORRY, GOLDIE. THEY COULDN'T REALLY LAND ON A GOOD DESIGN AESTHETIC FOR "DETECTIVE." YOU SHOULD SEE THEIR MOOD BOARDS, THEY'RE A MESS...
Heh.
HEY, WHAT'S THE MATTER WITH YOU?
Huh?
I DON'T THINK I'VE EVER SEEN YOU THIS QUIET. EVEN WHEN I WAS HALF CONSCIOUS IN THE HOSPITAL, YOU WOULDN'T STOP RAMBLING. SPILL.
I DUNNO. JUST FEELS LIKE I'VE BEEN IN KIND OF A SLUMP LATELY. NOT MUCH GOING ON IN THE DETECTIVE GAME THIS SEASON...
YOU? SLUMP? PLEASE. I SPENT THIRTEEN YEARS TRYING TO KEEP YOU DOWN. IT'LL NEVER HAPPEN. YOU ALWAYS BOUNCE BACK.
NOW, HURRY UP AND GET SETTLED. WE'VE GOT A LOT OF SIGHTS TO SEE BEFORE THE WEEKEND IS OUT, SO WE'VE GOTTA GET CRACKING.

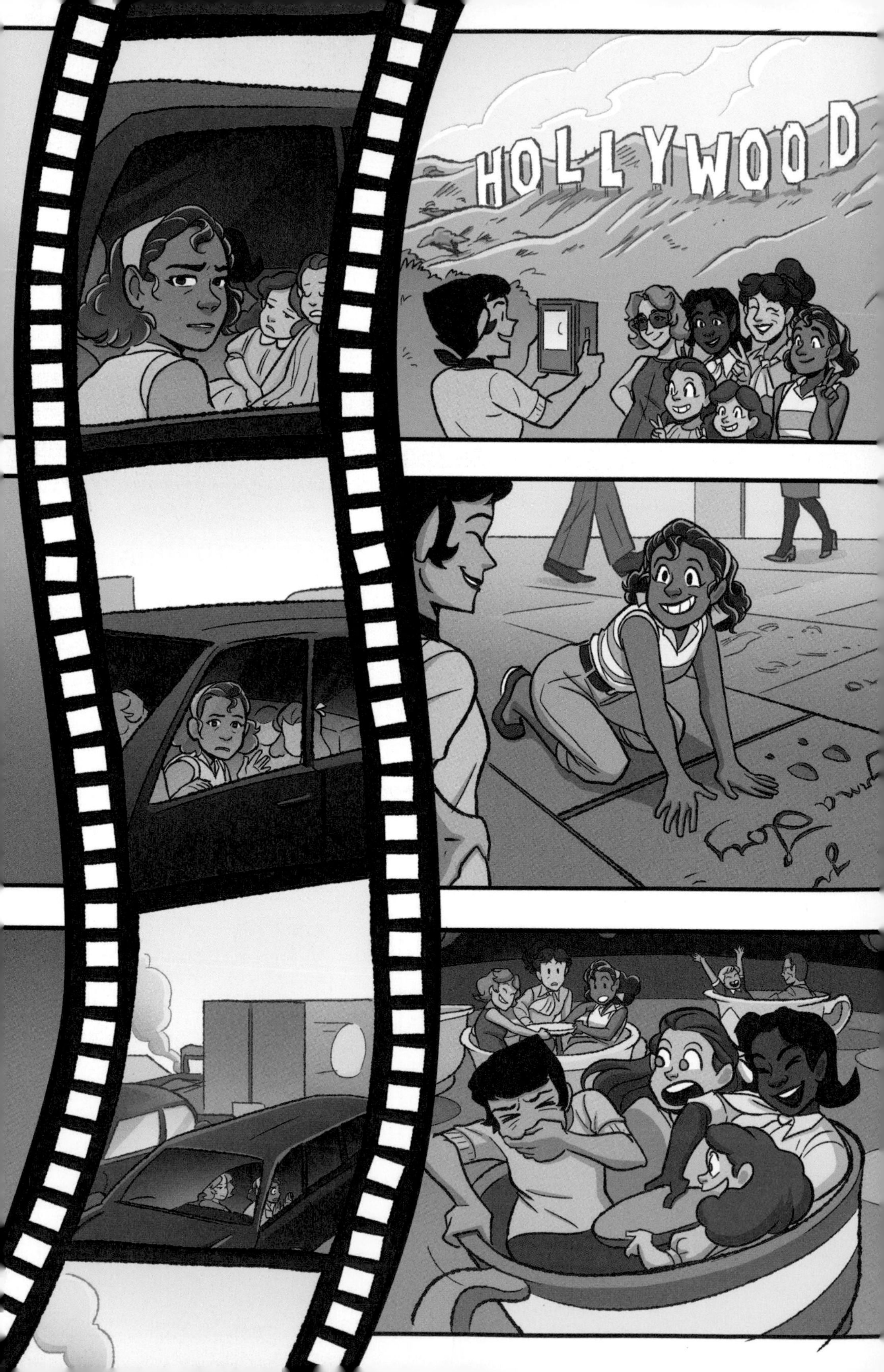
HOLLYWOOD

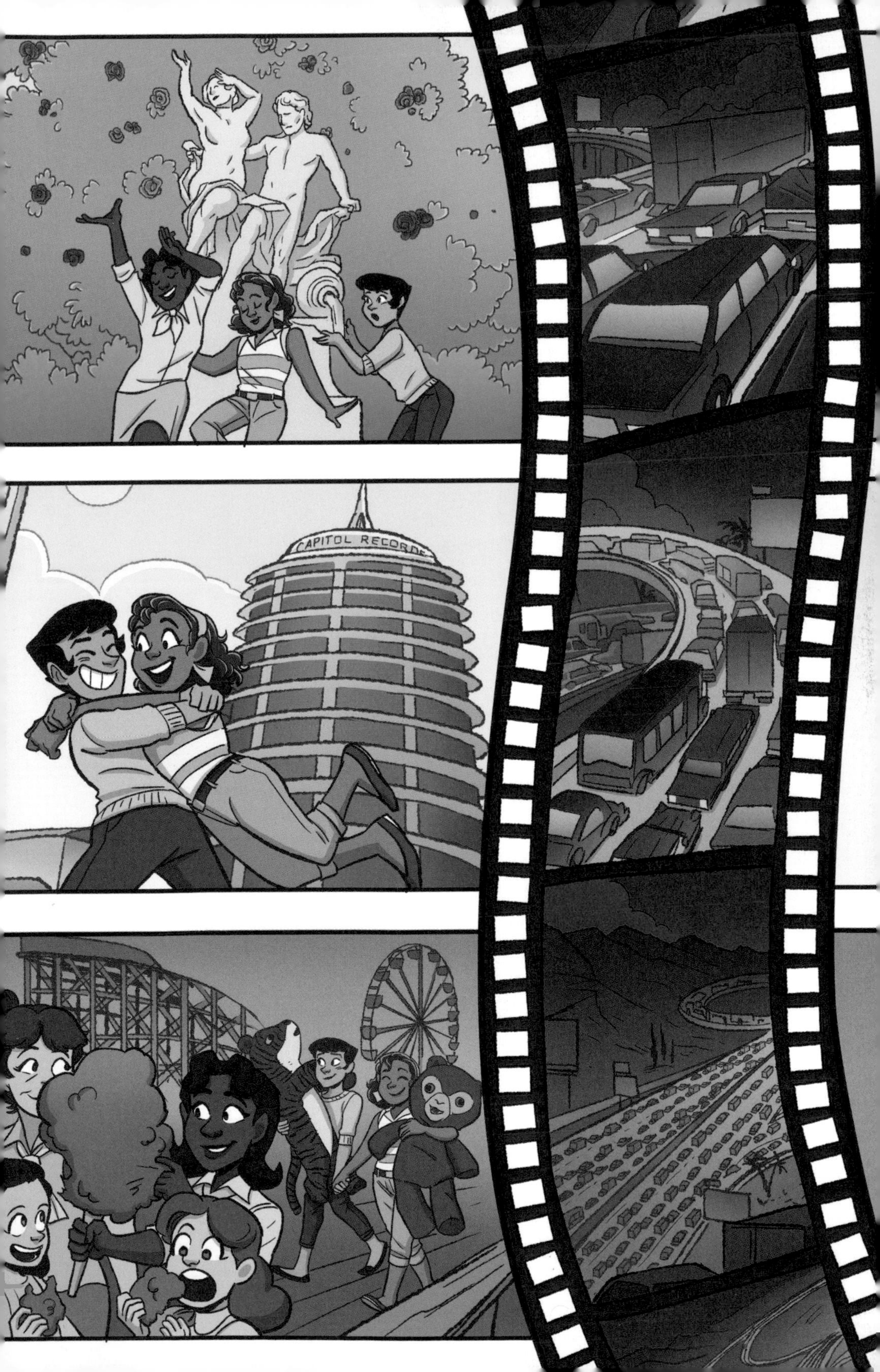
CAPITOL RECORD

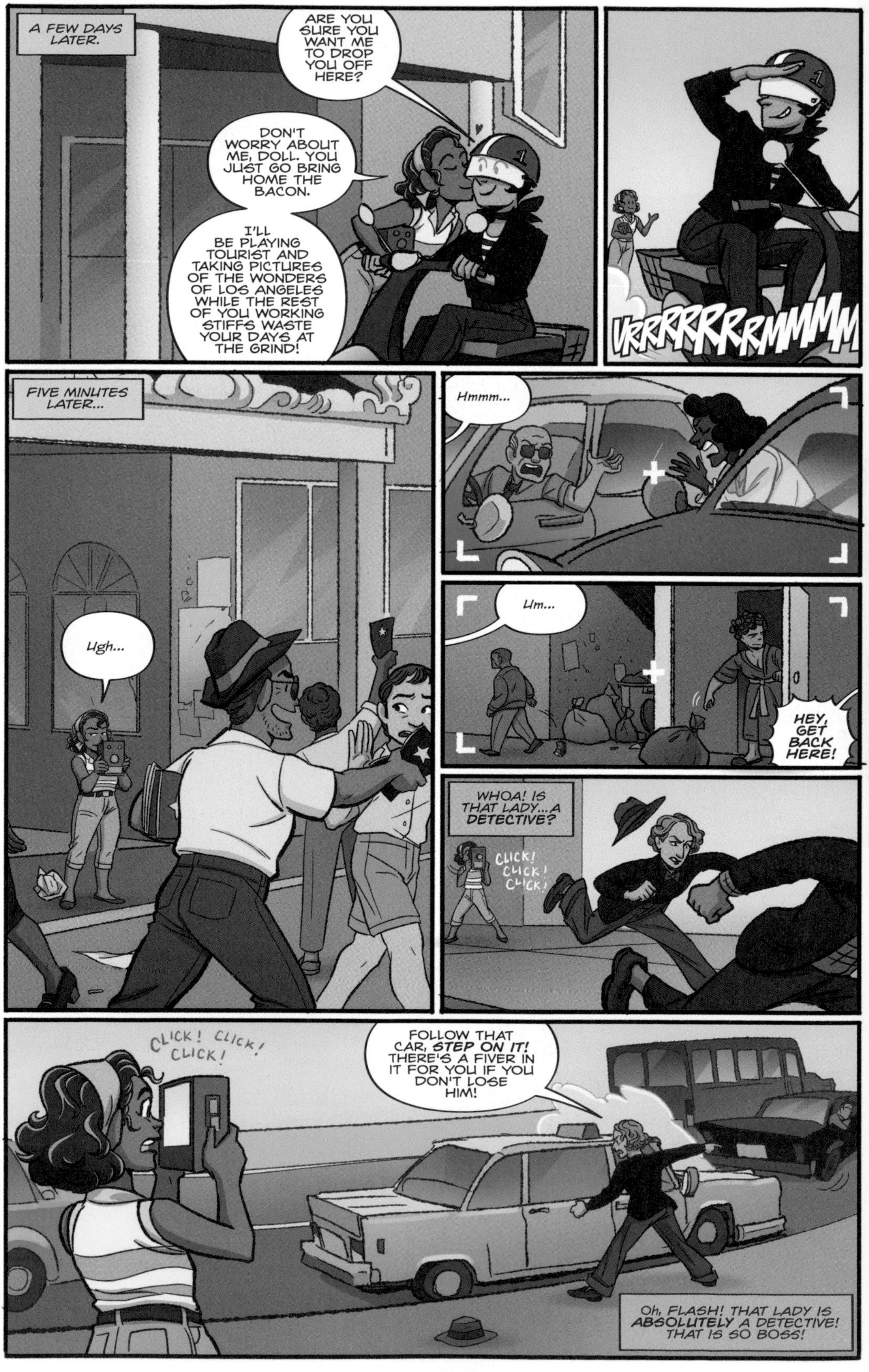

A FEW DAYS LATER.
ARE YOU SURE YOU WANT ME TO DROP YOU OFF HERE?
DON'T WORRY ABOUT ME, DOLL. YOU JUST GO BRING HOME THE BACON.
I'LL BE PLAYING TOURIST AND TAKING PICTURES OF THE WONDERS OF LOS ANGELES WHILE THE REST OF YOU WORKING STIFFS WASTE YOUR DAYS AT THE GRIND!
VRRRRRRRRMMMM
FIVE MINUTES LATER...
Ugh...
Hmmm...
Um...
HEY, GET BACK HERE!
WHOA! IS THAT LADY...A DETECTIVE?
CLICK! CLICK! CLICK!
CLICK! CLICK! CLICK!
FOLLOW THAT CAR, STEP ON IT! THERE'S A FIVER IN IT FOR YOU IF YOU DON'T LOSE HIM!
Oh, FLASH! THAT LADY IS ABSOLUTELY A DETECTIVE! THAT IS SO BOSS!

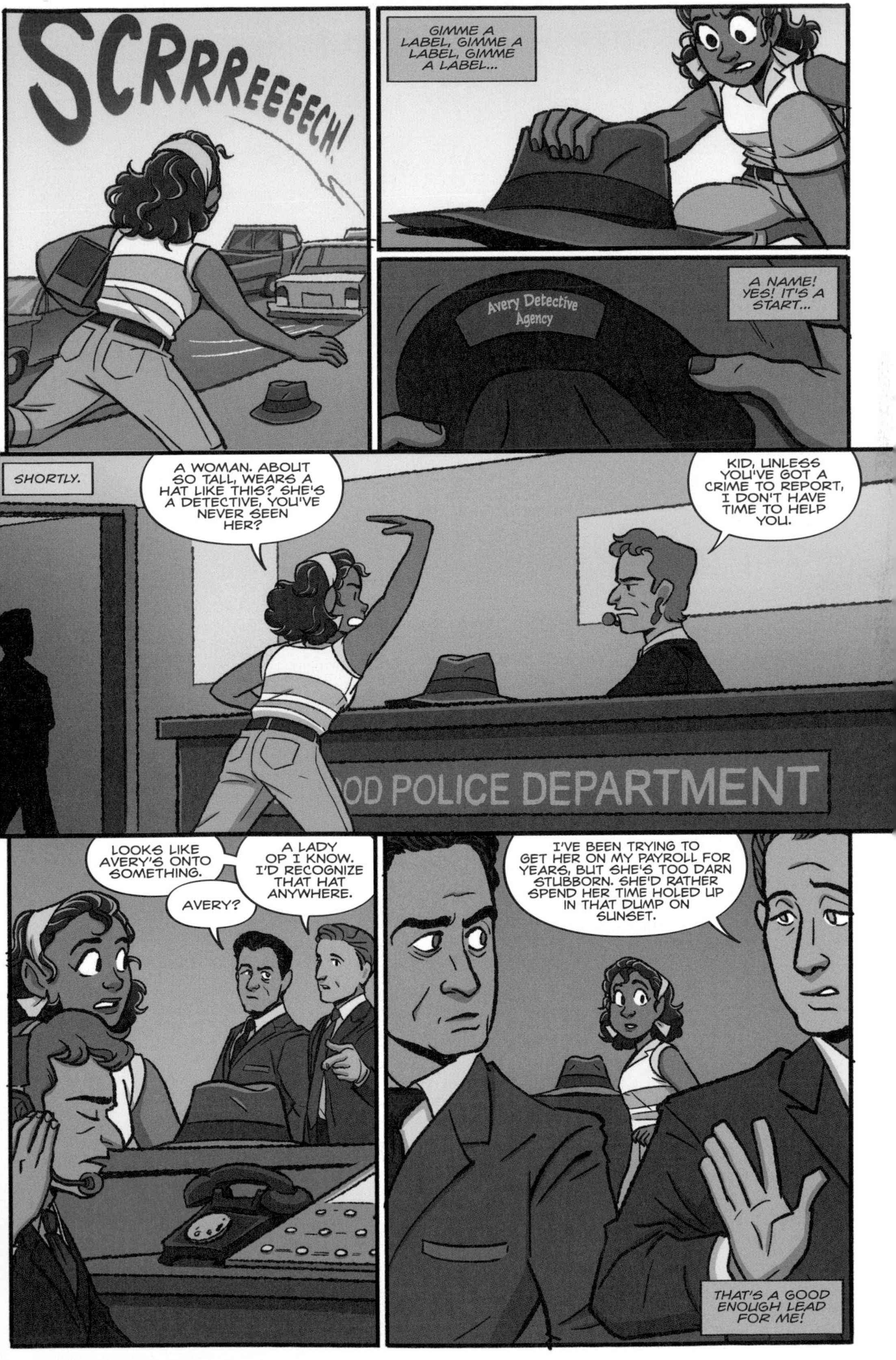
SCRRREEEECH!
GIMME A LABEL, GIMME A LABEL, GIMME A LABEL...
Avery Detective Agency
A NAME! YES! IT'S A START...
SHORTLY.
A WOMAN. ABOUT SO TALL, WEARS A HAT LIKE THIS? SHE'S A DETECTIVE, YOU'VE NEVER SEEN HER?
KID, UNLESS YOU'VE GOT A CRIME TO REPORT, I DON'T HAVE TIME TO HELP YOU.
OOD POLICE DEPARTMENT
LOOKS LIKE AVERY'S ONTO SOMETHING.
AVERY?
A LADY OP I KNOW. I'D RECOGNIZE THAT HAT ANYWHERE.
I'VE BEEN TRYING TO GET HER ON MY PAYROLL FOR YEARS, BUT SHE'S TOO DARN STUBBORN. SHE'D RATHER SPEND HER TIME HOLED UP IN THAT DUMP ON SUNSET.
THAT'S A GOOD ENOUGH LEAD FOR ME!

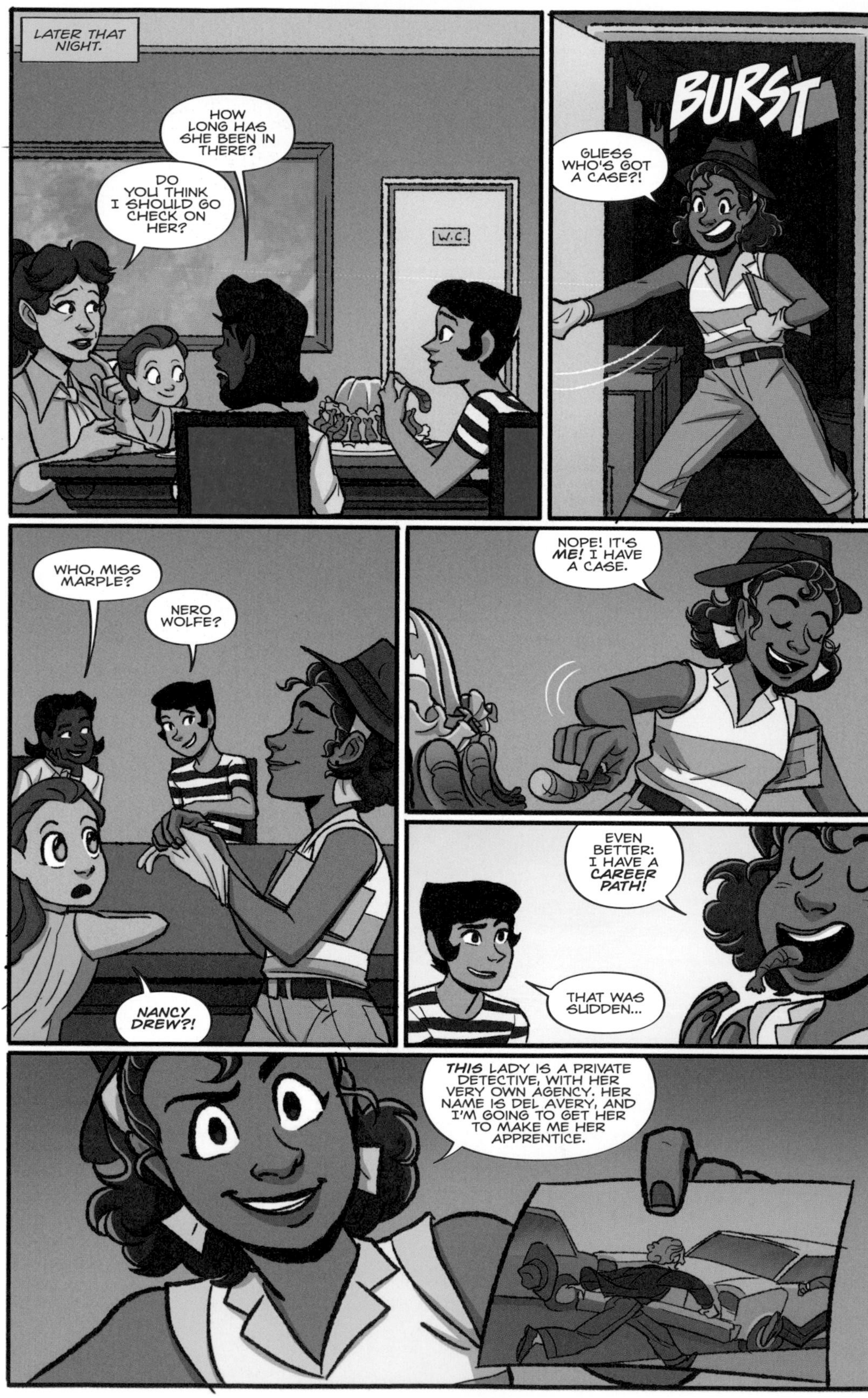
LATER THAT NIGHT.
HOW LONG HAS SHE BEEN IN THERE?
DO YOU THINK I SHOULD GO CHECK ON HER?
BURST
GUESS WHO'S GOT A CASE?!
WHO, MISS MARPLE?
NERO WOLFE?
NANCY DREW?!
NOPE! IT'S *ME!* I HAVE A CASE.
EVEN BETTER: I HAVE A *CAREER PATH!*
THAT WAS SUDDEN...
THIS LADY IS A PRIVATE DETECTIVE, WITH HER VERY OWN AGENCY. HER NAME IS DEL AVERY, AND I'M GOING TO GET HER TO MAKE ME HER APPRENTICE.
W.C.

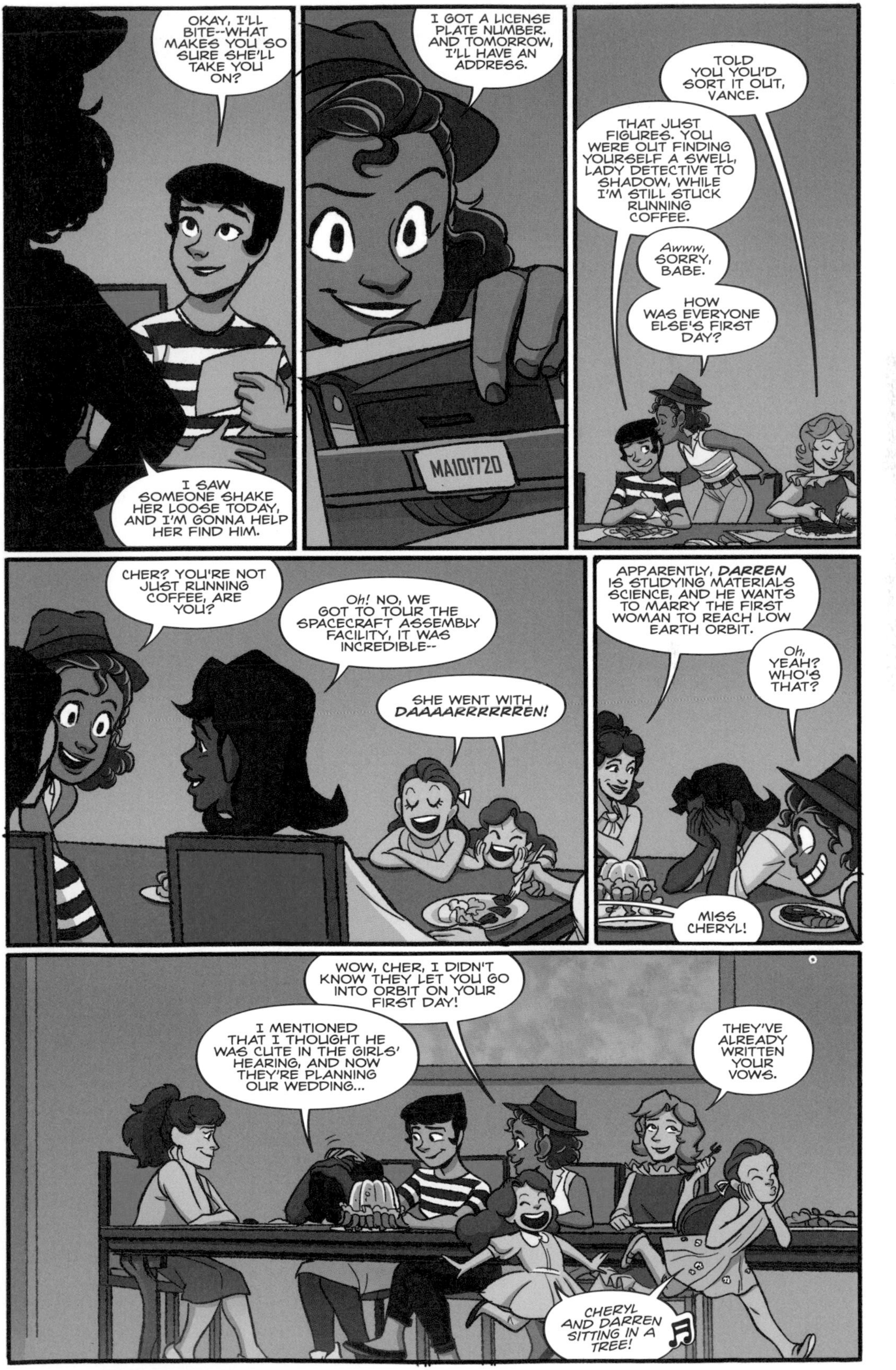

OKAY, I'LL BITE--WHAT MAKES YOU SO SURE SHE'LL TAKE YOU ON?
I SAW SOMEONE SHAKE HER LOOSE TODAY, AND I'M GONNA HELP HER FIND HIM.
I GOT A LICENSE PLATE NUMBER. AND TOMORROW, I'LL HAVE AN ADDRESS.
MA101720
TOLD YOU YOU'D SORT IT OUT, VANCE.
THAT JUST FIGURES. YOU WERE OUT FINDING YOURSELF A SWELL, LADY DETECTIVE TO SHADOW, WHILE I'M STILL STUCK RUNNING COFFEE.
Awww, SORRY, BABE.
HOW WAS EVERYONE ELSE'S FIRST DAY?
CHER? YOU'RE NOT JUST RUNNING COFFEE, ARE YOU?
Oh! NO, WE GOT TO TOUR THE SPACECRAFT ASSEMBLY FACILITY, IT WAS INCREDIBLE--
SHE WENT WITH DAAAARRRRRREN!
APPARENTLY, DARREN IS STUDYING MATERIALS SCIENCE, AND HE WANTS TO MARRY THE FIRST WOMAN TO REACH LOW EARTH ORBIT.
Oh, YEAH? WHO'S THAT?
MISS CHERYL!
WOW, CHER, I DIDN'T KNOW THEY LET YOU GO INTO ORBIT ON YOUR FIRST DAY!
I MENTIONED THAT I THOUGHT HE WAS CUTE IN THE GIRLS' HEARING, AND NOW THEY'RE PLANNING OUR WEDDING...
THEY'VE ALREADY WRITTEN YOUR VOWS.
CHERYL AND DARREN SITTING IN A TREE!

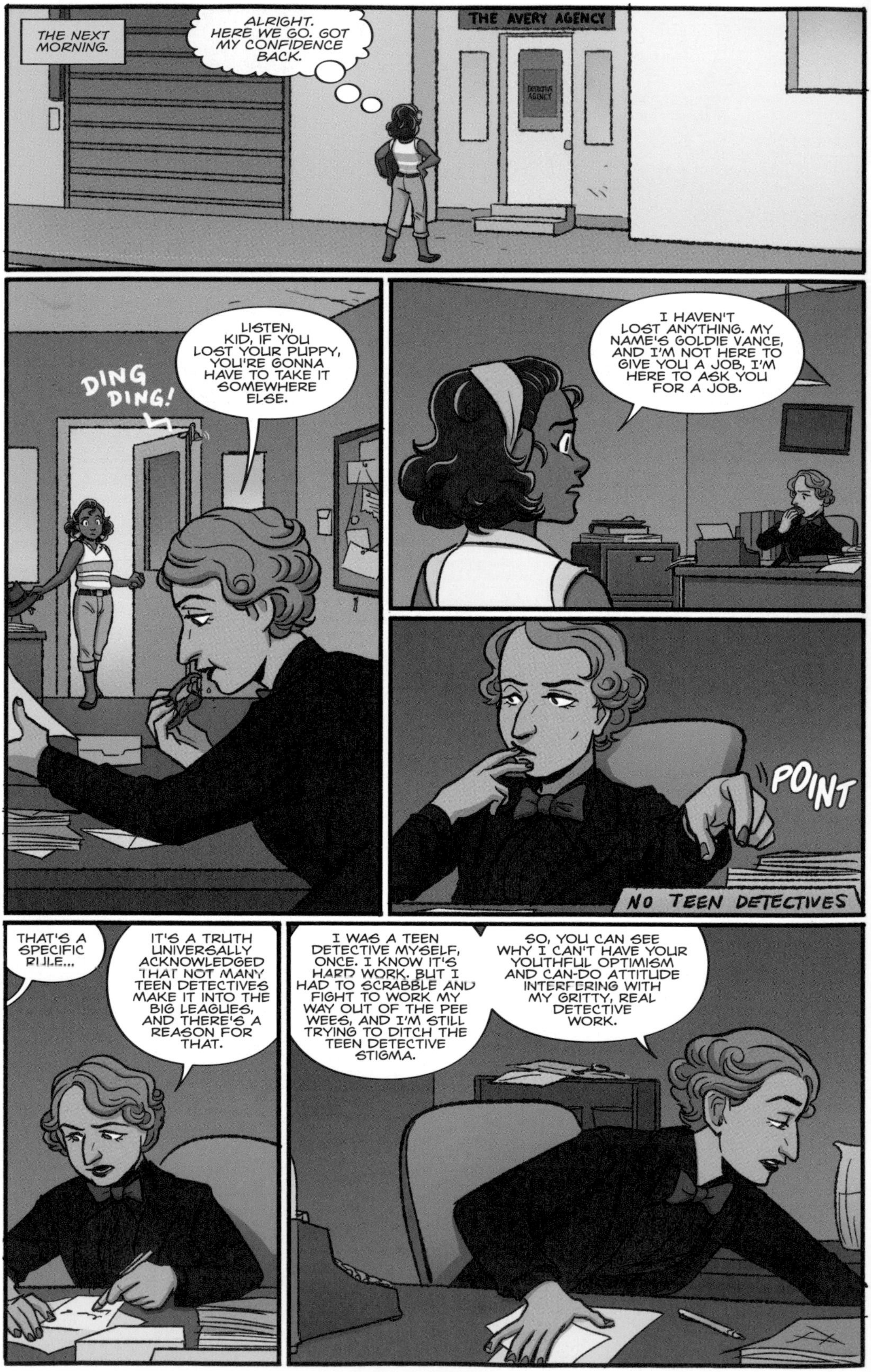
THE NEXT MORNING.
ALRIGHT. HERE WE GO. GOT MY CONFIDENCE BACK.
THE AVERY AGENCY
DETECTIVE AGENCY
DING DING!
LISTEN, KID, IF YOU LOST YOUR PUPPY, YOU'RE GONNA HAVE TO TAKE IT SOMEWHERE ELSE.
I HAVEN'T LOST ANYTHING. MY NAME'S GOLDIE VANCE, AND I'M NOT HERE TO GIVE YOU A JOB, I'M HERE TO ASK YOU FOR A JOB.
POINT
NO TEEN DETECTIVES
THAT'S A SPECIFIC RULE...
IT'S A TRUTH UNIVERSALLY ACKNOWLEDGED THAT NOT MANY TEEN DETECTIVES MAKE IT INTO THE BIG LEAGUES, AND THERE'S A REASON FOR THAT.
I WAS A TEEN DETECTIVE MYSELF, ONCE. I KNOW IT'S HARD WORK. BUT I HAD TO SCRABBLE AND FIGHT TO WORK MY WAY OUT OF THE PEE WEES, AND I'M STILL TRYING TO DITCH THE TEEN DETECTIVE STIGMA.
SO, YOU CAN SEE WHY I CAN'T HAVE YOUR YOUTHFUL OPTIMISM AND CAN-DO ATTITUDE INTERFERING WITH MY GRITTY, REAL DETECTIVE WORK.

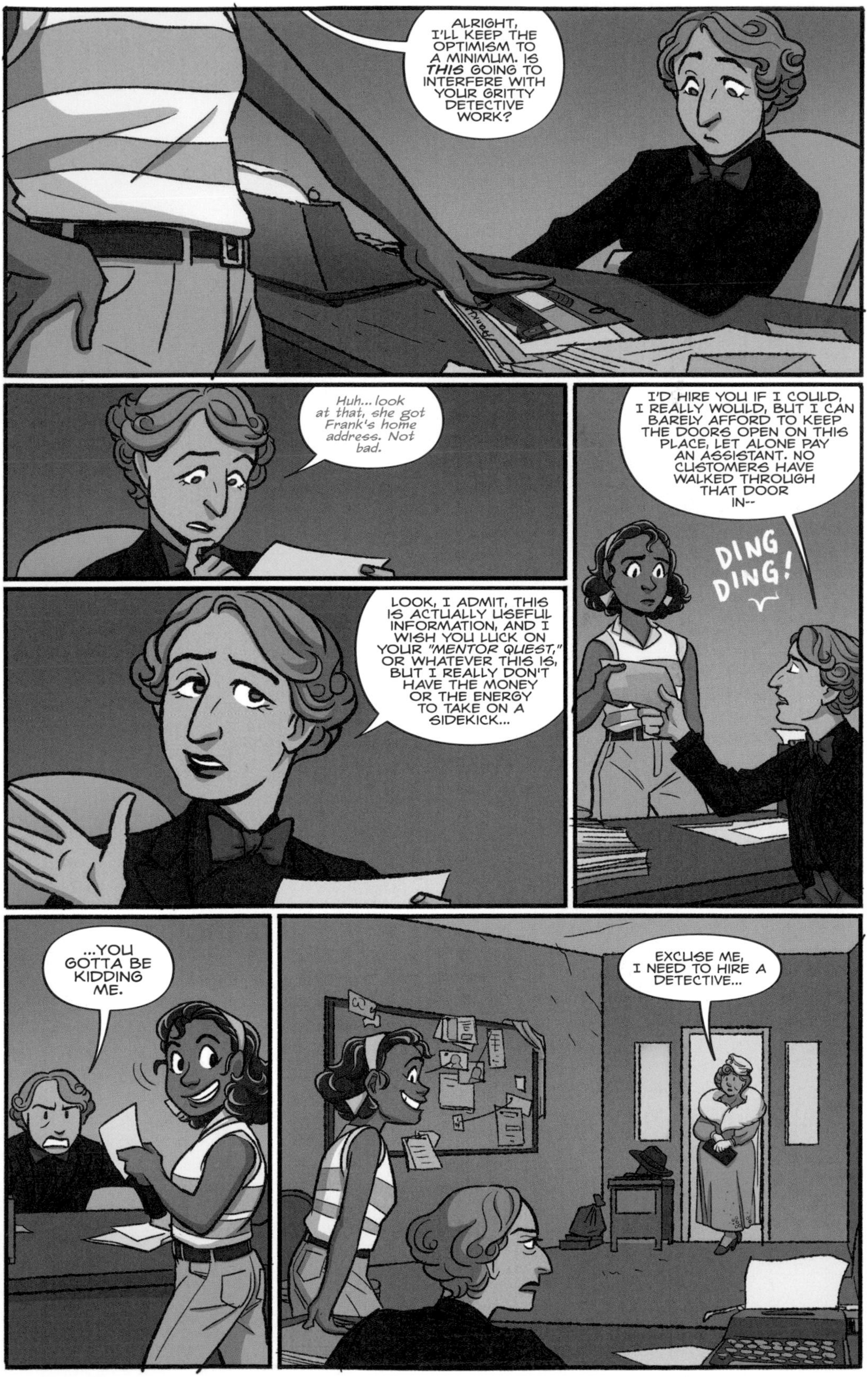
ALRIGHT, I'LL KEEP THE OPTIMISM TO A MINIMUM. IS *THIS* GOING TO INTERFERE WITH YOUR GRITTY DETECTIVE WORK?
Huh... look at that, she got Frank's home address. Not bad.
I'D HIRE YOU IF I COULD, I REALLY WOULD, BUT I CAN BARELY AFFORD TO KEEP THE DOORS OPEN ON THIS PLACE, LET ALONE PAY AN ASSISTANT. NO CUSTOMERS HAVE WALKED THROUGH THAT DOOR IN--
DING DING!
LOOK, I ADMIT, THIS IS ACTUALLY USEFUL INFORMATION, AND I WISH YOU LUCK ON YOUR *"MENTOR QUEST,"* OR WHATEVER THIS IS, BUT I REALLY DON'T HAVE THE MONEY OR THE ENERGY TO TAKE ON A SIDEKICK...
...YOU GOTTA BE KIDDING ME.
EXCUSE ME, I NEED TO HIRE A DETECTIVE...

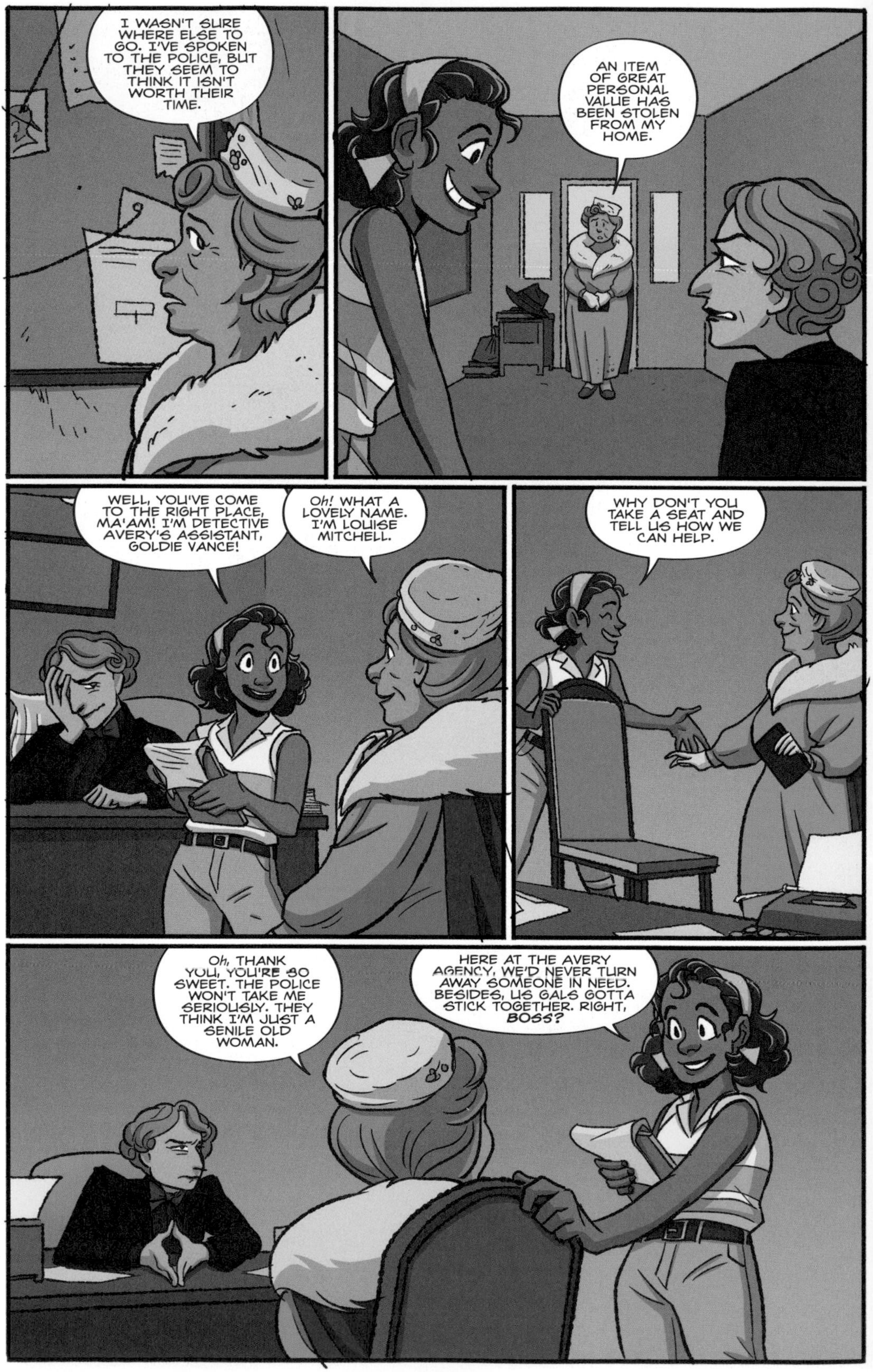
I WASN'T SURE WHERE ELSE TO GO. I'VE SPOKEN TO THE POLICE, BUT THEY SEEM TO THINK IT ISN'T WORTH THEIR TIME.
AN ITEM OF GREAT PERSONAL VALUE HAS BEEN STOLEN FROM MY HOME.
WELL, YOU'VE COME TO THE RIGHT PLACE, MA'AM! I'M DETECTIVE AVERY'S ASSISTANT, GOLDIE VANCE!
Oh! WHAT A LOVELY NAME. I'M LOUISE MITCHELL.
WHY DON'T YOU TAKE A SEAT AND TELL US HOW WE CAN HELP.
Oh, THANK YOU, YOU'RE SO SWEET. THE POLICE WON'T TAKE ME SERIOUSLY. THEY THINK I'M JUST A SENILE OLD WOMAN.
HERE AT THE AVERY AGENCY, WE'D NEVER TURN AWAY SOMEONE IN NEED. BESIDES, US GALS GOTTA STICK TOGETHER. RIGHT, ***BOSS?***

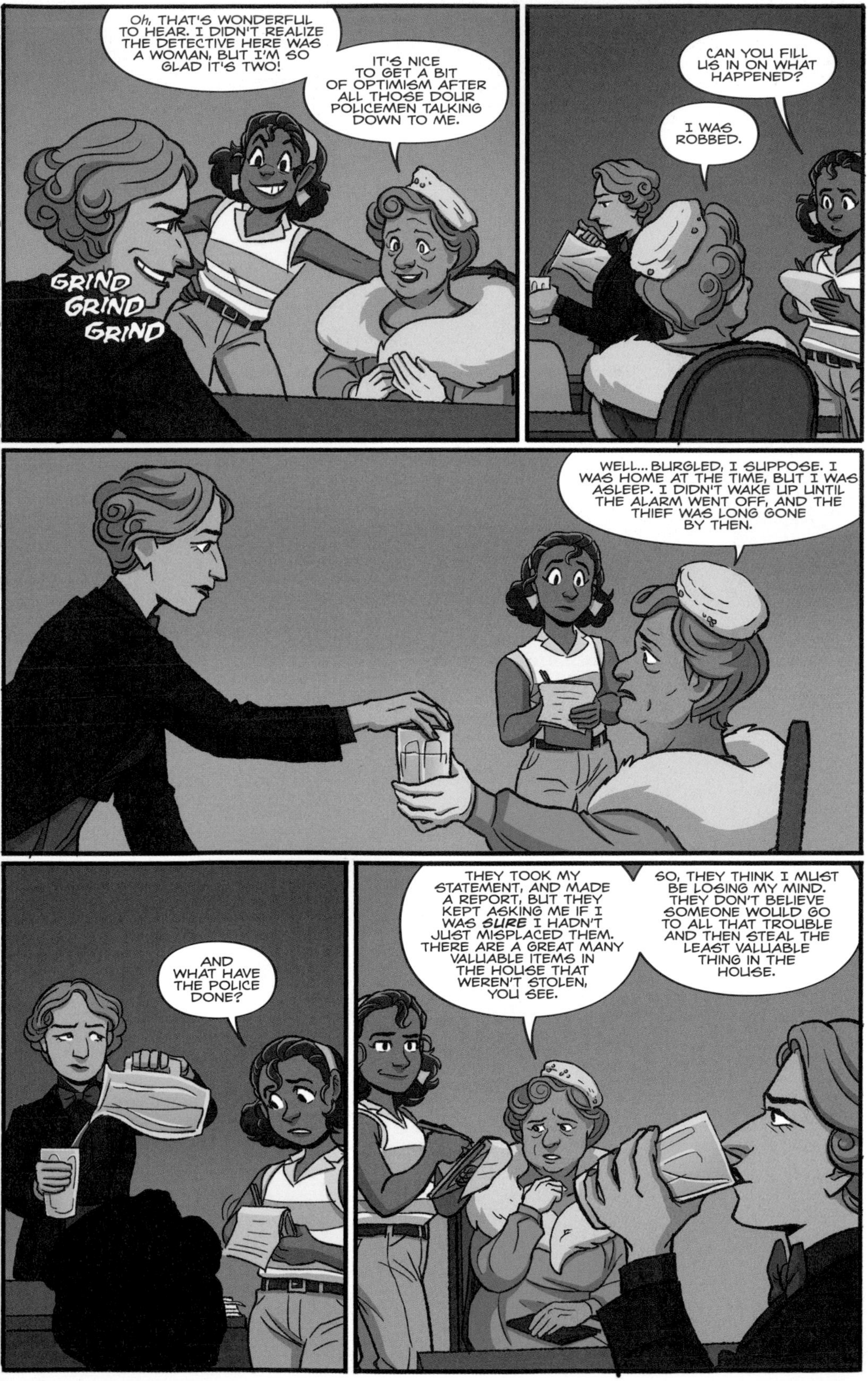
Oh, THAT'S WONDERFUL TO HEAR. I DIDN'T REALIZE THE DETECTIVE HERE WAS A WOMAN, BUT I'M SO GLAD IT'S TWO!
IT'S NICE TO GET A BIT OF OPTIMISM AFTER ALL THOSE DOUR POLICEMEN TALKING DOWN TO ME.
GRIND GRIND GRIND
CAN YOU FILL US IN ON WHAT HAPPENED?
I WAS ROBBED.
WELL... BURGLED, I SUPPOSE. I WAS HOME AT THE TIME, BUT I WAS ASLEEP. I DIDN'T WAKE UP UNTIL THE ALARM WENT OFF, AND THE THIEF WAS LONG GONE BY THEN.
AND WHAT HAVE THE POLICE DONE?
THEY TOOK MY STATEMENT, AND MADE A REPORT, BUT THEY KEPT ASKING ME IF I WAS SURE I HADN'T JUST MISPLACED THEM. THERE ARE A GREAT MANY VALUABLE ITEMS IN THE HOUSE THAT WEREN'T STOLEN, YOU SEE.
SO, THEY THINK I MUST BE LOSING MY MIND. THEY DON'T BELIEVE SOMEONE WOULD GO TO ALL THAT TROUBLE AND THEN STEAL THE LEAST VALUABLE THING IN THE HOUSE.

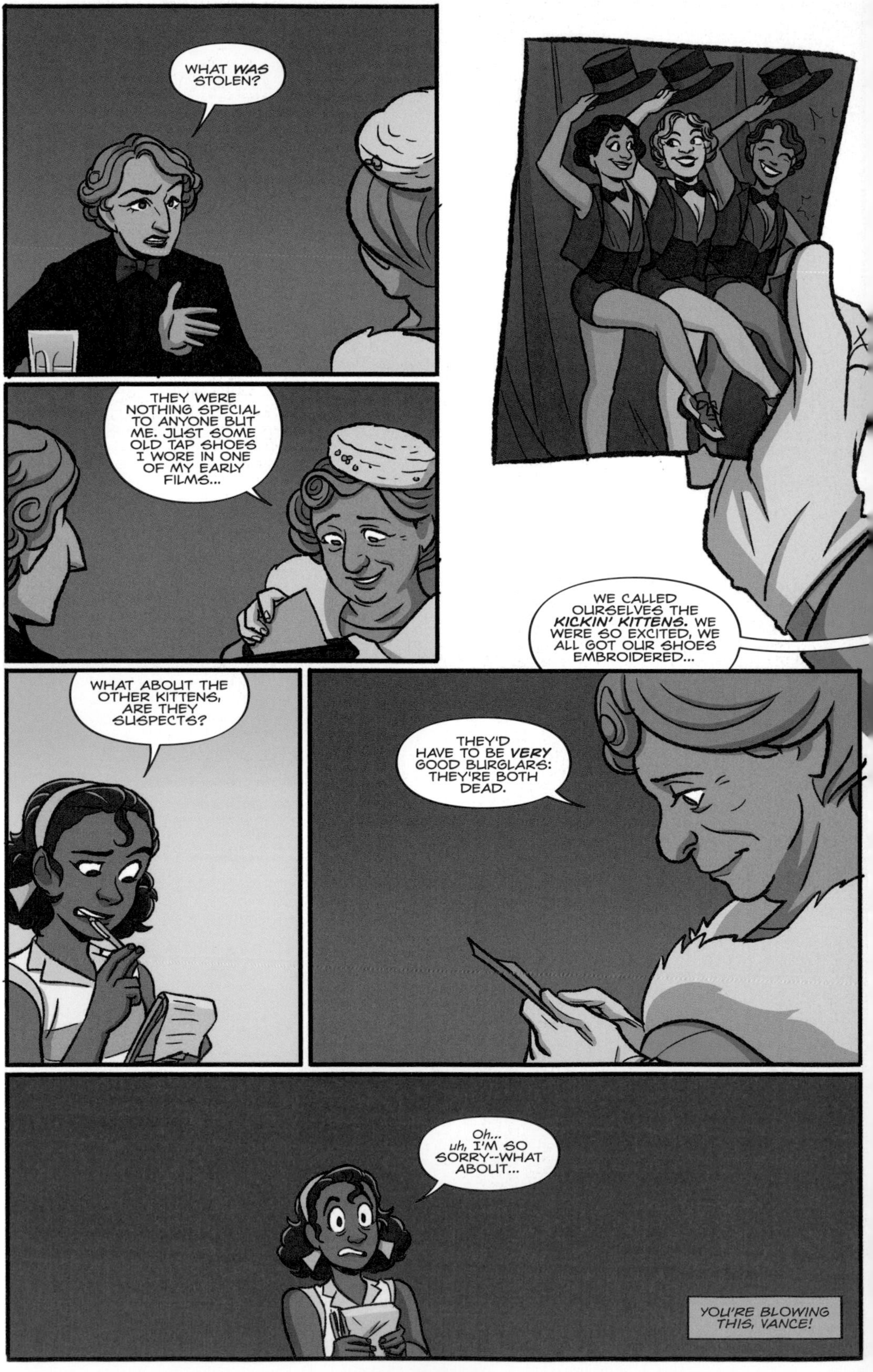
WHAT WAS STOLEN?
THEY WERE NOTHING SPECIAL TO ANYONE BUT ME. JUST SOME OLD TAP SHOES I WORE IN ONE OF MY EARLY FILMS...
WE CALLED OURSELVES THE KICKIN' KITTENS. WE WERE SO EXCITED, WE ALL GOT OUR SHOES EMBROIDERED...
WHAT ABOUT THE OTHER KITTENS, ARE THEY SUSPECTS?
THEY'D HAVE TO BE VERY GOOD BURGLARS: THEY'RE BOTH DEAD.
Oh... uh, I'M SO SORRY--WHAT ABOUT...
YOU'RE BLOWING THIS, VANCE!

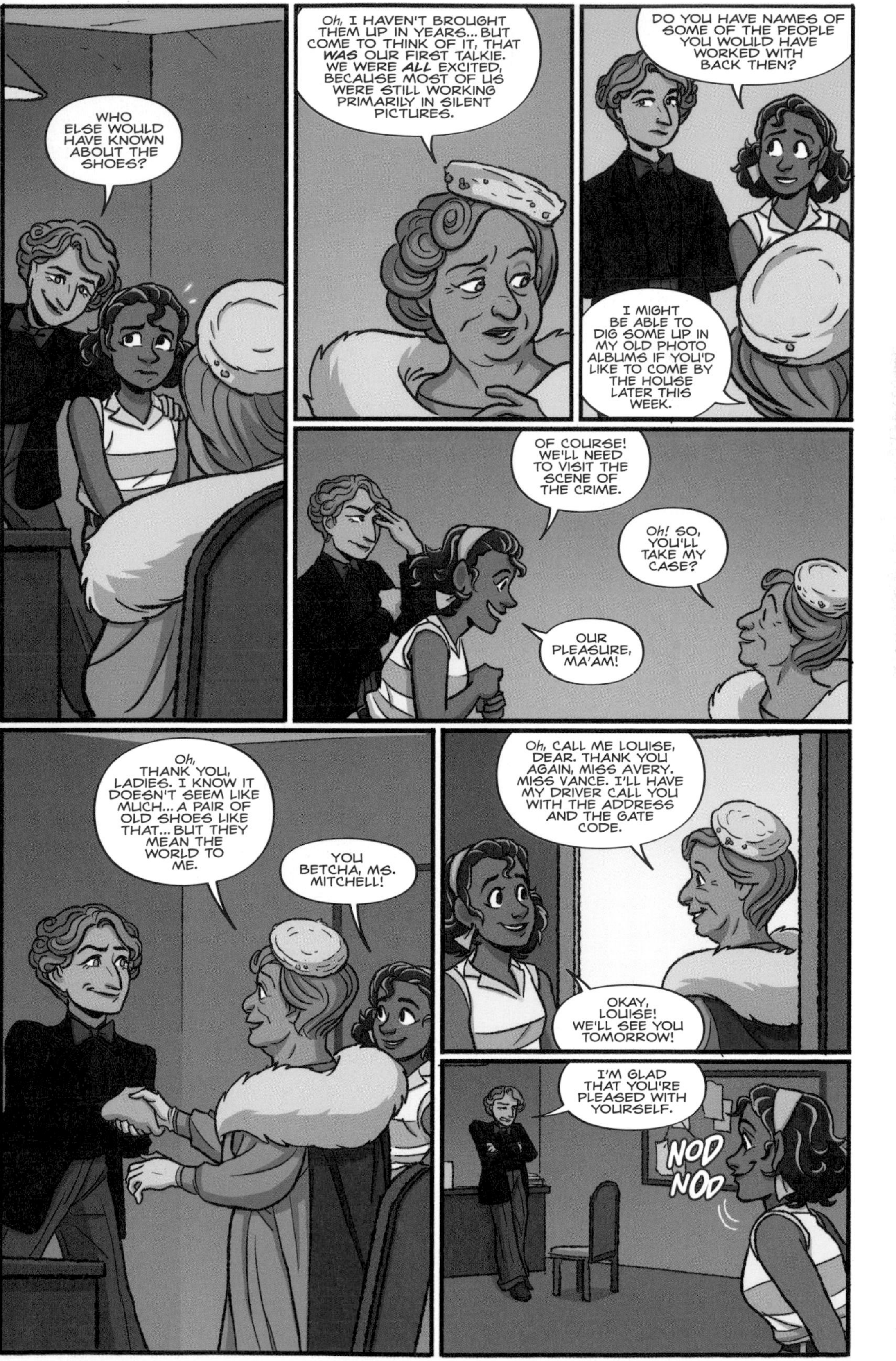

WHO ELSE WOULD HAVE KNOWN ABOUT THE SHOES?
Oh, I HAVEN'T BROUGHT THEM UP IN YEARS... BUT COME TO THINK OF IT, THAT ***WAS*** OUR FIRST TALKIE. WE WERE ***ALL*** EXCITED, BECAUSE MOST OF US WERE STILL WORKING PRIMARILY IN SILENT PICTURES.
DO YOU HAVE NAMES OF SOME OF THE PEOPLE YOU WOULD HAVE WORKED WITH BACK THEN?
I MIGHT BE ABLE TO DIG SOME UP IN MY OLD PHOTO ALBUMS IF YOU'D LIKE TO COME BY THE HOUSE LATER THIS WEEK.
OF COURSE! WE'LL NEED TO VISIT THE SCENE OF THE CRIME.
Oh! SO, YOU'LL TAKE MY CASE?
OUR PLEASURE, MA'AM!
Oh, THANK YOU, LADIES. I KNOW IT DOESN'T SEEM LIKE MUCH... A PAIR OF OLD SHOES LIKE THAT... BUT THEY MEAN THE WORLD TO ME.
YOU BETCHA, MS. MITCHELL!
Oh, CALL ME LOUISE, DEAR. THANK YOU AGAIN, MISS AVERY. MISS VANCE. I'LL HAVE MY DRIVER CALL YOU WITH THE ADDRESS AND THE GATE CODE.
OKAY, LOUISE! WE'LL SEE YOU TOMORROW!
I'M GLAD THAT YOU'RE PLEASED WITH YOURSELF.
NOD NOD

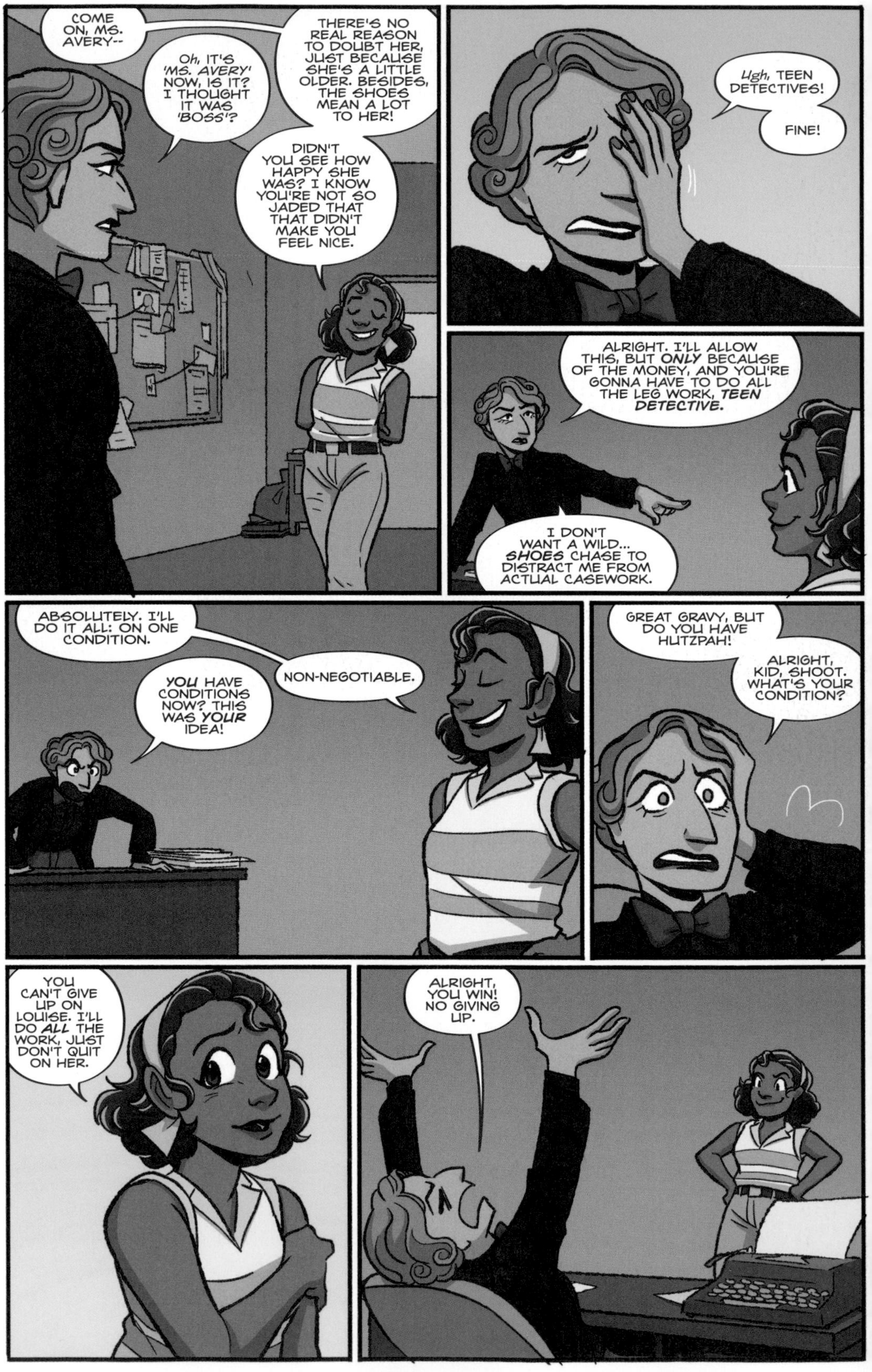

COME ON, MS. AVERY--
THERE'S NO REAL REASON TO DOUBT HER, JUST BECAUSE SHE'S A LITTLE OLDER. BESIDES, THE SHOES MEAN A LOT TO HER!
Oh, IT'S 'MS. AVERY' NOW, IS IT? I THOUGHT IT WAS 'BOSS'?
DIDN'T YOU SEE HOW HAPPY SHE WAS? I KNOW YOU'RE NOT SO JADED THAT THAT DIDN'T MAKE YOU FEEL NICE.
Ugh, TEEN DETECTIVES!
FINE!
ALRIGHT. I'LL ALLOW THIS, BUT ONLY BECAUSE OF THE MONEY, AND YOU'RE GONNA HAVE TO DO ALL THE LEG WORK, TEEN DETECTIVE.
I DON'T WANT A WILD... SHOES CHASE TO DISTRACT ME FROM ACTUAL CASEWORK.
ABSOLUTELY. I'LL DO IT ALL: ON ONE CONDITION.
NON-NEGOTIABLE.
YOU HAVE CONDITIONS NOW? THIS WAS YOUR IDEA!
GREAT GRAVY, BUT DO YOU HAVE HUTZPAH!
ALRIGHT, KID, SHOOT. WHAT'S YOUR CONDITION?
YOU CAN'T GIVE UP ON LOUISE. I'LL DO ALL THE WORK, JUST DON'T QUIT ON HER.
ALRIGHT, YOU WIN! NO GIVING UP.

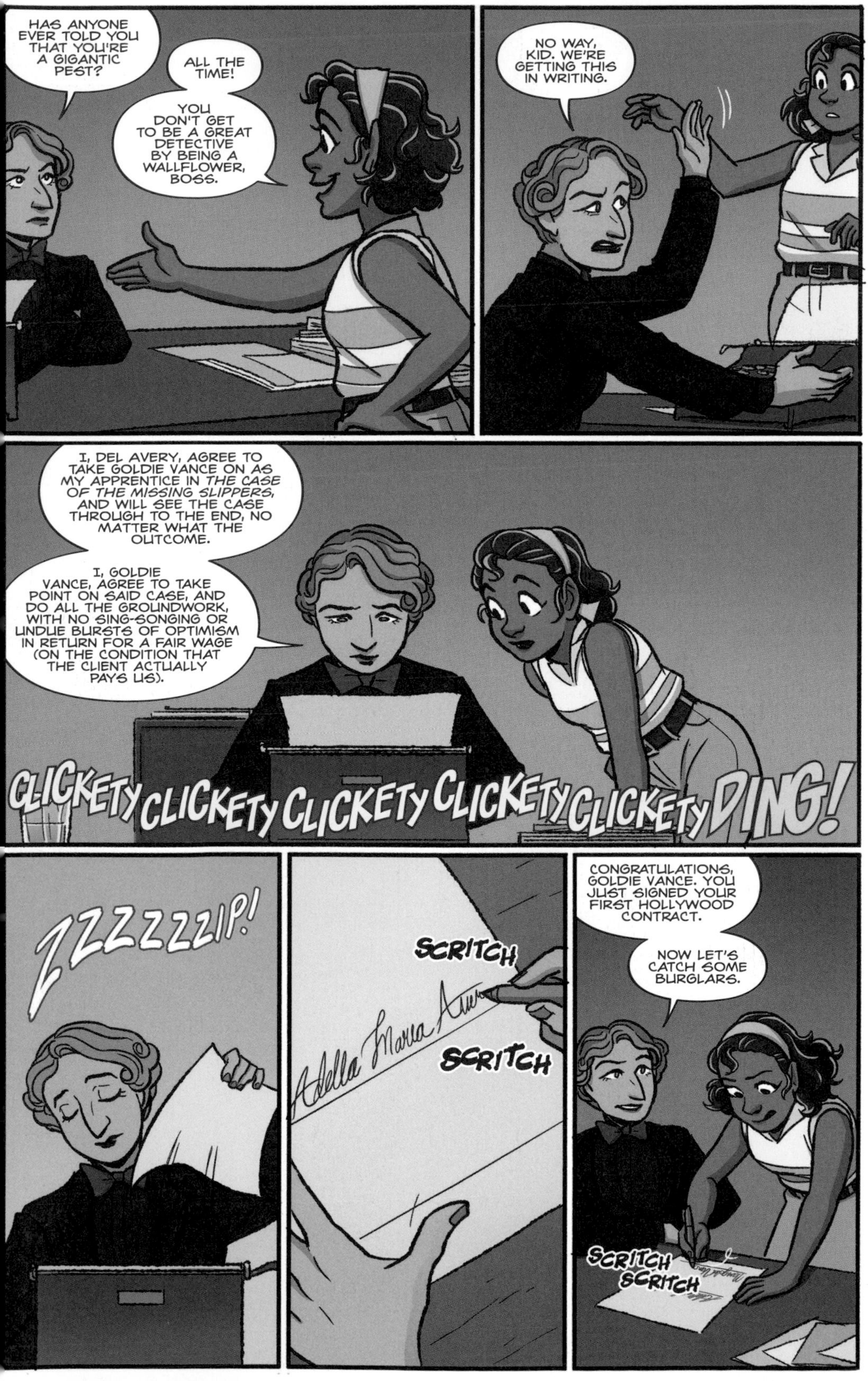
HAS ANYONE EVER TOLD YOU THAT YOU'RE A GIGANTIC PEST?
ALL THE TIME!
YOU DON'T GET TO BE A GREAT DETECTIVE BY BEING A WALLFLOWER, BOSS.
NO WAY, KID. WE'RE GETTING THIS IN WRITING.
I, DEL AVERY, AGREE TO TAKE GOLDIE VANCE ON AS MY APPRENTICE IN *THE CASE OF THE MISSING SLIPPERS*, AND WILL SEE THE CASE THROUGH TO THE END, NO MATTER WHAT THE OUTCOME.
I, GOLDIE VANCE, AGREE TO TAKE POINT ON SAID CASE, AND DO ALL THE GROUNDWORK, WITH NO SING-SONGING OR UNDUE BURSTS OF OPTIMISM IN RETURN FOR A FAIR WAGE (ON THE CONDITION THAT THE CLIENT ACTUALLY PAYS US).
CLICKETY CLICKETY CLICKETY CLICKETY CLICKETY DING!
ZZZZZZZIP!
SCRITCH
Adella Maria Avery
SCRITCH
CONGRATULATIONS, GOLDIE VANCE. YOU JUST SIGNED YOUR FIRST HOLLYWOOD CONTRACT.
NOW LET'S CATCH SOME BURGLARS.
SCRITCH
SCRITCH

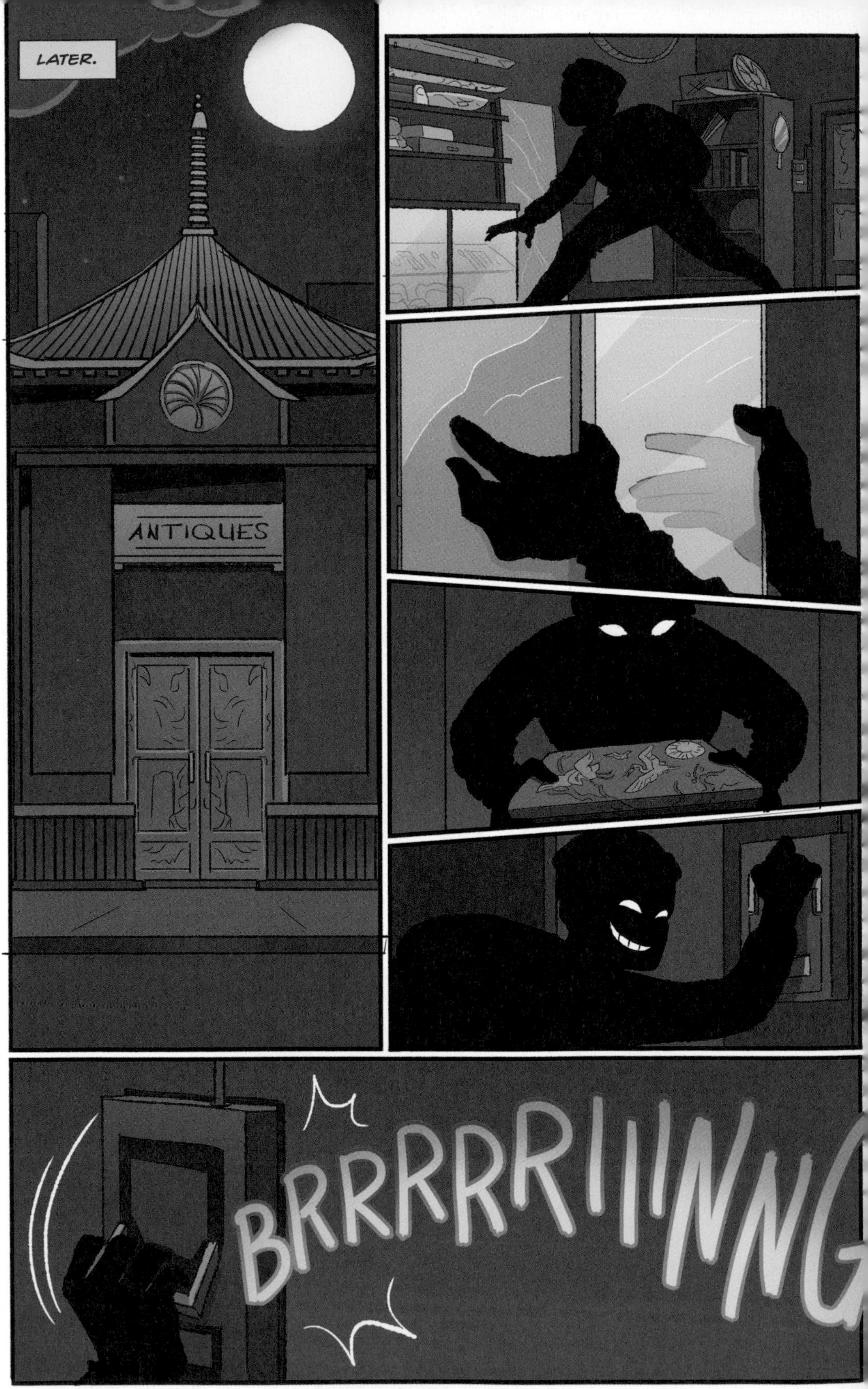
LATER.
ANTIQUES
BRRRRRIIINNG

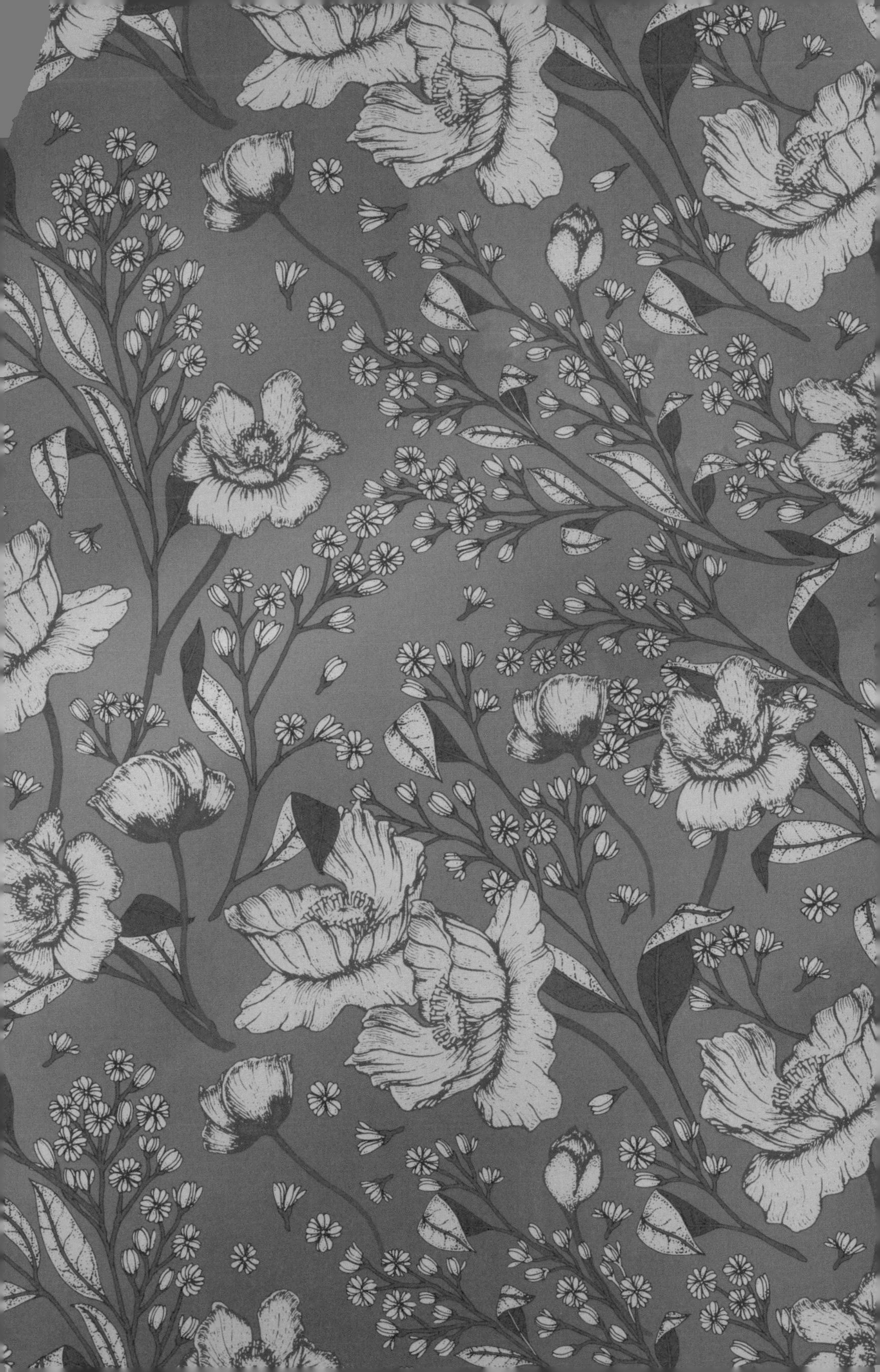

DISCOVER
ALL THE HITS

STEVENSON • ELLIS • WATTERS • ALLEN
LUMBERJANES
BEWARE THE KITTEN HOLY
NEW YORK TIMES BESTSELLING SERIES

Allison + Treiman + Cogar
GIANT DAYS
VOLUME ONE

RIBON • FISH • PEER
SLAM!
VOLUME ONE

Hope Larson • Brittney Williams • Sarah Stern
GOLDIE VANCE
"Scoot over Nancy Drew."
—Los Angeles Times
Volume One

JAMES TYNION IV • RIAN SYGH • WALTER BAIAMONTE
THE BACKSTAGERS

TYSON HESSE'S
DIESEL
IGNITION

BOOM! BOX™ **AVAILABLE AT YOUR LOCAL COMICS SHOP AND BOOKSTORE**
WWW.**BOOM-STUDIOS**.COM

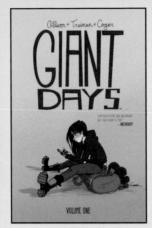

Lumberjanes
Noelle Stevenson, Shannon Watters, Grace Ellis, Brooklyn Allen, and Others
Volume 1: Beware the Kitten Holy
ISBN: 978-1-60886-687-8 | $14.99 US
Volume 2: Friendship to the Max
ISBN: 978-1-60886-737-0 | $14.99 US
Volume 3: A Terrible Plan
ISBN: 978-1-60886-803-2 | $14.99 US
Volume 4: Out of Time
ISBN: 978-1-60886-860-5 | $14.99 US
Volume 5: Band Together
ISBN: 978-1-60886-919-0 | $14.99 US

Giant Days
John Allison, Lissa Treiman, Max Sarin
Volume 1
ISBN: 978-1-60886-789-9 | $9.99 US
Volume 2
ISBN: 978-1-60886-804-9 | $14.99 US
Volume 3
ISBN: 978-1-60886-851-3 | $14.99 US

Jonesy
Sam Humphries, Caitlin Rose Boyle
Volume 1
ISBN: 978-1-60886-883-4 | $9.99 US
Volume 2
ISBN: 978-1-60886-999-2 | $14.99 US

Slam!
Pamela Ribon, Veronica Fish, Brittany Peer
Volume 1
ISBN: 978-1-68415-004-5 | $14.99 US

Goldie Vance
Hope Larson, Brittney Williams
Volume 1
ISBN: 978-1-60886-898-8 | $9.99 US
Volume 2
ISBN: 978-1-60886-974-9 | $14.99 US

The Backstagers
James Tynion IV, Rian Sygh
Volume 1
ISBN: 978-1-60886-993-0 | $14.99 US

Tyson Hesse's Diesel: Ignition
Tyson Hesse
ISBN: 978-1-60886-907-7 | $14.99 US

Coady & The Creepies
Liz Prince, Amanda Kirk, Hannah Fisher
ISBN: 978-1-68415-029-8 | $14.99 US